Reviews of Bestselling Novels by Steve Pieczenik

The Mind Palace

As the KGB tightens its grip on the Soviet Union, a compassionate American doctor discovers a grim truth about "treatment" in Soviet psychiatric hospitals—torture, mental barbarism and brutality—and helps a desperate political prisoner flee to freedom.

"Fast-paced...action-packed...and skillfully told."

—Publishers Weekly

"A bone-chilling look inside the Soviet system."

—Tom Clancy, author of *The Hunt for Red October*

Blood Heat

As the world plunges into an abyss of death and dying from a venomous new strain of the bubonic plague, disease specialist Dr. Russ Bradley begins a desperate hunt for a medical miracle and takes the reader on a roller coaster through Washington D.C.'s dark corridors of power.

"Hard to put down. It will intrigue and thrill."

—Baltimore Sun

"A chilling medical thriller of science and capitalism gone mad; Pieczenik does for medicine what Tom Clancy did for high technology warfare."

—James T. Grady, author of *Six Days of the Condor*

Pax Pacifica

Tensions between the United States and China are escalating when troubleshooter Assistant Secretary of State Dr. Dessaix Clark goes to Beijing to uncover the true Chinese agenda and finds a brutal power struggle and a vortex of deception where none of the players are actually who they seem.

"Insightful...a page-turner with plot twists."

—The Denver Post

*"Few authors have dramatized the protracted struggle between east and west as well as Steve Pieczenik. In **Pax Pacifica** he draws on his experience as an important actor in the struggle, and then creates a complex plot of high intrigue, deception, shifting loyalties, and war and peace in Asia."*

—James R. Lilly, former CIA chief in Beijing, for the
Washington Post Book World

State of Emergency

The governors of Utah, Colorado, Wyoming and Arizona threaten to have their states secede from the Union if not given full military control of their own borders and the rights to their own waterways. When Deputy Assistant Secretary of State Dr. Alison Carter is asked to negotiate with the renegade governors he finds himself inside a web of deceit and betrayal where the line between ally and enemy is never clear.

"A grandmaster of the geo-political chess game."

—Stephen Coonts, author of *Under Siege*

"Excellent...lots of action."

—Library Journal

Maximum Vigilance

As the President's personal psychiatrist, Dr. Dessaix Clark, a prominent international crisis manager, must decide whether the President of the United States is mentally competent to manage an international crisis that can precipitate World War III. Dr. Clark risks his life in a desperate race to uncover a shadowy enemy.

"Another cracking yarn about life on the inside track of power and politics by a man who has lived and worked there."

—Frederick Forsyth, author of *The Deceiver*

"An intricate psychological thriller and an excellent story. An accurate picture of the White House and the government in crisis as only an insider can provide."

—Larry Bond, author of *Red Phoenix*

Other Books by Steve Pieczenik

Novels Published under the name Alexander Court

Active Measures

Active Pursuit

Op Center Series (co-created with Tom Clancy)

Op Center

Op Center: Mirror Image

Op Center: Games of State

Op Center: Acts of War

Op Center: Balance of Power

Op Center: State of Siege

Op Center: Divide and Conquer

Op Center: Line of Control

Op Center: Mission of Honor

Op Center: Sea of Fire

Op Center: Call to Treason

Op Center: War of Eagles

Net Force Series (co-created with Tom Clancy)

Net Force

Net Force: Hidden Agendas

Net Force: Night Moves

Net Force: Breaking Point

Net Force: Point of Impact

Net Force: Cybernation

Net Force: Changing of the Guard

Net Force: State of War

Net Force: Springboard

Non-Fiction
My Life is Great, Why Do I Feel So Awful?

MY BELOVED TALLEYRAND

The Life of a Scoundrel by His Last Mistress

Steve Pieczenik

with
Roberta Rovner-Pieczenik

iUniverse, Inc.
New York Lincoln Shanghai

My Beloved Talleyrand
The Life of a Scoundrel by His Last Mistress

iUniverse books may be ordered through booksellers or by contacting:

iUniverse
2021 Pine Lake Road, Suite 100
Lincoln, NE 68512
www.iuniverse.com
1-800-Authors (1-800-288-4677)

WGAE Registered June 5, 2004

ISBN-13: 978-0-595-34208-2 (pbk)
ISBN-13: 978-0-595-80676-8 (cloth)
ISBN-13: 978-0-595-78978-8 (ebk)
ISBN-10: 0-595-34208-6 (pbk)
ISBN-10: 0-595-80676-7 (cloth)
ISBN-10: 0-595-78978-1 (ebk)

Printed in the United States of America

By necessity, life is a game of endless betrayals, deceits, and manipulations. Only a grand manipulator can utilize these machinations to achieve his personal ambitions, be they in domestic politics or foreign affairs or, above all else, in the sublime pursuit of amorous conquests.
—Charles-Maurice de Talleyrand-Perigord, 1812

Foreword

In the world of international affairs—a world in which I have worked for over thirty years—there is always a price to pay when a government is out of touch with reality. That price, all too frequently, is the lives of innocent civilians.

As a former State Department hostage negotiator and crisis manager—a position from which I have always attempted to save lives—I have found it increasingly difficult to watch my own country's blindness to global realities, and to listen to the absurd ideology of the neo-conservatives which has led the country into a spiral of self-destruction since the 9/11 attacks.

To gain perspective I turned to an historical analogue from which I discovered some forgotten truths. I found it in the era of the French Revolution and in the personage of Count Charles-Maurice de Talleyrand-Perigord, known to the world of the Enlightenment simply as Talleyrand.

I consider myself fortunate to have spent a great many summers of my youth in the region of France in which Talleyrand grew to manhood. I speak the French language fluently. And always seeking a political-psychological explanation of what happens in the world (as a trained psychiatrist and political scientist is wont to do), I was pleased to find one in 18th and 19th century France. For at that time, all of the idealism of liberty, equality and fraternity turned into a Reign of Terror, the loss of civil liberties for French citizens, and the decline of economic viability for the country. The disturbing similarity between 19th century France and America today—in the loss of civil liberties, declining economic viability, and perhaps an intellectual and spiritual reign of terror—may not have been brought about by an internal revolution, but the effects of an administration in which fantasy (if not lies) has overtaken reality have been just as disastrous.

Talleyrand was attractive to me as an historical figure who witnessed France and Europe's chaos, but who was able to bring about years of stability for the continent by the instrumental role he played at the Congress of Vienna (1814). Yes, he was a defrocked clergyman, a debauched bishop, a foreign minister who demanded bribes from other diplomats, a womanizer. An interesting main character for an historical novel!

But Talleyrand was also a brilliant diplomat who, when he recognized the men he worked for were out of touch with reality, sought to topple them from power—even if the men in question were King Louis XVI, the members of the Revolutionary Directory who ruled following the beheading of the king, and Napoleon himself. Through wile, intrigue, deceit and betrayal Talleyrand remained loyal to higher goals than expanding and maintaining power for the men who appointed him foreign minister—the goals of equality and justice for all, which we all took for granted, until recently. As readily as he helped the administrations he served build power, he worked even harder to destroy their powerful men and institutions when they began to harm France, its people, and the stability of Europe. And he was successful.

I hope my choice of main character becomes your "beloved Talleyrand." Enjoy!

Steve Pieczenik, M.D., PhD.

Talleyrand's Era

Charles-Maurice de Talleyrand-Perigord (1754–1838) lived during the French Revolution and the French Revolutionary Wars, a violent time that transformed the government of France and the face of Europe.

1774–1789: France is a monarchy under King Louis XVI of the house of Bourbon. Life in France is rigidly structured into social classes called estates.

1789–1791: France becomes a constitutional monarchy after angry Parisian mobs of commoners (the third estate) take to the streets and storm the Bastille (a fortress turned prison). The new National Assembly abolishes nobility's privileges and formulates a Declaration of Rights. King Louis XVI remains on the throne, but he is deprived of legislative power.

1791–1792: The government collapses, and a new Legislative Assembly declares war on Austria, believing it is instigating counter-revolutionary agitation. After Austrian and Prussian forces invade France, the palace is stormed, King Louis XVI and his family are imprisoned and beheaded, and state control is taken by the revolutionary Commune of Paris.

1793–1795: A civil war and widespread revolt in the provinces against the dictatorship of Paris leads to a Reign of Terror, a period of ruthless and bloody repression by a revolutionary tribunal. Anarchy and runaway inflation leads to the completion of another constitution.

1795-1799: France is led by an executive Directory and two assemblies. Rather than providing stability, the directors purge Royalists and moderates from the government, sending them to penal colonies. Corruption reigns until Napoleon Bonaparte overthrows the Directory.

1799–1804: A consulate government with Napoleon as first consul is formed. He centralizes political control, restores Catholicism, codifies civil laws, liberalizes education, and modernizes the banking system. He also instigates endless military campaigns against other European powers.

1804–1814: Napoleon crowns himself emperor and is viewed as invincible until his attack on Russia and retreat from Moscow, resulting in the loss of most of his troops. A coalition of Prussia, Russia, Britain, and Austria invade France, and Napoleon abdicates. He is exiled to the island of Elba.

1815–1860: The Congress of Vienna reestablishes a balance of power and stability on the continent. Napoleon escapes from Elba and forms an army, but he is defeated at Waterloo and exiled to the island of St. Helena. France restores the Bourbon dynasty to the throne, in the person of King Louis XVIII, who is advised by a chamber of deputies. King Louis is succeeded by King Louis-Philippe.

MY BELOVED
TALLEYRAND

PROLOGUE

▼

He was loathed by many but admired by more. His enemies blamed him for Napoleon's defeat at Waterloo. His supporters hailed him as France's most brilliant statesman, whose strategy at the Congress of Vienna secured peace for the continent. Late in his life, Charles-Maurice de Talleyrand-Perigord—the incomparable diplomat, friend to emperors and kings, master of seduction and reinvention—finally fell in love. With a wife and many love affairs behind him, he pursued a controversial union with me, a woman thirty years his junior, which lasted for more than twenty years until his death.

Some say our love took root on a hot August day in 1816, a year after my beloved's crowning success in Vienna. Talleyrand had been asked to preside over a duel in a sun-drenched, grassy field on the outskirts of Paris. Facing off were an Austrian nobleman, Count Clam-Martinitz, my lover, and Edmond de Perigord, my husband.

Both men had entrusted the details of the duel to Talleyrand. Neither appeared with seconds to witness the event, knowing that all who counted in Parisian society would be there to serve that purpose. The confrontation, of course, was a duel of honor. But the gravity of the day was largely feigned. At that time, it was forbidden for anyone in France to fight to the death in a duel. The drawing of blood was now sufficient to determine the outcome of the encounter. How could anything transpire in that duel that would be more than sport or theater?

Many of the onlookers also knew that the duel, itself, was irrelevant because my marriage had already failed. However, Edmond's honor (or was it mine) had to be defended.

Talleyrand had chosen the date of the duel, the judge, the attending physician, and even the audience. While he intended the day to be memorable, I wondered, even then, whose cause he was advancing, that of my dissolute husband or that of my ostentatious lover? Or his own?

Only a year before, he had asked me to accompany him to Austria as his hostess, to help with his work at the Congress of Vienna. It would be my role to oversee the parties, balls, and banquets he organized there in behalf of France, all part of the landscape of a changing Europe and the extravagant diplomacy facilitating it. He was the hope of France, especially the returning Bourbon king. I was the wife of his nephew, mere decoration and nothing more, despite what Talleyrand's wife and the gossips of the Parisian salons may have thought. Unfortunately, our life in Vienna caused tongues to clack, however innocent our relationship.

At noon, *les invitees,* the invited guests, began to assemble. Judging by the dress of many of the women, they could have been attending a palace garden party. Crinoline skirts rustled as nervous females rushed to huddle and embrace. The gentlemen behaved better, exhibiting some awareness of the ritualistic gravity surrounding the event.

In that verdant field, oppressed by the unforgiving sun, shirts were damp and cheeks were flushed. The only two not seeming to sweat were Talleyrand and a man I later learned was an Austrian spy, still in my uncle's pay since Vienna, where purchased information—both personal and diplomatic—was always at a premium. The gallant Talleyrand circulated among the ladies, kissing hands. My own was included, and I would allow that he did indeed hold mine longer than he held the others.

Standing tall with his gold-knobbed cane and formal dress, Talleyrand was the picture of elegance and calm. Everyone focused on his every move. Because of his role in the duel, what should have been an uninspired match between two men of uncertain scruples became a day of drama.

Since Edmond had provoked the duel, it was my lover's choice of weapon. Once he selected the sword, I knew Edmond would be at a disadvantage. As I expected, the awaited event did not last more than two minutes. After a few perfunctory lunges, Clam-Martinitz ran his sword across Edmond's left cheek, drawing blood. Edmond passed out, and my lover, who may have wished to inflict a fatal wound, simply walked away as custom demanded.

Talleyrand was the first to approach the fallen Edmond and take note of his healthy condition. He nodded to Clam-Martinitz, but he did not extend his hand. Anything more would have been an insult to Talleyrand's family. Once the physician took charge, Talleyrand walked over to me, taking the long, awkward strides that his clubfoot necessitated. For the second time, he took my hands, his eyes locking with my own.

In a deep voice, strengthened by experience and smoothed by years of successful conquests, personal and political, he said simply, "Have strength, my beauty."

I wondered if he suspected that I was glad Edmond had lost.

The onlookers bowed and deferred to him, holding onto his every word. Years later, he told me he was not deceived. He knew his enemies, and several were there that day.

Madame de Stael, one of his former mistresses and someone I admired greatly, was known to have said Talleyrand "would exchange his soul for a pile of dung, and he would be right to do so." But she was a jealous woman and a victim of her own temper.

Napoleon, that awful little Corsican, once had the audacity to say that Talleyrand was *"le merde dans le stockings de soie,"* the shit in silk stockings. But who was he to talk?

After the duel, my circumstances grew difficult. The gossip in Paris was unrelenting. Yet, once I decided to return to Vienna and to Clam-Martinitz, Talleyrand launched a campaign to deepen my attachment to him. Flowers came to my lodgings. Smartly dressed envoys delivered small packages.

In one, a note was attached. Written in Talleyrand's hand, it said, "We belong together, my beauty."

The attention overwhelmed me, and I knew I was entering unsheltered waters. For the diplomat who had outmaneuvered emperors and kings, presided over the fate of nations, and restored peace to a Europe emerging from years of war, Talleyrand's "love diplomacy" had become a new test of his skills.

During the winter of 1816, my beloved succeeded in his love campaign to win me to his side. I agreed to return to Paris to live with him at Rue St. Florentin, despite the protests of Clam-Martinitz. These many years later, I am pleased to record that Talleyrand was no less a genius in courtship than he was in international affairs. Whether it was true love—and only true love—that drove me into his arms that day in Vienna, I cannot say. But the result of our union served both of us well for two decades.

Years before the duel and the decisions that shaped our defiant love, Charles-Maurice de Talleyrand-Perigord had already lived a life that most would envy. Could it be true that, by the time I entered his life, his greatest days were behind him? It would be difficult to me to disagree entirely. Yet, it is precisely because of the life he had led—its passions and manipulations along with its victories and defeats—that the defiance itself was possible.

Talleyrand never disguised the fact that he wanted to be a man for the ages. Before I met him, he had begun composing his memoirs. However, not long after his death, a great portion of the papers that were created to assure his immortality simply vanished. Some believed (and probably still do) that I hid or destroyed selected records of what he had accomplished and those he loved because of my desire to control his story and protect my own reputation.

This is not so. The story I am reconstructing on these pages started toward the end of his life, under his close supervision. What I have added from my own memory and from letters kept by my beloved's colleagues and friends deviates in no way from Talleyrand's stated wishes. I know my motives will always remain suspect with my enemies. But, should it not finally be acknowledged that, as Talleyrand grew old, I played an increasingly important role in so many aspects of his life?

I have been to the publishers this morning, to that busy, steamy place on the Rue Montreux. There I met with Monsieur Claude Duclos, a very tidily dressed, dignified man, who told me he adored Talleyrand (one of countless men seduced by my beloved's words and deeds) and was grateful for this opportunity to get closer to him through this book. Monsieur Dugard stood by his side, perspiring and nodding a few times too many for me to be sure of the sincerity of Monsieur Duclos' statements. I worried that, like so many others, he was already judging my beloved, even as he was judging me.

I am first to admit that a woman, especially a young woman, does not attach herself to a brilliant, older, accomplished man without seeing some reward at the end. I may have been a master in the art of submission, but I am not without self-respect. If Talleyrand were here with me now, he would agree that what may have begun as a manipulation on both our parts turned into a wonderful partnership. This manuscript is first and foremost a record of my beloved's monumental life. It is also my chance to lend some meaning to my own trials on this earth.

CHAPTER 1

▼

My beloved was born on February 2,1754, the son of Charles-Daniel de Perigord, Count de Talleyrand, and Alexandrine-Marie-Victoire, Eleonore de Damas d'Antigny. Though possessed of a noble name, the young couple had scarcely enough income to maintain their residence in one of Paris' fashionable neighborhoods. Their poverty was so pronounced that it forced Alexandrine to appeal to her father, the Marquis d'Antigny, for money to purchase the linen necessary for her confinement during pregnancy.

But the lack of funds, however inconvenient, did not mean catastrophe for the couple. Talleyrand's father was a lieutenant general in King Louis XV's armies and a tutor to the future King Louis XVI. My beloved's mother was a *dame d'honneur* to King Louis XV's wife and a *dame du palais* to Marie-Antoinette, King Louis XVI's wife. They were each born to the nobility of the *ancien régime*, old regime, a fact of life that would supersede any considerations of material well-being. Attending court at Versailles, although unable to afford the cost of its extravagances, they were close to the center of power.

This noble lineage muted a harsh reality—the severe deformity of their newborn's right foot. It was a disability that later caused Talleyrand's parents to exclaim that Charles-Maurice was "fit for nothing," certainly not for the military service the Talleyrand-Perigords had performed for the monarchy for centuries.

His foot, of course, was the first thing anyone noticed when meeting Talleyrand. It is also part of my earliest memory of him. (I could have not been more than six or seven.) I do remember his hobbling among guests in the great hall of our country house, looking ever so handsome in a red velvet coat and making the ladies laugh.

They say that after the party I chanted, "Talleyrand, Talleyrand," and proceeded to imitate his limping gait. I believe I was as frightened as I was fascinated.

Charles-Maurice, a plucky child, minimized his disability by the use of extraordinarily interesting and precious canes. As he grew, his limping gait did not diminish his attractiveness. Anyone at court will tell you he appealed to an incomparable number of women, many of whom became his mistresses. While Talleyrand never gloated to me about these women, from information provided by friends, letters, and his own reminiscences, I believe I know a fair amount about all of them. I am pleased to report that each had won a place in his heart and in his bed, long before that fateful duel that placed me in his life forever.

From the beginning, his family's name shaped Charles-Maurice's future. If he had fewer toys or clothes than the local merchant's son, it was not a calamity because my beloved had ancestry. And that ancestry opened doors to government and the church.

During the reign of King Louis XIII, the family was issued papers in which the monarch recognized a branch of Charles-Maurice's family as *de Perigord (de* was—and still is—the French demarcation of nobility). However, years later, when King Louis XVIII was especially annoyed with my beloved, he remarked in a loud voice, making certain everyone in the room could hear, that the Talleyrands were *"du Perigord, et non de Perigord,"* from Perigord, but not of Perigord. It was an effrontery that Talleyrand accepted silently when uttered, but he was determined to repay tenfold at a later time.

In the bleak loneliness that often settled on my beloved as a young boy, he turned to the stories of his ancestors. At an early age, he identified himself with the rambunctious, irreverent, short-tempered Adalbert, the tenth-century Count of Perigord, who, after a purposefully contrived confrontation with Hugues Carpet, the King of France, was angrily asked by his sovereign, "Who then has made you a king?" While it was Adalbert's intemperate attitude toward knaves and fools that made an impression on young Talleyrand, he decided at an older age that a show of temper to accomplish a task revealed a weakness of character. Throughout his life, my beloved chose an attitude of insouciance and indifference to achieve his goals.

In the late twelfth century, on nothing more than a whim, Talleyrand's relative, Helie the First, ordered the bishop of Limoges' eyes to be gouged out. When the Viscount of Limoges had Helie arrested and thrown into a dungeon with the intention of exacting an "eye for an eye," so to speak, Helie escaped and exacted vengeance in his own way. He impregnated the only daughter of the viscount and then abandoned her. It was Helie's vengeance that intrigued my beloved, although he learned in time to control his own passion for revenge.

In 1331, the Dean of Richmond, an early Talleyrand who presided over the diocese of York, reigned as the power behind the papal throne. Petrarch, the historian and commentator, noted, "It amuses Talleyrand to make a pope rather than to be pope." Perhaps it was from this ancestor that Talleyrand learned to be content to stand one step behind the source of power.

From his ancestor Henri, Count of Chalais, Talleyrand learned the importance of developing strategies and tactics that won the day. It was said the count had tried to assassinate another relative, Cardinal Richelieu, the omnipotent minister of Louis XIII, on two different occasions, but he committed the most deadly of all sins. He failed. As a result, the cardinal had an apprentice executioner behead the count. It took thirty-four ungainly strokes of the axe to accomplish the deed successfully.

Thereafter, the dynasty of Talleyrand-Perigord settled into less dangerous professions. They became humble servants of the church and state, soldiers, diplomats, and prelates. Perhaps my beloved's most important link to his ancestors did not come through his parents, who were distant, cold, and put off by his lameness. Instead, it was through an early attachment to his paternal great-grandmother, the Princess of Chalais, who, at the age of seventy-two, took in the lame boy with the cascading ringlets and gave him a taste of a true home. At her *château* in Chalais, in the region of Perigord, he was initiated into the social graces and manners demanded of the nobility of the time: how to give a lady a compliment, how to dress for a ball, how to keep one's companions interested in one's conversation, and how to be graceful. These early lessons won my heart in later years, and they certainly served Talleyrand well when he became a man of international stature and influence. When his time with his elderly relative ended, my beloved was better able to navigate the sadness and isolation that stayed with him for many years to come.

CHAPTER 2

▼

It was through the motto of the Talleyrand-Perigord family, *"Rien que Dieu"* (No king but God), that my beloved learned a basic truth about man's power over man. He discovered personal power could flourish unimpeded, if one acted as if one were responsible to no one but God. This understanding foreshadowed his later decision to enter the clergy. To his dismay, it also shaped the views of the Bourbon king who Talleyrand restored to the throne of France after Napoleon Bonaparte's egomania lost him his empire.

In the meantime, there was the matter of Talleyrand's education. The idyllic days at Chalais ended when his parents sent Charles-Maurice to the College d'Harcourt in Paris, a preparatory school for the sons of nobility who were destined for the priesthood, at the age of eight. By age fifteen, he was entered into the most prestigious theological seminary in France by his uncle, the soon-to-be archbishop of Rheims. The seminary, administered by a society known as the Priests of St. Sulpice, was known throughout France for both the excellence of its teachings and the conservatism of its faculty.

Talleyrand rationalized his acquiescence to entering the seminary as the only way of escaping a life of shameful poverty. Years later, he wrote, "Seeing that my fate could not be avoided, my wearied mind surrendered, and I allowed myself to be taken to the Ecole de St. Sulpice."

I believe the year he spent with his uncle at Rheims and the lavish lifestyle he observed—sinners fed from silver and gold plates, lavish hunting parties, women-chasing—served only to impress this impoverished boy with the advantages of clerical life. His parents, determined to send him into the world with the family name respectably intact and unharmed by the family's persistent monetary problems, pressed this view upon him daily. However, it was only when Talleyrand came to the decision himself that it did take root. It happened, as he told me, one day on a walk near his home.

Dordogne, the region into which Talleyrand was born, has always been a hunter's paradise. Imagine a heavily wooded area, separating the western edge of the uplands of Massif Central, a dromedary-shaped mountain range, from the River Dordogne. A little way downstream sits Bergerac, a quiet town with tidy, animated public spaces adorned with an overabundance of wildflowers common to the area—bougainvilleas, trumpet flowers, bluebells, and yellow flox. The two tributaries flowing calmly from the river and the scenery of gently rolling, lush hills and miles of wooded land created a peaceful feeling that Talleyrand told me he never forgot. My beloved took refuge in these woods throughout his childhood.

Even now, it is painful for me to imagine a young Talleyrand limping down the dirt path that paralleled his family's neglected country estate in his oversized, scruffy, high black riding boots, ignoring the discomfort and limitations of his clubfoot. Later in his life, he chose to depend upon a cane and wear, as he called it, "a monstrosity of a contraption," a large, rounded shoe with a metal frame that extended up his leg to the knee, where it was attached with a leather strap. Did he wish then for an easier time of it? He must have, but it is hard to imagine so because, as an adult, he never dwelt upon his infirmities, either the passing small and ordinary ones or the ones another man would consider lasting and monumental.

On this day, the day of his epiphany, he had to content himself with a stub of a foot punctured by one toenail that was wrapped in a sock and placed into a regular boot. Even he had a hard time gazing at his own deformity, which looked to him as if someone had sadistically crushed his foot into a ragged ball of human flesh from which a yellow-stained, fungus-ridden nail grew. At one point in our life together, he told me that he had once gone so far as to grab a hammer with the full intention of mutilating his left foot so that it would appear like his right.

On the day in question, he proceeded, as I did with him many years later, into the uplands of the Plateau de Millevaches, where the tributaries plunge into a gorge and the woods are filled with beech, chestnut, and conifers. He was filled with excruciating pain that day. His malformation limited his physical mobility and perhaps should have stopped him, especially since he had been warned he might encounter wild animals in this particular area of the woods. However, danger was not on his mind. While he walked through the woods, absorbing its beauty and contemplating his life, he was suddenly confronted with a wild boar directly in front of him, sporting two large tusks and ready to attack.

These are the facts as I know them. Talleyrand spotted the boar and backed up ever so slowly. The boar, no doubt sensing his fear, advanced slightly. Thinking quickly, Talleyrand took off his right boot, the one covering the clubfoot. With screeching sounds and wild, bodily gesticulations, he threw it into the underbrush. The boar proceeded to chase the empty boot while my beloved hobbled home as quickly as he could. This was surely an example of his quick wit, but the incident also continued to remind him of his vulnerability and his mortality. He decided the church, with its mysteries and miracles, would be the means to transcend both.

Depending on the listener, the tale of the confrontation with the boar took on a wholly different character.

To the British ambassador after Napoleon's defeat at Waterloo he said, "When I was a young man confronted in the woods with a wild boar, I understood immediately that life is a long, continuous struggle in which shrewdness and calculation would trump the rage of the wildest of beasts."

To Czar Alexander of Russia, after promising to deliver to him the much sought-after prize of Austria, Talleyrand swore the experience had helped him understand how to make your enemies look left while you go right.

In our bedroom, retelling this early conquest, the event had taught an entirely different lesson. "I saw my life ahead of me, and I knew I needed to live in order to love."

Early triumphs, like later ones, could always be twisted just so in order to win the day.

My beloved's early bravery and resourcefulness did indeed reappear throughout his life. How exactly his indomitable will to succeed at whatever task confronting him was formed, I cannot say for sure, but I believe it was indelibly etched on his persona, in no small part, by his physical deformity. With an effort that came from within, because no praise certainly came from his family, he forced himself to overcome any sense of inadequacy and self-consciousness that, as long as he remembered, was at the source of his introvertedness and shyness. Ironically, these traits were mistaken in later years for arrogance and aloofness.

Since I did not know Talleyrand when he was young, there were few ways other than my beloved's remembrances for me to piece his early life together. I am thankful that children of servants who worked for his family throughout his life and who subsequently served us, related precious pieces and bits of information to me. Also, working backwards from full-sized portraits of him commissioned by paramours and kings, I was able to extract a rather complete portrait of my beloved as a young man. He spoke of those unhappy days only at my insistence, often dropping a significant nugget of information here or there.

What I understand is that he was small, with ringlets of reddish-brown hair cascading down the high collar of his everyday green topcoat, frayed from wear and inattention. His oval face was sharply cut by an aquiline nose, piercing brown eyes, and thick, full lips. Many thought him quite handsome, and I found him to be so until the end of his days. Yes, I would have liked to have known that young man. And yes, our age difference was a source of conflict at times. It was also a source of excitement and pleasure. When he related the story of his life to me, more than what others ever knew, it was all color and action. It was life lived vividly and ebulliently. It was a life for me to enjoy vicariously.

As a boy, he wondered if his misshapen foot denoted some kind of spiritual deficiency. Or had it been the result of his childhood nanny inadvertently dropping him on the hard ground when he was an infant, causing him to sustain a compound fracture that mended poorly? How was this story any more or less close to the truth than the one that stated that the de Perigord family was predisposed to such deformities? As was his wont at that particularly rebellious age, Talleyrand was reluctant to believe anything that absolved his parents of responsibility for his deformity. The theory that his parents possessed a defective component in their constitutional makeup appealed to both his sense of logic and, quite frankly, to the increasing rage against them that had been welling inside of him for many years. As painful as it might have been for him both physically and spiritually, in his early years, he thought himself to be a marked man, carrying the devil's handiwork, which could be passed onto his children and his children's children.

Fortunately, as he grew older and matured, the rage subsided, and Talleyrand no longer dwelled upon his physical limitations. Later on, in church or in government, he managed to erase any suspicions of deficiency from his mind. Women found him attractive and gave him their sexual favors, along with their hearts. Men of power found him intimidating, but they listened closely to his words. Kings distrusted him, but they relied on his advice. While there was no inherent safety in life, he always remembered he had outsmarted the beast that, given the chance, could have devoured him.

Talleyrand's years at home, with the exception of the affections of his great-grandmother, were loveless ones. In his own memoirs, he wrote that he regarded his first fifteen years of life as a *prisonnier sans barreaux,* prisoner without bars. He dreamed of leaving the family estate one day. He spent countless hours alone, reading history, theology, and the biographies of great men. Talleyrand's life, at that time, was a continuous struggle between what his family wanted him to do (enter the clergy) and his own, still unclear, hopes for a celebrated future. It was true that his uncle, Cardinal Richelieu, had served the Sun King, King Louis XIV, with ruthless loyalty, doing whatever it took to accomplish a task. Could admittance to the clergy lead Talleyrand to the palace at Versailles?

"I must assume a mask of self-denial so as to succeed in my ambitions, whatever they may be," he wrote on a piece of paper I discovered wedged between pages of the Perigord family prayer book. "I am being forced to enter the holy orders since no other career is open to a man of my name and condition."

At year's end, in 1770, Talleyrand submitted to his parents' wishes and agreed to attend St. Sulpice, the first of many decisions that proved a boost to both his status and fortunes.

CHAPTER 3

▼

My beloved left home for the seminary, located in a Parisian archdiocese some 800 kilometers away. He carried nothing with him other than the clothing he wore. His parents had provided him with a few francs, enough only to elevate his stature slightly above that of a beggar. Because his resources were so limited, Talleyrand had to choose between reaching the seminary on foot with some money left in his pocket or spending almost every franc he had on transportation and arriving at St. Sulpice penniless. Not surprisingly, he found abject poverty not to his taste and decided to take his chances with the uncertainties that accompany a journey on foot. The difficult road to Paris, past the fortified town of Cahors, was to be his gateway to opportunity.

Talleyrand recorded in his diary that, late in his first day of travel, while limping down that road, an elegant landau drawn by pair horses drew up alongside him. The coachman, a ruddy-complexioned man in livery, holding the reins in his left hand and a whip in his right shouted, "Young man, climb aboard!"

Talleyrand ignored the abrupt interruption of his own thoughts and continued to walk on in silence.

"Didn't you hear me, young man?" the driver asked, wondering whether the youth was deaf as well as crippled. "You may climb aboard the coach. I have plenty of room next to me."

"Thank you," Talleyrand responded, "but I prefer to walk."

"As you wish," the coachman muttered. But, just as he raised his whip to his horses, he heard a knock from the cab below, cautioning him not to proceed.

"May I invite you into my carriage?" A woman's hand opened a door gilded with the insignia of a noble family that Talleyrand did not recognize. Admittedly tired, thirsty, and hungry, he still resisted the temptation to enter the carriage, most likely out of pride or stubbornness. Whatever he had to do to reach the seminary would have to be done on his own terms, without any help. The idea that remaining on foot made him a target for ruffians and vagabonds had been dismissed by my beloved as unlikely (although, in reality, the probability was high). Now that he was on his own, he was determined to establish for himself a habit of self-reliance in the face of possible adversity. But, while he was planting his flag of independence, his right leg had already begun to feel the strain of the walk.

"Which way are you headed?" the woman asked, her voice somewhat muffled by the carriage's brocaded interior.

"I'm on my way to Paris," he answered.

"Paris?" she repeated. "That's a very long way. At least we can give you a bit of assistance to ease your journey."

As an adult, Talleyrand always remembered that faceless voice as sweetly seductive. I can imagine him, on that day, drawn to its mystery and intrigue. Still, he was not used to a voice such as this, gentle and coaxing as it was. His mother's voice always sounded so shrill, demanding and imperious when she spoke to him, with rarely a hint of care. It was not that she was cruel. She was simply not available…just like his father. To hear the mellifluous sounds of a female stranger besiege him with kindness must have seemed nothing short of a miracle.

So, a life of prodigious *amour* was off to a rather romantic start. I envy him that. Though I can remember my own amorous awakenings, they pale by comparison. A fearful touch. A stolen kiss. The breath of a man's desire was still the stuff of daydreams for me. And so it remained until my marriage. Talleyrand, who was determined to be a man of history, an immortal driving force, held onto the wooden rails on both sides of the metal steps and boosted his tired body into the carriage. He sat down on the cushioned bench opposite the woman from whom that heavenly voice emanated. She remained enveloped in the darkness of the cab.

"Thank you," he said.

"Please, make yourself comfortable," she coaxed. "Here, I think this will help."

With a delicate movement of her foot, she pushed her footstool over to Talleyrand. "I find that, on long journeys, even one's resting feet tend to tire, just simply from sitting. Strange, isn't it?"

"Oh, please, no!" Talleyrand responded, uncomfortable with the thought that the woman was taking pity on him.

"I insist!"

"Thank you once more," Talleyrand said, embarrassed by her generosity and, like most adolescents, transfixed by her graciousness and the possibility of her physical beauty.

Talleyrand's diary next describes the blue cape that attempted to conceal the woman's buxom body. She wore a wide-brimmed hat covered with white ostrich feathers, which swooped down in semicircular rings along its rim and hid her face in the shadows of a veil. Talleyrand imagined he caught a glimpse of dark, penetrating eyes and alabaster skin with a minute amount of rouge on the lips.

"What is your name?" she asked.

"Charles-Maurice…" He stopped, unsure whether he wanted her to know his family name, lest she be an acquaintance of his parents.

"Well, it is a pleasure to meet you Charles-Maurice," she said, extending an ungloved hand to him.

Talleyrand noticed a small ring on the second finger of her right hand with the same noble crest that adorned the carriage.

"Madame," he addressed her in a cracking voice, "may I be so presumptuous as to ask your name?"

"Of course, you may," she responded, attracted by the gentle awkwardness of the youth before her (or so my beloved thought at the time). "My name is Countess Marie-Therese de Perignod. But, if we are to make each other feel comfortable on this protracted journey, I think we should call each other by our given name. I insist that you address me as Marie-Therese."

Please forgive me, dear reader, for stopping Talleyrand's adventure at this ripe moment, but I believe you are probably confused by the similarity of names with which you have been presented. The de Perignod family of Countess Marie-Therese was a house of nobility that had no relationship to the de Perigord family of Talleyrand. They are two different *ancien régime* houses of nobility that happen to trace their respective ancestries to the southwest region of France. This distinction clarified, I return to what was taking place in the carriage.

The woman before him was clearly a woman of means. Yet, in Talleyrand's calculating mind, she was also a woman who might be seeking a reprieve from her otherwise boring life. He could identify with her in that respect. Wasn't he on the road to Paris to leave a numbing existence behind him? Despite his youth, he told me this episode proved to be one of the first times he totally trusted his instincts that, as the years went by, proved to be more accurate than purported facts.

"Then, Charles-Maurice, it shall be. And why, may I ask, are you going to Paris?"

"I am going there to study," he answered with increasing self-confidence in his voice.

"And what field of study would occupy a young man of such obvious vitality and intelligence?"

Despite a cynicism that lasted throughout his life, Talleyrand was young enough at this point to flush red upon hearing her flattery. "I will be attending the Ecole de St. Sulpice."

"The one attached to the Church of St. Sulpice?" she asked, bemused. She later told my beloved she had the notion she was in the presence of a religious apostate, most probably a virgin.

"Yes, the very same one," Talleyrand responded somewhat defensively this time.

"I presume you will become the abbé of Perigord one day?" she asked, revealing just a little bit more than she had intended.

"Well, yes," he muttered. "I will, if all goes well, become an abbé."

His face flushed red again. He had been discovered. And he had made such a determined effort to conceal his identity so that he could be treated on the basis of who he was, not what he represented.

"Please forgive me if I have ruined your attempt at anonymity." Marie-Therese leaned forward and gently touched his left hand, the one on which he wore a half-silver ring with his family's crest. "Talleyrand-Perigord is a well-known family in this area of the Dordogne. I can assure you that it is nothing of which to be ashamed."

"I am not ashamed of what or who I am," he responded brusquely. But he allowed her hand to continue resting upon his.

"Of course, you're not," Marie-Therese replied soothingly, fearful she might have hurt his feelings. She leaned toward him and raised her veil so that he could have full view of her face.

"I..." He hesitated, not knowing what to say. All his fantasies were ruined. With the veil removed, this gracious lady exhibited a half-moon scar over her left eye, which greatly diminished her beauty, and creases over her brow revealing a greater difference in age than he had imagined.

"Don't be afraid, Charles-Maurice," Marie-Therese said, holding both of his cold hands in her warm palms. "My scar was a present from my parents during one of their bacchanalian feasts. At the age of five, I had the grand privilege of stopping a bottle of wine while it was in flight and traversing the room."

"What can I..."

"The accidents of life are intended either to make us bitter or enhance our gratefulness of what we have," she interrupted. "I have chosen the latter. For that, I am at peace with myself, as I hope you will be one day." She glanced at his crippled leg. "The scars you and I wear are apparent to all those who want to gawk. But the scars of the heart are hidden so well that even we are not aware of them."

He felt his hands warm to hers. Suddenly, he understood the reason for her initial invitation into the carriage. She had seen him limping along the road and sensed he was a kinsman by both birthright and physical handicap. With this appreciation, her face became more beautiful. It would even seem enhanced by its imperfection.

Marie-Therese drew Talleyrand closer and placed a gentle kiss on his lips. His entire body shook. For the first time in his life, he told me he felt totally alive. He could feel the rush of adrenaline coursing through his veins and the fullness enveloping his groin. His heart beat quickly, matched only by his rapid breathing. Marie-Therese pulled him to her, and both descended gradually to the bottom of the carriage, where they remained for the rest of the voyage.

This incident, each time my beloved retold it, made me both happy and sad. I was happy Talleyrand had finally received tenderness from a woman of his station. Yet, I was sad that I was never able to share with him the exquisite sensations of a first love. To my regret, Edmond was chosen by others to be mine. As an obedient daughter, I accepted life as it was supposed to be lived and love as it was supposed to be given. Was I Edmond's great love? I preferred not to ask the question at the time of our marriage, afraid to hear the answer.

As someone who loved Talleyrand very much and who is trying to tell his...no, our...story faithfully, I hope my beginning goes a long way toward maintaining your confidence in my abilities and the selflessness of my words.

CHAPTER 4

▼

In spite of himself, Talleyrand became an abbé and was forever resentful he had gone through the charade of piety to please his parents, who never once visited him in the five years he studied at the seminary of St. Sulpice.

In the letters Talleyrand occasionally wrote to them, which were returned to his possession after their deaths, there is a sadly beautiful self-portrait of one still in his youth:

> People think I am haughty and often reproach me for it. When they do, I do not bother to reply. For it seems to me that, if they knew me better, they would not think me so. Some say my arrogance is beyond endurance. *Mon Dieu*, My God! I am neither haughty nor arrogant. I am merely an innocent adolescent and an extremely miserable and confused one. I hold feelings of resentment against my teachers and even against you, *cher*, dear, mama and papa, but especially against the concept of 'social propriety' to which I have been forced to surrender. In spite of my personal frustrations, resentments, and desire to abandon this entire charade, I promise to become a priest. Against my nature, I will wear that silly piece of cloth, signifying the ultimate hypocrisy, the clerical cassock.

Throughout his years at St. Sulpice, Talleyrand found some measure of solace in the only place where intellectual hunger interlaces with emotional restlessness, the seminary's library. It was no larger than a village chapel, but it was filled with oversized, leatherbound books that were frayed at the edges and reeked with a smell of staleness that Talleyrand always found inviting. He entered the poorly lit structure daily and pulled down each book from its perch on a sagging shelf with almost religious reverence, anticipating an escape into a new world, a world shaped and defined only by its author. From each author (no doubt all were men because, in those times, as now, we women hold so little sway), he devoured words, phrases, and ideas that ameliorated his confusion and illuminated his destiny. It was in that small, musty, dark library that Talleyrand found his intellectual passions inflamed.

Shortly after his death, when I needed to console myself, I often turned to his diary to find comfort and feel his presence. Reading the following passage always brought me closer to the man I adored, his vulnerability being so obvious and so revealing when he confessed his feelings during his years at St. Sulpice:

> As a child, unappreciated as I was by my parents, I often believed what they said—that I was fit for nothing. But once they were removed from my daily experience, my despondency gave way to a strong and comforting feeling that usually would come over me as I sat in the library—that I was indeed fit for something. I spent my days reading the works of great historians; the private lives of statesmen, philosophers, and moralists; and much poetry. This was my recreation. I chose. I devoured the most revolutionary books I could find, and I fed my mind with histories describing revolts, sedition, and revolution in every land, knowing that, in spirit, I was one with the rebel.

All was not books and solitude for Talleyrand. He made ample time to advance his skills with women. Often, he ignored his theology courses to slip away with Marie-Therese. There were others, probably more than he was willing to tell me about. I knew from the smile on his face when he mentioned this period of his life that, with all its frolics and experiments in physical passion, he was far more devil than saint. I must say that this never displeased me. By the time we consummated our physical relationship, I was more excited by his mental strength than his physical prowess.

His deformity, which I always felt added character to his person, persisted in being a source of self-consciousness for him during this period of his sexual awakening. Who, at that time of life, does not give in to feelings of self-pity? I had fretted that my eyes were set too far apart, my brow was too broad. When older, watching my coquettish friends banter with ease, it seemed I always had to struggle to keep pace.

One evening, during an interlude with Marie-Therese at her apartment near the Louvre, he confessed to her, "Even after all these years we have spent together, sharing a bed, I still feel uncomfortable when you place my foot in your hand, stroking and fondling it. I am embarrassed. I find my foot so ugly. So hideous!"

Marie-Therese responded with her usual wisdom. "You are still too young to appreciate what a woman really wants."

He told me that she gazed into his eyes and at the locks of curly hair falling haphazardly over his face. She gently kissed his lips, his eyelids, his cheeks. She nibbled his right earlobe, whispering, *"Je t'aime,"* I love you.

"Why?" he asked, running his fingers lightly over the scar near her temple. "You are twelve years older than I."

As frequently as he tried to provoke her, he knew he loved her as much as he could ever love anyone, and I am grateful to her for giving him so much pleasure and understanding. She was the only woman who had ever touched…no…caressed his body as if every part was precious. She made him feel alive. And, when she spent time kissing his foot, which they named *mon petit ami*, my little friend, she made him feel complete, whole, and normal. She teased him that the foot was the price he paid for his prodigious intellect. For indeed, his mind was, for her as for all of his women, the ultimate aphrodisiac.

When he looked around the small room in which they held their assignations, a place sparsely furnished save for the draped mahogany bed that Marie-Therese had imported from England, he realized what she had sacrificed to be with him. Being a married woman with children, she risked her own social standing by spending so much time with this novice. Only years later, when it was I who was the novice to his tender embraces, could I truly appreciate the role Marie-Therese had played in his life.

"My dear, Charles-Maurice," she answered, "if you were twice handicapped and carried a small hump on your back, I would love you just the same." She smiled slyly. "Maybe even more."

"Then the answer is clear!" he said decisively. "We love each other because each of us has been marked unfairly."

"Would you love me any less if I didn't have this scar on my face?" Without waiting for the sweet answer she was confident he would give, she placed her naked body over his and started to slide back and forth, clearly exciting him.

Talleyrand knew that no verbal response was required while he felt himself become aroused.

"Answer me!" she demanded innocently while she gently took him inside her. Looking at his head against the pillow with his eyes closed, he still looked like the cherubic boy she had seduced as he limped on his way toward St. Sulpice. But they both knew he no longer was the innocent. Over those five years, he had become a proficient lover, learning everything she could teach him about pleasing a woman and discovering new avenues through his own powerful imagination. He was no longer in a rush for satisfaction…no longer besieged by a thirst he felt could never be quenched. He knew how to take his time, stroke her body with his delicate hands, and whisper the most incredible and stimulating obscenities of love.

Some of this early relationship Talleyrand shared with me. I read about other relationships in his diaries. A great deal I simply imagined, assured that what my beloved and I shared, while special, had been rehearsed by him countless times before with more women than I cared to learn about. You might imagine how extremely difficult it is for me to recount this story of my beloved's pleasure with his first mistress. Yet I greatly appreciated my inheritance from Marie-Therese and his other loves when my role changed from niece-by-marriage, to hostess, to mistress, and to live-in companion. I am convinced that, whatever the course Talleyrand's lovemaking took and whatever new delights he brought to the bed, it was always his voice and his words that sent women, myself included, into complete submission. Marie-Therese may have wondered how many times she would have to explain to him that his charm rested on his ability to make her feel beautiful, intelligent, and needed. Although she must have realized the day would come when he would leave her, she seemed to live her moments with him to the fullest. I met her by chance many years later when she was already elderly, and she was kind enough to share a thought with me.

"My dear, Charles-Maurice was an eager student of love, but it was always his words. It was the way he could take a moment in time and possess it through his intelligence. When he shared his knowledge and thoughts with me, I was the novice. I was the one to learn and grow. It was my turn to be flattered by his conversation, as if we were equals."

Apparently, Talleyrand was also instinctively clever about how to let a woman down. For when Marie-Therese asked him how she should be addressed when he became the abbé de Perigord, he replied, "Madame, Abbé de Perigord! Of course! What else!"

According to her, "We laughed like children then, but I sensed then that I would soon be seeing him no more." Marie-Therese grew somber. "You are a very lucky woman," she said to me.

The last year at the seminary, my beloved precipitated a major confrontation with Abbé Couturier, a sagacious old man who was familiar with the worldly ways of his novitiates. When the abbé confronted Talleyrand with a recounting of his transgressions, which, by the fifth year, had taken on proportions that seemed to defy his commitment to the church, Talleyrand countered, as always, with, "I do whatever is necessary and leave it to others to argue over whether it was right or wrong. If my consorting with the countess be sin, then you, my superior, and your colleagues must accept it."

It was then, with Abbé Couturier's response, that Talleyrand learned one of his many lessons about political power, lessons that held him in good stead throughout his life. "I have developed the art of being blind when necessary. I merely caution a student who is regarded as destined to fill high posts in the clergy, especially one who may become the coadjutor to the archbishop of Rheims, a cardinal, or even a minister delegated by the king's authority to distribute benefices."

No one, my beloved realized at that moment, not even a high member of the church, would dare risk his future on reprimanding the nephew of the archbishop of Rheims. Ultimately, it was brute power and connections that enabled him to become the abbé of Perigord, rather than piety or personal achievement.

In the diary he kept throughout his years at St. Sulpice, Talleyrand complained how he detested the seminary and how much energy and emotion it took from him not to leave. At several entries, he questioned his belief in God.

I must admit that these sentiments of skepticism were not so different from my own throughout my youth, but I dared not express them aloud to anyone. In truth, I appeared to submit to God more easily than Talleyrand did because I respected what was expected of me by my parents. Surrounded as I was by my brothers and sisters, I was also less lonely, less combative. Yet, listening to my beloved's sentiments endeared him to me more than you might imagine. My heart raced when I thought about how he stood fast against so much hypocrisy in his family, his school, and his church. While I tried many times to tell him of my pride in him, I fear, in retrospect, that I should have tried harder.

CHAPTER 5

▼

When Talleyrand was incardinated into his uncle's diocese in Rheims as the new abbé of Perigord, he was well aware that, while a cleric must be accredited to a diocese, he is not required to live in it. With the influence of his uncle, Archbishop Alexandre-Angelique, my beloved managed to have himself posted to Paris, the only place he felt an intelligent, ambitious young man should reside.

The archbishop, a shrewd man in his late sixties, was easily co-opted by Talleyrand's arguments for staying in Paris. In part, it was out of fondness for his nephew. In part, it was out of pity for his deformity. In part, it was out of admiration for his audacity. Years later, when Talleyrand was more politically sophisticated, he realized the archbishop also recognized an opportunity to have a family member act as a spy for him in the city. Providing him with information about who was considered to be on his way up or on his way down the social and political ladders of Paris was the least a grateful nephew could do for an uncle who had favored him with his patronage. So, Talleyrand, as he would do throughout his life, found resolution to a personal desire, which also served the interests of others (in this case, his uncle) without having to create an enemy or confront anyone unnecessarily.

Talleyrand remained living at the rectory of St. Sulpice, where he continued to sleep on a wooden cot in a room no larger than a prison cell with all his worldly belongings either in a chest at the foot of his bed or at his side on a sturdy, oak nightstand from Brittany. Given the many years he lived in this condition, I find it very easy to understand why he developed his lifelong yearning for ornamental and well-crafted furnishings. Deprivation was a good teacher.

Dear reader, let it be known now that, throughout his life, Talleyrand, a master of diplomacy, was fearful of direct confrontation. When he disagreed strongly, it was never "I am angry" because of this or that. Rather, his discussion went more like, "Would it not be a more practical idea if…"

Sometimes, I wished him to raise his voice or throw a plate when we argued, but he always seemed too indifferent for that, which served to make me even angrier. I could pound a table or break a plate as easily as I drew a breath. Then, how I had to beg for forgiveness. To this day, so many years later, I choose to deny those memories that make it appear that I built my life around the virtue of submission. I would rather see my decisions to act—or not to act—as carefully chosen manipulations. Were they as clever as those of my beloved, whose entire life was built on manipulating people and events in order to control them? Of course not. Yet, they worked well.

Talleyrand once told me he avoided confrontation because he could not predict its consequences. Too much emotion…too little control. At the Congress of Vienna, when the stakes were so great, he mentioned this one and that one who yielded the upper hand merely because of an uncontrollable temper. When colleagues asked him how he successfully abided both conflict and confrontation, he informed them that anything less was simply *déclassé*, beneath him. I believe it was at St. Sulpice where he began to create an approach to life that would become his trademark behavior—aggressive opportunism combined with the appearance of indifference. My own, in retrospect, was just draped in the costumes used by women.

As a result of his uncle's influence, he was soon made deacon of Rheims. In May 1780, he was appointed one of two agents-general of the clergy. In this post, he served as liaison between the church and the government in matters pertaining to the income and expenditures of the church. He also dealt in matters pertaining to the maintenance of the privileges of the church and the clergy. Years later, when Talleyrand had acquired enemies in the royal court, they attempted to malign his reputation by pointing out the personal wealth he had managed to acquire during his years in the clergy. While I never cared that he chose not to lend credence to the innuendoes of larceny by responding to his critics, I was disappointed that he also never chose to contradict their charges when discussing financial matters with me.

I believe it was in this liaison position that he sharpened his skills in diplomacy and developed considerable patience in all matters. I also warn the reader right now that, while his later actions might seem anticlerical and his reversal of opinions on the church confusing, in his position as agent-general, there was no better spokesperson for the church than my beloved. He created a better administrative structure for communications between the king's ministers and the clergy. He withstood the attacks made on the church's temporal powers, the attempts to seize its property, and end its right to tithe. He defended the opulence of the upper church hierarchy against the lower clergy's resentment. My beloved played his institutional role for five years with resourcefulness, sensitivity, and statesmanship. No doubt, he was learning and practicing many of the techniques he was soon to use in service to the king.

Talleyrand, however, spent as little time as possible at St. Sulpice. Instead, he attacked the social scene in Paris with the intensity of a general attempting a military objective. Like the brilliant strategist he was, he approached the problem of access to Parisian society by reversing the typical strategy of seeming social and garrulous. Instead, he was determined to appear aloof and reserved in order to seem more interesting.

I hope it is not blasphemous for me to thank God for the social world that presented itself to my beloved as a youthful cleric. Decades before my birth, I have been told that France had established increasingly repressive laws, preventing unsupervised and unlicensed gatherings of men who were considered possible plotters against the monarchy. Large dinners could not be held, and club life did not develop. It was only after the king's death that a series of remarkable women appeared in Paris to carry on and, perhaps, perfect the salons that had begun decades before. Soon, there were aristocratic salons, like those of the duke of Chartres at the Palais-Royal, salons of financiers, and literary salons. By the contrivance of women in salons, men became princes of the church, ministers of state, and members of the Academy. Some were given protection, as was Voltaire, my beloved's inspiration, by Madame de Richelieu, to whom the keeper of the seals revealed secret government measures proposed against the philosopher for his revolutionary ideas.

During Talleyrand's days as a youthful abbé, Paris was again awash in private parties, salons, balls, and all manner of amusements that appealed to his physical and mental senses. He told me the women dressed in long, flowing, diaphanous dresses, leaving nothing to the imagination. They exchanged their favors with anyone who was within proximity, man or woman. Other parties, of course, were more sedate (that is, rather discreet), where only the undercurrents of sexual tension vibrated. It was at one of those parties that Talleyrand first introduced himself to Parisian society, calculating correctly that he should seem as demure and dignified as possible. Once he had established himself as "the guest one must always have," he would allow himself to take more liberties.

By the time Parisian society accepted my beloved, he had recognized and recorded that:

> Most senior clerics were able to remain in the church because worldly temptations were readily accessible to them without having to alter their façade of piety, self-abnegation, and chastity. The church, like most social institutions, simply provided a cover for the true nature of man. It was the ultimate refuge of the hedonist, the depraved, and the hypocrite.

CHAPTER 6

▼

Talleyrand's *entrée*, entrance, into Parisian society was through Madame de Gramont, the daughter of the duke of Choiseul, the first minister to the king. As soon as she heard there was a young, witty abbé in Paris from a far nobler lineage than hers (who was also a distant relative), she decided that, as a *doyenne* of Paris society, it was her duty to assess this young man. She would test him in company and put him in his proper place if need be. Through her dear friend, Auguste de Comte, she invited this young cleric to one of her celebrated dinner parties. Until her dying day, she never realized Talleyrand had manipulated de Comte into pressing Madame de Gramont for an invitation.

When young Talleyrand arrived at the *château* on Rue de Montaigne dressed in a frayed, black frock coat and white silk ascot with his hair cascading in ringlets, a woman in her late forties greeted him. She had a sharp, pointed nose, a small chin, and a permanent expression of disdain on her face. Consistent with the fashion of the day, she had her hair combed up into a chignon that was tied with two red ribbons, intended to match the brilliantly colored red silk brocade dress that billowed over her heavyset frame in a vain attempt to disguise ungainly curvatures. In her hand, she held a cabriolet fan. My beloved told me he remembered thinking her silver earrings, shaped like undulating ribbon bows with diamonds and other precious stones, gave her a garish, rather than refined, appearance.

Talleyrand could not help but stare at her until he realized he was making her uncomfortable. In turn, she focused on his right boot as if she could actually see the misshapen foot inside, his unconscious humiliation of her paid for in kind. She took an instant dislike to this coarsely dressed, rude young man and immediately decided that, in the salons of Paris, where every gesture, conversation, and joke was a strategic move as much as it was a point of social grace, she was going to teach him a lesson.

"Welcome to my home," she said in an overly sweet tone of voice, pulling him closer and kissing him on both cheeks. "I have been looking forward to this evening for quite some time."

"It is very kind of you to invite me to your home," Talleyrand responded politely, scanning the large entry hall and sweeping staircase. "Your décor is quite exquisite. I must compliment you on your taste."

My beloved was unexpectedly impressed by the entire wardrobe, from its *canapés, bergeres, faut evils,* and *chaises,* all *en suite* and upholstered to match. The marquetry console, with its concealed drawers, was the newest fashion in Paris. Talleyrand had grown up, however, to admire the typically heavy-wooded walnut furniture of Provençal, every piece looking as if it had been carved out of a single piece of wood. Although beveled floor-to-ceiling mirrors in intricately carved wooden frames graced the walls and alabaster nymphs rested and played with their naked young on a rich, red Isfahan carpet in the center of the entry hall, to Talleyrand, it was the décor of a bordello crossed with the insecure monies of the upstart *bourgeoisie,* middle class.

"The console you are admiring was designed by none other than Bernard van Risenburgh," said Madame de Gramont, pointing to the piece that seemed to catch the young man's eye. "I'm certain the de Perigord family must own a few of his pieces. He is the most sought-after designer in Paris."

"I don't believe my family is in the habit of patronizing anyone but French artisans," my beloved responded, delighted to watch her overly powdered face blanch under the implied insult that she was not loyal to things French.

Her response was to ignore his words and take his arm. She led him to a commode attributed to Boulle, a supreme French craftsman known throughout Parisian society for his new technique of clamping together sheets of tortoise shell and brass. Making a point of being solicitous about his limp, she still walked more quickly across the room than he could manage with ease. He, in turn, decided to walk as slowly as he could to frustrate her. It was in this fashion that the war of manners was played out in every drawing room in Paris, except that Madame de Gramont's was known to be the most vitriolic and, therefore, the most challenging for anyone with social aspirations.

Talleyrand released himself from her grip and stopped before the portrait of a tall, lithe, beautiful woman dressed in a gold brocade gown with a *décolletage,* low cut neckline, that provided a sensuous setting for the emerald-studded necklace that sat as a collar around her neck. A backdrop of obvious fake foliage surrounded her. The painter had asked the woman to lean against a sepia-toned marble statue of a seated woman suckling a newborn child.

"Fascinating, isn't she?" Madame de Gramont asked, pleased by the fact that something she prized had captivated this ill-cultured young man's attention.

"The delicacy of her face…" Talleyrand responded, "her arms, her hands…"

"Refined, isn't she?" Madame Gramont responded, eager for his comments. She always told her lady friends that, if you find a man's proclivities, you control his activities.

"Most certainly!" Talleyrand replied, realizing too late that his interest in the portrait would only serve to provide his relative with another verbal thrust and parry.

"Who is she?" he asked.

"In Paris, we have a saying…" she replied, gloating over the fact that she was privy to a secret that would soon surprise him, "don't start the dessert until you've eaten the main course."

"What's her name?" he asked again, enchanted by the simplicity and innocence of the woman in the elegant gown. Her slightly oval face held delicate features—high cheekbones, green slanted eyes, thinly arched brows—that mesmerized him.

"The painting was done by Francois Boucher," she said, avoiding his question. "I'm certain your family would be proud to know this painter is a true Frenchman."

"Her name, Madame de Gramont?" Talleyrand demanded quietly, finding his relative intolerably sadistic. While he wished to put her in her place with a well-turned phrase, he feared he might lose control of himself, which would make him look the fool. To look foolish would be an unpardonable sin.

"Come, let us go toward the dining room, where I can introduce you to my guests," she continued, still avoiding his question. She was pleased by the fact that she already knew how to exasperate him. This meant she also had the power to make him feel gratitude, a most useful ability in the ethereal world of social diplomacy.

When they entered the anteroom to the dining room, Talleyrand stopped short, as if he had seen an apparition. His heart started to beat quickly. He could feel the flush in his neck ascend as if it was a tube of mercury measuring a rising temperature. In front of him, there she stood, the woman in the painting, wearing the same gown with its *décolletage,* except this gown was blue and the jewels caressing her neck were red. Her skin was as delicate as it was in the portrait. Only she was more petite and thinner than she had been painted.

"Abbé," Madame de Gramont said, "I would like you to meet the marquise of Boudreaux."

"Madame," Talleyrand said as he bent over to kiss her delicate right hand. "I am most honored…" Having Auguste de Comte familiarize him with the names of likely guests, he now realized the woman to whom he was being introduced, the woman in the portrait, was King Louis XVI's favorite mistress. Talleyrand's entire body quivered. He was literally one hand removed from kissing the hand of the king. Suddenly, all his dreams of power, his ambition for greatness, seemed possible.

"I am also pleased…" she smiled, realizing the handsome young man before her was extremely nervous.

"Allow me to express my admiration for your beauty." Talleyrand realized he was on the verge of making a fool of himself and released her hand. "I was only just admiring your portrait. But, quite frankly, how shall I continue without offending you or my hostess?"

"As honestly as possible," the marquise said with a laugh. "I would hate to think that an abbé of the church would need to lie in any way."

"Then you have given me no other choice except to say that the portrait by Monsieur Boucher, as fine as it is, does not do you the justice you deserve." It must have been difficult for my beloved to gaze into the marquise's green eyes and maintain his composure. He told me that, as they stood together talking, he wondered what she thought of him and what the king would think of him once she told him—or if she told him—about a young cleric's awkward shyness.

"How quickly compliments and insults flow from the abbé's mouth," Madame de Gramont interjected. "But rest assured, I take no offense."

"You are very kind, *monsieur* abbé," the marquise said, "but please feel free to call me Antoinette Manon or, better yet, Manon. This way, we can dismiss all unnecessary formalities and become better acquainted that much sooner."

They stood looking at each other in awkward silence. Manon liked this young cleric, whom she calculated to be ten years her junior. She later told my beloved there was something attractive about both his youthful intensity and boldness. She had met and bedded countless young men like him, each eager to enter the unctuous game of political opportunism, making all the necessary social contacts to advance their careers. But there was something different about him. Perhaps it was an incredible self-assurance that stood behind the surface shyness. Perhaps it stemmed from knowing he was born of an *ancien* pedigree, according to Madame de Gramont's gossip earlier in the day, that was far older and nobler than most of the other pedigrees in the room. Perhaps it was his limp, which, at one and the same time, made him appear both vulnerable and imperturbable.

"Then I insist you call me Charles," he responded, "or Charles-Maurice, if you become annoyed with me."

"So," she said with a coy smile, "you are already warning me that you can become mischievous."

"Let us proceed to the dinner table, where many of my guests await an introduction to my young relative," Madame de Gramont interjected, disturbed by the fact that these two were already flirting and the first course had not yet been served.

"I strongly support that idea," Talleyrand responded, gathering the arms of both women as he escorted them into the dining room.

The table was set with one of the most lavish turquoise-blue services ever produced at Sevres, shining silver candelabras decorated with a combination of embossing and *repoussé,* and a grand silver soup tureen and plateau that was obviously on the table to be admired. Gold silk cloth covered the walls. A handful of guests were already seated, each of whom nodded his head as Talleyrand was introduced. In his imagination, Talleyrand felt as if he was a king and these people were paying their proper homage to him. In reality, of course, he was there in order to make their acquaintance and be evaluated by them, a position of weakness in which he tried to make sure, in his later years, he did not find himself again.

The men wore the latest fashion in formal wear, black jackets with long tails and white ascots. The women wore ruffled, billowing dresses, their hair was tied in tight chignons, and their faces were covered with white powder and rouge to make them attractive in the style of the day. Madame de Gramont introduced my beloved to her distinguished guests, most of the names he entered into his diary later that night, a habit that was to become lifelong: Maurepas, Louis XVI's minister of state who held all the power of a prime minister; Turgot, the comptroller general of France; Malesherbes, president of the Tax Court; and Charles-Alexandre de Calonne, Turgot's soon-to-be successor as comptroller general.

Of the women, he remembered only two names: Louise de Rohan, countess of Brionne, and her striking daughter, the princess of Vaudemont. All night long, while the food was served and the *bon mots,* witticisms, were being exchanged, Talleyrand could think only of one person, Manon. My beloved had never dreamed he would ever meet her—tonight or any other night. As King Louis

XVI's favorite mistress, she exerted an immense amount of cultural, intellectual, and political influence at the French court. The king had installed her to be his official mistress only a few years before. From that position, she was known to arrange the king's entertainment, influence the appointment of ministers, and even help design the Ecole Militaire. Having been born into an extremely rich family of financiers had allowed her to move easily into fashionable, Enlightenment-oriented Parisian circles.

As far as Talleyrand was concerned, she was an exceptional woman whose good graces he had to cultivate slowly and meticulously. She was not the kind of person who was easily impressed, so he would have to monitor his performance at the table very carefully. Not too much aggressiveness…nor any undue shyness. He would wait, listen, and interject himself into the conversation only at the proper moments, lest she think of him as foolish and immature. It was a most delicate balancing act for him at this early stage in his life. But he sensed she liked him. Years later, when I compared her to the marquise de Pompadour, mistress and confidante of King Louis XV, Talleyrand rebuked me for it. I suspect he was too taken with Manon to accept the reality of her numerous liaisons.

It soon became apparent to my beloved that there were houses in which to be a guest was considered so important that a mere invitation caused one to be ranked among the most distinguished men of the day. Talleyrand was surprised to learn how highly certain people spoke of him simply because they had been introduced at a particular dinner party. His invitation made his reputation. On the other hand, he also discovered there were some houses he had to avoid so as not to appear too indiscriminate in his socializing.

However, this evening at Madame de Gramont's *château*, would be truly memorable for two reasons. The first was that Manon smiled at him throughout the evening and allowed him to escort her home. The second was an insight into life that he shared with the other dinner guests and that I take the liberty to paraphrase: one must learn to control each situation that arises by means of nothing more complicated than a gesture or a sign. Even as my beloved wrote these last words, he wondered how he had had the presumption to lecture to these celebrated guests.

I have no doubt that, after escorting Manon home, their post-party activity had far greater impact on his future than did the intellectual epiphany he had shared with Madame de Gramont's guests.

CHAPTER 7

▼

King Louis XVI, unlike many of his predecessors, was a man of the Scriptures. To Talleyrand's profound disappointment, the king was a relatively moral, devout, and self-righteous man, despite the fact he had installed Manon as his mistress. With perfect Cartesian reasoning, the king was able to rationalize his deep devotion to the sanctity of the Holy Spirit while, at the same time, maintain his passionate liaison with the marquise of Boudreaux. My beloved denounced the king as a hypocrite, somehow forgetting his own inclinations. I have always found it amusing, as I hope the reader does, to contemplate the logic incorporated into the notion of "truth" as spoken by two hypocrites simultaneously.

"To succeed in the world, it is not enough to be stupid. You must also be well-mannered," Talleyrand responded to Manon's disappointing news that King Louis XVI would not grant him an appointment to become archbishop of Bourges.

Perhaps it was unfortunate that my beloved's uncle had been accorded that position at relatively the same age as Talleyrand. Clearly, precedent had been set in Talleyrand's mind. And who was to say that Talleyrand was less deserving or less ambitious than his uncle. What Manon had neglected to tell him was that the king was extremely angry when she had broached the subject with him. Resenting my beloved's liaison with her and knowing him to be a clergyman of "uncertain morals and unprincipled behavior," the king was also disturbed that Talleyrand had used his friendship with Charles-Alexandre de Calonne, comptroller general of the finances, to obtain state information and successfully use it for personal financial gain on the stock exchange. As far as the king was concerned, the abbé was *persona non grata.*

Manon ignored the rumors sweeping through the salons of Paris that she was playing a dangerous, double-dealing game. A talented courtesan, she concentrated her energies on advancing the career of her unusual paramour. To be frank, my beloved had become an obsession, despite the fact she knew he was still spending a significant amount of time with her ostensible rival, Marie-Therese, and was also known to frequent houses that were considered to be less than respectable.

I suspect Manon was taken with Talleyrand's wit and intelligence, as attractive to her as they were enchanting to me. Or was it his sense of vulnerability that she could allay with her caresses? Or was it his lovemaking ability that was taught to him by Marie-Therese? For me, so many years later, it was still his power and presence that drew me close, a life well-lived, and the feeling he was the right person to give me the status in life I sought. At least, I felt that way in the beginning.

My beloved's desire for Manon was easy to understand, although I grew jealous when he told me how he was consumed by her pristine beauty and the adoration she lavished upon him. His notes indicate he found her as gentle as she was passionate, but, in a faded hand, he wrote, *"Que elle manque quelque chose, je ne sais pas quoi,"* She lacks a certain quality, but I don't know what.

While Talleyrand and Manon's relationship was the talk of Paris, my beloved continued to see Marie-Therese. She was anything but a fool. Many times, she asked him outright whether he had other mistresses.

True to his nonconfrontational nature, he responded, "Several mistresses would be a luxury the future archbishop of Bourges can little afford."

With this lie, he signaled her that what consumed him for the present was his all-consuming ambition. Once said, Marie-Therese knew it to be a gracious lie and realized her remaining time with Talleyrand was limited. She would soon return to her family and forgo the fantasy of a life filled with passion.

The relationship between Manon and Talleyrand soon got to the point that, any time spent away from her, she took as time away from *them.* The converse, however, did not seem to apply. Her only retort to spending time with the king, feeble as it was, was, "But you can't be jealous. After all, he is the king."

"All kings are rogues," Talleyrand retorted, reclining on Manon's alcove bed one evening after having attended a most uninteresting reception. Upon further reflection, he amended the statement, "One of the strongest natural proofs of the folly of the hereditary right of kings is that nature disapproves it. Otherwise, she would not so frequently turn it into ridicule by giving mankind an ass in place of a lion."

Manon smiled to herself, set down on the bureau the floral brooch she had been struggling to remove from her gown, and kissed my beloved upon the lips. She understand she—and not the king—had really disappointed him. Of course, he was using her to propel his ambitions. That was irrelevant. Most of her lovers wanted to exploit her access to the king. Talleyrand, at least, cared for her well-being. He cautioned her about what to say and what not to say in public. He pointed out to her the intrigues that swirled around the court that could harm her. He taught her many lessons in surviving her enemies in the Royal Court. For that, she would always be grateful. And he was always able to break through the false wall of self-sufficiency she presented to the world and allow her to feel vulnerable.

"The kiss is a lovely trick designed by nature to stop speech when words become superfluous," he whispered in her ear.

"Don't mock me!" she said, pushing him away while still holding onto his vest.

"The kiss is a peculiar proposition," Talleyrand continued, "of no use to one…yet absolute bliss to two. The small boy gets it for nothing, the young man has to lie for it, and the old man has to buy it. The baby's right, the lover's privilege, and the hypocrite's mask."

"And to a young girl?" Manon asked, flirtatiously.

"Faith," my beloved responded. "Hope to a married woman and charity to an old maid."

This playful side of Talleyrand could always seduce. Early on, he had mastered the art of using words to excite the passions of others, both in the political arena and in bed.

Manon, a willing victim to my beloved's captivating charm, raised her hand to strike him with a mock blow. "How intolerable you have become with your insatiable ambition to become an archbishop."

I am sure she wanted to strangle him and make love to him at the same time. Damn him, she must have thought (for I have felt the same way so many times in my beloved's presence) for being so deft at eliciting so many conflicting emotions.

"If I wish to reach the highest position in the French government," he replied, "I must begin with the lowest." Of course, his double entendre was not lost on her. He was not only speaking of his ambition, but of the women with whom he was consorting. Presumably, Manon was at the lowest end of his hierarchy, and Marie-Therese was at the highest.

"Then go back to your instructress, if she hasn't already fled to that cow pasture in the southwest," Manon retaliated with a terrible feeling in the pit of her stomach. Talleyrand was starting to push her away, as he had done to countless other women. Yes, he was going to leave her. She would not hold onto him much longer, unless she could help satisfy his ambitions.

"Marie-Therese was my first love, the one a young man always remembers." Talleyrand could not help himself. His response was a biting sarcasm he knew could mortally wound their relationship.

"I am surprised the good abbé is admitting there is any woman he would remember. Or any woman to whom he could be true," Manon retorted.

Talleyrand's diary notes he left hurriedly. Despite her venom, he knew Manon was absolutely correct. He could not tolerate intimacy. Sexuality? Yes. Passion? Yes. Continuous vulnerability to a woman? Not possible. At least, not yet. Perhaps…when he was older…when he was more settled…and when some of his ambitions were realized. For now, he could not worry about the damaged feelings of paramours, only about his own future.

You can imagine, dear readers, how relieved I was to find this notation.

By 1785, Talleyrand was thirty-one. In his mind, he was long overdue for a major advancement in life. If he was to achieve his ambition of becoming minister of foreign affairs of France and prove to the world it was individuals who determine the course of history, he would have to take his ecclesiastical duties more seriously. He could no longer simply rely on the social acquaintances he was making in Paris.

As an abbé, his religious life had remained minimal. He had given no masses and endured no confessions. Nevertheless, for the first time in his short career as a cleric, he immersed himself in a religious project he decided would impress the Assembly of the Clergy, the individuals who guarded the doors to power in the church. The senior clergy needed to be overwhelmed with both his diligence and organizational abilities if he was to be promoted to archbishop of Bourges.

After deliberating for weeks over which project would facilitate his promotion within the church and then isolating himself from his social world for months to work on the project, Talleyrand presented the Assembly with a series of reports on the works of public assistance maintained by the church in France. This included help provided to schools, hospitals, orphanages, and poorhouses. Through this seemingly innocuous subject matter, he was able to develop and demonstrate a mastery of the income, expenses, assets, and liabilities of the church and its holdings, providing the Assembly with its first comprehensive picture of the church's financial state.

The bishops of France were appropriately impressed by Talleyrand's initiative and diligence, and they were pleased to receive confirmation of the Church's vast holdings and wealth. The archbishop of Bordeaux publicly expressed the Assembly's gratitude to my beloved by recognizing "our everlasting gratitude to the able hands that prepared (the study)." To make certain their acknowledgment was truly appreciated, they gave my beloved 30,000 francs in gratitude, a handsome amount of money at that time.

Like most ambitious and talented men, Talleyrand was pleased by the project's reception and the gift. But, like most narcissistic men, he was still dissatisfied. He could feel within himself not only the call of destiny beckoning, but the equally powerful imperative of his ancestral heritage. The fact he was of noble birth was beginning to affect his sense of entitlement.

How frustrating it must have been for my beloved to know that many clerics, at even an earlier age than he, had been able to exchange the somber black cassock of the ordinary priest for the violet of the bishop, even if they had to lie about their sexual adventures. While the sins of those who were appointed bishop were played out in the quiet corners of Paris, they did not flaunt their mistresses all over the city, the way he did, or at the king's court at Versailles. The Church, he concluded, really asked very little of its clerics beyond performing some ritual duties and avoiding scandal. Had he taken several fatal missteps? For the first time, he began to have some misgivings about the gap between his present position and his future ambitions, and he grew despondent.

At that point in my beloved's life, destiny entered and toyed with him with the same whimsy a paramour might employ. A lover he could always manipulate. Fate, he knew, was an entirely different matter, especially when it entered his life in the guise of the eternal reaper.

CHAPTER 8

▼

Death is an indiscriminate visitor. Those who wish it to befall them rarely succeed in achieving their goal. Those who desperately try to avoid death find it to be an unrelenting nuisance preying upon their worst fears. Death made its unexpected entry into Talleyrand's life with his father's request that his son return home.

According to his memoirs, Talleyrand was extremely reluctant to see his father. He could never forgive the dying man for not having been a parent to him when he was young, even though it was quite common for children of the *ancien régime* to be living with relatives away from their home for years at a time. To my beloved, both parents had been heartless and self-absorbed. Why did they not attend his graduation from St. Sulpice or his ordination as an abbé? His father had always had the habit of making Talleyrand feel as if his birth was an unwanted accident, and that a clubfoot child in a noble family whose history was in giving military service to the monarchy was unacceptable and inappropriate.

Given their relationship, nothing could have been more distasteful to Talleyrand than his filial obligation of making the arduous journey from Paris to his ancestral home in the Dordognes in order to see his father for the last time. It was not to hear the old man's deathbed confession because, as an abbé, he had heard enough deathbed confessions to have become immune to the notion that salvation would come to the dying. He had always said a person's contrition was usually related to nothing more than guilt. The more contrition, the more guilt. As far as Talleyrand was concerned, deathbed confessions were as meaningless as they were burdensome to the listener. He certainly expected no less from this visit, whether in his role as son or priest.

The count of Perigord lay in his bed in a room made dark by heavily brocaded curtains, looking the way my beloved might have expected—withered, sallow, and exceedingly frail. It was hard, even for Talleyrand, to conjure up the image of the man he once feared and hated while he watched his father's parched lips try to form words and sentences between coughs. The dying man placed a sweat-soaked hand upon his son's hand.

"I've come to pay my respects," Talleyrand said coldly, gently removing his father's hand, "and to perform the last rites, if you wish me to."

"This is not a time for penitence for either of us," the count responded, "but I wanted to see you before my eyelids close permanently." He paused to try to find a breath with which to continue. "There are two things I have left unfinished in my life, both of which, not surprisingly, involve you."

Talleyrand remained silent, hoping his impatience was not apparent.

"I know I have not been a good father," the count continued. "It would be both inappropriate and too late to say I am sorry. But I am a dying man, and it is my prerogative to define the final rules of whatever life I have left."

Talleyrand nodded his head in agreement, impressed by his father's attempt at honesty. Or, on second thought, perhaps he had only underestimated the power of unresolved guilt.

"You are as clever as I thought you might turn out to be…" the count began.

The compliment took Talleyrand by surprise. For a moment, he wondered whether he had misread his father all these years. Had he merely been waiting for his son to become an accomplished individual without having to use the family name before he displayed his admiration?

"…but always listen carefully," he continued. "That's why God gave you two ears and one mouth. So that you could listen twice as much as you talked."

"But God only gave me one functioning foot," Talleyrand retorted cynically, dismissing the possibility he had miscalculated his father's feelings for him.

"How easy," he thought, "to be taken in by a dying man."

"Does that mean God had intended for me to walk half as far as anyone else and twice as slowly?"

"I see that what they say about you is true."

"And what is that?

"That you have a clever way with words," the count replied.

"What else do they say, Father?"

"The usual things that make you infamous."

"And what would they be?"

"Womanizing in public," the count began, coughing ever so slightly, "defiance of clerical authority, obvious political ambition without any semblance of the piety one might expect for an abbé. Especially, the abbé of Perigord."

"I see you have followed my career," Talleyrand smiled and saw a similar smile creep onto his father's face.

"You are fortunate, Charles, that you did not have an extraordinary father. Otherwise, you would have had to prove yourself very early in your career. Yes, I have taken an interest in your life in Paris, but I am still not certain what you mean your career to be."

"I am the abbé of Perigord," Talleyrand responded, puzzled by the tone of his father's feeble-sounding voice.

"In name only," his father replied. "You do not live in the region. You do not practice the faith. And, from what I have been told, you most certainly do not live in the manner of a man of the cloth. You are supposed to be pious, chaste, abstinent, and humble. All of which, we both know, you are not."

"Is this why you called me to come back? To chastise me one last time?"

"In part," the count replied, "and in part to see what can be done to correct your ways before it is too late."

"Too late? Too late for what?"

"Even in the wilderness of the Dordognes, a dying man can learn about the mischievous life his son leads in the salons of Paris rather than in prayer...meditation...study...administering to the feeble and ill..."

"I'm afraid this talk is coming a little late in our...relationship for me to alter the impression you have formed."

"You might be right," the count responded, "or you might be wrong."

"What do you mean?"

"I did not ask you to come home to ask for your forgiveness for having been a poor father, nor do I ask you to explain yourself to me. I realize I am not entitled to an explanation. So, I have only one option left with regards to you...before I die..."

The count tried to prop himself up on his elbows, but he sank slowly back onto his pillows. He waved away the offer of his son's assistance. "Are you serious about wanting a future of importance?"

"Yes, very much so, Father," Talleyrand replied, cringing at his childish use of the word "Father."

"Such ambitions can be dangerous and lead to the destruction of the individual."

"I am not afraid!"

"Are you willing to give up your vices?"

My beloved hesitated, unsure at this point whether what he answered would be a lie to his father or a lie to himself. Did he truly have the ability to give up his vices?

"If the reason be compelling enough," he answered, in what he thought was good faith.

"...to ensure your future?"

"Then the answer is yes," Talleyrand replied shamelessly, realizing a libertine who is addicted to pleasure will say and do whatever is necessary in order to maintain his addiction.

"I will make you a promise, if you, in turn, promise me to give up your current ways."

"And the promise?"

"I promise I will speak to King Louis about your becoming the bishop of Autun."

"Father! Please don't trouble yourself," Talleyrand exclaimed. He did not mean to sound ungrateful, but he did not also believe his father was capable of doing anything he might say at that moment.

Once again, Talleyrand felt betrayed by his father's ineffectiveness, but he responded the way he knew he should. "Most certainly, I would appreciate any efforts on my behalf."

Talleyrand bent over and kissed his father's forehead, not wanting to insult his father needlessly. "If you no longer need my presence, I will be departing for Paris. Despite what you have heard, there are many important functions at which, as abbé, I must officiate."

"Au revoir, mon fils," good-bye, my son, the count responded, knowing better than to bid farewell to his son with the customary à bientôt, until we meet again.

This was to be the final visit between father and son. But the count was true to his word. Because his ancestry was intermingled with that of the Bourbons through the Carolingian kings, according to the customs of the time, the Talleyrands were les cousins of the king. As a close friend and distant relative of King Louis XV and a former tutor of the present king, my beloved's father would see to it that his son's future was assured.

So, Talleyrand learned, from the father he despised, about the use of influence and the importance of attaching oneself to those of great stature. This was a lesson he imparted to me in Paris when I was not yet his niece-by-marriage, on one of those blue sky mornings in which everything seems perfect. Over coffee and croissants at the Café Pierre, he instructed me to seek out those influential women, such as Madame de Stael, who could be of benefit.

Years later, when we lived together in Rue St. Florentin and awaited a new piece of furniture that reminded Talleyrand of a small *secretaire* in his father's bedroom, he told me the king had, in fact, arrived in Perigord before the count's death. King Louis XVI listened carefully to his friend's request for his son and, despite his own misgivings, signed the document nominating Charles-Maurice de Talleyrand-Perigord to be bishop of Autun on December 10, 1788.

Two days later, count of Perigord closed his eyes, having fulfilled his only promise to his wayward son.

CHAPTER 9

▼

"I, Charles-Maurice de Talleyrand-Perigord, chosen for the Church of Autun…"

My beloved spoke the words slowly and deliberately, clearly demonstrating to both King Louis XVI and his Austrian-born queen, Marie-Antoinette, that he was already bored with the ritual of being appointed bishop of Autun in the small royal chapel. The ceremony was encapsulated—one could say overpowered—in a ceiling of endless mosaics of an obese Madonna reaching out to naked cherubs flying about her as if they were swarms of bees ready to attack with little bows and arrows. He quietly enjoyed the thought that, if the bows and arrows were filled with potions of love, then placing the Madonna so close to this sort of event was surely a sacrilege.

The king and queen, in turn, were not happy with the religious hypocrite standing before them who, by their intervention, was now taking a sacred oath. King Louis XVI was fulfilling his promise to his father's old friend, but he did not enjoy doing it. My beloved believed Marie-Antoinette was wary of him simply because he had not attempted to seduce her. I personally think he might have been flattering himself, as many men will do from time to time. But, as his adoring mistress so much later in his life, my own actions only manage to substantiate Talleyrand's supposition, however arrogant it may seem.

"…from this day forward will be faithful and obedient to St. Peter the Apostle…"

Talleyrand did try to enjoy what was becoming a circus atmosphere. He had watched the men saunter into the royal chapel wearing their powdered wigs, embroidered silk or velvet suits, silk stockings, and buckled shoes with pearl-handled swords on their hips.

"...to the Holy Roman Church..." Talleyrand continued speaking slowly in a monotonous voice, scanning the ladies. They wore low-cut silk or brocade dresses stretched wide over *panniers* with a train appropriate to their respective rank in society. Each woman wore a perfectly round patch of bright rouge on each cheek, precisely three inches across, starkly shaded with the colors making them look like images of American Indians he had seen in the colored sections of the magazine, *Le Monde.*

"...to our Holy Father, the Pope..."

Talleyrand droned on, standing before the small altar and wearing the appropriate costume for the part he was about to play in the church hierarchy. The new bishop of Autun was dressed in an elaborate golden-brocaded white linen robe, puffing over his small shoulders and dragging on the floor behind his feet. Over his shoulder hung a white linen stole with golden borders and five, white, embroidered tassels, representing his status as a bishop.

"...and legitimate successors."

With great seriousness, King Louis XVI bestowed upon Talleyrand the miter, the pastoral staff, and the half-gold, half-silver ring with its replica of the five tassels on his garment. To every courtier's delight, the choir sang "*Ecce Sacerdos Magnus,*" Behold a Great Priest, who, in his time, has pleased the Lord.

Talleyrand bowed his head in humble gratitude, to the degree he could affect such an emotion, quietly reaffirming to himself his skepticism about the religious aspects of his new offices. It was not the bishop's prerogatives he wanted, and he certainly did not care to ordain priests and confer the sacrament of confirmation. In truth, his ambition was for neither place, title, nor apostolic authority. Autun, comprising the entire region of Saone et Loire, was to be Talleyrand's venue into the larger world of power.

"There is one favor the queen and I would ask of you," King Louis XVI said as he concluded the ordination ritual.

"Whatever Your Majesty and the queen might desire," Talleyrand replied, taken completely by surprise.

"You would be doing a great honor to the crown if you would conduct your first mass...now...in this chapel," King Louis XVI said with a sly smile.

Talleyrand was caught off guard. "Your Majesty, the excitement of the day has overwhelmed me. Tomorrow, I would be most happy to conduct a mass," my beloved responded, trying to disguise his apprehension.

"No," King Louis XVI replied emphatically. "We request a mass be said right now."

With that, he puffed up his corpulent frame, no doubt pleased he had been able to place this manipulator of men and seducer of women into a position of possible embarrassment.

"It would please us, our new bishop of Autun." The king emphasized Talleyrand's new title with great condescension.

"It would be my extreme pleasure, Your Majesty!" Talleyrand replied, compensating for his lack of preparation with an attitude of bravado. He decided that all he needed to do was imagine himself as an actor playing the part of a sacrosanct priest. He would speak largely in Latin, knowing the royal couple as well as most of the court, had little mastery of the language or knowledge of the conduct of the mass itself. Yes, a performance it would be…by an actor named Talleyrand playing the part of the bishop of Autun.

Snickering spread throughout the chapel like a mist of snuff. Everyone was aware Talleyrand knew little and cared even less about religious rites, and each was prepared to witness a spectacle of humiliation.

"*Pater Noster, Ave Maria, Credo.*" Talleyrand genuflected in front of the cross. He turned toward the audience and pronounced the Latin words again in as slurred a fashion as he could, so the assembled would feel it was their fault if they did not understand what was being said.

"*Domine, Deus ominipotens, qui ad prinicpum hujus diei nos pervnire feceisti tua nos hodie salva virtue…Per Christum Dominum nostrum. Amen.*"

Unfortunately, as my beloved turned and walked toward the altar to kiss the cross, he tripped over his trailing vestments. All who saw the accident guffawed so loudly that Talleyrand was forced to raise his voice. Needing the comfort of language, he recited the rest of the mass in French, despite the intolerable pain in his crippled leg.

"Angel of God, to whose care I have been committed by Divine Goodness, enlighten, direct, defend, and protect me."

He glared at the royal couple, who were having difficulty hiding their own laughter. With a quiet "*amen,*" Talleyrand ended his first performance as bishop of Autun, bowed respectfully to the king and queen, and limped out of the royal chapel.

He exhibited no anger, he told me with great pride, given the humiliating situation and refused to allow himself any self-pity. He would do now what he would do for the rest of his life when emotionally wounded. He would isolate himself for a short while to plan his next actions and will himself to recuperate quickly.

Disappearing into the grounds of Versailles after the debacle at the royal chapel was the best palliative for the moment. As he walked, he kept reminding himself that Versailles was the center of power in France and power was what he wanted.

By the time I was born in 1784, thirty years after Talleyrand, so much had changed that I could barely fathom what it must have been like for my beloved to walk those extraordinary gardens, Le Notre's masterpiece of design, before they were destroyed in the upheaval of 1789. I have heard the story that, in the 1680s, a workforce of 36,000 was made busy planting and building the additions to the small family *château* that more than tripled its size. I sometimes watch my beloved, in my mind, walking down the Rue Royal by the topiary with its clipped hedges and geometric beds. Did he notice the hidden delights, the surprise changes around corners, the diversionary structures, and resting places? I suspect not. He was still in shock about what had transpired, and his humiliation and feelings of inadequacy did not dissipate as quickly as he had hoped. However, at the moment when the walkway of fine gravel and crushed brick ended, he had vowed to outlast and outmaneuver the subtle and snide attitudes of the court.

CHAPTER 10

▼

Talleyrand despised the architecture of Versailles, its gardens notwithstanding. He always believed it lacked both architectural grace and drama, particularly when compared to his family's estate. Started as a hunting lodge, the original *château* at Versailles had been built to be a relatively standard country house of brick and pale gray stone. That lodge, which had been added onto several times, was now a quarter of a mile long and contained hundreds of rooms. To either side of the central block of rooms were tremendous wings containing ministerial offices, a theater, and other secondary premises. The royal chapel was of lesser physical interest than the monumental horseshoe-shaped stables and dog kennels. Both King Louis XVI and King Louis XV before him had equated the hunt with divine rule so that both church and steeplechase were deemed part of the same plan put forth by God to place kings above all other mortals.

Versailles served its current king as a physical sanctuary. The royal couple rarely ventured into Paris. The grounds were a billet for officers in the seventeen squadrons of the king's household troops, in addition to the gendarmes, Swiss Guards, bodyguards, and musketeers. These military and paramilitary warriors, each with its distinctive uniform of various combinations of blue, white, and red, were lodged there to defend the king from his enemies. After officers retired, many assumed important positions at the court, such as marshal of the diplomatic corps or governor of the royal princes. They remained at Versailles until they died.

Talleyrand estimated there were approximately 1,000 courtiers at Versailles as well, each accompanied by twice as many servants. For the most part, the courtiers were nobleman, but any Frenchman, whatever his birthright might be, could purchase one of 4,000 offices in service of the king.

Not many men were enamored of wearing the sword because, once so ennobled, a man might not engage in lucrative businesses such as manufacturing or trade, which commoners rightly and shrewdly insisted were their specific province. A smart man, Talleyrand believed, would trade off the potential of becoming part of the nobility through the purchase of a title for the practicality of assuming a more humble, but significantly more lucrative, role of a merchant. At least that was what my beloved would have done if he had not been born to the sword. Since childhood, Talleyrand had been made aware by his parents that the income of the nobility was declining while the income of commoners was increasing.

Everything about life at Versailles was extremely ritualized, a fact of daily existence from which I believe Talleyrand drew comfort. In his own published memoirs, which have already been shared with the world, my beloved wrote:

> In place of one class (of nobility), there were seven or eight—of the Sword, of the Bar, of the Court, of the Provinces, old and new, large and small. Each pretended to be superior to the other, which, in turn, claimed to be equal to the former.

According to my beloved, in the years before the Revolution, ritual demands permeated all aspects of life at court—from how to enter a room, how to bow, and how to walk, stand, or sit to advantage. Talleyrand became a master at such "silliness," as he called it. He admired those of the nobility who competed for and were honored by the king by being allowed to wear the *justaucorps à brevet*, the blue coat lined with scarlet and embroidered in gold.

Versailles was also a center for the arts, and it was this aspect of palace life that my beloved appreciated most. He relished seeing the new plays and operas by Goldoni of Venice, resident writer and Italian tutor to the king's daughters. The chapel supported one of the best orchestras and choirs in France. Paintings by Lorrain, Poussin, Watteau, Nattier, and a multitude of other great masters were displayed in the state apartments. Skilled craftsmen turned out a profusion of marquetry tables and delicately carved chairs, cabinets, and bookcases. Craftsmen (silversmiths, dressmakers, enamellers, pyrotechnicians, and bakers) abounded. It was a world of rich wonders. My beloved's lifelong love of fine possessions was both ignited and refined at Versailles, with its silk and brocades from Lyon and

Tours, its tapestries and carpets from Gobeling and Savonnerie, its mirrors from St. Gobain, and its porcelain from Sevres.

And the gardens! When my beloved was not despondent, I am sure he could not help but admire Le Notre's living geometry. Circular pools set off by lines of box bushes, and trees kept continually trimmed. Each spring, the brocade-patterned flower beds were replanted. Each winter, the orange trees were taken inside to the warmth. Fruits and vegetables were grown in newly developed hothouses. Numerous ponds were stocked with the most varied assortment of fish. The gondolas on the lake were regilded every season. Had I been there with him, I would have made sure he noticed it all.

He did, however, notice that Versailles was populated by hordes of shopkeepers, hidden away in the nooks and crannies of the outbuildings, and selling everything from millinery, to the *Gazette de France,* to trusses. At least a dozen courtiers owned presses, printing their own invitations, poetic verses written for their mistresses, or short political diatribes which passed from hand to hand.

As he described the daily excitement of people living and working in Versailles, "This stately palace was nothing more than a veritable marketplace, which even sold forbidden copies of Voltaire's *Candide* and various other satirical pieces that derided the king and queen." Over the years, Talleyrand was featured in many of these satires, but he enjoyed the prominence of position it implied.

What made Versailles most important to him (no less than to the rest of France) was the fact it was the seat of government. It was from this *château* that the king ruled. His ministers lived and worked in the same building. The council chamber was a mere thirty seconds stroll from the *boudoirs* and ballrooms.

It did not take Talleyrand long, however, to understand the ultimate secret of Versailles was its ability to maintain an illusion. It was there that ordinary Frenchmen supposed that godlike masters had only to lift their fingers to secure justice, issue a decree, or implement a command. The reality, as Talleyrand discovered it to be, was that this king, like any other man of power, had to reckon with myriad layers of subordinates, any of whom could effectively sabotage his will.

Talleyrand told me Versailles exemplified Aristotle's mystery of the one and the many. Although, on my first encounter with that idea, I was too naïve to understand its profundity. The palace housed thousands of sophisticated Frenchmen of varied opinions and one king, who was preordained to embody all divergent views. How then could one man speak for so many? The answer lay in the fact that the French monarchy was absolute. The monarchy and the state were one, and the king's will was ultimately the supreme law. Consequently, the nobility and parliament were always subordinate. Yet, in some ways, they remained in perpetual opposition to the king.

The fundamental flaw of the entire *ancien régime*, however, was not the structure of the government. According to my beloved, it was the system of taxation that was harder on the poor than on the rich. When King Louis XVI began his rule, he kept delaying needed tax reforms. He backed down when his bishops pleaded with him to exempt the clergy from taxes, and he backed down when the nobility, whose traditional service in the army or the navy earned little pay, pleaded with him to exempt them from the *taille,* one of the three taxes paid by most Frenchmen. The persistence of the king's critics in exercising their voice was keeping the government dangerously weak. The government was at an impasse over the question of tax reform.

Later in his career, Talleyrand employed spies to keep him informed of the intrigues of the court. At this point, he was still naïve to many of its ways and depended largely on his intuition.

Several days after his coronation at the royal chapel, my beloved committed a very foolish act, something no doubt linked to the earlier effrontery dealt him by the king and queen. It was a cloudless Thursday in Paris, a day of no particular importance, when a crowd began to gather in the square just below the Place de la Concorde. A very old man walked slowly through the assembled mass. As he did, people moved to the side to make way for him. He could have been Moses parting the Red Sea, but this aged man, this hero, was a more earthly, more recent legend. He was Voltaire, the "Patriarch of the Enlightenment," finally returned from a four-year exile for his relentless attacks, both in print and onstage, against the Roman Catholic Church and the king.

In an instant, an event transpired that caused the crowd first to gasp and then to cheer. There was my beloved, the bishop of Autun, for all to see, bestowing his blessing upon a man who had published moral, religious, political, and philosophical critiques of his own nation and who had been banished from Paris. That act, on Talleyrand's part, certainly helped to fan the heady promise of change already in the air. Talleyrand took this to be one of the great, spontaneous dramatic moments in his life, and he relived it with me often.

CHAPTER 11

▼

Throughout the first half of the eighteenth century, before my beloved's birth, Paris had been a tapestry of different groups—the clergy, the nobility, the sovereign courts, the universities, the academies, the financial companies. Custom and hierarchy was their organizing principles. Each individual, according to his or her rank and station, had rights and obligations that had been formed by tradition. By the time my beloved arrived at the court of King Louis XVI, these traditions were being challenged daily by new ideologies and social practices.

Enlightened ideas of "equality" were being disseminated throughout Parisian cafés. It must have been an intoxicating time. Artists and writers frequented the Café Procope. Officers frequented the Café Meletane. Actors and actresses frequented the Café des Barecheries. Financiers frequented the Café du Prophite Elie. Talleyrand's idol, Voltaire, along with Rousseau and Diderot, frequented several of these cafés, and café life became intensely political. The ideas of the Enlightenment were circulated and discussed by people from varying social backgrounds. New forums for social and political action had been created, such as the *Société Philanthropique*, which gained the respect of Talleyrand, along with his alarm, by proclaiming the equality of all its varied members.

Life in the court of King Louis XVI, however, had not changed very much. Social rank remained visible with brocades, linings, furs, feathers, lace, and gold and silver trimming preserving the hierarchy of power. Political and sexual intrigues and gossip still dominated the balls given by the nobility. After several months in Versailles, it was clear to my beloved that he was at the center of a political maelstrom that would soon erupt.

King Louis' grandfather, Louis XIV, had been hated for isolating the monarchy from Paris, his capital, by constructing the palace at Versailles and moving the court there, rarely to visit Paris again. His mistresses and illegitimate children were less a reason for Parisian discontent. King Louis' father, Louis XV, had managed to inspire both hatred and disrespect. My beloved showed me several pieces written about King Louis XV's immoral life that were in circulation in 1775. So, King Louis XVI of the House of Bourbon had taken over a monarchy about which the public held a negative attitude. His political clumsiness and ineptness at being unable to control his queen, who had a reputation for siphoning money from a depleted royal treasury to pay for her clothes and extravagances, did not earn him either respect or popularity. I still feel blessed that my beloved lived through those years in safety, while the king and Marie-Antoinette were destined to be placed on trial during the Revolution and lose their lives to the guillotine.

By 1789, the mood of the French had changed markedly since the king had been crowned fourteen years earlier. Talleyrand wrote in his diary:

> The king has great difficulty being an enlightened monarch. He faces an impossible task, trying to be both loved and feared at the same time.

Increasing financial burdens imposed upon the country by King Louis XVI were taking their toll. At every level of society, from blacksmith to nobleman, Talleyrand detected a sense of unease. An air of expectation concerning portentous change spun about Paris with the fury of a whirling dervish. It was, as we know now, the irreversible force of revolutionary change.

Like a heavily scented perfume, these same sentiments permeated the salons of Paris. The conversations in Madame Brionne's salon, which Talleyrand frequently attended, shifted from gossip, scandal, and entertainment to the more ominous topics of economic and political upheaval—even revolution. One evening at the aging matron's home near Faubourg St. Germaine, an area of Paris that housed (and still houses) a great number of nobility, a most unusual event occurred. As my beloved recounted the story to me, a young man whom no one recognized proceeded to go on at length about what Jean-Jacques Rousseau, an Enlightenment philosopher with the rank of Voltaire, believed to be a woman's place in society.

With the women clucking together in one corner, each with hair assembled to towering perfection with ribbons and ornaments, and the men posturing on yet another side of the room fussing about the cost of their shoe buckles, the subject of "equality" brought all activity in the ornate room to a chilly halt.

In England, the young man offered, equality was the rage. Old Jean-Luc Neuf, upon hearing these words, pounded a nearby table with his fist and said he would rather be dead than see a woman rise above her station. His mousy wife puffed herself up to broader proportions and scowled. Talleyrand, always the mediator, deferred to Neuf but questioned if the time might be right for women to come into their own. Were there not gifted women who could get most anything with a well-placed word or the lifting of an eyebrow? Neuf demurred, and his wife beamed in my beloved's direction.

Growing up in these times, I must admit to being confused about being female. While I enjoyed the comforts of my home and the adoration of Papa, I wondered about a life with more freedom than Maman seemed to have. Of course, I assumed I would one day wed a young man of noble lineage who would provide me with those social and material benefits a young woman of my background was due—furs, brocades, feathers, and gold trimming on my cloak. Yet, as my engagement to Edmond was announced, a decision my family made for me, I began to ask myself whether I was being treated as an object, something to be bartered and traded. I knew the answer and resented it.

Even after all these years, I do not understand why I was so different from my sisters. While they read such sentimental sop as *Manon Lescaut,* a tale of passion triumphing over every obstacle except death, I much preferred *Les Liaisons Dangereuses,* and the perverse psychology of a cynical seducer of women. While they enjoyed an evening at the theater with Beaumarchais' comedy, *The Barber of Seville,* I gladly remained at home reading Rousseau's *La Nouvelle Heloise,* which presented me with questions about life I could not answer, but which I somehow knew were important to ponder. On those occasions when we were permitted to be present at the start of a ball Maman had arranged in our home, my sisters chattered endlessly about the gowns worn by the women while I strained to overhear conversation coming from the circle of men about recent government edicts or new demands being made by their servants. Talleyrand, of course, always claimed full responsibility for my independence of spirit and my intellectual awakening.

However, I digress too far from Talleyrand's evening with Jean-Luc Neuf. The conversation among the men worked its way toward the news of the day, and Talleyrand listened for the rumbling sounds of a throne tottering. Patting stuffed paunches and gazing with sad eyes to the gilded ceilings covering their heads, everyone spoke of economic want and financial ruin. The cost of France's participation in the American Revolution, the enormous debts incurred by the reigns of King Louis XIV and King Louis XV, the current excessive and unregulated expenditures of the state, and the wastefulness of King Louis XVI which was draining the treasury and the people.

Talleyrand was very near to all of this because Jacques Turgot, the minister of France for King Louis XVI, was his close friend. So, he watched carefully as Turgot worked diligently to improve the economy of one of France's poorer provinces. He started by eliminating excessive expenses, but it was at the cost of offending almost everyone in the Clermont-Ferrand province. He abolished state-controlled commerce, but, by doing so, he antagonized the speculators and merchants. He eliminated trade guilds, which controlled the number of workers in each industry, but he alienated both ordinary workers and organized labor. When Turgot freed the peasants from their obligation to repair public roads, he earned the animosity of the landowners who were now burdened by the expense of such maintenance. The result of Turgot's actions was that whoever had prospered under the *ancien régime* (the nobility, the clergy, and the *bourgeoisie*), now joined together with the insistence of the queen, to force him out of office. Talleyrand always quoted Turgot's parting words to his colleagues, "Remember, my friends, it was weakness which brought King Charles I to the chopping block."

CHAPTER 12

▼

At the age of thirty-four, as Talleyrand watched the economy of France decline, he was still on the fringes of power. However, a timely and electrifying conversation with an extremely bright and capable Englishman, William Pitt, changed the direction of his life. Mr. Pitt, at the age of twenty-nine, had been Chancellor of the Exchequer. Talleyrand was envious and shocked to learn that, in England, power was open to men of ability—regardless of age or class—by way of Parliament. The contrast to France was great, where it was only open to ambitious men by way of inheritance, the purchase of title, or elaborate court intrigue.

One evening, Talleyrand brought Pitt to Madame Brionne's apartments, where Pitt regaled her guests with how very different things were in England. Whether or not the listeners cared about these differences, I do not know, but the conversation was seminal. It fortified my beloved's desire to enter politics and convinced him his method would be to become a deputy to the first National Assembly from Autun. Within the week, he returned to his diocese to convince his parishioners he had spent his time in Paris attending to their concerns so that they could send him back to Paris with a new title and mission.

Talleyrand understood the concept of leveraging money, power, and work. While he lived in Paris, he had assigned capable prelates to attend to the needs of the citizens of Autun. Although the citizens may not have seen Talleyrand often, his representatives plied their trade (if I do not sound too cynical) in his name. In this way, my beloved had, without any work on his part, created a constituency and an organization. When he decided to enter the political arena as a deputy, he also decided to retain his prestigious clerical identity. My beloved was no fool. He placed his chips on both sides of the roulette table—the red and the black. He would play all sides if it would allow him to achieve his goals, an approach he took to all of life.

I think it only appropriate that I provide a brief description of Autun, but I must quickly traverse Talleyrand's time there because it was no more than a quick means to an end. In approximately 1 BC, when its amphitheater held 20,000 people, Autun was a large, thriving center of learning and culture. By the time of my beloved's consecration as bishop, Autun had turned into a rather small provincial town with only several thousand inhabitants. Perhaps the town's most important feature was (and probably will always be) the Cathedral of St. Lazare, which houses a collection of sculptures by a twelfth-century artist named Giselebertius, whose *The Last Judgment* still remains one of the finest figurative pieces of the Middle Ages. It was this religious community to which Talleyrand returned in order to advance his political aspirations.

When Talleyrand arrived in Autun at the beginning of March, he had only two weeks to ingratiate himself to the electorate. Following the socially and politically astute example set by Madame Brionne, he gave frequent dinners at the bishop's palace to which everyone from the local nobility, the *bourgeoisie,* and the commoners were invited, dinners that were long remembered by all to be the highlight of Talleyrand's brief tenure as bishop. During the day, Talleyrand campaigned tirelessly, limping from street to alleyway and conversing with everyone he thought could be of some value—shopkeepers, tradesman, women, and even children in the faint hope they might influence their parents. His message was as simple as it was direct, "Tell me what you want me to do, and I will do it." Oh yes, he also conducted Mass regularly at the cathedral.

One day, after agreeing to conduct High Mass on the Feast of the Annunciation, Talleyrand maneuvered to use the occasion to advance his campaign for deputy. After Mass, he provided the entire congregation with good food and good wine. He assembled them to listen to a speech he might want to deliver to Parliament, if elected. He mounted a chair, taking care not to trip over his trailing vestments, and began an oration on the need for social and economic reform.

I quote verbatim from his speech, "On the Necessity for a Responsible Government":

> No public act shall be made the law of the land unless the people have solemnly consented to it. No taxes shall be recognized which are not established, modified, limited, or revoked by the people. Public order must be

restored to France, and public order rests on two foundations: liberty and property. Both are sacred, but the time has come to consider whether or not 'property' which belongs to any individual or group should, in fact, belong to the nation as a whole. Liberty must be proclaimed anew and reinforced. Freedom of speech and of the press must be guaranteed by law. Citizens must be granted the right to trial by jury, and they must be protected from unjust prosecution by *habeas corpus*.

By the time he mentioned the issue of extending the right of education to all classes of citizens and of financing that action by abolishing old tax exemptions and selling crown lands, his congregation had broken into spontaneous applause.

It was certainly an ambitious statement about needed reforms. But, without such reforms, Talleyrand's own chances for advancement would be minimal because he was currently out of favor with the influential men at court. Associating himself with the reform faction among the nobility was his best (and possibly only) chance at continued power.

My beloved put to the test another lesson he had learned while he limped through Autun, speaking with everyone he met. If he appeared sincere about his convictions and could articulate his ideas in an understandable way, he knew he could seduce the common man. Did Talleyrand believe all that he told his congregants? I am not entirely sure. I am proud to record that he was elected with an overwhelming majority, one of several men from Autun sent to Paris with the mandate to reform France and give it a constitution. As a deputy, he would now be in a position to advance himself without hiding behind the bishop's collar or his family name and without the *noblesse oblige* from King Louis XVI or favors from former mistresses. The lame boy from Perigord, my beloved, was on his way back to Paris, never to return to Autun again.

CHAPTER 13

▼

On May 4, 1789, Talleyrand felt invincible. He had returned to the center of power and was once again in Versailles. If politics is theater, then the stage could not have been more perfectly set for the new deputy from Autun. On that spring morning, he had a definite expectation that this would be a momentous day in what might well turn out to be a momentous year.

The courtyard in front of the palace of Versailles had its three roadways guarded by soldiers for this special day. The main entrance from the avenue leading to Paris was to be used only by the royal family and princes of the blood. Carriages of the nobility were to be admitted to the side gates. Everyone else either walked or was carried for six *sous* in one of the "blue chairs" with blue-liveried carriers provided by a *concessionaire*. Any respectably dressed person, however, was admitted to the palace grounds that day.

The procession of deputies entering the royal chapel was an impressive sight. Ordinary citizens of the third estate might have been mistaken to be part of a funeral procession because they were bedecked in black, sleeveless cloaks worn over even more somber clothing, their Sunday best. In contrast, the second estate, the noblemen, were flamboyant. They wore hats adorned with peacock feathers and velvet robes of intense colors that were ample and flowing. Their shoe buckles were encrusted with diamonds. The clergy, not to be outshone, arrived in the most vibrant and commanding red and black capes that befit their position within the hierarchy of the church.

My father told my sisters and me that he marched with the noblemen. Throughout my childhood, he often spoke of this grand day. Looking back, it now seems improbable that he would have displayed himself so ostentatiously in public because he was a reserved man. He was also a man who enjoyed ceremony, and he took great pains in our growing years to give us lessons in rank and power, using the details of the procession as his guide.

Sometimes, when we were young, my sisters and I reenacted royal processions of our own. I was always the queen, which meant I was in a position to command. I mention this particularly to contrast my childhood games with those of Talleyrand, who was never so foolish. From an early age, he knew it was not important to be king or cardinal if, from a subordinate role, one could exercise power.

Given the optimism of the day, it would have been impossible to believe Robespierre, also part of the new National Assembly, would be beheaded within five years by some of the men standing next to him. As a child of ten, I remember being told the details of Robespierre's death by my tutor, who blamed him for the Terror. How my sisters squealed in delight at the gory tale of bloody box carts, a hastily constructed guillotine in the courtyard of the Palace of Justice, and the filth that was thrown on the group of condemned men by women who danced around them. While frightened by the images, I was more interested in why so much blood must be shed for life, as I knew it, to go on. I wondered who was responsible for starting and stopping the bloodshed and what I would say to him—for it was certain to be a man—if we met.

My beloved, as was his place in the procession, wore his regal, red bishop's robe with its yellow brocade shawl falling into a cascade of silk, twisted cords. He must have looked magisterial. A vivid portrait of him has come from a diary written by Manon, who remained his mistress throughout this period. I do not know how her slim volume came into Talleyrand's possession, but I am not surprised that Talleyrand enjoyed owning it. Manon wrote:

> Talleyrand's appearance was not without a certain attraction. I was struck less by his good features than by his posture of indifference that, when combined with a certain malevolence, had the effect of giving him the head of an angel, animated by the spirit of a demon.

I suspect Talleyrand felt unusually attractive despite his limp and the gold-knobbed cane that accompanied him on such occasions.

In his youth, my beloved must have been something to behold. Some faded color drawings from that time reveal a head of reddish-brown hair with curls bordering an angular face. His highly arched eyebrows give his deep brown eyes a menacingly attractive look. In all etchings, his lips are full and tightly pressed, giving an air of determination to his firm jaw. Then, of course, there is the dimple on his chin that made him always appear so adorable to me. Early in our relationship, I was vexed to have missed knowing the young Talleyrand because I do not fool myself that his physical appearance must have been far more vital than that of the man to whom I committed. Yet, even old age never robbed him of his attractiveness.

Talleyrand was impressed by the festive atmosphere that momentous day. Everyone applauded and cheered everyone else. They shouted, as they should have, *"Vive le roi!"* Long live the king! when the king's carriage approached the royal chapel and the king stepped down. They took a very different tone, however, when Queen Marie-Antoinette appeared. Well-bred women changed their smiles into frowns. *Doyennes* of the city's best salons became brazen vulgarians, calling out the vilest curses against the queen and challenging her to try to buy her way out of their fury.

Suddenly, there was another turn in the bearing of the onlookers when the duke of Orleans, the popular heir of King Louis XVI, approached. *"Vive le duc d'Orleans!"* Long live the duke of Orleans! they shouted ecstatically. *"Vive le duc,"* Long live the duke. The crowd murmured how better life would be with the duke as king. Standing on the steps of the royal chapel, my beloved noted, with dismay, how quickly the crowd could turn.

After the Mass of the Holy Spirit, which was fortunately not conducted by Talleyrand, all the deputies, led by the king and the noblemen, walked from the royal chapel to the *salle des Menus-Plaisirs* of the palace. The first elected National Assembly was about to be held in which merchants, trade unions, and intellectuals were being allowed to participate. Even the king hoped the trappings of democracy would help salvage the monarchy and keep the country from bankruptcy and political chaos.

The assembly hall was a dark bronze color with highly polished wooden floors. The ceiling was largely unadorned, with only small areas of gilded florettes. Its walls were draped with multicolored Flemish tapestries filled with hunting themes replete with hunters and deer and storybook themes of unrequited love filled with plump women and cherubs flying about. According to my beloved, this hall was considerably less ornamental than others in the palace.

Unfortunately, the National Assembly had maintained its symbols of status in what should have been a more egalitarian convocation. The nobility and clergy sat in upholstered chairs to the left of the king. To his right were the dignitaries and officials of the Royal Court, seated according to their rank in the social hierarchy, on chairs or armchairs. Facing the king were the commoners, sitting on hard benches without any backs or cushions. For Talleyrand, this was a bad omen.

"The day I have desired in my heart for so long has finally arrived, and I am now surrounded by the representatives of the nation that is my glory to command." With these words, King Louis XVI opened the first democratic parliament in France.

Everyone in the room applauded loudly. Some were thought to be crying with joy. Then the mood of the National Assembly turned surly and somber when Jacques Necker, the minister of finance and the only minister not of noble birth, stood up and gave a long, tedious report on the revenues and expenses of the state.

Talleyrand did not like Necker personally, but he had great respect for his financial abilities. The finance minister was extremely unpopular in the Royal Court because he insisted to all who would listen to him that the predominant expenses of the state were incurred by the courtiers. Unless they curtailed their expenditures, the budget would not balance. His conclusions that day were met by cries from the nobility for his immediate resignation. Talleyrand said nothing, but he took note that the major divisions within the National Assembly were even more intransigent than he had suspected.

Soon after Necker's soporific speech, one nobleman and one cleric stood up to reaffirm the right of the first and second estates to exercise the prerogative that allowed them to remain separate from the reforms required of the third estate. They were immediately shouted down by the representatives of the commoners, who outnumbered them.

Talleyrand found himself shocked by the vehemence with which several leaders of the commoners—Mirabeau, Bailly, Sieyes, and Malouet—demanded "their inalienable rights." He disliked extremism in any form.

"The greatest mistake was to authorize the third estate to elect as many deputies as the other two orders together," Talleyrand whispered to the duke of Orleans while they listened to the ferocity of the debate raging around them. "That part of the third estate, which sits in this room, is composed almost exclusively of lawyers, a class of men whose method of thinking generally makes them dangerous in public affairs."

Both men were members of the Society of Thirty, a political club comprised largely of nobles, but still worked toward the same reform goals as the commoners. Yet, while Talleyrand agreed on the need for a written constitution, he still wanted to preserve a separate noble order. He was certainly a reformer, but he was not yet a revolutionary. The duke, according to my beloved, was even more conservative.

"The way these *parvenus*, upstarts, deal with our king and the nobility is despicable," the duke responded. "I must admit I still have my doubts about the feasibility of allowing this type of riffraff into the National Assembly."

"The best posture to assume in this maelstrom of verbiage is one of prudence, silence, and passivity," Talleyrand replied.

"My dear friend," the duke responded, placing an arm around Talleyrand's shoulders, "I will assure you of one thing. Neither my friends nor I will give way on our inherent right to our ancestral privileges."

"I am afraid there may be little choice."

"What do you mean by that?"

"If you look carefully," Talleyrand continued, "the abbé of Sieyes is inching his way toward Mirabeau's position, that of the commoner's, and taking along with him all the county pastors who have been elected by their parishioners."

"Ah, my dear Charles," the duke declared, "once again, you exhibit your keen powers of observation."

"You flatter me," my beloved responded disingenuously. "But watch. By the time we end the day, one of those representatives of the commoners, probably Mirabeau, will confront the king directly and threaten him with an ultimatum."

"How do you know?"

"By watching the falcons in Perigord eat the weaker birds. I can recognize a definite similarity to what I am watching here."

"Oh, come now, Charles!" the duke replied half-heartedly. "You are being cynical, even by your own standards. I must admit your statement alone is worth a wager."

"Shame on you! Don't you know that trying to tempt a priest…" Talleyrand wondered whether the duke was aware my beloved knew he frequented gaming houses throughout Paris and was known to wager heavily when gambling at Versailles.

"And a bishop at that!" the duke interrupted him.

"You are in luck. Any wager would have been lost," Talleyrand said as they watched Mirabeau and his cohorts approach the king.

"Your Majesty, we, the representatives of the first estate," Mirabeau announced in a loud, deliberate voice, "are determined to see that a constitution of the realm and public reform are established and implemented."

"That's the beginning of the revolution," Talleyrand whispered to the duke.

"Don't get your hopes up too high," he responded. "It's just a group of legal upstarts testing out their newly acquired powers with the help of traitors to the first estate, like Mirabeau."

"Never underestimate the fury of patient men. What we just witnessed was a direct and public challenge to the king."

The duke was amused by the seriousness with which Talleyrand seemed to be taking the process of politics. As far as the duke was concerned, this National Assembly was nothing more than the continuation of the ongoing charade of power sharing that had been transpiring for centuries among kings, nobility, and commoners.

By the end of the day, after much shouting and demanding, a proclamation was passed by King Louis XVI that, in effect, took away the commoner's voice in the decisions of the Assembly.

"We will dismiss the National Assembly," the king proclaimed, "and reconvene in two months."

"We are here by the will of the people, and we will leave only at the point of a bayonet," cried Mirabeau.

"Remain here as long as you want," the king responded angrily. "I, the queen, and my counselors are leaving." King Louis XVI stood up and, followed by his entourage, left a wave of rumbling that filled the hall.

My beloved watched the king leave and realized this new parliamentary system had created two immutable groups: the aristocrats and the commoners.

He carefully examined his own beliefs. His head replayed the arguments jettisoned back and forth that day, and he suffered *une crise de conscience,* a crisis of conscience. On the one hand, he was a proponent of the need of the *ancien régime* for change. On the other hand, he could not fight against the beliefs instilled in him since childhood that affairs of state were the province of the nobility and upper classes. It was not for commoners, who were too ignorant about or indifferent to such important matters. The radical statements he had made as bishop of Autun concerning the rights of the people to liberty, prosperity, and protection from oppression had been sincere. Like his hereditary compatriots, however, Talleyrand could not help feeling that it remained the prerogative of the aristocracy to recognize and implement these rights he had so eloquently espoused. The ethos of paternalism was an integral part of my beloved's heritage as a de Perigord.

Talleyrand surveyed the political landscape and drew his inevitable conclusion. The monarchy was already lost.

CHAPTER 14

▼

The games of my childhood were often piecemeal reenactments of what I had heard about the days just before and after the Revolution. It was a tumultuous time, distilled by my still youthful mind into threads of those who had power and those who were losing it. Violent images of angry mobs were ever-present in stories we were told. There was always the guillotine. My sisters and I played with history as our backdrop. I lost my imaginary crown more than once, and, later raising the stakes, my sisters condemned me to an imaginary beheading. While our mother was horrified at our choice of games, Talleyrand was witness to the real events, and there was no playacting the toll it took upon the nation.

Whirlpools of unrest swirled relentlessly throughout French society and clearly could be seen on the streets of Paris. The commoners were demanding food. It was 1789, and the harvests had been extremely poor the year before. Of course, it did not help that the balmy weather of a beautiful spring was fanning the flames of discontent. It was no accident, Talleyrand wrote in his memoirs, that revolutions begin in the springtime, for that is the season in which passions are stirred.

That spring, there was neither enough food to eat in France nor money to buy it. The middle class, the *bourgeoisie,* which had perceived the newly constructed National Assembly to be its primary hope, was forced to bankrupt its small shops, businesses, and landholdings in order to feed families. Typical of both the intellectual and *bourgeoisie,* both agitated the lower class.

King Louis XVI listened to his advisors as well as to his wife, all of whom urged him to quell the riots by using force. The French Guards, normally responsive to their king, openly defied his orders to contain the restless masses milling about Paris, looting and destroying property. In a matter of weeks, this disorder evolved into riots that, in turn, resolved into complete anarchy. The government, as Talleyrand had foreseen, had deteriorated to the point that it could truly be said that no one was in charge of maintaining the sovereign nation of France.

My beloved had a visceral dislike for allying himself against the king. By doing so, he was defying the mores and edicts of his own heritage as a member of the nobility. But, the king was unwilling or unable to understand the populist movement that was taking place. (It was a blindness for which he would soon pay with his life.) So, Talleyrand quietly allied himself with one of the most vocal leaders of the revolutionary movement, Count Honore Mirabeau, a flamboyant orator who, Talleyrand would admit, was as concerned with hearing his own words and mobilizing the crowds as he was with stating the facts properly. This alliance, however, along with Talleyrand's own reputation as a moderate, kept him on good terms with the commoners for the next three years.

Mirabeau and my beloved had been the kind of friends whose relationship had always been tempestuous. He was a renegade nobleman whom Talleyrand had helped acquire a position as spy for the French foreign ministry. Mirabeau had repaid the favor by supporting Talleyrand's bid for the bishopric of Autun. But, relations between the two had become strained. Mirabeau accused Talleyrand of posting him to Berlin so that he could seduce his mistress with impunity. According to Talleyrand's notes, my beloved fully admitted to this and with great pleasure. As an act of revenge, Mirabeau spread the rumor that, in Talleyrand's position of deputy to the National Assembly, he had benefited financially from his association with Minister of Finance Calonne. The minister, while teaching him the intricacies of government finances, had shown my beloved how to speculate with the state trust for personal gain. Mirabeau also reminded his colleagues in the National Assembly that King Louis XVI had always questioned the personal fortune that Talleyrand had amassed after the financial study he had undertaken for the church.

All of Paris questioned his purchase of a residence that was to be designed and built by Claude-Nicolas Ledoux, an architect for many of the nobility. The home was a brilliant treatment of a site near the Tuileries and the king's palace on Rue St. Florentin with rococo complexity and ingenuity behind a sober neoclassical façade. Ionic columns graced the main entrance. Ledoux had designed a circular drive that would place the visitor's carriage directly at the base of an imposing ceremonial staircase. Once the outside staircase had been managed, a servant in an ornate vestibule would greet the visitor. From which, he would then pass through to the gallery and onto the library, Talleyrand's favorite room. Horses were stabled near the secondary door, which was driven through by carriages that had no room to turn about in the front drive.

My beloved, to say it diplomatically, was extremely astute when it came to finances. That would be to his credit (and discredit) over the rest of his life. Even in his later years, as foreign minister, he demanded payment of a considerable fee before a foreign ambassador could see either him or the king. Without trying to defend such actions, I can only remind you that, despite his prestigious noble title, he was born into poverty and swore early in his years that he would never live without wealth.

History has now recorded that the Revolution began on July 14, 1789, when the king ordered his troops to move into Paris and quell the riots. The city erupted into a day of fury. Men, women, and children screamed obscenities as they climbed an outer wall of the Bastille, the massive stone fortress with 100-foot-high-walls that was surrounded by a seventy-five-foot-wide moat filled with water and capped by turrets from which soldiers were shooting down at the crowd. When the mob swarmed into the inner courtyard, they threw whatever they had picked up along the way—pitchforks, rocks, bricks—as the king's soldiers fired at will.

This monstrosity of a fort had been transformed into a prison in which paupers, prostitutes, and political radicals were incarcerated. Voltaire, for one, had spent weeks in the Bastille for challenging a member of the aristocracy to a duel. The sensational *Memoires de la Bastille,* published in 1783 by a well-known Parisian lawyer, had inflamed emotions with its description of the despotism of the Paris police and the arbitrariness of government. Although Talleyrand would be the first to admit that the Bastille was found to be holding only seven prisoners guarded only by eighty aged soldiers and thirty Swiss Guards when it was overrun by citizens that day, to the people of Paris, it represented all the suppression and terror by which the king and nobility continued to rule France.

As a deputy of the National Assembly, Talleyrand had befriended the young marquis de Lafayette, who, like my beloved, was born of the nobility but personally invested in changing the social order. Lafayette had recently returned from a successful adventure assisting the American revolutionaries in their struggle against the British and had just been appointed commander of the newly formed National Guard in France. The two men stood in a protected building nearby, watching the National Guard attempt to aid the royal troops against the anger of the citizens.

"Why are you investing yourself in this new revolutionary enterprise?" Talleyrand asked Lafayette, knowing him to be more a man of the people than my beloved. The general had relished fighting alongside the American terrorists who had proclaimed their revolution by dumping tea into the Boston harbor.

"Because it is just that, my friend. New." Lafayette responded. "What we are about to go through, Talleyrand, will make the American revolution pale by comparison. And it will be our very own. I believe our ancestors would run from their graves if they knew what is coming."

"Yet, you are doing your job, carrying out the king's will. You and I both know we can't desert Louis," Talleyrand responded with less conviction than he wished.

"My dear Talleyrand, you are at heart a sentimentalist. No, let me say, you are a romantic, still yearning for the golden days of our past. We both know all too well that our ineffectual Louis and his Austrian cow..."

"I remind you, as members of the nobility, we are still his cousins."

"Then what would you have us do?" Lafayette interrupted, shamed by Talleyrand's ambivalence, yet himself holding a lingering contempt for the rioting masses.

"Honor dictates that we stand firm until the king himself has signified his intention of deserting his own interests and those of the monarchy."

"I think the king has made his intentions quite clear," Lafayette responded, "by having sent in his troops. At this moment, we seek to imprison the rabble, but later, after the Revolution, troops will come for us."

"So we must reason with the king. We must present our case face-to-face. We must make him understand that the future of France is at stake. He would not sacrifice France for some minor royal privileges."

"My dear friend," Lafayette continued, "I am genuinely touched by your concern for our king. But I don't think that even you have completely comprehended that he would be acting too late. And, in history, as in love, timing is everything."

"I still maintain that if we talk to him directly..." Talleyrand stopped in mid-sentence, nauseated as he watched men urinate on city walls, defecate in alleyways, and throw excrement at the soldiers. The crowds that filled the streets and surrounded the buildings made him feel as if he was about to die from suffocation. While he would not admit the following to anyone other than me, his fear of confrontation took hold of him, the fear that confrontation leads to anger that, in turn, leads to fighting that, in turn, leads into chaos. And, once chaos exists, only force, repression, and counter-force could maintain law and order. As much as Talleyrand tried to distance himself from his past, the de Perigords had served the French kings since the thirteenth century. And yet, he knew Lafayette was correct.

"Talleyrand," Lafayette responded, incredulous that his politically sophisticated friend could be wavering at such an auspicious moment in history, "perhaps it is time to leave the country and go to London. Or America."

"I would find that cowardly and despicable."

"Do you know the king's brother, the count of Artois, who is next in line to the throne if Louis was to die, is immigrating to the new world?"

"Reprehensible," Talleyrand answered.

"That is why you were made a bishop," Lafayette laughed, "so that you could pass judgment on your fellow countrymen. Condemn your class! Then give them absolution!"

"My options are limited."

"On the contrary. Many options are available to a man who knows finances and administration. Just get rid of that ridiculous red robe. The sooner you return to the secular world, the better you will feel. By disposition and ambition, you are a politician, not a priest, nursemaid, or guarantor of the royal monarchy."

For weeks after this fateful day, Talleyrand thought about what Lafayette had said. His diaries are filled with notes of subsequent conversations with his respected friend. At one point in these conversations, he decided he could no longer vacillate. A social contract had to be created in which rights would be granted to the state, but only in return for personal security and equal treatment before the law for its citizens. And neither race, religion, nor ancestry should determine any citizen's rights. But could that occur without a revolution?

Many of his peers also wanted reform. But most left their own privileges intact. The nobles might give up some fiscal privileges, but they would not give up their privileged political position. The clergy might give up some fiscal privileges, but they would not give up church property.

Talleyrand's own vision of humanity had been shaped in great part by the writings of Voltaire, Diderot, Rousseau, and the fathers of the American Constitution. But I do wonder (and this was a question I feared to press too hard when my beloved was alive) how much of their principles he really took as his own. A shrewd man, it is easy to suspect he may have embraced these philosophies fervently at times, merely to enliven the salons of Paris.

A sadness crept over my own home following the fall of the Bastille. I was five or six—my sisters a little older—when the Revolution brought equality before the law to France. It scared Maman, who told us to be respectful of our servants because they might be conspiring against us. We were also to smile pleasingly at the peasants working our land when our carriage passed them because they were undoubtedly angry over the authority Maman and Papa exercised over them.

When I grew to marriageable age, I recognized Maman's cautions as nothing less than fear. Fear that the noble class in France would disappear. Fear that she and Papa would be reduced to the status of mere citizens. Fear that she would be required to live a life for which she was entirely unprepared. Although my sisters exhibited those same fears, my relative youth may have shielded me from them. Perhaps I also had a natural inclination to admire the ideals of the Revolution, liberty and equality. These were ideals my beloved took years of ambivalence to fully embrace and advocate.

Mirabeau, a manipulator of considerable ability, decided to direct Talleyrand's intensity and intelligence. He suggested that his friend become a member of the Constitutional Committee of the National Assembly, and my beloved did not hesitate. For several months, Talleyrand immersed himself in the work of the committee that had the task of creating a new constitution for France, one in which the rights of citizens were to be clearly defined and the organizing principles of the state were to be efficiently structured.

Although I find it difficult to believe, the price he paid for his political ambitions was the complete estrangement of his mistresses. Manon and Marie-Therese saw very little of Talleyrand, and his other mistresses (I have heard there were more than a few) also did not fare well. His women correctly concluded that he had uncovered a passion far greater than the one he claimed to have for them.

When the Declaration of the Rights of Man, containing twenty-two articles, was completed, it was widely known that Talleyrand had contributed significantly to Article VI, an article that allowed my beloved to resolve many ambivalent personal feelings toward the *ancien régime*.

His personal notes indicate that, at the time he was to give the presentation speech, he was extremely nervous, concerned that members of the National Assembly would heckle him and scream "hypocrite" because of his many incarnations. His nights were filled with tormented dreams and nightmares. Always, the clubfoot, with its solitary nail, was prominent during some vision of humiliation.

What did Talleyrand believe the dreams revealed? That he was a solitary, deformed man who dreamed of power beyond his grasp? Or, did they tell him that, in spite of his constraints, he was the person to lead France out of its terrible darkness? I believe you can guess.

When it was time, Talleyrand stood up in front of the 423 men who comprised the National Assembly and spoke with the firm voice he had used in Autun:

> Article VI: The law is an expression of the will of the community. All citizens have a right to concur, either personally or by their representatives, in its formation. It should be the same to all, whether it protects or punishes; and all being equal in its sight, are equally eligible to all honors, places, and employments, according to their different abilities, without any other distinction than that created by their virtues and talents.

When he finished, he received a thunderous ovation. One dissenter, born of a distinguished *ancien* family, shouted out that he would renounce his own noble heritage when it was state policy that all men were created equal. From another, he heard the newly created French constitution would guarantee all citizens—be they pauper or king—freedom from oppression. Several women sitting in the back of the room, who frequently attended the meetings, conducted their own noisy commentary on human liberties and freedom of the press.

While Talleyrand now had the National Assembly's support, he also knew he would have to move quickly because deputies were fickle. After exhaustive nights preparing a second speech from his temporary residence in the palace of the archbishop of Paris, my beloved, using his now-familiar gold-headed cane, limped up the wooden steps toward the podium of the assembly. He looked around the room, which was so small that many deputies had to stand in the back or listen from adjoining rooms, and saw all those faces, which only a few years ago would have ignored him because he was either part of the nobility or a member of the clergy, waiting attentively. He knew what they were about to hear would shock them.

"France is bankrupt," he announced bluntly.

The deputies shouted and whistled with impatience, being reminded only of something of which they were already aware.

"The ordinary means of revenue are now exhausted," Talleyrand continued, unperturbed by the hecklers. "The people are in the direst of straits and are unable to bear the smallest increase in taxes, however justifiable such an increase might be."

"We know all that," some of the deputies shouted. "Is this why you convened a special session?"

Five months had already passed, and impatience was a staple of daily life in the National Assembly.

"There is, however, another source of revenue, as immense as it is as yet untapped, which, in my opinion, may be utilized without offending the rights of property even in its strictest sense." My beloved paused and carefully took measure of his audience, restless, intense, eager, and unforgiving.

"This source of immeasurable revenue is the property of the church."

The National Assembly broke into an uncontrollable uproar when the deputies realized the bishop of Autun was proposing nothing less than the expropriation of church property.

"I propose that the National Assembly declare all ecclesiastical property be at the disposal of the nation."

The uproar continued. Some delegates stood on their wooden benches shouting out accolades. Others sat silently in disbelief. While a similar proposal had been made several times over the last months, it had never come from a bishop of the church. The motion passed by a nearly unanimous vote, and Talleyrand limped quietly back to his seat in triumph.

Talleyrand's revolution had begun. Citizens applauded as his carriage passed by them. He awoke each morning to groups gathered in the street, chanting his name. He was now considered a man to be trusted by the members of the third estate, even though he was both a nobleman and member of the clergy—both natural enemies of the people.

CHAPTER 15

▼

There was no doubt in the National Assembly that, with his words, Talleyrand had eliminated the stronghold of the Roman Papacy over the French Catholic Church. His motion set the stage for the expropriation of all church property and the allocation of its wealth and holdings to the state. He began a process that Napoleon would continue years later—to restructure the political, economic, and social structure of France, but without the use of force, the destruction of property, or the imposition of intolerable taxes.

Mirabeau, to my beloved's chagrin, continued to sit in his seat, shaking his leonine head with tears coursing down his pockmarked cheeks. He was heard to remark to a mutual friend his disbelief that this "aristocratic cockroach," as he called my beloved, "dressed in his full ecclesiastical splendor was a member of the clergy." Privately, Mirabeau would never forgive Talleyrand his speech, calling it "a theatrical gesture" designed to serve no other purpose than to secure the presidency of the National Assembly, the same position that Mirabeau himself sought.

The contest for president between these two men of stature was a short one. Within weeks of Talleyrand's speech, Mirabeau died. In his eulogy for his departed rival and friend, Talleyrand said,

> I will not dwell on the emotion excited by some of his addresses. Monsieur de Mirabeau remained a loyal statesman throughout his life. He will always be remembered for his words and those precious deeds that ensured the preservation of France.

What my beloved purposefully omitted at the graveside was Mirabeau's final declaration to him, "My friend, I take with me into the grave the last shreds of the monarchy."

"I swear, with uplifted hand, to diligently fulfill my duties, to be faithful to the Constitution, to the nation, and to the king."

Talleyrand, the new president of the National Assembly, stood in the assembly hall on February 16, 1790, and pronounced these somber words of allegiance with a distinct sense of irony and cynicism. As a clergyman swearing allegiance to the new constitution, no longer only to the pope in Rome, he was issuing the death knell of the Catholic Church. As he stood facing King Louis XVI, bedecked for this occasion in full regal splendor with blue silk vestment, emerald crown, and golden scepter, Talleyrand lied as he also swore allegiance to the Catholic Church, knowing full well he would resign his position as bishop in a very short time. He wondered whether King Louis XVI knew that the decision had already been made by the National Assembly to dispose of its monarch.

It was a curious moment in Talleyrand's life. A bishop, whose loyalty was first to the state (as specified by the provisions of the constitution), was in a precarious position, especially under a king who detested him. As the only bishop in the National Assembly who had taken the oath of acceptance of the new constitution (now a requirement for all priests who desired to maintain their civic rights and pension), he was also in a precarious position with the clergy. The ecclesiastical robes that had given him a position and constituency from which to rise in government in the past would now only restrict his political upward mobility.

What was he to do? While it may have seemed a precipitous action to most of his colleagues, Talleyrand resigned as bishop of Autun. He wrote in his diary:

> I resigned the bishopric of Autun and was surprisingly saddened to abandon the first career I had followed. But, I put myself at the disposition of events, and, provided I remained a Frenchman, all else was of indifference to me. The Revolution promised new destinies for the nation. I followed its course and took my chances.

By the time I reached the age of eight in 1792, I had determined that piety and religion were fine for Maman and Papa, but I questioned my own need for the church. While to this day I am unaware of the root of my distaste for religion, it may have come from nothing more than the foul smell of the old abbé who lived with us as a secretary/companion/tutor after the Revolution when so many churches were closed and he could no longer make a living. I found his heavy wig with its knotted locks disgusting. I wanted to run from the chapel when he leaned close to me, and his stale breath spewed forth droplets as he spoke. Should such things have produced a lifelong antipathy for religion? Certainly not. But they did. In later years, my readings reinforced these feelings. My agnosticism, well-concealed in public, proved to be both a surprise and a delight to my beloved.

As president of the National Assembly, Talleyrand's first notes reflect his melancholia over the loss of Mirabeau. While my beloved had many acquaintances, he had few friends, and this would not change as long as I knew him. After several days of dull headaches and lethargy, he immersed himself completely in the intimidating amount of work required in the first years after the Revolution.

There were momentous changes in Paris between 1789 and 1792. The smell of revolution pervaded the atmosphere, and nothing escaped its penumbra. The king was a virtual prisoner in his palace in the beautifully coiffured gardens of the Tuileries. The splendor of the court had vanished, and many of the great names that had illustrated the glories of the *ancien régime* and animated the life of the city were now seen only on the ever-growing list of émigrés. Gambling and lovemaking continued at an even more frenetic pace, as if elaborate dinner parties and salons hosted by famous courtesans were also soon to be pleasures of the past.

It was not until years later that I understood why Maman became so angry when she discovered my sisters and me in our playroom one day, dressing our servants in her best clothes. To us, it was make-believe. How were we to know that, as the Revolution unfolded, servants would buy the old clothing of the nobility from dealers on Rue St. Honore and wear the fluted caps that Maman felt were only the privilege of the aristocracy.

Despite Maman's teachings, I grew up with egalitarian ideas. When Babette, my science tutor, came into my room, I refused to care which of us sat on the chair and which sat on the stool. Maman cared and took pains to rearrange us whenever she felt she should. I also grew up questioning why she and Papa required the assistance of so many maids, valets, hairdressers, tailors, and dressmakers, all having assistants of their own. Maman would have locked me in my room if I had even hinted to her that I harbored the dream of every pretty street girl of the lowest origins—to become an *artiste* and perform onstage. Of course, at my age, I was spared the knowledge that such girls were "kept" by men of my father's class, an idea that would have appalled me. It took me many more years to realize that my own husband would seek out such pleasures, assuming they were his by birthright. No, in my child's eye, I saw only glittering sequined costumes, rouged cheeks, waving plumes, and the mystery of a dim, candlelit room.

During this period of transition in Paris, Talleyrand encountered a young American, Robert Morris, who had arrived in Paris on behalf of his family's financial interests to buy tobacco and flour contracts. Both he and his cousin, Gouverneur Morris of Philadelphia, had been instrumental in the formation of the Continental Congress and in writing the American Constitution. But, what made Morris particularly attractive to Talleyrand—as a friend and companion— was the fact he was single, clever, experienced in financial matters, spoke excellent French, and had come to France fortified with letters of introduction to members of the highest nobility and leaders in public affairs. With these letters, he secured immediate admission to the most exclusive social and political circles in which he and Talleyrand met on a daily basis.

The sight of these two men strolling the streets of Paris in their waistcoats, taking dinner together in cafés reputed to be owned by revolutionaries, must have stirred the hearts of the hopeful and chilled the hearts of the entrenched. The Bastille was gone. Chatelet prison had been demolished. Hundreds of churches had closed. With the sale and subdivision of convent gardens, whole new living quarters appeared for the people. And nobility, such as Talleyrand, chose to walk in the streets rather than be taken places in elaborately decorated carriages.

With the death of Mirabeau, Talleyrand felt he single-handedly had to stem the deleterious tide of extremism arising from Danton and Robespierre, two of the most influential leaders of the Revolution, and from the Cordelier and Jacobin clubs, two of the most revolutionary of the political clubs. The rise of these men and their clubs portended discontent with both the National Assembly and the monarchy. Soon, it would be spreading throughout the city with unprecedented consequences. Political pamphlets issued by the National Assembly, already circulating the city, demanded the abolition of the monarchy and the immediate replacement of the power vacuum with democratic institutions.

Talleyrand recoiled with horror as a crowd of French citizens assaulted the king's Swiss Guards protecting the royal family at their new residence in the Tuileries. Wherever he looked, he saw everything he detested. Rampage…looting…confrontation…chaos…the destabilization of the French state. The army, previously under the command of the king, now allied itself with the revolutionary leaders. The shift in the balance of power meant only one thing to my beloved, the inevitability of civil war.

In the spring of 1791, an incident occurred that served to heighten my beloved's fear that royal blood might soon be shed. King Louis XVI and his family attempted to flee Paris, under cover of night, to a fortified town near the eastern border of France. The escape of the royal family from *de facto* imprisonment in the palace, arranged by the queen's lover, Count Axel Ferson, proved to be a humiliating disaster for all involved. Talleyrand recorded the execution of the plan, as reconstructed by members of the National Assembly in the days following the incident, "could have formed the basis of a comedy."

His *ancien* sensibilities had been shamed by the blundering nature of the attempted escape. The dauphin had been made to wear a girl's dress. Marie-Antoinette had worn a simple frock of a governess and a hat with a long veil hiding her face. The king had taken on the role of a steward, donning *bourgeois* clothing and wig. After several stops at relay inns by the coach containing the royal family and exceedingly reckless behavior on the part of the king, the royal family was recognized. Once that occurred, word quickly spread from relay station to relay station that the royal family would be passing through in disguise. To compound the problems, the detachment of troops that was supposed to meet the carriage at an agreed-upon station never appeared.

By the time the king's carriage arrived in the small town of Varennes to change horses, it was nearly midnight, and the drivers did not know where to go. Arriving at the center of town, the carriage found itself surrounded by men with rifles and bayonets. It seems a postmaster from another town had ridden to Varennes and informed the local grocer, who was also a municipal representative, that, if the royal family was allowed to flee, he and other Varennois would be charged with treason. So, by the cock's crow and with an increasingly large group of angry citizens converging on the town to see their king, the coach carrying the royal family worked its way back to Paris.

In truth, the thought of the royal family fleeing like thieves in the night repulsed my beloved so much that he took to his bed with headaches for two days. His shame turned to anger, however, when he realized that, as the royal family fled, the king must certainly have been aware that Prussia, Austria, and Russia were armed and mobilizing on France's borders, poised to invade, fearful the Revolution might spread across the continent and destabilize their own monarchies.

My beloved wrote, "Only a fool or a desperate man would chance to welcome foreign troops to French soil. Was King Louis XVI so divorced from reality to think these foreign armies would save his throne?"

Talleyrand was horrified that war might be thrust upon France. He had always agreed with Voltaire's position that peace was the natural state of man. War, as represented by the conquest of one nation by another, was the victory of irrationality over reason. Although Voltaire's philosophy was now being criticized, my beloved recalled with fondness that day in 1778 when he had blessed an old man of eighty-four and watched crowds of admirers wave to Voltaire as he walked through the city. Talleyrand had never forgotten the man or his words and always maintained that the first duty of a sovereign was to obtain a lasting peace for his people. Little did he suspect at the time that the Congress of Vienna would give him that chance for France.

Within a day after the royal family's return to Paris, the Jacobins and the Cordeliers demanded the king be stripped of his powers and executed. The National Assembly, unable to reach a decision on the king's fate, did nothing. Once again, the royal family were prisoners inside their palace.

I now wonder if my beloved would have behaved any differently had he been able to predict the course of history as we now know it. The beheading of the king in January of 1793…a reign of terror by the Revolutionary Council that was installed to protect the people…a new form of government called the Directory in which five men were chosen by the legislature to lead France…the overthrow of this increasingly corrupt and unpopular Directory by Napoleon Bonaparte on November 9,1799…and its replacement with the Consulate form of government.

Talleyrand was to say later on that he never abandoned a regime until it had abandoned itself. Perhaps this was true. He would abandon the Revolution only when it began to spill the blood of Frenchmen. He would abandon Napoleon when his decisions made continuing war for France inevitable. He would abandon the Restoration of King Louis XVI to the throne when the king's blindness brought France to the brink of civil war.

This matter of abandonings defined our relationship as well. My beloved had to abandon a wife to pursue me, his nephew's wife. To be with Talleyrand, I had to abandon a husband, a lover, my children, and the regard of my family. And, in our early days together, I feared I would be abandoned by Talleyrand when he saw fit to do so. This thought kept me always wary.

Although I write of abandoning my children with what might seem to the reader as callous disregard, I assure you it was not done without bouts of melancholia and long periods of sleepless nights and ghostlike days. I have rationalized my behavior by assuring myself that governesses and tutors would have always played a much more prominent role in my children's life than I would have. Yet, I have never been able to think of my actions without some sorrow. Not remorse, just sorrow. What does this say about my character? My natural motherly affections? My capacity to love? I will never know, for deep introspection is not part of my nature and, for purposes of this manuscript, Talleyrand remains my focus.

CHAPTER 16

▼

Talleyrand could not remember a time when he had felt so ill for so long. While his diaries refer to periodic, dull headaches beginning during the summer of 1791 and a stiffening of his "good" leg during the fall months, it is clear to me as I write of this period that, as he sat before the hearth in his library on a cold day in January 1793, his constitution had adapted poorly to the portent of regicide. Melancholia, as is universally known, comes in many forms, and, if I had been his doctor at the time, this would have been my diagnosis.

My beloved, according to his notes, had risen earlier than usual. Perhaps he had been awakened by the sound of drum rolls, real or imagined. Perhaps his sleep had been disturbed by the insults and rocks hurled onto the grounds of the Tuileries at a king that was no longer living there. But knowing he would not venture out in the cold of the day and certain no one would be calling on him, he had delayed making his toilette and had moved slowly all morning between his bedroom and his library.

It was approximately nine o'clock in the morning, and he was certain he heard the drum roll begin. Then, for an hour, an eerie silence settled over the city. At ten o'clock, when the drum roll renewed and he heard several cannon shots, Talleyrand knew the king had been beheaded.

My beloved was barely conscious when his manservant entered the room to add logs to the fire. His head had again begun its dull ache, his brain decrying the act of putting the king to the guillotine by madmen who had no respect for either France or its history. He knew he could be next because the guillotine was being reserved for all moderates, who were now viewed as enemies of the Revolution by the extremist Jacobins and Cordeliers. Over the prior six months, since the king had been forced to accept the National Assembly's constitution, Paris had become a city awaiting the next day's horror. Even as King Louis XVI had acquiesced and taken an oath to accept a constitution that limited his powers, Talleyrand had been mortified that the king had been given only a simple armchair in which to sit. No deputy rose or took off his hat as the king stood to sign the document. *Quel humiliation!* What humiliation!

Celebrations the royal family had attended—the public masses, the ballets, the carriage rides in the open air—were little consolation for the trimming of royal power and the royal family's imprisonment in their palace. The "old" National Assembly became the new Legislative Assembly, but the king's acceptance of their declaration of war against the Austrian emperor in April 1792 only fanned rumors that the king and queen were betraying the nation by encouraging foreign forces to march on Paris to liberate them.

While the royal family remained in the Tuileries over the spring of 1792, Talleyrand lived in darkness and fear, closing both windows and curtains and curtailing the use of his garden in order to muffle the insults coming from venomous tongues outside and to avoid seeing the daily pamphlets that insisted on either prison or death for the royal family.

During the month of June, a mob smashed through the gates surrounding the grounds of the palace as well as the doors to the *château* while the National Guard did little more than turn out the unruly crowd. By August, on order of the Legislative Assembly, the royal family was moved to a medieval dungeon next to a seventeenth-century palace owned by the count of Artois that only years earlier had been the site of parties given by the king's younger brother. The Temple, as the dungeon was called, had been a political prison for many years. Throughout the fall and winter months, Talleyrand's sources of information were limited. He realized there was little he could do for the king.

Perhaps my beloved's worst moment came, not at the expected beheading of King Louis XVI, but months earlier in September when the head of the Princess de Lamballe was paraded throughout Paris on a pike and brought before his windows as it was walked around the Tuileries by an angry mob.

The king's official trial before the Revolutionary Tribunal, a court created to try anyone suspected of royalist sympathies, had taken place in December. By January 21, the monarchy that was voted out of existence in September by the Legislative Assembly, no longer had its monarch. The king was dead. And next would be his queen.

Maman tells me that, when King Louis XVI was beheaded, I slept without disturbance, the faint noise of the cannons not reaching my consciousness. My own recollections are of the silence of a crowd, the laughter of executioners, and a little dog licking the blood flowing from the scaffold. Of course, Maman was correct. I was merely a child with an overactive imagination. But she does not contradict my later memories of tumbrels laden with the dead of the day, rumbling over cobbled streets next to our carriage, or that our trips through Paris became less frequent.

After several weeks of anguish and sadness, Talleyrand did what Talleyrand did best. He maneuvered. As a member of the "old" National Assembly, he was automatically excluded from election to the new Legislative Assembly. So my beloved stepped down as president and was given the post of diplomat to London, just at the moment he knew he could no longer be effective working with the meglomaniacal Jacobins, whom he was certain would destroy France.

It was a disastrous posting. Although my beloved always had a deep-seated admiration and affection for the English way of life and their egalitarian institutions, once he stepped onto its shores, he found the English completely unsympathetic to the French struggle. Opinion against the Revolution had already been formed by countless numbers of angry French émigrés. Everywhere my beloved traveled, he heard both the French and English gentry refer to him as a traitor, a renegade, and a defrocked priest. Fortunately, he was able to use his considerable negotiating skills to convince the English foreign minister to sign a treaty that stated it was the official policy of England not to interfere in the internal affairs of a foreign country, which included France.

When Talleyrand was asked to return to Paris at the height of continued political unrest, he was certain he had to leave France if he was to survive, politically and personally. Danton, the feared leader of the Jacobins, informed him he could not guarantee his personal safety. He admitted that the people's revolution was out of control and it would be best for Talleyrand to leave France until the currents of hysteria and cruelty subsided.

The unstated implications of Danton's words were also clear. The Revolutionary Council's tentacles could easily reach across the English Channel, if England was the country to which Talleyrand would flee. And, once there, my beloved knew he could not insulate himself from the angry French *émigré* community. With the destruction of the British navy at the French port of Toulon by an audacious, young, Corsican artillery captain named Napoleon Bonaparte, Talleyrand decided he had to find an alternative country in which to live.

On a wintry morning in 1794, my beloved set sail for an unspecified duration to America.

CHAPTER   17

▼

After thirty-eight days on turbulent seas, my beloved reached the port of Philadelphia. Knowing Talleyrand as I did, it was not hard for me to assume that, after the splendor of Versailles and the stately mansions of Paris and Perigord, Philadelphia would prove to be an architectural wasteland. But he was genuinely impressed by the bustling city of 90,000 citizens. Each person, so it seemed, scurried about on meticulously clean cobblestone sidewalks in front of row upon row of identical three-story, gable-roofed townhouses constructed of red brick.

According to my beloved's notes, upon his arrival, he contacted Gouverneur Morris, with whom he felt he could confide his sentiments:

> My mind was totally immune to the novelties which, as a rule, excite the interest of travelers. I had the greatest difficulty in rousing my curiosity…Thus, meeting with neither opposition, advice, nor direction, my instinct alone guided me, and I was led to contemplate more attentively the grand sight under my eyes.

I will sketch my beloved's two years in a land that fascinated him (but holds no interest for me) out of a sense of duty and needed completion. I can best provide a sense of his journey by directly quoting from a selection of his diary entries.

> *8 May 1793* I was pleased to meet with Alexander Hamilton today through an introduction by my dear friend Gouverneur Morris. Here is a true leader who has successfully accomplished in this new world what my colleagues and I have yet to be able to achieve in France—liberty, equality, and justice.

5 June 1793 Gouverneur Morris has relayed a message that President Washington will not meet with me due to issues that leave me to suspect prudishness in the man. Morris insisted to the president that, with respect to morals, none of the French leaders is exemplary. The former bishop, meaning me, should not be blamed unduly. I believe Washington strongly objected to my gambling and stock-jobbing during my tenure in government. Morris said he tried to extol my virtues, but to no avail.

30 July 1793 It was particularly hot in Moreau's Bookstore this evening. Beaumetz, my manservant, the viscount of Noailles, the marquis de Blacons, Omer Talon, the duke of Rochefoucauld-Liancourt, and a handful of other émigrés heretofore unknown to me are filling my evenings with their gossip and goodwill and making me yearn, once again, for France. I feel as if I can open my heart to these men without sounding maudlin.

25 August 1793 As much as I admire the Americans I meet, I am unsure whether it is constitutionally possible for me to be as 'respectable' as is called for in daily conduct. I am incapable of appearing more virtuous than I am. My dear friend Hamilton has informed me in a private correspondence that, despite my great amiability, I can never attain in Philadelphia society the success I might merit. I wonder if such a statement is due to my close friendship with a beauty of Caribbean origin. As she and I promenade through Philadelphia, I see shocked expressions on my Quaker hosts.

9 September 1793 There are more chances to make one's fortune in America than in any country I have ever visited! Yet, my new friend, Alex de Tocqueville, told me tonight at Moreau's that America, unlike France, is a country in which, when you have a good idea, someone is more than happy to steal it and make it his own. "Americans all smile in front of your face and seem enchanted by your quaint French manners and accent," de Tocqueville said, "but don't underestimate these rogues. They are mongrels who are quite ruthless in business and almost as pious in church." What a pessimist the man is, when he thinks he is a realist. Lefrevre told me that de Toqueville's patron, Benjamin Franklin, appears to be an ascetic puritan in public, but his private life would even embarrass me.

7 December 1793 I have asked some of my Swedish acquaintances to send over goods to sell either in New York or in Philadelphia. I am in a position to do good business for those who place themselves entirely in my hands. America is a place in which to be an entrepreneur. My friends admonish me, and they mean well. But, most are men who are not used to taking large risks.

10 December 1793 One can make a great deal of money here, either by commissions in public funds or commissions in the purchase of land. The reputations of American agents are so uncertain that European merchants are always at a disadvantage in trying to find someone to represent them here. I will offer myself for the job since I have some qualifications in financial assessment. The accusations that I embezzled church funds and state monies in France were entirely false. I merely invested wisely when an opportunity arose.

30 July 1794 My voyage to the largely unoccupied state of Maine was a wonder to the senses. There were forests as old as the world itself…green and luxuriant grasses hugging the banks of the rivers, large natural meadows, and strange and delicate flowers quite new to me. Here and there were traces of tornadoes that had carried everything before them…In the face of the immense solitude, my friends and I gave free vent to our imagination. Our minds built cities and villages. There is an inexpressible charm in thinking of the future when traveling in such a country. It is impossible to move a step without feeling convinced that nature requires that an immense population will someday use the land which now lies idle but which requires only the touch of the human hand to produce everything in abundance.

12 August 1794 I cannot say which state I prefer—New York, Connecticut, Massachusetts, or Maine. Each has its own beauty. I have learned all about timber to be able to sell parcels of land to émigrés. I now know the differences between oak, pine, and cedar, their growth and planting seasons, the cost of cutting down an individual tree and carrying it from one state to another, the poll taxes involved, and the buying and selling patterns of the businessmen.

3 September 1794 To me, the only purpose of money is to buy articles I would enjoy possessing—luxurious surroundings, books, clocks, paintings, fine clothing, and presents for friends. Money gives me the ability to be independent of anyone who might think he or she could control me. But I find that money means something very different to Americans. They see it as a means of measuring social and political rank in a system in which I understood all men to have been created equal. I find the luxury displayed by Americans quite unbecoming. I admit that my own possessions often demonstrate my improvidence and frivolity, but in America, luxury only serves to emphasize defects that prove that refinement does not exist in this country—either in the daily conduct of life or in its incidentals.

28 September 1794 Every day, the differences between France and America are more apparent to me. In France, rich men become richer as they hold state office. But, in America, where money is worshipped with an astounding devotion, public servants resign and seek other employment in order to support their families. I find this practice of not enriching yourself at the expense of the public somewhat childish.

When Talleyrand was in America, my parents began to seek a match for me and decided upon, of all people, Edmond, Talleyrand's nephew. Never could a man be more unlike his elder relative. Talleyrand could woo across continents. Edmond was lucky to hold the attention of a corner of a drawing room. But, keep in mind, I was only ten when my parents and Edmond's parents entered into discussions about our future betrothal. I now believe it was a crime, if it weren't so laughable. I was told years later by Maman that "negotiations" began one day when she innocently invited Edmond's parents to lunch. His parents were of noble blood, so the invitation was quite appropriate. My mother told me the conversation soon turned into a discussion of dowry, one that particularly delighted my father. The discussion remained quite friendly until Edmond's mother became serious.

"Let us formalize," she said once and then thrice, her ample chest heaving at each assertion. "Let us formalize."

So, while I was barely able to dress myself, my parents were giving me away with the cows and the cutlery.

Still, my mother, bless her soul, held greater hopes for me than a well-placed marriage. Like Talleyrand's journey to a new world, she knew I was being reared on the cusp of a new France. Yet who could have known that Edmond would become my albatross!

At the end of Talleyrand's second year in America, during which my beloved prospered greatly, Robespierre was guillotined. According to both history and my beloved, his death marked the beginning of the last phase of the Revolution. All of the reports that reached America stated the French were exhausted by tyranny and disgusted by the excessive and brutal shedding of blood. A universal cry for peace, order, and civility seemed to be rising. The moderate Girondans, who had been expelled from the Constitutional Convention, were now recalled. The separation of church and state was complete. The Committee of Public Safety that had exercised decisions over life and death was disbanded. The Jacobin Club was abolished, as was the Revolutionary Tribunal. Most importantly, my beloved, who had always been in contact with agents in the government, was recalled to France to assume an unspecified position within the foreign ministry.

Talleyrand told me how he sat one evening in October with his friends at the Philadelphia bookstore (from which he had received so much sustenance) and proudly read the following letter:

The   National   Convention   decrees   that   Charles-Maurice   de Talleyrand-Perigord, former bishop of Autun, is authorized to reenter the territory of the French Republic and that his name shall be removed from the list of émigrés. Accordingly, the Convention rescinds the decree of accusations issued against him.

Little did anyone in that small room in the back of the bookstore realize, this letter of pardon had cost Talleyrand all the money he had earned over the past two years in America.

CHAPTER 18

▼

When Talleyrand returned to Paris, he saw only a shadow of its past. The grandeur that a monarchy had once conferred upon the ambience of a city had disappeared like a once-cherished dream. There were no longer gilded coaches in the streets or richly dressed nobility strolling in public to show off the latest fashion. The most ornate buildings in the sixteenth *arrondissement*, district, were in disrepair. Even the sounds and smells of the city had changed, with the aroma of incense and candles disappearing along with so many churches. Perhaps worst of all, the Seine, that glorious river that runs through the heart of Paris, looked as if it had been desecrated by excrement, mud, and sewage. Talleyrand limped along the banks of the river daily, wondering if this was not the perfect symbol for the stagnant, blood-tinged tyranny and terror that had gripped the city.

As my beloved walked the relatively empty streets of the Right Bank, accosted by beggars, prostitutes, and homeless mothers in doorways of dilapidated buildings begging for their starving children, the pathos of the situation overwhelmed him. He handed out a few francs to the needy, but he knew he was simply going through the motions of charity. He told me that, for the first time in his life, he was speechless and disgusted by what he saw—the rape and ravage of Europe's most beautiful city, Paris.

This was the world in which I was raised and the cesspool of corruption that would shape my husband Edmond's life. Would my life be marked by the legacy of the city's dark turn? Many individuals were consumed by wiping out the "old," assuming this was the only way for change to be secured. The statues of King Louis XIV and Joan of Arc, while left standing in Place de Beau Rivage, were completely destroyed. The monuments in Place de la Concorde, representing the victories France had won, were defaced by obscene phrases and large painted letters spelling "*La Revolution.*"

I was born in 1784, a mere five years before the Revolution began, with noble roots as deep and wide as those of the house of Perigord. My mother, a duchess, could boast of ties to the Russian crown. My father, whose properties extended through the richest areas of the Loire, was most proud of his service to kings. When I came into this world, I have since been told that the usual fuss was made with the usual titled guests in attendance. But the festivities were muted by the times. Nobility had to watch what they said, how they dressed, and where they went.

The Reign of Terror cast a pall over much of my family's daily life, and I was not indifferent to those changes. Although I laughed at my sisters' imitations of the beheadings during the day, many of my nights were filled with images of men with knives between their teeth, yelling, shouting, and trying to climb over the stone wall surrounding our estate. Papa's trusted menservants always drove them back. Some would slip beneath the hooves of horses; others would be crushed between the wheels of carriages. This same hideous and sinister dream haunted me throughout my childhood. I suspect my early interest in politics and power, what men seemed to fight over and share so poorly, grew as my own life was increasingly constrained.

By the time I turned ten years old in 1794, my sisters and I rarely took carriage rides through Paris any longer because Maman would say "the filthy streets reflect the poverty and crimes of all its inhabitants." When she did allow us a visit to the Louvre, I saw few fine carriages in the streets, only decrepit coaches drawn by old nags harnessed with rope. Was this what the men who visited Maman and Papa discussed?

Unknown to my parents, I had decided by the time I was fifteen years old who my husband would be, and it would not be Edmond. Even when we played together as children, I mistrusted his sincerity. My girlish love, which lasted for years, was given to one of the heroes of Polish independence, the handsome Prince Adam Czartoryski, who had once appeared at my home. When my secret was discovered, my entire family laughed for days, and I felt the smaller for it. Many years later, when the match between Edmond and I was made, they tried to convince me how perfectly suited for me he was, pointing to his resemblance to the prince.

"Ha!" I said then and "Ha!" I say now. Many years later, the fact the adults could not tell the difference between a stallion and an ox became a private joke between Talleyrand and me.

All along the elegant Rue du Faubourg St. Honore, Talleyrand found that *châteaux* of noblemen he had once visited had been transformed into public warehouses filled with stalls from which merchants sold everything from food to clothing to livestock. Pigs, chickens, and ducks ran free, spattering mud wherever they went. The squeals of the animals and shouts from the merchants chasing them made Talleyrand wonder about how quickly man could descend into a state of primitive behavior when law and order is eliminated. He recognized merchandise that rolled by on carts that had been looted by the citizens in the name of justice and equality—furniture from salons he had visited in addition to silver, china, and oil paintings belonging to families he had once called on socially. He became nauseated upon seeing a breakfront that belonged to Madame de Stael covered with painted letters advertising the sale of eggs, thankful she was not standing there to see what had happened to her possessions. He was looking into the face of chaos in the name of revolution, and he despised it, along with those former colleagues and friends—Danton, Robespierre and Mirabeau—with whom he had worked so hard to transform a beautiful world into a living hell.

He could not help viewing Paris as if a tornado had swept through, destroying everything in its path and randomly tossing about all objects that belonged to the *ancien régime.* Gone were etiquette and restraint. Messengers now dressed indifferently. They did not bow or remove their hats. People in the street had become rude, abrasive, demanding, scared, and clearly uncertain about their future. Defamatory words like *merde, couchon,* and *cretin* replaced civil dialogue among Parisians.

Yet Talleyrand also recorded that the oppressiveness of the Revolution was gone, the constant sense of terror that existed under the tyranny of the Jacobins. In its place was an atmosphere of banter and jocularity that he had not witnessed outside the salons of the nobility. Peasants danced in the cemetery of his former parish, St. Sulpice. Spectacles and fireworks replaced prisons and revolutionary committees. The fashions of a new merchant class, earmarked by seminudity, gaudy laces, crinolines, and saches, mirrored the excesses of the times. *Les merveilleuses,* the marvelous ones, had taken the place of the vanished ladies of the court, who, like the latter, were imitations of whores competing for the prize in sensuous extravagance.

According to my beloved's notes, "Their arms and legs were bare, and it distressed me to see such wantonness."

The women wore silver and gold rings on their toes. Unlike the *nouveaux riches* of Philadelphia, the men of this new revolution wore gigantic *cravats,* ties that were pulled up over their lower lips so that only their nose and eyes were visible. Their hats, pulled down over their eyebrows, caused a look that Talleyrand labeled *les incroyables,* the unbelievable ones. Talleyrand wrote that, despite the looting he detested, the pervasive sensuousness excited him. These were changes I heard about from my tutors, but with which I had no daily experience. To a large extent, my schooling remained within the grounds of our estate.

One day, as he walked the streets, seeking to understand its new ways, he recognized some church vestments and sacred vessels being carried carelessly by beggars. He told me he felt obliged to act.

"Stop!" Talleyrand shouted, limping quickly after the filthy robbers.

"Don't bother us, cripple!" shouted back a one-armed man, wearing the tattered red and blue uniform of what was once the formidable French army.

"That belongs to the church!" Talleyrand waved his gold-headed cane and attempted to catch up to the laughing thieves.

"Then ask God for another sacred vestment!" the one-armed man screamed back as he and his two companions ran from Talleyrand's sight. *"C'est un Dieu que nous a donne que merde!"* It is a God who gave us this shit!

Talleyrand leaned against a nearby building, exhausted, dizzy, and disgusted. Not only was France being raped, but so was the church, the church that had given legitimacy and sanctity to generations of Frenchmen, including the Talleyrand-Perigord dynasty. As he tried to compose himself, he could not help but wonder whether he, as the proponent of the nationalization of church property, was partly responsible for this desecration. What had he helped to create? Chaos? Anarchy? In the name of equality and justice? He was finding it difficult to hold on to some vision that would allow him to maintain his emotional equilibrium. Wasn't he in agreement with the street urchins who were ransacking the same institution that had humiliated him so many times? Perhaps with some of them, he thought, but certainly not with all. They were out of control in a way he could never be and which he had never anticipated. At that moment, he knew he would have to undo the havoc he had helped to create.

Talleyrand quickly set about to discover where the new center of power lay. Much to his pleasant surprise, he found it centered around a woman called "the Queen of Society," who could be a found nibbling ice or gaping at fireworks while talking politics. The woman he described in his notes was a beautiful Creole aristocrat by the name of Josephine de Beauhamais, who had been married to the Viscount Alexandre de Beauhamais, who, as president of the National Assembly, had been guillotined by Robespierre. Josephine had been spared from death only by the timely execution of Robespierre himself and had since sought nurturance and assistance from a succession of prominent men, including Paul Barras, General Hoche, and, perhaps most importantly, a young army officer who was in the middle of attacking Italy in the name of France. His name was Napoleone Buonaparte, a Corsican by birth, who had literally learned to speak French only after Corsica was given to France by the Italian state of Genoa. Sent to a French military academy speaking French with a heavy Italian accent, he changed his name to Napoleon Bonaparte in order for it to sound more French and deserted his homeland of Corsica in order to dedicate himself to climbing his way up the ladder of power in France. I gain on my story, however, for what I am trying to say at this moment is that Talleyrand went out of his way to befriend Josephine.

Paul Barras, a man now at the center of power in Paris, had helped to free France from the terror that occurred after the beheading of King Louis XVI. Born of Gascon nobility, Barras was one of five members of the Directory, a group that had been formed among the political elite to control France immediately after the Revolution. The Directory had risen out of the ruins of a bloodthirsty reign that used the guillotine, so it seemed to Talleyrand as punishment of first resort. It was to be advised by a legislature that consisted of the Council of Ancients and the Council of Five Hundred. Its goals, Talleyrand found out, had already changed from liberty and equality for all citizens to that of increasing and protecting their own profits. Within a few years, the Directory's corruption and military defeats would make it increasingly unpopular.

To thrust himself once again into the midst of power, Talleyrand realized his name would have to regain its prominence in the public domain. Through *protégés*, he was invited to deliver two academic papers at the prestigious Institute of Moral and Political Sciences. Housed in one of the new buildings of Paris, it had been developed under codes that coordinated the height of structures with the width of streets in order to ensure the penetration of sunlight to the trees, a definite improvement over prior land development schemes.

The first paper, "On Commercial Relations Between England and the United States," concluded that there really was no opportunity for the French to take advantage of America as a trading partner. Despite the fact that Americans admired the French, America remained a British colony through its common heritage, language, education, history, and laws.

Talleyrand's second paper, "On The Advantage of Acquiring New Colonies," made a significantly more profound and far-reaching statement. He pointed out that hope for the future of France lay primarily in colonial expansion. France, he concluded, should send its citizens into new lands and export the values of the new revolution—fraternity, equality, and justice. This would open up new horizons for French industry and culture and offer unlimited opportunity for French entrepreneurs. In this way, France would be able to compete with England commercially without entering into direct conflict. At long last, the two countries could work in a spirit of cooperation and mutual interests.

His reception by the French and foreign dignitaries attending each lecture went far beyond anything he might have imagined. Grey heads nodded in approval. Men joked and patted him on his back. Everyone was impressed by his ability to assess differences in national character and how important they now seemed to be in the formulation of a foreign policy. Once again, Talleyrand's name was bandied about in the Legislative Assembly for the position of minister of foreign affairs, buttressed by the fact that those who had worked with him in the past recognized him to be a brilliant statesman.

True to his original strategy of keeping a low political profile, he spent much of his time merely greeting and meeting new members of the Academy and the Directory. At a small dinner party of venison and wild boar he gave at his home on Rue St. Florentin, he toasted his guests and made certain that all who spoke with him knew that, under no conditions, would he take an active role in politics. Of course, it was a ruse, as distracting as was the champagne he served with the meal. Politics was his eventual goal, but he was still waiting and carefully monitoring the tide of change that was sweeping ashore. For the guests who remained leery of his intentions, he had just two words, "More champagne?"

Talleyrand, in his love life and his political life, was a master planner. I would later learn it was he who had encouraged Edmond's parents to pursue the possibility of their son's engagement to me. Did he already have plans for his young nephew, playing the role that his uncle, the archbishop, had played for him? Or, if I were as Machiavellian as was my beloved, I would ask whether he already had future plans for me. But I am getting ahead of my story. First, my beloved had to order his own world.

A choice had to be made between restoring the Bourbon monarchy, establishing a Republican form of government, or maintaining the revolutionary Directory, which was proving unable to control the poverty, rampant crime, and social unrest that had overtaken France. The choice was clear, but the timing was poor. Then suddenly, it wasn't.

A political crisis unexpectedly occurred with France's attempt to land a force in Ireland with the hope of sparking a revolt against England. The landing failed, but, in the process, the supporting Spanish fleet was destroyed, and England was left the ruling power on the seas. At the same time, the French armies in Germany were in retreat. Only the French army in Italy, under the command of now General Napoleon Bonaparte, was finding success, having defeated five Austrian armies. This Italian victory had resulted in large measure from Napoleon's brilliant strategy and tactics, abilities with which Talleyrand felt that he, too, had been blessed. My beloved quickly realized that, for the masses, Napoleon was the man of the hour, the deity of the army, the hero of France, and, possibly, the savior of the Republic.

At the same time, the citizens of France were finally turning against the members of the Directory, largely because of their incorrigible corruption and ineptitude. The political stage was now set for a major confrontation. On one side were the Royalist-controlled legislative chambers. On the opposing side were members of the Directory, determined to retain power regardless of the opposition.

Talleyrand knew a confluence of events was building up to a political confrontation. If he did not act soon, he would miss his moment of opportunity. To reenter the political arena and seek office, he decided to join the most influential of all political groups, the Constitutional Club. At that time, the Club's membership was composed of moderate and progressive Jacobins, many of whom Talleyrand knew personally. Within months of his diligence in attending meetings and cajoling friends and foes alike, his name was placed on a short list of potential candidates to become the next minister of foreign affairs.

But, when the appointment was introduced at the Assembly, the reactions of some were quite vitriolic.

"This little priest of yours," one Jacobin leader shouted, "will sell the country from under us for any amount he can get!"

"What has he sold thus far?" Barras asked.

"His God, to begin with," the Jacobin replied.

"How is that possible? He does not believe in God!"

The legislators laughed, and the Jacobin recognized he was trapped by his own logic. He responded, "Talleyrand is a traitor to his own class and to the king."

"It seems to me," Barras replied, "we are the last ones who can hold that against him."

Not long after, while Talleyrand lay in bed one night with his mistress, Madame de Stael, daughter of the king's financial advisor, a servant entered the room and handed her mistress a sealed envelope. She opened it up, read it, and smiled.

"Well," she said to my beloved, "in the beginning of our tryst, I was making love to an ordinary citizen of France. Now I am in bed with no less than its new foreign minister."

And so, as always, my beloved got what he wanted. He had learned to choose the right allies, make the right case, and, most of all, cultivate patience. These skills would be essential in later years, not only in the exercise of diplomacy, but in his purposeful courtship of me, his nephew's wife.

CHAPTER 19

▼

Talleyrand often said that, when the gods are cruel, they grant one's wishes. After being appointed minister of foreign affairs in July 1794, he quickly discovered his powers were, to say the least, truncated. He was nothing more than a lackey for the five-member Directory, excluded from most important decisions concerning France's relations with foreign powers. Perhaps even worse, he had to tolerate their boorish, pugnacious ways of interacting, screaming, and physically fighting with one another over even minor disagreements. I can well imagine how their behavior deeply offended my beloved's need for order and decorum.

At this point in his life, he was frequently in the company of Madame de Stael, much admired for her political salon and hostessing skills. She had married the Swedish ambassador to France, the Baron de Stael, in 1786, but she was living quite independently when my beloved first bedded her. Considered by many to be an outstanding literary figure, she was the only mistress of Talleyrand's whom I both envied and resented.

Not one to be satisfied by merely one dalliance at a time, within weeks of his appointment as foreign minister, Talleyrand dispatched his predecessor, Charles Delacroix, as a diplomat outside the country so that he could bed Madame Delacroix, a dignified thirty-nine-year-old beauty, who my beloved informed me was more than willing to indulge in an amorous escapade because her husband had been unable to fulfill his marital obligations for quite some time. Within nine months, Madame Delacroix gave birth to a boy she named Eugene Delacroix, who is just now becoming a respected artist, but who has never recognized Talleyrand as his biological father.

Talleyrand also had a chance encounter with one Catherine-Noel Worlee Grand, who arrived on his doorstep one night. She asked him to protect the money she had left in an English bank and was afraid that, with any French invasion of England, she would lose her considerable fortune. Talleyrand, well-informed about matters that had to do with both money and affairs of the heart, was well-aware of the woman's amorous adventures with several influential men in Paris. Why I bother at this point in Talleyrand's life to even mention Catherine, rather than several additional mistresses of my beloved who were smarter and cleverer, is that Catherine eventually became the princess of Talleyrand, Talleyrand's wife. Unlike his previous mistresses, who were largely of noble birth, refined, well-educated, and intelligent, it was Catherine's simplicity and docile qualities that somehow appealed to Talleyrand, who was becoming fatigued by the imperious brilliance of Madame de Stael and her class of women.

This segment of Talleyrand's life is somewhat painful for me to acknowledge, but I am told that, if an accurate portrait of my beloved's life is to be made, it cannot be made without Catherine. So, it should be said at the outset that a permanent relationship with that woman was to be a shock to all of his friends, a far greater shock even than his later liaison with me.

Catherine was born in India (to be exact, in Tranquebar, a Danish possession) in 1762. She was the daughter of a low-ranking French official. At the age of fifteen, she moved to Chandernagore, where she became the mistress of George Francis Grand, an English civil servant who married her a year later. When she and her husband were transferred back to India, she was caught *in flagrante* by her outraged husband while making love to Sir Philip Francis, a member of the King's Council. Sir Francis, a most "modern" gentleman, asked her to move into his household with him and his wife. Surprisingly, the arrangement seemed to work for a while. At the time of Catherine's encounter with Talleyrand, she had returned to France and had several more affairs of the heart.

From what I understood from my beloved, Catherine was the youngest mistress he ever had, she was in constant good humor, and, of course, she was beautiful. She was svelte and had thick masses of blond hair. She had blue eyes accentuated by dark eyebrows, alabaster skin, and exquisite grace of movement. But her lack of intelligence became the gossip of the salons of Paris, and her *gaffes*, blunders, and *gaucheries*, awkwardness, were a source of entertainment. Although I race ahead of my story, I must note with irony that it was in one of Madame de Stael's salons that Catherine made her first appearance as Talleyrand's wife. She did well...for a short while.

"How beautiful," clucked the elderly wives of the statesmen.

"How delicious," clucked the lascivious statesmen themselves.

Everyone agreed that, if she was mute, she would be an incredible adornment to anyone's household. Yet, despite the whispers throughout the Parisian salons of this unlikely liaison, my beloved decided to set up Catherine in a house of her own at Montmorency.

Although I always listened particularly attentively when my beloved talked about his amorous years before we met, I must confess that I sometimes wished I had also bedded more young gentlemen before I started my life with Talleyrand.

As my beloved arranged his personal life, he started to assess his position and ambitions. Did he really want to remain minister of foreign affairs, a position so controlled by others that it sometimes seemed he was no better than, to quote his notes, "a eunuch"? He was subjected to sadistic statements ("Let our limping *abbé* implement our plan!") and insults ("Lying? Don't worry! Talleyrand is the master of the lie!") The comments served to remind him of his dreaded school days at St. Sulpice. The men of the Directory made Talleyrand's task of trying to conclude treaties with England, Portugal, or Austria, all of which had been in a state of war with France, impossible. It took only a few months for him to conclude that his fate could no longer be linked to the incompetent, wasteful, and corrupt Directory. When he proclaimed to Madame de Stael in a fit of pique that "The Directory was a corpse waiting to be buried, the destiny of all despotism," he realized he would have to disengage himself from any association with both competing political parties, the Jacobins and the Royalists.

As a man with impeccable timing, he had begun to listen to the murmur of the name "Bonaparte" in the streets and decided to write the general a letter that was to set the course of their personal and professional future together:

18 July 1797

General Bonaparte,

I have the honor to inform you that the Directory has appointed me minister of foreign affairs. Fully aware of the fearful responsibility that my duties entail, I gain confidence from the knowledge that your glory cannot fail to facilitate any negotiations that I may be required to undertake. The mere name of Bonaparte will remove all obstacles.

I shall diligently acquaint you with all matters which the Directory may instruct me to bring to your attention, though your fame, which so quickly spreads news of your achievements, will often deprive me of the pleasure of informing the Directors of the manner in which you will have executed their policies.

Your servant,

Foreign Minister Charles-Maurice de Talleyrand

As usual, Talleyrand had done his homework. He had discovered that Napoleon was in desperate need of an ally within the Directory, understanding that his fame had already engendered envy, jealously, and vindictiveness among its five petty members. So, in writing the letter, Talleyrand was not only trying to co-opt Napoleon, but he was simultaneously letting him know he was available as a worthy ally.

The memory of this first letter always gave my beloved pleasure because Napoleon immediately responded:

30 August 1797

Minister Talleyrand,

The government's choice of you as minister of foreign affairs is a tribute to its good judgment. It also demonstrates that you possess great talents. You are, as I have been informed, a pure civic spirit and no stranger to the aberrations that have dishonored the Revolution.

I will be flattered to exchange letters with you often, so as to keep you fully informed of my victories, and also to persuade you of my esteem and respect for you.

General Napoleon Bonaparte

Talleyrand was pleased to see that Napoleon had understood everything he was trying to convey. It was a satisfactory, prudent, yet appropriately guarded response. It was everything Talleyrand could have hoped for from an initial correspondence. Napoleon's praise of Talleyrand's "pure civic spirit" was an admission that the general's sentiments, like those of the foreign minister's, lay with the noncontaminated spirit of the Legislative Assembly and in opposition to the Royalists of the right who had now risen to power in the councils of the

Directory. The reference to the "aberrations that have dishonored the Revolution" was an overt rejection of the policies of the extremists of the left, the new Jacobins.

Talleyrand congratulated himself. He had calculated correctly. Of course, at the very beginning of what was to become an extensive correspondence between the two men, it was difficult for him to know what, if anything, they had in common. But it was soon clear to Talleyrand that the brilliant young general was a man of the political center, like himself. There was also no doubt that Napoleon would welcome the presence of a reliable informant and ally in the Directory. They were kindred spirits who could help each other achieve greatness for themselves and, of course, for France.

---

21 September 1797

General Bonaparte,

Once again, the tides of internal chaos and civil war have erupted in France. Each of the factions within the Directory is maneuvering for greater suzerainty. This cannot stand as is. The discontent of the citizenry is being mimicked by the military. Discipline and focus is threatened. I know your intervention would be most appreciated.

Foreign Minister Charles-Maurice de Talleyrand

Three weeks later, Napoleon's answer arrived:

---

12 October 1797

Minister Talleyrand,

Speaking in the name of 80,000 men, I warn you that the days when cowardly lawyers and contemptible chatterers could send valiant soldiers to be butchered are over and done with! They will never become like those in Paris who I hear are tearing up the shops and destroying the streets. I will forbid it!

General Napoleon Bonaparte

Two weeks later:

---

25 October 1797

General Bonaparte,

Your certainty reassures me, but, in the coming weeks, I hope it will assert itself in appropriate punishment of those who stray from the goal of protecting the common good. Much is to be gained from your wise and continuous intervention.

Foreign Minister Charles-Maurice de Talleyrand

Two weeks later:

---

7 November 1797

Minister Talleyrand,

They will die before they defy me further.

General Napoleon Bonaparte

Months into their interchange of letters, Talleyrand had taken the measure of the man. For Napoleon, power and its ancillary offspring, glory, were both means and ends, justification for his existence. For the glorification of General Napoleon Bonaparte and to obtain any additional iota of power, he would do anything—destroy, ravage, pillage, lie, and cheat. Before these two ever met, Talleyrand came to consider Napoleon a megalomaniac who could not distinguish the difference between what was or was not impossible. He once told me that he shuddered when he began to suspect this very factor would ultimately lead to a major rift in their relationship. But, for the moment, they needed one another, and Talleyrand was too judicious to confront someone as volatile as Napoleon.

By the end of 1797, the relationship between them was no longer one Talleyrand could categorize as a foreign minister to a vainglorious field general.

Rather, it took the form of co-conspirators who realized that each was indispensable to the other in gaining ascendancy in France.

As foreign minister, Talleyrand had the constitutional mandate to supersede any treaties Napoleon might want to negotiate with a country with which he was fighting or had fought. But, openly contradicting or reprimanding Napoleon would be to court serious trouble and incur animosity that Talleyrand could ill afford. He needed the sword and shield of the general to help him affect his own agenda. So, when Napoleon ignored the wishes of both Talleyrand and the Directory and gave the city of Venice to the Emperor of Austria, my beloved still sent him a cable of support:

28 November 1797

General Bonaparte,

You have concluded the peace, and it is a peace in the best style of Bonaparte. You have my heartfelt congratulations. Words do not suffice to express what I feel at this moment. The Directors are content, and the people are delighted. There may be some outcry in Italy, but that is not important.

Foreign Minister Charles-Maurice de Talleyrand

Despite the niceties of the letter, Napoleon's action seriously tarnished the image of France as a liberator, making her appear to the rest of Europe as an autocratic nation trafficking in other nations. Yet, as furious as Talleyrand was with Napoleon, my beloved swallowed his pride and reigned in his anger and disappointment, skills he was still perfecting and which he would hone in the coming years.

When Napoleon came to Paris on December 6, 1797, he asked to meet Talleyrand at Rue St. Florentin. At the request of Madame de Stael, to whom my beloved was deeply indebted for personal, financial, and political favors, Talleyrand invited her to be present at the meeting in his home. Throughout the evening, Napoleon ignored de Stael, entering into a lively dialogue with Talleyrand as if his mistress was not present. Their first face-to-face conversation was highly solicitous on both their parts. Napoleon spoke in kind terms of my beloved's appointment as foreign minister and insisted on the pleasure it gave him to correspond with a person so different from the men of the Directory.

As Napoleon spoke, Talleyrand realized that, despite his victories on the field, the general was intimidated in the presence of a member of a famous noble family.

Yet, he thought to himself, "What would one expect from the son of a poor Corsican family?"

"Yes," my beloved responded to some compliment given to his lineage. "I have both the pleasure and pride of belonging to the house of de Talleyrand-Perigord."

"I also have an uncle who is an archdeacon in Corsica. It was he who helped educate me. You know that, in Corsica, an archdeacon is the same as a bishop in France?"

It was on hearing that statement that Talleyrand suddenly realized the general would be both a formidable ally and opponent for the same reasons: jealously and envy, the twin-headed monsters of self-destruction. On the one hand, Napoleon wanted to express his admiration for Talleyrand's heritage, but, on the other hand, he needed to see himself as my beloved's equal.

In their later days, I am sorry to report that, when Napoleon indulged his uncontrollable feelings of jealousy to attack Talleyrand, my beloved would remind me he had predicted the course of their relationship from its start. By the end of this first meeting, it was clear to Talleyrand that he would have to learn how to manage this mercurial general because my beloved's future in the foreign ministry would depend not on such formidable matters as war and peace, but on whether a French nobleman could appease a Corsican peasant with unlimited pretenses. *Quel horreur!* What horror!

CHAPTER 20

▼

"The hesitations and jealousies of the Directors are causing Bonaparte a certain annoyance," Talleyrand observed to Madame de Stael after dinner one evening in her home.

Madame de Stael gave my beloved little more than an indifferent silence, still resentful for having been ignored by "that ruffian" Napoleon.

"I sense a strong strain of self-destruction that could ultimately harm France," Talleyrand continued, more to give vent to his concerns than because of having an interested listener. He had already begun to resent the large amount of time needed to spend orchestrating Napoleon's appearances before the Directory, most of whose members felt threatened by the "Corsican thug." The time he spent arranging Napoleon's appearances before the hordes of Frenchmen who stormed the general's hotel daily to catch a glimpse of the "new hero of France" was far more satisfying.

"All of Paris rings with his name. The people throng in such vast numbers to cheer 'the conqueror of Italy' that the sentries stationed at the gateway to his hotel can hardly hold them back."

"It's such a pity the French always have to have a hero," Madame de Stael responded sarcastically, "and to resort to that midget! *Quel dommage!*" What a pity!

When Talleyrand left his mistress' house at Rue de Faubourg St. Honore, he made sure he remembered his cane because he had planned to walk to his own mansion near Place de la Concorde. As soon as he entered his home (what would become my home as well in twenty years), I suspect he walked to the library, his favorite room. Its walls, where not covered by books, were hung with tapestries.

His eyes probably scanned some of his most pleasing possessions: a cabinet with mirrored panels that was crowned by a double-arched pediment with an ornamental filial, a carved beechwood sofa with Aubusson tapestry upholstering, and a highly ornate mantel clock made from ormolu and marble that was festooned with flowers signed by Andre Ribaucourt. For a moment, it was likely he forgot what such luxury represented to the citizenry on the streets of Paris, pleased his luxurious manor of living was now so very different from that of his childhood. But only for a moment.

"People would flock just as eagerly to see me if I were on my way to the guillotine," Napoleon had uttered to Talleyrand with disgust, only days before as he waved to the crowd cheering outside his residence window.

Knowing the statement to be quite true, my beloved decided to plan Napoleon's visit not as the "conquering hero" he was, but as a military officer of modesty who had risen up through the ranks because of his unusual military acumen. Throughout Napoleon's stay in Paris, Talleyrand made a point of referring to him as "Citizen Bonaparte." Napoleon, in turn, took his cues from Talleyrand's judicious direction and barely ventured out of the hotel alone. My beloved would invite only small circles of friends and colleagues to his own residence to meet the remarkable military officer. When Talleyrand accompanied Napoleon to the theater and the audience cheered him, Napoleon would withdraw into the recesses of his box, as my beloved directed, so that no one could accuse him of pandering.

Talleyrand's plan seemed to be working until the evening of a small dinner party given in Napoleon's honor by the daughter of the president of a provincial parliament. While I would never tell my beloved that his judgment in affairs of the heart cannot compare with his judgment in diplomatic affairs, I let you, the reader, be the judge of the wisdom of Talleyrand's actions.

Madame de Stael had insisted on meeting Napoleon again in order to test her charm and intellect against the young conqueror. Talleyrand felt he could not deny her request. What subsequently transpired, however, would affect Talleyrand's relations with each of these two figures for the rest of his life.

"General," Madame de Stael said, "once again I have the unique privilege of meeting you." She smiled at the hatchet-faced, thin, young man with coarse features and an uncomfortable air.

"Yes, I recall we have met before," Napoleon responded brusquely.

"If I may be so bold," Madame de Stael continued in her most coquettish tone, "who is the woman you would love the most?"

"My wife, of course, madame. If I had one..."

"Of course. But who is the one you would consider most successful among her sex?"

"The one who bears the greatest number of my children."

With this statement, Napoleon nodded curtly, turned on his heels, and left to join another group of guests.

"Clearly, this Bonaparte's passions are of a very basic nature," de Stael said to Talleyrand in a particularly loud voice. "I see he can be made easily content with Josephine's lovely face and empty head. But, is it true she is barren?"

Those in the room who heard the remark grew awkwardly silent. No one would disagree Josephine was of limited intelligence, but few would dare to infer anything about her relationship with Napoleon in his presence, especially of such an intimate nature.

"My dear," Talleyrand responded, trying to contain his fury over this unnecessary insult, "I think you should lower your voice and then leave the battles of the will to Napoleon and his enemies on the field. Try to remain content with seducing lesser men, like myself, Narbonne, and Constant."

With that rebuke, Talleyrand also turned his back to Madame de Stael, leaving her standing alone in a corner of the room. Although he wrote in his diary that it was reprehensible behavior on his part to leave her in that unmannered way, she had placed my beloved in the awkward position of having to make a choice between her and Napoleon. And there was not much doubt in his mind which one he would choose.

I had the good fortune to meet Germaine de Stael several years later in my position as the new niece-by-marriage of her former lover, Talleyrand. Edmond had acceded to my wishes and escorted me to her salon, the most politically sophisticated in all of Paris, although his own interest in politics rated far below that of his interest in dog wagering. I knew of de Stael only through her writings, which I admired, and from the whisperings within the family about her relationship with my new uncle. It was common knowledge that she had bullied and charmed most of the men in the room that night to have Talleyrand's name stricken from the list of *émigrés,* which enabled him to return to France from America.

It was said the most powerful and influential men of the day passed through her salon. That evening, at one end of a drawing room appointed with the *chinoiserie* that was so popular at the time, chatted known adversaries of Napoleon. A group of moderates stood at the other end, as close to the regime as the first consul's own brother. Talleyrand, while introducing Edmond and me to de Stael, was interrupted by several loud male voices.

"What a ridiculous man he is, your first consul," de Stael said to Talleyrand, as if he was responsible for all of Napoleon's shortcomings.

"Those men over there are cretins," she continued, nodding in the direction of the loud men. "They are nothing but police, gathering information on my guests and me. Yet, they are not even capable of understanding what they are hearing."

"You are quite right," I interjected. "But I must tell you how much I admire what you have to say."

I sounded brash, even to my own ears, but I wanted very much to engage the woman who outshone most of the men in the room with her courage, knowledge, and wit.

"Does not the first consul realize that, while we may differ on religious issues, I am in full agreement with him on most political matters? If he could read French, he would know that." De Stael ignored my compliment and continued to address Talleyrand.

"I believe he might fear you decry his placing politics above liberty, which also reinforces the authority of men over women," I interjected.

This time, all took notice of me. Talleyrand and de Stael seemed to stare in disbelief, wondering if I had, in fact, uttered those words. Edmond (poor dear) almost dropped the glass of claret he was holding. But they were reactions I had anticipated. My readings during the prior months had been well considered.

Both Talleyrand's and de Stael's stares turned to smiles as I continued to both engage and flatter her with words from her own books. Edmond's face spoke only of confusion. It was a night I will always remember fondly as it proved seminal in my relationship with Talleyrand. After that evening, admiration and respect always greeted me in my new uncle's eyes, those same feelings I always saw in his eyes for Madame de Stael.

Over the course of Napoleon's visit, Talleyrand found a very clever way of occupying the general's time, a way that would serve both Talleyrand's purposes and those of the general's equally well. Instigated by Napoleon's continuous whining and complaining about being restless after having conquered Austria and cannibalizing Italy, my beloved prodded the Directory to offer Napoleon a command that would take him to England. Surprisingly, Napoleon turned down the commission, feeling there was little chance of successfully invading England at that time.

As I write these words, years after Napoleon's reign and at a point in time when France and England are now allies, I am amused at the hostilities between France and England over the last 100 years. Before Napoleon even began rearranging the map of Europe, the two countries had almost continuously waged both economic and military warfare. Perhaps it was merely the heightened arrogance of Napoleon to believe he could counter England's naval supremacy or conduct an economic blockade of the island, and that would lead to bankruptcy and surrender.

Talleyrand would not be deterred. He deigned to tell the great military strategist that the way to attack England was indirectly, that is, by forcibly taking over her vital supply lines to India. For Napoleon, that meant mounting an expedition against Egypt and the Island of Malta, both of which were positioned strategically to control England's commercial trade with the East.

Talleyrand was extremely pleased with himself when he made this entry to his diary:

> Through my own manipulations, I have carefully steered Napoleon to his own conclusion that France must obtain colonies along the Mediterranean shores and not to directly engage England in a commercial war. Conquering Egypt certainly would be a propitious beginning.

To gather supporters for what my beloved felt was a brilliant strategy, he reminded the Directory that the Mamluk beys who had ruled Egypt as feudal warlords were now subjecting French merchants to intolerable harassment. Recommending military invasion under the color of protecting French interests, Talleyrand made an invasion palatable to the Directory.

Talleyrand, the master tactician, had still another reason to encourage Napoleon to invade Egypt. As my beloved understood the current political situation in Europe, its leaders were already afraid that this young, impetuous general carrying France's revolutionary ideals might destabilize other European capitals. An invasion of Egypt would take Napoleon far away from the continent and relax its leaders.

That May afternoon in 1798, before Napoleon was to set sail for Egypt, he visited Talleyrand at his home and found him in his library. Napoleon cried out in desperation to the man he considered "one of my closest friends" that he did not have sufficient funds to support his personal needs during the military campaign.

"While I have sent a fortune to the Directory, as my campaigns proved successful, they have not shared any part of the immense wealth with me."

"Open that desk," a slightly ill Talleyrand responded, pointing to a carved fall-front cabinet with small compartments, "and you will find 100,000 francs in the lower drawer on the right side. Take them. You may repay the loan when you return."

"I cannot thank you enough for your beneficence," Napoleon answered in a sincere, if not whining, voice.

Many years later, when he became first consul, he repaid the loan, asking, "What was your reason for lending me the money? I tried a hundred times to fathom your motive."

"I had no motive. I was feeling ill, and I realized I might never see you again. You were young, and you had made a great impression on me. I decided, without any ulterior motive, to help you."

"In that case," Napoleon replied, "you were a fool."

By this time, Napoleon's statement was neither shocking nor disappointing. Talleyrand had already taken the measure of the man.

Ironically, several of Talleyrand's diplomatic problems involved the United States of America. Since 1793, hostilities had existed on the high seas with the ships of the Directory, manned by red-bonneted ruffians claiming to be Jacobins, seizing American ships under the pretext they were trading with England. Over 300 American ships had been captured by French warships and privateers, mostly in the West Indies. Relations between the two countries had deteriorated so badly that it looked as if war were about to be declared.

John Adams, the American president, sent a delegation of three men to Paris to present America's case to the Directory in order to maintain a neutral posture in the battle he foresaw between England and France. However, when these men arrived in Paris, Talleyrand's agents informed them it would be useless to pursue negotiations until they had made a substantial gift of cash to the foreign minister and agreed to a loan that was to profit the five members of the Directory. The American emissaries were so outraged and insulted by this request that they publicized their treatment by the French in American newspapers under the title, "the XYZ Affair."

When word spread throughout Parisian society that Talleyrand was once again demanding bribes from anyone wanting to receive an audience with him, he retreated to the comfort of old friends at Madame de Stael's salon. To his surprise, everyone there was also scornful, questioning his behavior and integrity.

"What did you think you were doing, my dear Charles?" Madame de Stael asked Talleyrand as they sipped a glass of port in the privacy of her drawing room.

Talleyrand told me he was torn between responding to her question and continuing to admire the furnishings, which now favored the neoclassic style. He sat on a blue velvet chair, resting his head on the knob of his highly polished cane.

"You have done many foolish things," Madame de Stael continued, "and I have never berated you for them or for any other indiscretions you may have committed in public. But consider your precarious political position. It is no longer wise to encourage those who would drag your family name through the verbal streets of mud. I beseech you to change your behavior and act solely in the interests of France."

Apparently, my beloved simply remained in the chair, silent.

"I ask you, as both your friend and mistress, if these titles hold any meaning for you, to clear your name of these egregious charges," Madame de Stael repeated, somewhat angrily now, for Talleyrand's lack of response.

"No one instructs a de Perigord how he should or should not behave," my beloved said, rising from his seat. "I thank you for your consideration of my welfare, but I bid you a fond farewell until we meet again."

Once again, Talleyrand left Madame de Stael alone, shocked by his reaction to her words.

Was it his avarice or merely my beloved's pride that dictated his behavior toward a woman he cared for and respected? Talleyrand's response to my question was that he allowed for only a few "sins." Madame de Stael had committed several by trying to force herself upon Napoleon on occasions when it was quite apparent he did not want her near him. Now she was committing another by questioning Talleyrand's judgment. This, my beloved said, he could not forgive. As hard-hearted and reckless as it may sound, Talleyrand made a decision at that precise moment to terminate his relationship with his mistress of so many years.

Whether right or wrong, throughout his career, Talleyrand never declared himself above receiving gratuities, either as abbé, bishop, foreign minister, or, in later years, ambassador. Only a few years after settling "the XYZ Affair," Talleyrand collected the handsome sum of 16,000,000 francs for his efforts to avoid potential wars with Austria, England, and Russia. For Talleyrand, there was no intimation that he had sold his conscience for money or abandoned his principles. Rather, he was "entitled to remuneration for the advantages which my talents have secured for both France and the interests of foreign countries." In a very primordial sense, he felt Count de Talleyrand-Perigord was France and the tributes being paid to France were due him. It would remain so for the rest of his life.

As someone who has spent a great deal of time reviewing and absorbing my beloved's writings, I have few indications of how difficult the times were becoming for him. Internal insurrections were arising in the army for lack of pay, but there was no money to disperse after Napoleon's forays in Egypt had bled the treasury dry. While many archeological treasures were taken out of Egypt and sent to France, no gold was found to fill the coffers of the French treasury. The Turkish Empire had been provoked beyond endurance by Napoleon's Egyptian expedition and decided to declare war on France. Austria, incensed by France's insistence on propagating republican institutions in Italy, broke off negotiations with Talleyrand and declared war on France…as did Russia.

It was 1799, and previously defeated Italian troops had moved northward. England was about to attack them in Holland from the sea. The Swiss were in rebellion against their French masters, and Germany was bellicose. This was the situation that Talleyrand found France in without his most useful, if not trusted and powerful ally, Napoleon Bonaparte. My beloved was truly worried. No one knew whether Napoleon was dead or alive. The ruling Directors were bickering among themselves.

"As long as the French armies appear victorious, the people hate their rule, but fear their power," Talleyrand wrote in his memoirs. "But, when the hour of defeat arrives, the government will be met with universal contempt."

Talleyrand understood, better than anyone I ever met, that governments might survive opposition, defeat, and even revolution. But, no government could ever survive the contempt of those they governed. Bearing this in mind, he decided to insert his own candidate into the Directory. Someone, of course, who would be under his control.

CHAPTER 21

▼

In the blur of my childhood, I remember large rooms with enormously high ceilings in which there were all manner of celebrations. I imagine the contours of expansive spaces crowned with crystal chandeliers and one smaller room with hanging tapestries and a collection of Italian clocks that my sisters and I were warned never to touch. It was in the smaller room—with its most precious items—that Maman entertained ladies of substance and Papa amused men of influence. Their salon was among the most sought after at the century's end, and just about everyone of importance in Paris made an appearance.

I must have been twelve or thirteen when as many gentlemen in fine waistcoats appeared in the foyer. Though memory plays games, I believe Talleyrand was one of these men. Even at my very young age, it was easy to see he was someone very important because my mother fussed over him in ways that revealed it. She made long introductions of him to the other guests, circling the room with him on her arm as if he was a prize. Tall and elegant, he chatted amiably with everyone. I remember him because he was handsome. I also remember him because he limped, which held a particular fascination for me.

This evening, there seemed to be more excitement than usual as my sisters and I stood at the top of the winding staircase, watching the gentlemen and ladies in their finery flit from group to laughing group. The door was suddenly thrown wide, and a gruff, uniformed man entered with two attendants. One attendant asked for my father in a manner that was frightening, but, when my father saw the man, he smiled broadly.

"Napoleon," whispered one of my sisters. "Napoleon," she said again.

He was much shorter than the other men, but he was broader across the chest. He removed his tri-cornered hat and handed it to one of his attendants. I watched him with fascination, watched his bluster, and watched how nearly all the others in the room sought his attention.

All, that is, except the man I believe was Talleyrand, who was holding one of Maman's most precious vases, a Japanese porcelain with a scene of a river and birds, and describing what the delicate painting signified to a very attractive woman.

Now who can say for certain that I spied both Napoleon and Talleyrand on the same evening? Memory teases, and I was only just coming into some awareness of the larger world, years away from understanding how these men would eventually shape my life. Later, when I was living with Talleyrand, I came to imagine that Napoleon, though long since dead, still lived with us. So much of what Talleyrand had accomplished in the world was accelerated after his stormy dealings with this brusque, haunting warrior. Talleyrand never stopped talking about Napoleon, posing issues and arguing each position. By that time in our relationship, I was rarely jealous of Talleyrand's former mistresses, but Napoleon was another matter entirely.

While my youthful eyes saw nothing but remarkably elaborate wigs and even more remarkable crinolines, chaos reigned in France where once law and order had existed. Talleyrand's writings at the time reveal he understood that, for the government to survive, he had to consolidate his own power. Although he would not be able to take direct control of the ruling Directory, he could take indirect control by maneuvering to have men who were loyal to him appointed to influential positions. So, my beloved set out to choose men whom he could control, not only through his appreciation of their specific talents, but also because he knew a great deal about their vices and weaknesses. Although I am not proud to admit it, Talleyrand had few qualms about manipulating men's frailties when necessary. He only selected men who understood that, once a favor was granted, they were forever indebted to him.

Talleyrand's first selection for an appointment was Emmanuel-Joseph Sieyes, a friend from his earliest days when he was a young man newly liberated from the seminary. By Talleyrand's intervention, Sieyes had recently been appointed the French ambassador to Berlin. Sieyes was a clever man and an astute politician, but he was one of those public officials who existed in a state of continuous dissatisfaction, employed far below his level of capabilities. He had always been afraid to firmly choose one or another side of an issue for fear of making a mistake. To Talleyrand, this trait would indicate a coward, although, to most politicians, it would characterize a diplomat as "prudent."

It was only a matter of Talleyrand's time and maneuvering before Sieyes succeeded Robespierre as one of the five members of the Directory. Sieyes was a man sufficiently identified with the Revolution to be acceptable to the less rabid Jacobins; yet, he was not so much so as to be unacceptable to the Royalists. Known among his colleagues as a revisionist, Sieyes took his oath and, as Talleyrand predicted, announced to the group that the first order of the day would be its reformation. To this end, he proposed to and succeeded in eliminating three of the Directory's most radical members. Years later, when Sieyes was asked what was his greatest accomplishment during the chaotic days of the Revolution, he calmly replied, "I survived."

Perhaps Talleyrand's most important appointment was his choice for minister of police, a man who had been a minor functionary in the ministry of foreign affairs at the time. His name was Joseph Fouche, a staunch Jacobin and extremist revolutionary who had personally beheaded many royalty.

"At this moment," Talleyrand strategized to Sieyes, "when we are being attacked so daringly and so violently by the Jacobins, we must make use of a Jacobin as our weapon. A Jacobin capable of storming into battle, coming to grips with the enemy, and wrestling them to a standstill. For such a man, you need look no further. There is Fouche."

According to all I have read and heard, Fouche was one of the most sinister figures of that period. In addition to the ideological differences standing between him and my beloved, Fouche was uncouth in manner, brutal in his relationships, filthy in dress and personal habits, and loud and coarse in conversation. He was also committed to the precept that politics was based on torturing or imprisoning one's enemy and then extracting whatever information was desired. Yet, given all I have just written, Talleyrand believed Fouche was precisely the man for the times. As a new minister, his talents would be at the service of Sieyes and, by extension, my beloved.

Talleyrand harbored no delusions that his maneuverings and appointments would not take a toll on his own political relationships. The enemies he incurred in the process of quietly "packing" the government ultimately impeded his own effectiveness. According to his memoirs, one Director spoke the following words before the group:

> The man responsible for our collective miseries is no other than the bishop of Autun, who, being a great nobleman, seems to know everything, even though

he has never troubled himself to learn anything…One must even be more stupid than this vile, vicious, manipulative pervert not to see that he had himself named minister of foreign affairs solely for the purpose of destroying the Revolution from within…He is a lover of the English, an *émigré*, the betrayer and the assassin of his country.

Such attacks went on for months. Talleyrand was charged with being a Royalist, an adulterer, a thief, an English spy, and a perjurer. Whether his memoirs lie at this moment, I cannot judge. But, according to them, he bore the assaults well, even using them to his advantage. He ignored the accusations, but he prepared to extricate himself from a government on the verge of collapse.

Having secured his political flanks through a number of important appointments, Talleyrand turned to the task of securing his military flanks. Napoleon Bonaparte, of course, was his ideal candidate, but he was in Egypt then. In order for Napoleon and the French army to return to French soil, where my beloved felt they were urgently needed, Talleyrand must conclude negotiations with Turkey. And so, he did.

By the time Talleyrand tendered his resignation, which was accepted by the Directory without hint of anyone's misgivings, he was already in the midst of preparing his return to power. The same day the directors accepted Talleyrand's resignation, Fouche became minister of police. From that moment onward, anything of importance that transpired in Paris or the provinces immediately reached the ears of both men. Everything was now in place for a *coup d'état* that Talleyrand had orchestrated before his resignation from yet another French government he considered ineffective, corrupt, and destructive to his country.

CHAPTER 22

▼

"There was an outburst of affection, which had to be seen to be believed and which will never be equaled," Talleyrand wrote after witnessing Napoleon's return to Paris—to a hero's welcome. He was embraced warmly by the general as an old trusted friend, and the two men spent a considerable amount of time together during Napoleon's stay. My beloved congratulated himself at having picked the right man to be both the idol of the nation and the sword of the coming *coup*.

While the present seemed fixed in place, Talleyrand's skepticism of Napoleon's mercurial nature left him to worry about the future. France, Talleyrand knew all too well, quickly tired of its heroes and, as it did with the previous royal family, would eventually devour its own. Accordingly, Talleyrand instructed Napoleon to assume the modest public posture he had successfully exhibited after his triumphant return from Italy.

Listening to this wise advice, Napoleon absented himself from appearing at many public affairs and declined most theater invitations. Much of his time was spent reconciling himself with Josephine, whom he discovered had made a series of amorous conquests in Paris while he was winning his military campaigns in Egypt. Most evenings, Napoleon attended political meetings arranged by Talleyrand and Sieyes to discuss the current political situation with small groups of military officials, statesmen, and financiers. When talk turned, as it frequently did, to the possibility of a military *coup*, Talleyrand always made it seem as if he was a neutral listener who would bow to the wishes of the majority.

"Charles lounged nonchalantly on a sofa, his face immobile, undecipherable, his hair powdered, saying little, occasionally interjecting a subtle or telling phrase, and then lapsing into his usual posture of distinguished lassitude and indifference." This was Napoleon's description in his own memoirs of my beloved's insouciant attitude throughout their conspiratorial meetings.

"Napoleon's prestige," according to my beloved, "was such that the mere invocation of his name created an impression among all political parties of a man who could not only be called to account for his actions, but one whom circumstances made indispensable and whose favor it was essential to win." So, Talleyrand invoked Napoleon's name in order to court reluctant politicians.

"For the most part, I set the stage for a group of potential conspirators and then acted as their liaison," Talleyrand wrote, describing his role in the overthrow of the government.

It was a role he enjoyed, being by nature both a conciliator and catalyst of men and ideas. During his years in Paris, he had made a point of knowing everyone of importance, and every "relevant" person knew of him as well. He kept himself apprised of what transpired throughout the government by agents discreetly placed in critical positions. The people whom he invited to meet the general were all deeply in debt to my beloved for favors rendered during his tenure as minister.

According to the group's plan, Napoleon would be the pivotal figure, the one who would be immediately vaulted to power over a prostrate Directory. Sieyes, Fouche, and Napoleon's brother, Lucien Bonaparte, were to assume active roles in the execution of the plot. But, it was Talleyrand alone who would weave together the threads of a rather complicated intrigue so that the group maintained its objectives and followed a well-delineated blueprint. As I reread my beloved's notes on planning the *coup*, I could not help but view Talleyrand as no less than remarkable in maneuvering people and events.

Once the plans were in place, Talleyrand turned his manipulative genius toward co-opting the head of the Directory, whose *château* was located near Talleyrand's own place of residence. Quite understandably, Paul Barras had begun to grow suspicious of the important men and the exceedingly large number of carriages arriving at and departing from Talleyrand's home at all hours of the day.

"My dear friend, Charles," Barras said to Talleyrand one afternoon as they met walking on the Rue de Rivoli, "it seems as if your house was a way station for people in need of food or lodging. Could it be that you are entering a new profession of which I and the Directory are not aware?"

"My dear friend, Barras," Talleyrand responded in kind, having prepared himself for this moment of confrontation, "how pleased I am to know that my neighbor is so concerned about my personal well-being that he watches my house so closely."

"Charles," Barras responded with an edge of annoyance to his voice, "I am your friend, but there are others in the Directory who are not so well-disposed to you or your clandestine activities. They are not fools, believe me!"

"If they were fools," Talleyrand responded, "I would not have consented to work with them. But remember, Barras, my primary loyalty is always to France." My beloved offered this last statement as a point of purposeful ambiguity so that Barras might interpret it any way he chose.

"No one questions your loyalty to France," Barras retorted, "only to those who rule France."

"Then, as I suspected," Talleyrand replied with a knowing grin, "you have understood the nuance of my words."

"I warn you again that your nuances and well-recognized ability to play with words have gotten you into enough trouble to last for several lifetimes. I am certain you recognize the Directory is not an institution with which you can trifle."

"Trifle?" Talleyrand laughed. "My God, no!"

"Why are you laughing?"

"Trifle is too subtle a word for these boorish killers!" Talleyrand replied with venom he chose to no longer disguise. He wondered if his hopes for Barras had been misplaced. Perhaps the man would not understand what lay beneath his words. The moment had come to take his greatest risk.

"The people of France and the political parties of France see in Napoleon not only a man who can be called to account for his actions," Talleyrand said in a conspiratorial voice, "but one whom circumstances have made indispensable and whose favor it is essential to win."

"Is there no way I can get you to speak more plainly?"

"Only if what I am about to tell you remains within the sanctity of our friendship," Talleyrand said. He was hoping for a favorable response, but he was not entirely sure what he would do if one did not come.

"Your words will be received as they are spoken...to a friend. No other consideration will interfere with that."

"Then let me assure you that I have strong personal assurances from Napoleon himself," Talleyrand continued, "that, if a new regime is to replace the old, he wants a complete reorganization of the Directory and the government."

"What specifically does he have in mind?" Barras asked, wondering whether Napoleon had ever mentioned him, personally, to Talleyrand.

"What I am about to tell you requires the ultimate discretion." Talleyrand purposefully did not respond to the question, heightening the drama of the moment.

"You have my word," Barras said impatiently.

"Napoleon wants a severe reduction in the number of directors."

"But there are only five directors now. He knows that."

"He only wants one powerful director, and your name is the only one which I have heard on his lips."

"That's quite bold of the general!" Barras responded, obviously pleased.

"Furthermore, he wants this director to become the undisputed ruler of France."

Barras was appropriately shocked, pleased, curious, and then disappointed when my beloved proffered a fond à *bientôt*, citing an event he must rush to and telling Barras to be discreet about the matter until he could provide him with more details.

One week later, Talleyrand called upon Barras at his home on Rue St. Honore, accompanied by Lucien Bonaparte, now president of the Council of Five Hundred, and Fouche, minister of police. This time, no mention was made of the specific man who was to become the sole director to remain in the Directory. The men talked and plotted for much of that afternoon, lifting glasses of wine and setting them atop a mahogany table whose legs were crowned by carvings resembling gargoyles grimacing at the discussion taking place above them. To Talleyrand's amusement, Barras' suspicions were never aroused. He had correctly calculated the man's ambitions and vanity would blind him. Until the moment of the *coup*, Barras considered himself a part of it, a conspirator in the very plot designed by Talleyrand to remove him from office.

The day before the *coup*, November 8, 1799, in what became known as the Eighteenth Brumaire of the Year VIII, Talleyrand spent a quiet afternoon at home, playing whist with a few friends. Barras arrived, clearly anxious. Napoleon, as commanding general of the Army of Italy, would be marching into Paris with his troops to replace a failing Directory. As the afternoon wore on and the sun began to set, my beloved led Barras to the window to view the citizens milling in the streets and the soldiers befriending them. He pointed out a solitary figure, a man who had fallen from wealth and influence. His clothes, once fashionable, were now outdated and worn-looking. The man made his way, trying to be as invisible as he could. My beloved's subsequent discourse on how easily the once-mighty lose their power and influence was delivered with particular emphasis on the failings of Barras as a member of the Directory. Talleyrand's clear-eyed gaze could not be misunderstood.

When Barras realized that Talleyrand was asking him to relinquish power, he sank down into a chair, not to rise again for one hour. My beloved first appealed to Barras' love of country, then to his intelligence, and finally, more satisfactorily, to his greed. Talleyrand mentioned the sum of three million francs that he realized a former head of the Directory would require to "retire to his estate in the country." Barras, with appropriate reluctance, rose to the occasion and accepted the sum. He left Talleyrand's home in the company of dragoons that had been sent by Napoleon to "protect" the fallen ruler of France.

The following day, the drama continued. Napoleon, his troops having secured the city, attended a combined meeting of the two remaining councils of the Revolution—the Council of Ancients and the Council of Five Hundred. The meeting took place in a building that had belonged to one of Marie-Antoinette's courtesans. The large chamber used was a cruelly frivolous place. Clusters of cherubs painted on the ceiling, edged by sculpted cornices, kept watch like so many plump, intruding voyeurs. The angry, disheveled men assembling beneath them in front of their boasting general all held high opinions of themselves. When they began to direct their venom at Napoleon, he bore their insults like a pelted tiger waiting for his time to pounce. And pounce he did.

Talleyrand had managed to lodge himself at a safe distance from the arguing group, which he would later do at the Congress of Vienna and again at the duel that set in motion our future together. He manipulated and calculated, always keeping his hands clean and always at a distance. These were traits that frequently became a source of friction between us.

Napoleon was surprised by the reception he received from the assembled functionaries, so different from that given by the masses. Instead of accolades, he heard deputies shout, "No dictatorship! No bayonets! Down with the tyrant!" Some became so physically threatening that Napoleon called upon his men to escort him from the chamber. Once outside, he gathered his troops, re-entered the hall and physically threw out all the men inside. With this one action, the Reign of Terror begun by the deputies of the Revolution was officially over. In a few months, a consulate form of government would be in place with Napoleon as first consul.

Though Maman and Papa showed little outward signs of emotion, the day that Paris went to bed under the Directory and woke up under a Consulate found them all smiles and laughter. When they told my sisters and me that liberty had once again returned to France, I could have sworn that Maman's eyes glistened with tears. After dinner, she confided that all of Paris was shouting, "Down with the Jacobins! Long live Bonaparte! Long live peace!"

I admit that I fantasized about the man. A warrior. A conqueror. A deliverer. He was a man who would save France from itself. No more bad dreams for me. No more jeers as our carriage rolled through the streets of Paris. No more surly servants. I could not have been more pleased.

Over the next few years, my admiration for Napoleon only increased. It was hard not to be impressed with his military victories. My sisters and I experienced the changes taking place in our city. We could now sit in the Café du Caveau near the royal palace and listen to a harpist sing ballads in honor of Napoleon and not feel out of place. We could walk down the Boulevard du Temple at dusk to enjoy the tumblers, little theatres, and rope dancers who were no longer afraid to appear in the streets. All because Napoleon was now in charge of the government. I made it a point to listen very closely to all of my parents' whisperings about Napoleon and France. Little did I suspect the first procession I would attend, several years later at my husband's side, would be heralding Napoleon's defeat.

When it came time to choose a new foreign minister, Napoleon chose Talleyrand, certainly not to anyone's surprise.

As Napoleon explained to one of his commanders, who had also sought the position, "Talleyrand understands the world. He is excellent at negotiations. He knows the courts of Europe. He never reveals what he is thinking. And, finally, he bears a great name."

And so, the new first consul of France, General Napoleon Bonaparte, appointed Charles-Maurice de Talleyrand-Perigord as minister of foreign affairs. Once again, my beloved held on to the position that was so dear to him for so much of his life.

CHAPTER 23

▼

Sometimes I wished Talleyrand was not always right because it is a trait in a loved one that is very hard to live with day after day. I suppose I was always somewhat jealous of his predictive abilities, which were as accurate in our domestic life as they were in matters pertaining to foreign relations.

Napoleon Bonaparte did restore political, economic, and social order to France, accomplishing what Talleyrand knew no other man could at that moment in history. By June 1800, he had fought and beat the Austrians at Marengo in a major military battle, and the citizens of France were euphoric. Yet, my beloved, who referred to Napoleon in his private notes as "that Corsican peasant" because of "his crass manners and unintelligible French" was worried that, at some not so distant point in time, Napoleon could also be "the catalyst for the downfall of France." Napoleon's appetite for power was writ large on everything he said and did.

The salons of Paris had been alive that spring with all matter of gossip before the news of Napoleon's victory had even reached the city and without the kindling Talleyrand frequently provided.

Huddled in corners of grand salons, dodging the brushes of billowing curtains that looked out over luxuriant gardens at the homes of anyone of a number of esteemed hostesses, nobility whispered to each other, "What will happen if the Battle of Marengo will be a disaster rather than a victory? What will happen to France if Napoleon, upon whom all our hopes are founded, should be killed?"

There was much gossip to the effect that Talleyrand and Fouche were planning still another *coup* if Napoleon's consular regime foundered. Rumors abounded that the duke of Orleans would be crowned the next king, Louis XVIII, and the Bourbon dynasty would return to power once again.

When Napoleon returned to France victorious, the tone of the note with which he summoned Talleyrand and Fouche to his quarters one morning was one of outrage. His taste for appearance and ostentation were easy to see even then, preferring to reside at the Tuileries of the kings rather than at the Luxembourg of the directors. Each man sat in an upholstered *bergère*, an armchair set upon carved cabriole legs. Napoleon wore a red uniform, his form of court dress. His sword, adorned with the Regent Diamond, lay across his knees. My beloved's concern escalated when Napoleon offered them no refreshments from the plates standing on the marble-topped console.

"They thought I was to die? Do they think I am Louis XVI? If so, they are seriously mistaken. For me, a battle lost is the same as a battle won!" Napoleon screamed at both men.

"I will save France in spite of traitors and incompetents! I know what you two are doing," he continued, as if Talleyrand and Fouche were conspirators. "My agents have informed me of your secret meetings…your discussions concerning my death."

"I must compliment your agents," Talleyrand smiled back to Napoleon. "They were not wrong."

"So you admit that you two are plotting against me!" He carefully placed the sword upon the console and began to pace up and down in front of my beloved and Fouche as if he was inspecting his troops.

"No, General," Fouche responded in his most sycophant tone, "we were simply creating a possible scenario for France if you found yourself in difficulties."

"*Alors,*" Napoleon exclaimed in his heavy Italian accent, "*dites-mois que'est ce que vous avez pense?*" Then tell me what you thought.

"Any good minister to the first consul would be obligated to do what we have done," Talleyrand proceeded, taking Fouche's cue. "We imagined what France might be like without the rule of…"

Fouche's lips tightened, which always denoted seriousness. "You jest with us. But, if someone wanted to kill you…and as you well know from my previous reports that there are both Royalists and Jacobins who would be more than happy…"

"It's only prudent," Talleyrand interrupted, trying to relieve both Fouche's and Napoleon's anxiety, "for the minister of police to collaborate with the minister of foreign affairs to discuss both the domestic and foreign policy implications of such a misfortune..."

"Which, of course, my two trusted ministers do not think is very probable," Napoleon responded sarcastically.

"The increased probability of your death rises proportionally with your growing popularity with the French citizenry," Talleyrand responded, nonplussed, but aware Napoleon was trying to bait him into an altercation.

"Apres moi, les deluges!" Let all hell break out if I am to die, Napoleon responded.

"Think what you may, General," Talleyrand said in his most authoritative voice, "but remember that you fight foreign armies so that ministers like Monsieur Fouche and I can maintain peace and order at home."

Napoleon continued to pace the room with both hands linked behind his back. If the general continued any longer, Talleyrand decided, a groove would be made in the inlaid parquet floor lit by the sunlight pouring in through green velvet curtains tied back with fine ropes of braided gold. Talleyrand smiled, thinking Napoleon was just being Napoleon. He knew the general did not really believe either he or Fouche were co-conspirators or that there was a *coup* being planned. Napoleon was well aware Fouche was his eyes and ears in France, and Talleyrand was his mind and mouth before the rest of the world. The meeting ended, according to my beloved's notes, with some sort of guttural sound on Napoleon's part and their dismissal with no more than an arm gesture.

Several days after the attempted reprimand, Napoleon ordered Talleyrand to negotiate a peace treaty with Austria. After weeks of working on what became known as the Treaty of Luneville, Talleyrand returned from Vienna with more land and concessions than even Napoleon's victory at Marengo had extracted. His treaty expanded France's borders through the acquisition of Luxembourg, Belgium, and substantial parts of Italy. My beloved had gained for France the largest territory in its history.

The ordinary French citizen was overwhelmed with joy. Europe was in a state of shock. Only my beloved was uneasy about what everyone considered his "brilliant accomplishment," sensing that a new standard had been set by the treaty, which would affect Napoleon's expectations for all future dealings with defeated nations.

"Two roads are open to the first consul with each new victory," Talleyrand commented to Fouche one day as they walked around the Galerie du Palais, taking note of the linen drapers, lace makers, glovers and other shops now catering to the needs of the new *bourgeoisie*. "The first is the road to federation, in which Napoleon would leave a defeated ruler as master of his own lands, but with whom he would negotiate other terms and boundaries. If, on the other hand, Napoleon intends to unite and incorporate all his victories under France's flag, he enters upon a road to which there can be no end."

In reality, the position of first consul was that of a limited monarchy, with my beloved having unlimited access to Napoleon, the monarch. It was Talleyrand's strategy that, of the three consuls appointed, the first consul would control everything relating to politics, the police for internal affairs, the minister for external affairs, as well as to the means of making war. It was also Talleyrand who urged Napoleon to take all the power he could. The additional consuls were to do little more than supply the first consul with advice, which he could either accept or reject. Their appointment was for appearances more than need.

Because both the general and my beloved despised the Jacobins and looked sympathetically upon the Royalists, neither man was insensitive to the attraction of a system that placed an immense amount of power in both their hands. The only vice of the Royalists, they agreed, was their hopeless attachment to the lost cause of the Bourbons and their king. So, it was left to Talleyrand to develop a strategy that would maintain the support of the nobility for Napoleon, which my beloved felt they both would need in turbulent times.

Together, Talleyrand and Napoleon issued a decree abolishing all penalties against *émigrés*, who were largely of the nobility, inviting them to return to France. They made certain that all but the most militant members of the Bourbon supporters were included in this general absolution. More importantly, those *émigrés* who returned were to receive any deeded properties that had been seized during the Revolution. To their pleasant surprise, over 40,000 *émigrés* returned to France, largely from England and Germany.

Upon their return, Talleyrand made certain that Napoleon met the most illustrious of these *ancien régime* families. At one of many sumptuous dinners held in Napoleon's behalf (this one at the Hotel Galliffet), my beloved took the first consul around by the arm and introduced him to the chevalier of Coigny, the duke of Rochefoucauld-Liancourt, as well as the attractive Madame de Custine, the duchess of Aiguillon, the duchess of Fleury, the countess of Noailles, and Madame de Flahaut. Talleyrand often told me how much he relished the company of so many former friends who had been living abroad.

The assembled enjoyed appetizers of the finest *foie gras* and an *entrée* of duck with finely sliced apples, accompanied by abundant fruit and vegetables brought in from the surrounding countryside. Champagne flowed, and the conversation was animated. Needless to say, several women attending that evening had been

Talleyrand's mistresses. The only one missing from his guest list was Madame de Stael, largely because my beloved told me he could not risk another confrontation between her and the general. Napoleon's initial aversion to the lady had been exacerbated—rather than mitigated—by the passage of time, having been informed of her opposition to him that appeared in her political and philosophical writings and of the snide comments about him she continued to spread throughout the Parisian salons.

Napoleon and Talleyrand were a match of opposites, as I discern from the writings of both men. The general was a demon for work, never happier than when dictating to several secretaries at once, keeping an eye on every detail of every military and political campaign, and maintaining an intrusive involvement in everything he touched. The workday was never long enough.

In contrast, by nature, Talleyrand was lazy. He had cultivated the image of indolence so carefully that he was as famous for this as he was for his intelligence. His approach to work, in general, started and ended with a single immutable rule: Never undertake anything that can be avoided or delegated to another. Nor did he ever dictate a memorandum. He would set down on paper a few ideas he wished to issue from his ministry and then turn the formless outline over to a trusted lieutenant, Desrenaudes, who had learned to interpret Talleyrand's mind and decipher his handwriting over the years.

Although opposites, Talleyrand and Napoleon worked together quite productively for the first few years. Napoleon respected the fact my beloved was not cowed by anyone in power, including the general, nor did he try to flatter him. For the most part, he also respected Talleyrand's advice and enjoyed his companionship. Talleyrand, in turn, cherished his access to Napoleon and his influence over the de facto ruler of France. Whether a genuine friendship formed, the one I felt jealous of for so many years, I do not know for sure to this very day. But mutual benefit went a long way for a number of years.

It is with regret that I must inform the reader that, despite interesting evenings Talleyrand and Napoleon spent together, competition between these two began increasing at a worrisome pace. To illustrate, Talleyrand's writings, years earlier, were very clear about the importance of France's relations with the Roman Catholic Church. Napoleon agreed, realizing that, to bring a sense of order back to France, he needed to regularize relations between government and the church. The schism provoked by the constitution in 1792, which placed the clergy under civilian—rather than papal—control by the time of Napoleon's first consulate, had largely disappeared. Despite a brief flirtation with the *culte decadaire,* decadent cult, as the "religion" of the Revolution was known, the majority of Frenchmen remained Roman Catholic.

Napoleon knew that, as long as France was alienated from Rome, there would be justifiable criticisms leveled against him by the Royalists. He strategized that, if he could reach an understanding with the church, represented by Pope Pius VII, he would strengthen his hold on the loyalty of the ordinary citizen.

Before Napoleon could act on his beliefs, however, Talleyrand entered into secret negotiations with the Vatican. This resulted in the Concordat of 1801, in which Roman Catholicism was recognized to be the religion of France and its free exercise permitted. In turn for such an agreement and being the tactician he was, Talleyrand extracted a heavy price from the Pope. First, the Pope agreed that properties appropriated during the Revolution need not be returned to the Vatican. Second (and perhaps more important), the Pope agreed that both bishops and priests were to be paid by the first consul and would take an oath of loyalty to him. This concession, in practice, turned the clergy into officials of the state who could be fired at will by Napoleon or his representatives, ultimately weakening the power of the clergy.

As always, Talleyrand would not let an opportunity to leverage a situation slip by him. While initially opposed to Napoleon's proposed *rapprochement*, coming together, with the clergy, he wrote public treatises praising the wisdom and leadership of Napoleon on this issue:

> When Napoleon reestablished religion in France, he performed an act not only of justice, but of great cleverness. The Napoleon of the Concordat is the truly great Napoleon, the man enlightened, the man guided by genius.

Of course, to his friends and colleagues, he promoted his own leading role in the reconciliation with the Vatican.

Given the importance of the issues involving Talleyrand at the time, Edmond was both honored and surprised when his uncle invited my family to afternoon tea. I was excited beyond measure because I would finally meet the uncle who had claimed Maman's interest, Papa's respect, and Edmond's envy. It was to be an afternoon that introduced me to a world of politics and international affairs that I had only experienced through books and my tutors' opinions. I prepared for the day by getting Maman to tell me everything she knew about my celebrated uncle-to-be.

Until Talleyrand made his appearance, one hour late, witless gossip relieved only my mindless games, such as hide-and-seek, in the courtyard. But, once he entered, looking very dashing with his gold-knobbed cane, the nature of the conversation turned serious, enlightening, and educational. How was Voltaire getting on in his estate at Ferney? Would Austria be amenable to diplomatic overtures? Will there be war with Britain? Even if I was not expected to have answers to such important questions, standing next to the man who asked and discussed them was more exciting than any of my mundane conversations with Edmond. My husband-to-be thought the afternoon to be a bit too serious. I was already planning to get to know my uncle-to-be much better.

CHAPTER 24

▼

I wish that I, as Talleyrand's future hostess, could recount the following story without the anger and sadness I always feel upon its telling. But I cannot, and you shall soon know why. With relations between France and the Vatican normalized, Napoleon felt the need to reinstate a veneer of respectability in France. Although not prudish by nature, he was a puritan by policy when he decided to eliminate the appearance of sexual laxity in the government that had characterized the Directory. His greatest embarrassment before the family of European nations, so he proclaimed, was now none other than my beloved, a defrocked bishop living in mortal sin with his mistress, Catherine Grand.

As was his habit, Napoleon confronted Talleyrand mid-morning as they sat together in the Tuileries, ostensibly on a break from a morning of business. The first consul had decided that his foreign minister must either return to the fold of the church and divest himself of his mistress...or leave the church for all time and marry her. Mindful of the fact that no one ever said "no" to Napoleon, my beloved tried to reason his edict out of existence...but to no avail.

Talleyrand went into a lengthy discussion of how he had been forced into the priesthood against his own will. He pointed out that the happiest day of his life had been when he had divested himself of his bishopric. He explained he had no intention of ever again taking up a profession that he not only disliked, but to which he was so unsuited...but to no avail.

Napoleon was impressed by Talleyrand's arguments, but he insisted upon trying to make Talleyrand appear respectable to the world. He offered Talleyrand a cardinal's hat if he would give up Catherine, but Talleyrand dismissed this offer out of hand. So, Napoleon shifted strategy, insisting that, with the sanction of the Pope, Talleyrand would marry Catherine Grand.

Without Talleyrand's knowledge (and certainly without his permission), Napoleon announced publicly that his foreign minister would marry Madame Grand in both civil and religious ceremonies. The first consul's self-satisfaction was equaled only by the astonishment of all of Paris. No one could believe Talleyrand, of all men, could have acquiesced to such a misalliance, a match between a member of the highest and most ancient aristocracy and a woman of low origins and even lower reputation.

Talleyrand initially tried to deny any intention of marriage.

When Catherine heard rumors Talleyrand might give her up for the clergy rather than marry her, she wrote to him, "Abandon me indeed! If you think you will be rid of me so easily, you are very wrong. Do you hear? Wrong! If you, *piedcourt*, short foot, are not careful, I will make you shorter by another foot."

I need say no more than her own words to render her character.

The confluence of Napoleon's insistence, Talleyrand's natural indolence, and his lifelong contempt for public censure finally convinced him to withdraw any objections he may have had to the marriage.

According to Josephine Bonaparte, "This wench of a woman, without more effort than spreading her legs apart, will be transformed into the wife of the good foreign minister of France, to whom ambassadors from all over the world will have to pay their respects."

Her tone reflected all her anger at knowing that, while Napoleon had been pressuring Talleyrand to marry, both he and Fouche had been pressuring Napoleon to abandon her and marry into one of Europe's dynasties to produce an heir.

As I write of Talleyrand confronting the decision to marry Catherine, I am reminded of my own wedding to his nephew three years later. I was almost twenty-one years old when Edmond and I exchanged vows in the small white church where I took my first communion. It was an elegant wedding with all of France's nobility turned out to witness what everyone said would be a fortunate union for both families. My hair was dressed *a la grecque* with braids and coronets. My long, flowing gown had been created for me by one of the best dressmakers in Paris. Made of white satin, the skirt was slightly gorged with a hem edged with a lace ruffle. In the years after the Revolution, fashion had taken a turn for the simpler so as not to invite comparisons to Marie-Antoinette. My one regret about my wedding dress was that it was simple to the point of being austere in its design. But, looking back, what could have been more appropriate? I had six bridesmaids, including my beautiful sisters.

The *crème* of Parisian society attended, and all nodded when I walked down the aisle of the church. The women dabbed their eyes when the vows were exchanged, but they stopped the second that Talleyrand and his wife walked in to take their place with Edmond's family. After a long glance at me, he patted Edmond on the back. When the ceremony was over, Talleyrand asked my husband for permission to kiss the bride. It was a brief kiss, but it was a memorable one because it generated a warmth that circulated my cheeks.

I did not think much of it then. I felt beautiful, Edmond looked handsome, and there was every reason to think we would remain together for eternity. I hoped for the financial support of a man I could respect and a marriage that offered the ability to see more of the world. Although our interests diverged, my independence was almost assured by a man who spent most of his time at the gaming tables with his friends. I now believe Edmond expected no more from me than the dutiful support of a beautiful possession that would raise his esteem in the eyes of his friends and colleagues. The match, by all measures, should have been good for each of us. In all truthfulness, we did care for each other. At least, at first.

One incident above all others stands out from my glorious day. At the reception at my family's home, Edmond got very drunk and rushed a kitchen maid into the garden bushes, thinking they could not be seen. But, they were…by me, several cousins, and Talleyrand, my new uncle-by-marriage. With great discretion and elegance, he interrupted the rude frolic, grabbing Edmond by his *cravat,* tie, and pointing a finger at his nose, a gesture I might have replaced with the statement, *"Tu est un cochon!"* You are a pig! if circumstances had been different. When they reentered the reception, Edmond had his head bowed. Talleyrand was smiling. I knew then who was beast and who was hunter, and I knew I would never forget.

CHAPTER 25

▼

By 1802, my beloved had won his struggles with rival contenders and had become one of the most important figures in Napoleon's government. Yet, his relations with Napoleon had become increasingly strained over two major issues. The first involved Catherine, my beloved's new wife, and the lack of respect shown to her by the man who had forced him to marry. The second revolved around Napoleon's desire to conquer Britain. Of the two issues, the one that bothered my beloved the most was Napoleon's opinion of Catherine as "plainly stupid."

One evening at a formal dinner attended by several of Napoleon's ministers and their wives, he impolitely remarked to Catherine in a voice that others could overhear, "I hope the good conduct of the Citizeness Talleyrand will soon cause the indiscretions of Madame Grand to be forgotten."

"In that respect, I surely cannot do better than follow the example of Citizeness Bonaparte," Catherine retorted, her wide blue eyes innocently staring into Napoleon's intense, focused frown.

A hush spread across the table. Crystal wine glasses were eased back onto the damask tablecloth with some clinking, which added a faint levity to a very tense moment.

My beloved noted in his diaries that Napoleon never forgave Catherine for her implied criticism of Josephine. Ten years later, he would still be complaining that, "In spite of my objection and to the great scandal of all Europe, Talleyrand married his shameless mistress, with whom he could not even hope to have children."

Of course, my beloved and I never had children together either, though he was most kind to my daughter, Pauline, when I had a reconciliation with her years later. We were also no strangers to the label of shame that came with my residing at Rue St. Florentin for the last twenty years of his life. But, beyond these similarities, no one could ever think to compare Catherine with me, a point I made repeatedly to Talleyrand in later years.

"*Monsieur* foreign minister," Napoleon said to Talleyrand the very next morning when they met in a corridor of the Tuileries palace, "I want to inform you that, from this moment onward, your wife will no longer be welcome within my presence."

"Then, my dear general," Talleyrand responded angrily, "if that is what your disposition compels you to do, as a member of an aristocracy that takes marriage vows seriously, I find I have no other recourse than to resign my position."

"*Alors, laissez-moi tranquille!*" Napoleon responded with his sing-song Corsican accent, emphasizing the *laissez-moi*, leave me. "We shall resolve this matter another time."

Two days later, meeting again in that same corridor, Napoleon again brought up the issue.

"Catherine will be received in my residence with one stipulation," Napoleon grumbled.

"And what might that be?"

"You must assure me that she will come as infrequently as possible."

"I can only assure you that I will try to accommodate to your wishes while at the same time fulfill my wife's."

Each man continued past the other, both unclear about what had truly transpired.

Unfortunately, my beloved discovered that Napoleon was not the only man in Paris who had the need to insult Catherine.

"Talleyrand," General Macdonald whispered, "wanted four things out of life: to be a bishop, to be a minister of state, to be rich, and to be the husband of a fool. He succeeded in all four."

Soon, no one could resist the temptation to meet the "fallen woman" who the infamous Talleyrand had redeemed by marriage. Beyond the English Channel, a fashionable British socialite with an even more scandalous past than Catherine, compared Talleyrand's wife to the duchess of Cumberland, who was known to be "the silliest woman in the world."

To the honor of my beloved, Talleyrand treated Catherine with unfailing kindness and consideration so long as they lived together. No one was allowed in his presence who did not show her proper respect and deference. Talleyrand himself never revealed any embarrassment over Catherine's foolishness, and he never pretended she was other than what she was.

"Stupid," he would say and then add, "as a rose."

Sometimes, he defended her indirectly by explaining that his wife, for all her faults, was preferable to the more gifted ladies.

"A clever woman usually compromises her husband. But a foolish one compromises only herself."

Comparing Catherine to Madame de Stael in his notes, Talleyrand wrote, "One must have loved a genius in order to appreciate the simplicity of loving a fool."

If my beloved seemed to have won his battle with Napoleon over the place of Catherine at court, he also made headway on the issue of Napoleon's animosity toward the English. After repeated urgings, Napoleon gave in to his request to negotiate a peace treaty with England, with which France was at war. If truth be known, by the date of Napoleon's acquiescence, Talleyrand had already dispatched an English-speaking *aide-de-camp* and confidential secretary to begin talks with senior officials in the British foreign ministry.

According to the best information Talleyrand received from his agents abroad, England was experiencing serious domestic difficulties in addition to facing an insurrection in Ireland. By my beloved's calculations, the British would soon be desperate for peace. In a meeting that took place in Napoleon's offices, my beloved countenanced "moderation" in France's demands of England, convinced a strong England was essential to the well-being of Europe. He preferred that the peace he would negotiate would not lead to future wars.

Napoleon, true to his own aggressive nature, did not agree with his foreign minister. He wanted France to control as much land as she could and insisted on a weak England with little chance of recovery in the immediate future.

Arguments between them became so heated that Napoleon sent his eldest brother, Joseph, to England to sign a preliminary treaty rather than send Talleyrand. Once the preliminary treaty was signed, Joseph Bonaparte worsened an already regrettable situation by corresponding directly with his brother rather than have Talleyrand respond, a clear violation of protocol. As one might imagine, Talleyrand did not take kindly to the professional humiliation. Not one to allow a grievance to pass without repayment, that day soon came.

In March 1802, when the final treaty between France and England was signed at Amiens, Talleyrand made certain he was the first to learn of it. The next day, he spent the morning with Napoleon going over routine business. As they stood

together looking over papers laid out on a rolltop desk made especially for
Napoleon by Jean-Francois Oeben, my beloved nonchalantly handed the first
consul a stack of papers.

"Oh, here is something you may find interesting. It is the Treaty of Amiens,
which has just been signed." Talleyrand continued to gather up and review other
papers, seemingly indifferent to any reaction by Napoleon.

"Why didn't you tell me at once?" Napoleon demanded.

"Because," Talleyrand responded, like a father to an irresponsible child, "I
knew that, if I did, you would not have paid attention to any other business this
morning."

Then, taking his own stack of papers, my beloved bowed and withdrew,
leaving the first consul to deal with his rage as best he could.

Yet, Talleyrand was still not content. Napoleon was being praised throughout
France as its savior, and few knew it was my beloved who had shaped the peace
with England. To Talleyrand's manner of thinking, it was he who had literally
dragged France up from the depths of ignominy, into which the Directory had
plunged her, to become a country in Europe of the first rank. And all could
vanish in a moment if Napoleon's impetuousness was not restrained.

No sooner had the ink dried on the Treaty of Amiens than were Talleyrand's
worst fears realized. Over his vehement protests, the former Kingdom of
Piedmont was formally annexed to France by Napoleon's swift, unannounced
conquest of those Italian lands.

During the summer of 1802, Napoleon saw to it that the three-consulate form
of government was disbanded and that he was declared consul for life, a title that
enabled him to name his own successor. When Napoleon had also taken the title
of president of the Italian Republic, my beloved realized that "this little Corsican"
had become greater than a king in all but name. Would there be no end to his
self-aggrandizement?

One snowy day in February 1803, during a meeting in the Tuileries palace
with ministers of both England and France, Napoleon started to rail against
British demands to void the Treaty of Amiens on the grounds that Napoleon had
taken ownership of Piedmont (which he had promised not to) and refused to
withdraw troops from Holland, as he had promised to do. After what seemed like
hours of wild threats of war aimed at Lord Whitworth, the British ambassador,
Napoleon slammed shut the door to the chamber behind him and walked quickly
down the corridor.

"We shall be fighting in two weeks" were Napoleon's final words.

"He must be mad!" Lord Whitworth exclaimed, realizing there was no way to stop Napoleon other than with an ultimatum of war. "France must evacuate Holland immediately. Only then will Britain agree to limit her interests in Malta to ten years."

To this, Whitworth added, "I must have a reply within seven days!" Then he, too, stormed out of the room.

As Talleyrand expected, Napoleon was still furious when they came together the next day in the ministry.

"The word 'ultimatum,'" Napoleon screamed at Talleyrand, "implied war and worse. In fact, England's manner of negotiating was entirely insulting, that of a superior with an inferior."

"General," Talleyrand pleaded in a desperate effort to avert another war, "perhaps Malta could be turned over to one of the nations guaranteeing the Treaty of Amiens."

Napoleon's response was an unintelligible grunt as he brushed past my beloved.

Unfortunately, too many insults had been incurred by both the French and the British to curtail the fever of war. None of Talleyrand's efforts to preserve the peace had the slightest effect. On May 20, 1803, after fourteen months of an uneasy peace, France declared war on Great Britain.

Talleyrand stood in Napoleon's library in dumbfounded silence as he listened to Napoleon's plans for war.

"I intend to do something that will be the most difficult undertaking ever conceived of by a French military leader," Napoleon stated in the histrionic manner of a man who realized he is about to make history. "With some foggy weather and relatively favorable circumstances, I can land troops on British soil and, in three days time, be master of London, Parliament, and the Bank of England."

"There will be dire consequences for such a bold intervention!" Talleyrand interjected, appalled by the audacity of the strategy.

"What we need to do immediately is reactivate the port of Boulougne, from which we can launch the invasion," Napoleon continued, completely ignoring Talleyrand's words. "I will also order the construction of flat-bottomed barges with which to transport my armies across the Channel."

Talleyrand knew Napoleon's plan to be a self-destructive undertaking. He continued to protest the first consul's actions, but to no avail.

"The future is now upon us," my beloved wrote in his diary. "Napoleon is headed for a major catastrophe and may bring down France in his attempts to conquer the world."

My concerns at that time were far less complicated. Talleyrand was the most interesting man I had ever met, a man with whom I wanted to discuss books I had read and ideas forming in my head. The pleasant afternoons my family and I spent at Rue St. Florentin, however, did not ever offer us any privacy of conversation. To gain that, I was forced to devise a strategy that some might call devious, but which solved my problem in an acceptable way.

Parisians have always chosen to walk where it was fashionable to show themselves. Walkways of the royal palace, the Champs-Elysee, and the Tuileries, during any hour of the day, were likely to be filled with well-dressed women of means conversing rapidly on a variety of topical subjects. Talleyrand, it was made known to me, would often take late morning walks along a favorite path in the Tuileries near his home to clear his mind of the morning's correspondence and business. Once known, it was not difficult for me to arrange an "accidental" meeting with my uncle-to-be along that path. Until he died, Talleyrand never knew that several years of meetings with him, both before and after my marriage to Edmond, had been so "arranged."

My beloved always maintained he remembered our first meeting quite distinctly because he was taken with my fancifully plumed hat and parasol. While I do not remember my dress, I had braided my hair in the fashion of the day, clubbing it up in back of my neck to catch his eye, and I recall it had taken hours of my time. The overall effect, however, was according to plan. Talleyrand took notice of me.

With the help of my science tutor, I was able to escape the company of Maman for the afternoon. At this first meeting in the Tuileries, we spoke of little more than minor family matters and the weather. Both of us were somewhat awkward until we shared a laugh as a pet poodle, on a promenade with his mistress, escaped from its leash and spent an adventurous few minutes in the grass. Though the minutes we spent together during this first meeting were small in number, when we parted and continued down our own paths, the eyes that left mine offered more than familial approval.

CHAPTER 26

▼

There is a painting in the Louvre I enjoy looking at even now, so many years after my beloved's death. It is Louis David's *Coronation of Napoleon,* in which my beloved is standing among the new dignitaries of the empire with a slight smile upon his lips. Perhaps this expression of half-amusement and half-disdain represents Talleyrand's satisfaction that, despite occasional public protestations to the contrary and after fourteen years of wandering, France had been brought safely into the secure haven of a monarchical system.

Napoleon, already well-versed in how to flatter his cynical, independent-minded foreign minister, anointed Talleyrand with the newly created title of grand chamberlain of the imperial court. My beloved accepted the honor with the appropriate gratitude, as the painting bears witness. Perhaps his half-smile signals his amusement that Napoleon, usurping the Pope's prerogative, had crowned himself emperor during the winter of 1804 in Notre Dame Cathedral, indicating that his crown and his power came, not from heaven through the hands of the Pope, but from the people of France by virtue of his own deeds.

Whatever the reason for the smile, my beloved cringed a few months later when he heard the Senate proclamation:

> ...that Napoleon Bonaparte be named emperor and that, in this capacity, responsible for the government of the French Republic; and that the title of emperor and the imperial resides with it be made hereditary in his family, from male to male, by primogeniture...

My own romantic image of Napoleon only increased that year of his coronation. Although a bout of flu placed me in bed that wintry December morning, Maman and Papa witnessed the entire double procession of Pope and emperor. Papa reported to me that soldiers held back four ranks of citizens who lined the streets leading to the cathedral. Maman provided me with every detail of dress, of the choir, the mass, and the crowning. She reported that the cloak Napoleon wore contained 10,000 francs worth of laurel leaves and bees embroidered in gold. Two orchestras struck up a march when Napoleon and Josephine appeared in the nave. All those present rose and cried, "Long live the emperor!" I found it very romantic that Napoleon had finally married his consort the night before in a short, civil ceremony. My own wedding, lovely as it was, would never have the drama of an illicit love affair made legitimate.

Despite several tempestuous years, Talleyrand served Napoleon with fealty and good advice, even when his opinions were not taken. Domestically, Talleyrand had reconciled some outstanding differences between the nobility and the emperor. In the realm of foreign affairs, however, his diary notes he was very concerned. My beloved's policies depended on prudence and moderation, virtues that were foreign to Napoleon's temperament. The emperor's love of power and his embrace of glory both depended upon the notion of conquest.

"Vanity is his driving force," Talleyrand wrote. "It is not enough he was proclaimed emperor of the French. He wants to become the equal of the house of Austria."

According to my beloved, it was only a matter of time before the interests of France and those of Napoleon would come into direct conflict.

In a feat of military agility, however, Napoleon's troops surrounded Ulm, a city that General Baron von Mack, the Austrian commander, controlled. Without firing a shot at Austrian troops, Napoleon acquired an unconditional surrender.

Knowing his position would anger Napoleon, but also certain it was the best possible alternative for France, Talleyrand pressed the emperor not to enfeeble Austria. Instead, he was to make it an ally that could help neutralize Russia's expansionist tendencies toward the west. According to Talleyrand, Russia would look east and encounter the British. If all went as my beloved felt it would, Russia and Britain would exhaust each other, fighting out their differences in the Orient. The result would be a Europe left in peace. Although no more than a dilettante in military matters, even I would have recognized Talleyrand's strategy as brilliant.

One spring day in 1804, a year prior to my marriage to Edmond, this very same topic was discussed by my uncle-to-be and my husband-to-be with me as the onlooker. In another of my "arranged" meetings, Talleyrand spotted Edmond and I on horseback one Saturday afternoon in the Tuileries. After we tethered our horses, the two men spoke with seriousness about the 200,000 troops Napoleon was mobilizing along the English Channel in preparation to invade England, and the 250,000 Austrian soldiers moving toward the Inn River to invade France's ally, Bavaria. Knowing Edmond as I did, I realized that the rapt look in his eyes masked a mind that was likely to be elsewhere while my eyes glistened with pride in listening to a man whose family I was soon going to join. I only wished his remarks might have been more directed toward me. When I look back on this day, I am reminded of Madame de Stael's first meeting with Napoleon and how invisible she must have felt throughout his discussions with Talleyrand.

When Talleyrand took his leave, however, it was clear he had noticed me. He complimented the riding coat I had carefully selected for the occasion, a triple-collared coat of puce-colored shantung with ivory studs at the front and pockets. When he also commented on the green and white plumes in my yellow felt hat, I knew his attention had been as much on the figure cut by his niece-to-be as it had been on his politics. The sensation I felt in the center of my being when he bent forward to kiss my hand as he departed was more forceful than any Edmond ever elicited in the darkness of our *boudoir*.

Napoleon, however, remained unconvinced by Talleyrand. When he defeated both Austria and Prussia, in what history would recognize as the Battle of Austeriitz, he again ignored Talleyrand's arguments for co-opting Austria rather than dismembering her. He compelled Austria to concede Venetia, the Tyrol and Vrorlberg, Bavaria, Baden, and Wurttemberg to France, amounting to 2.5 million subjects and one-sixth of Austria's revenues. In addition, Austria agreed to pay France 40 million francs as war indemnity.

When my beloved handed the signed treaty to Napoleon, Talleyrand was taken aback by the ingratitude he received.

"You have created a treaty that annoys me a great deal!" Napoleon screamed at him. "You allowed those Austrian peacocks to keep too much territory and money. Are you nothing but an Austrian sympathizer? You certainly don't represent my interests or those of France!"

"Never before has France dictated such an encompassing treaty," Talleyrand responded nonplussed, "and never before has Austria signed one as onerous."

According to my beloved, this "peace" treaty became a sore between he and Napoleon that never healed.

Despite Napoleon's impressive military victories, what my beloved saw stretched out in front of France were not the blessings of peace, but endless years of war and bloodshed. And, once he realized this, Talleyrand began to prepare himself for the day when catastrophe would overwhelm France and her armies.

Perhaps it is also appropriate at this time to mention the name of someone of great importance to both my beloved and me in years to come. Prince Klemens von Metternich, Austria's acclaimed foreign minister, reported to his king that there was no "one" France. From his point of view, France was divided into the militarists, whose fortunes were inextricably bound up with the Napoleonic idea of conquest and a Europe ruled by France, and a group comprised of those who foresaw Napoleon's ambitions would end in ruin. Chief among the latter group, Metternich reported to the other ministers of state in Europe, was Talleyrand. So, without his even knowing it, Talleyrand had sown some of the seeds that would lead to his own glorious moment at the Congress of Vienna, only nine years away.

Napoleon's defeat of the Prussian Army, professional warriors trained under Frederick the Great, resulted in another argument between my beloved and the emperor. Napoleon demanded Prussia, like Austria, be deprived of half of its population and half of its revenue and pay an indemnity of 160,000 francs. He was again in no mood to grant any favorable conditions to a defeated country.

Talleyrand, still confident in his own assessment, evaluated this new "alliance" with Prussia as no alliance at all. Instead, he felt it would introduce into the bosom of Europe a malevolent and dangerous enemy. Like Austria, Prussia would be deprived of its self-respect and pride, leading to ill will and an eventual desire to regain lost territories. While my beloved tried to explain this to Napoleon at one of their many volatile meetings, the emperor would not listen.

The one act that most likely led to Talleyrand's resignation as minister of foreign affairs was Napoleon ordering my beloved to draft a document declaring a formal blockade against England, closing all ports France controlled to British shipping.

"I will conquer the sea by land power," Napoleon declared emphatically to Talleyrand's vehement objections. "In fact, any country that refuses to cooperate with us will face invasion by France's armies."

"If this is the direction in which you are taking France," Talleyrand replied, "I have no alternative than to cease to be your foreign minister."

Before my beloved's words could be put to paper and without informing Talleyrand, Napoleon invaded East Prussia at Eylau in order to destroy a large concentration of Russian troops massing there. He quickly followed this attack by chasing the Russian army eastward, away from French soil. Attempting to mollify Talleyrand and be magnanimous, Napoleon asked him to negotiate a generous peace treaty with Czar Alexander.

The treaty was so generous that Talleyrand later wrote, "If Czar Alexander were a woman, Napoleon could have made him his mistress."

As I have learned over these many years, little can be taken at face value in either love or war. A secret alliance between France and Russia was proposed by my beloved that stated, if England refused to make peace with France on favorable terms, Russia would declare war against the island. Both France and Russia would then require their allies and client states to do likewise. In addition, if Napoleon's mediation between Constantinople and St. Petersburg failed, France pledged to join Russia in a war against the Turks.

Talleyrand then did something that was typically Talleyrand…he leaked the secret treaty to his contacts in London. His motive was pure, he told me somewhat defensively, more times than required to make his point. He wanted to show England how easy it was to turn Russia, Napoleon's mightiest enemy, into a conspirator. While senior officials in London were informed that Talleyrand opposed the secret treaty, he was no fool and knew the British always suspected him of being the treaty's architect.

Only three months after my marriage to Edmond, Talleyrand and I met again in the Tuileries. At the time, I convinced myself that my motives were solely to further my education, although I was thrilled to have the attention and conversation of such a celebrated man. When I asked myself what Talleyrand gained by these meetings, I thought it to be an attractive and intelligent companion. In later years, following the Congress of Vienna, I often wondered whether Talleyrand already had me bedded…in his mind.

My first impulse, upon hearing Talleyrand's opinions of Napoleon and his tactics with other countries, was to voice concern that he would be considered a traitor and, possibly worse, an opportunist. Weren't those the criticisms I had heard whispered in salons when the speaker was unaware I was his niece?

"You are still a naïve young woman," Talleyrand responded, "and, by being naïve, you are a danger to your country."

My eyes flamed, and my lips tightened. Was I never to be an adult in his eyes, with opinions worthy of his consideration?

"What do you hold, dear, if it isn't loyalty to your emperor? A crown for yourself? Yes, how that would impress all the admiring…" I stopped myself short, suddenly not knowing whether my words reflected my newly acquired political opinions or my own jealousies.

"If you are asking whether I hold you dear to me," he continued, aware of my confusion, "I assure you that I do. But, if you are questioning my judgment on a matter that I consider a direct threat to our country, then let us continue talking."

I sat on the bench, as if frozen.

"I believe you have heard my opinions on anyone who places himself above both his men and his country. If you cannot understand my reasoning, then these past months of conversation have been a waste of both our time. Have you not sickened to the news of French blood being shed on foreign soil?"

When I realized it to be a rhetorical question, I wanted nothing more than to ask his forgiveness. How could I have even entertained the idea that, despite his manipulations, his ultimate loyalty was to nothing and no one but France?

Whether the reader agrees or disagrees with Talleyrand's motives, by that time, he had begun his long process of undermining Napoleon. The more the emperor was determined to follow his own path, the more Talleyrand knew France was in danger. The actual end of their collaboration was in 1807 when Talleyrand formally tendered his resignation to Napoleon. With a steady hand, my beloved wrote:

> I served Napoleon while he was emperor as I had served him when he was first consul, that is, with devotion so long as I could believe that he himself was devoted to the interests of France. But, as soon as I saw him begin to undertake those irrational enterprises, which were to lead to his and France's doom, I resigned my ministry. For this, he never forgave me.

Napoleon "saved face," according to Talleyrand, by claiming he was forced to fire his minister of foreign affairs because of complaints received from the King of Bavaria and the King of Wurtemberg regarding Talleyrand's extortions and rapacious financial demands.

I do not relish stating that, with my beloved's resignation, a downward spiral began for Napoleon. Though he always remained a phantom rival for my beloved's attention, I shared with my countrymen the excitement of his achievements. I was a child when he led and won his most extravagant campaigns, and I remember the songs that accompanied each triumph. I sing them still. But, when the end was near for him, as I assembled the details of his life from my beloved's journal, I began to see not so much the end of Napoleon, but the ascendancy of my beloved.

CHAPTER 27

▼

Although their formal relationship had been officially severed, the emperor continued to request my beloved's advice in matters of foreign affairs. A modest, incompetent civil servant, whose name is not worth even mentioning, but was under the complete control of Napoleon, was now foreign minister. Talleyrand retained the title of grand chamberlain, but his only duty was to sign already-negotiated treaties.

It was during this period that the nature of my relationship with Talleyrand changed forever. I remember the day well. It was almost summer, and Talleyrand discovered me lounging on one of the long line of chairs bordering the great alley of Tuilleries, reading a treatise by Madame de Stael, which had been published several years earlier. The choice of book, I must admit, was made partly to impress Talleyrand with my intellectual interests, partly to understand what had made Madame de Stael so appealing to my new uncle, and partly to join with everyone else in Paris who seemed to have begun to read. No matter where one looked, a book appeared in the hand of a coachman in his box, a soldier at his post, or a seamstress outside her work area.

"Good day, my beauty," Talleyrand said as he came upon me, his hand taking hold of my book so that he could see it's title. "A woman with a fine mind and capable pen. I applaud your taste. As you know, Madame de Stael is a good friend."

"Edmond discouraged it, but philosophy and politics have even reached the streets. I am sure you have noticed. These days, there is no truth that is too strong to be known."

"And do you agree with de Stael's opinions that literature should be an educative philosophy, not an elegant art?"

"I am still thinking about it, but I certainly agree with her ideas on the perfectibility of civilizations," I responded, spoken as if it was an idea that constantly preoccupied me. My eyes never left his as I recited a well-rehearsed list of topics I had memorized for the occasion.

We chatted briefly, and I could see Talleyrand was impressed with my conversation. Looking back at what might seem to the reader as manipulative on my part, I counter that the books I had read prior to and following my marriage and the ideas that filled my head—even when they had motives other than education—did become a part of me. And, as Talleyrand, my best mentor, would be the first to say, "Ends can be justified by many means."

One of the more enjoyable requests made of Talleyrand during this period by Napoleon was that Talleyrand purchase a *château* for himself (at state expense) for the primary purpose of holding the Spanish heir to the throne, Ferdinand, Prince of the Asturias, under house arrest. My beloved's notes state he had vehemently opposed dethroning and detaining the Bourbon king in order to place one of Napoleon's relatives upon the throne. However, the prospect of buying "a handsome property," as Napoleon suggested, "so that you are able to entertain heads of state and other distinguished foreigners as brilliantly as possible" was not at all distasteful.

Napoleon, I suspect, was appealing to my beloved's *ancien* sense of place when he said, "People must enjoy being there, and an invitation from you must come to be regarded as a mark of distinction for the ambassadors of those sovereigns with whom I am pleased."

Talleyrand's response came within a week as he stood in Napoleon's library, admiring the vivid enamel colors of the seventeenth-century porcelain vase that had been given to the emperor that very morning by a foreign diplomat.

"Your Excellency, I have my eye on an estate called Valençay in the Department of Indre, 180 miles south of Paris. The property includes a magnificent *château* containing twenty-five master suites, enclosed by 360 tended acres, 40,000 acres of forest, and twenty-three villages."

"I am not surprised my former minister would be so quickly prepared with an appropriately rich setting," Napoleon responded, no doubt noting the inflated price Talleyrand suggested.

"At my age, Your Excellency, a man must think of his retirement," Talleyrand confessed, knowing full well both men were talking about large sums of money that would be expropriated directly from the French treasury for this purchase.

Once again, they played their games, and the discussion bore its usual dance-like ritual. Napoleon paced the room, fitful and distracted. Talleyrand relaxed into a comfortable chair, seeming unconcerned by anything distasteful Napoleon said. Talleyrand was an established luminary now. Napoleon was still an icon.

My beloved, unwilling to afford and maintain such a costly *château* using his own funds, but hoping to continue the life of grandeur he had always revered as a relatively poor child, accepted Napoleon's Spanish "guests." Although this implicated him in the crime of their captivity, he did not seem to care. If I were asked my opinion regarding the "winner" of this particular contest, I would readily choose Napoleon, at least during the years he was in power. For every day my beloved spent in Valençay with his houseguests, as exquisite as the property was, he was reminded he was still the servant of the emperor and, as such, at his disposal.

As anyone who knew Talleyrand might have suspected, he was his most gracious self to the princes of Spain when they arrived at Valençay in May 1808, although I doubt he knew they would remain there under house arrest for the next six years. He made certain the entire Spanish contingency in his charge was treated well and with respect. I almost hesitate to indulge the rumor that Talleyrand encouraged his own wife to have an affair with the pretender to the Spanish throne, proud that Catherine could attract such a sensible, distinguished nobleman.

A year later, Napoleon requested Talleyrand's personal services again, asking my beloved accompany him to Saxony to meet with Czar Alexander of Russia to construct a new peace treaty. Although flattered by Napoleon's frequent kind notes and small gifts, I wonder whether Talleyrand would have agreed to the voyage if he knew that, once he left, he would not be returning to his treasured Valençay for nearly a decade.

Talleyrand has recorded the passing years had cured Czar Alexander of any infatuation he might have once felt for Napoleon. The emperor had gotten stronger in the intervening period, and the czar was of the opinion that France would eventually attack Russia. The only question was *when.*

During their workdays in the *château* in Saxony, Napoleon would try to charm the czar by offering to draft a mutually advantageous treaty. The chamber's tall windows provided a glorious view of the expansive gardens below, and Talleyrand frequently commented to me that, not even at Valençay, was there so much compatibility between exterior and interior. Each evening, however, Talleyrand would meet secretly with the czar in the sitting room of the princess of Thurn, sister of the queen of Prussia.

Before going on, I must confess to having had a special fascination for the czar. Years before meeting him at the Congress of Vienna, I knew of his reputation as a strikingly handsome, cultured man, and Talleyrand did not disabuse me of this opinion. On this particular evening in Saxony, as on those that preceded it, Talleyrand took as his task the continuing education of the Russian ruler.

"Sire, it is in your power to save Europe, but you can do so only by standing up to Napoleon," Talleyrand began. "The French are civilized, but their sovereign is not. The sovereign of Russia is civilized, but his people are not. What could be more fitting than the sovereign of Russia becoming the ally of the people of France?"

My beloved paused, assuring himself of the czar's attentiveness before he continued. "All Frenchmen desire nothing more than peace, but, unless you oppose Napoleon's designs on Europe, even they will become victims of their emperor's desires."

The czar remained silent, hesitant to trust the man standing before him. He fiddled with a glass miniature of a Roman soldier produced in Nevers as a toy for young Louis XVIII, which Napoleon had presented to him in a display of friendship. How many times had Talleyrand talked so eloquently and persuasively, the czar wondered, yet destroyed the careers of those whom he counseled? The czar's mother, who had counseled her son before he had left Russia, had been less than diplomatic in her assessment of Talleyrand, as my beloved was informed years after these meetings took place.

"Be cautious of that snake in the grass," she had told her son. "God marked him with a limp so that all could see that he was the devil in disguise. He would destroy Russia as easily as he destroyed the influence of the Roman Catholic Church in France."

"You are a wise ruler," Talleyrand continued seductively, "but time and history respect those who act quickly and effectively. Time, Your Excellency, is not your friend at this moment."

Evening after evening, Talleyrand and the czar met late into the night, discussing the matters that were talked about earlier in the day when the czar had met with Napoleon. The meetings ended only when the czar was persuaded that Talleyrand's opinion was the opinion of "all the sensible people of France." Arguments and counterarguments were outlined in detail, with Talleyrand always suggesting to the czar some new approach to the next day's meeting.

According to my beloved, the czar was a very good student. One day, when Napoleon arrived unexpectedly at my beloved's quarters, he complained to Talleyrand that the czar was being surprisingly clever and obstinate.

"If he cares as much for me as he makes me believe he does, why does he not sign the agreement?"

"The czar is perhaps more naïve than us and does not understand the need for complicated treaties between men of honor," Talleyrand replied disingenuously. "He believes his word and his affection for you are more binding than any piece of paper that we might call a treaty."

"Merde!" Shit! Napoleon offered in response.

Was it wise for my beloved to initiate such a dangerous, complex game of international diplomacy, playing two world leaders against each another? In effect, Talleyrand was making a conspirator of Czar Alexander and a dupe of Napoleon. My beloved knew he risked exposure and disgrace. Everything he possessed—his position, his wealth, his honor, and perhaps even his life—could be forfeited if his duplicity was discovered by Napoleon. It was an issue we frequently discussed years later during our walks in the woods at Valençay when Talleyrand was reflecting on his life. Even upon reassessment, however, he genuinely felt he was preserving the integrity of both France and Europe against the aggrandizing and destabilizing policies of his emperor. I must admit that, toward the end of my beloved's life, it became very important to him that I be convinced of the necessity of his actions that others might view as treacherous on his part. And I can honestly say he did convince me.

After countless days of what appeared to Napoleon to be fruitless negotiations, Czar Alexander finally gave in on several unimportant points, and a treaty was signed. The czar agreed that, if Austria attacked France, he and Napoleon would join forces against her. This would leave Napoleon free to attack Spain and Portugal. In exchange for such backing, Napoleon would allow Czar Alexander to invade Finland and annex the Danubian provinces he had always coveted.

"I am well pleased with the czar, and he should be equally pleased with me," a triumphant Napoleon told Talleyrand.

I suspect Napoleon would have been less pleased had he known the czar had accepted his proposal of Russia's intervention against Austria only after accepting Talleyrand's advice that Russia not honor it. Later that week, the czar wrote to Emperor Francis of Austria assuring him he would attack his forces under no condition.

The next day, when Talleyrand met with Napoleon to assess the success of the delicate balancing act he had constructed, he found a man whose attention had already turned to other matters. They spoke in the two-story library of the *château*, a room that provided warmth to their often-heated discussions, with its coffered ceiling, large Beavais tapestries, and Savonnerie rugs. Talleyrand stood uneasily, not yet confident of the new cane an admirer had given him, carved out of a soft wood by the man himself.

"Divorce," Napoleon blurted out without any context. "Sadly, my destiny requires it! The tranquility of France demands it. I have no successor. I can found a dynasty only by marrying a princess from one of the reigning houses of Europe. Czar Alexander is now an ally. He has sisters. There must be one whose age is suitable."

"I will discuss this very sensitive issue with the czar," Talleyrand responded.

"Remember, it must not sound as if it is coming from me."

To Talleyrand's chagrin, Czar Alexander, when told of Napoleon's proposition, told my beloved he must first seek the approval of his mother, the Empress Dowager.

"I would expect no less," Talleyrand responded with a pose of deep respect. The Empress Dowager, as all Europe knew, would sooner have one of her daughters become a prostitute than marry that "Corsican murderer."

The following day, at a meeting arranged by Talleyrand, Czar Alexander brought up the idea of a marriage between Napoleon and one of his sisters, the Grand Duchess Catherine, to seal the growing friendship between their countries. Napoleon replied he was honored and left the meeting extremely pleased he would have to reply to the offer of the grand duchess's hand rather than ask for it. Although the match was not destined to take place, just as Talleyrand hoped, each statesman returned to his respective country ostensibly enamored of the other.

As proof of the czar's newly found trust in Talleyrand, he sent two ambassadors to France. The official one reported directly to Napoleon. The other man presented his credentials only to Talleyrand, papers that documented he would be responsible for delivering any private correspondence directly to and from the czar.

CHAPTER 28

▼

In 1809, at the age of fifty-five, Talleyrand had, in his own words, "settled into the insignificant life of a 'Grand Dignitary of the Empire,'" playing his role largely in the shadows. He was feeling despondent and shrouded his depression with self-pity, a characteristic that permeated the rest of his life. *"Je suis comme un etranger dans mon pays. Personne ne me veut pas. Je suis deplace."* I am like a stranger in my own country. Nobody wants me. I am displaced.

For want of a significant governmental mission, he dedicated himself to the personal destruction of Napoleon. While he continued to press upon me that he found Napoleon a threat to the peace of Europe, I always felt these two strong personalities would have clashed sooner or later, if only over the merits of truffles or Brie. To maintain harmony in our relationship, then and later on, I usually adopted Talleyrand's point of view, not only for harmony's sake, but because my beloved's tutelage had, in fact, educated me to accept his view of the world.

With the annexation of Holland and northwest Germany, the French Empire consisted of 130 departments. Members of Napoleon's family had been set upon the thrones of Holland, Naples, Westphalia, Spain, and Tuscany. Napoleon and France predominated on the continent. Talleyrand was not pleased and made a purposeful effort to tell all with whom he spoke that he was thoroughly in opposition to Napoleon's policies. Holding no official position in the government, he felt free to say whatever pleased him, and certainly put his thoughts in his diary:

> The emperor has become so successful at conquest that he has convinced himself he is as talented as he would like to be. One day, I predict that Corsican's self-delusions will not only bring himself down, but France as well.

I often ask myself why Talleyrand, so circumspect in his personal and public life, who abhorred confrontation, would now be so bold about stating such negative opinions about his emperor. Given Napoleon's political and military strength and his need to extract revenge, one could reasonably argue that my beloved was being indiscreet, at best, and foolish, at worst. Neither, I think, was the case. Rather, consistent with Talleyrand's style, he had a very clear objective, and that was to uncover and gather around his person individuals who were also in opposition to Napoleon's rule.

If I were organizing this manuscript around the life of Napoleon, I would certainly be remiss not to dwell upon the constructive years of the Consulate, 1799 through 1804, when he transformed the administrative, financial, legal, and religious institutions that formed the framework of the France I knew as a child. But this is Talleyrand's story, and, by 1808, it was clear to my beloved that Napoleon was not about to allow France to remain at peace for very long.

The true genius of Talleyrand's new anti-Napoleonic stance was his reconciliation with Minister of Police Fouche, their antagonisms over the years well-known throughout Paris. Personally, they had struggled as rival contenders for Napoleon's attention. Their professional differences usually found Talleyrand leaning toward a restoration of monarchical structures and Fouche toward republican principles. In the salons, they were known to attack each other's veracity and integrity in the harshest of terms. At one point in 1802, Talleyrand had even precipitated Fouche's dismissal. Their unexpected *rapprochement*, reconciliation, only enhanced Talleyrand's image of conspiratorial adeptness in the eyes of the diplomatic community.

Austria's Foreign Minister Metternich, well-respected throughout official and unofficial Paris, continued to report to his king that Talleyrand was the man to watch, even without portfolio:

> He is a veritable genius who can make all things possible. There are now two parties in France that are opposed to one another. The leader of one faction is the emperor. At the head of the other faction lies Talleyrand and Fouche. This second alliance, based on Fouche's ability to be ruthless with internal security and Talleyrand's adeptness in external matters, leaves no political room for the emperor other than to undertake military expeditions outside of France.

According to Talleyrand, Metternich reflected the pervasive opinion throughout Europe. He also agreed with my beloved that a divorce from Josephine and a marriage into one of the royal families of Europe was essential to both the stability of his regime and the stability of Europe.

It did not take long before news of the unholy alliance between Talleyrand and Fouche reached the emperor. Fearful of an impending coup, Napoleon rushed back to France from Spain and convened his principal advisers, including my beloved. They met in the damp library of the Tuileries, seven men seated around an impressive mahogany table with gilt carvings and ormolu mounts of stars and medallions, no doubt to create the impression of the grandeur that was Napoleon. Talleyrand, the only *ex-officio* minister present, leaned nonchalantly against the fireplace mantle, fingering his gold and lacquer snuffbox, ignoring the slander directed at him. Napoleon paced the room, shouting invectives. His brown eyes burned with the concept to which his homeland had given birth, the "vendetta."

"You all were appointed by me and can be dismissed by me!" Napoleon shouted in his high-pitched voice. "You must cease giving free rein to your private thoughts."

He paused and looked at the impassive face of Talleyrand, which made him all the more infuriated.

"All of you exist as a result of my will alone! To doubt your emperor is to betray him! To defy the will of the emperor is grounds for treason!"

Talleyrand watched with amusement as Napoleon worked himself into a fury, all the time pacing back and forth between the table and the mantle against which Talleyrand leaned. For more than an hour, the men listened to a litany of invectives and accusations fall from Napoleon's lips—traitors, liars, ingrates, miscreants, political whores. All in the room felt these were primarily directed at Talleyrand. But my beloved listened patiently, revealing no emotion and watching the emperor make a fool of himself before his ministers.

"You," Napoleon finally screamed straight at Talleyrand, "say you were not involved in the murder of the duke of Enghien. Have you forgotten it was you who advised me, in writing, to have him killed?"

Napoleon won the moment. The ministers appeared shocked, some capable of accepting everything Talleyrand had ever been accused of as true.

The argument continued without a response from Talleyrand. "Have you forgotten it was you who advised me to become involved in the Spanish War?"

Napoleon could barely pause to catch his breath. "Have you forgotten it was you who insisted I adopt the stupid policies of King Louis XIV?"

Talleyrand remained silent, making Napoleon ever angrier. He stared straight ahead, giving no indication he was even aware of being addressed.

"You are an ingrate, a thief, a liar, a coward, and…and an atheist," Napoleon screamed.

It was at this point that my beloved wrote in his diary that Napoleon lost all control, as Talleyrand almost did.

"You are nothing but a cripple whose stupid wife could have no other sexual pleasure than to fornicate with the lowly Spanish lodged at Valençay—at my cost and at my request, may I add."

Napoleon paused again to catch his breath, "Your precious Valençay, which I bought and which rightfully belongs to me."

Still, Talleyrand said nothing.

"What is your scheme? What is it that you want? Do you dare to tell me? I could break you into a thousand pieces. I have the power to do it! But, I hold you in too much contempt to take the trouble!"

The entire room remained silent

"You are a shit in silk stockings!"

Having exhausted his repertoire of insults, the emperor stormed out of the room, but not before pointing an accusatory finger at both Fouche and Talleyrand.

"Remember this! If a revolution comes, you two will be the first ones to be crushed by it!"

The silence that remained after Napoleon had gone was broken only by Talleyrand's insouciant comment, "What a pity that so great a man should be so ill-bred."

There were those who, having later heard of the incident, asked indignantly, "You listened to that? You did not snatch up a chair, a poker, or the bellows and smash it over his head?"

"More men are destroyed by the tongues of the Faubourg St. Germain than by the cannons of the emperor," Talleyrand responded with deep satisfaction.

I ask you, dear reader, do you see the devil Talleyrand could be? Carefully and craftily, he accrued his power in the way he wanted. The staging of his betrayal of Napoleon was merely a dress rehearsal for what he would do to my poor Edmond in a few short years. Edmond, the lesser man, the weaker man, the man who, not a year into our married life, I had already grown to despise.

CHAPTER 29

▼

Talleyrand, as usual, was correct. It was just a matter of time and bloodshed until Napoleon would fail. When his armies were forced to retreat from Vienna, Napoleon's first major military defeat, the news spread like the bubonic plague throughout Europe. England made immediate plans to invade France. The King of Prussia swore he would also soon go to war against Napoleon. Czar Alexander carefully moved his troops from one end of Russia's frontier to the other. And, while Napoleon informed his ministers with his usual audacity that "they are all expecting to have a rendezvous on my grave, but I shall disappoint them," his words had a hollow ring.

The sycophants he had appointed to the ministries could offer no suggestions about when the English would invade the continent. Although, they did guess that, whenever it was, the invasion would come through the Netherlands. In desperation and in need of Talleyrand's range of intelligence, Napoleon invited my beloved to help him plan for a coming war.

I was all of twenty-five years old, coming into awareness of the world as a married woman with one child crawling and a second on the way. Talleyrand was fifty-five years old and being told by the gossips in Paris that he was past his prime. He no longer had direct political power, to be sure, but both he and I knew he exercised immense influence in government through appointments to both the foreign and interior ministries he had helped secure over the decades.

Over several years of both pre-arranged and chance meetings, our conversations had shifted from the banal to the substantive. We spoke increasingly as friends who were not separated by thirty years of life's experiences. While nothing of an intimate nature was ever in my thoughts, proximity to this man of power and intelligence was always intoxicating and educating. His own protective feelings toward me came clear one day when, I dare to admit it, he learned of my desire to learn billiards.

As we walked the paths of the Tuileries, I informed him that, although many noble houses had their own billiard rooms, it was fashionable for both men and women to visit a public billiard hall together. I told him I had suggested to Edmond that we pay such a visit, but he had dismissed my request out of hand with the statement, "I'll stay with my own wagers—my cocking, prizefights, and horse races—thank you."

When I proceeded to make the same suggestion to Talleyrand, I believe he took it too much to heart.

"You shall not be found in such places while I am your uncle," Talleyrand said with vehemence as we watched three superbly dressed "established" women stroll past.

"I find your concern for my reputation touching, but unenlightened, dear uncle." My choice of words was purposeful, for being "enlightened" was exactly what Talleyrand espoused.

"Do you value your reputation so little? Is there anything to be gotten from being in the presence of young women who are exhibiting their bodies in provocative gowns and wearing a minimum of underwear? I offer to you that there are many ways for you to exhibit your independent spirit without compromising your family's name. And that is what a visit to a billiard hall will do."

His tone was such that I knew it to be disrespectful to press my point. Perhaps that decision to give in to Talleyrand's opinion on face value began a pattern of submission and dominance in our relationship that did not truly end until I established my own identity as an independent woman through my liaison with Count Clam-Martinitz in Vienna. Perhaps it never really ended. But, I made peace with myself that day by believing my uncle was merely being protective of me, and it was only a matter of time before I would either convince or charm him into changing his mind. Shall I admit right now that I was wrong in that assessment?

Talleyrand made a small concession that day by taking me to the Café Beau Rivage in a questionable neighborhood of Paris to meet the ex-chef of a nobleman who had left for London after the Revolution. The chef was now offering food of noble quality to any passerby with a few francs in his pocket. We all spent several hours in animated conversation, and I felt Talleyrand's dalliance there was his way of showing his respect for me.

While Talleyrand and I were getting to know each other better, the emperor, out of spite or necessity, continued to employ my beloved in a largely ceremonial position. When asked by Fouche why he kept my beloved as grand chamberlain because *"Talleyrand, c'est un vieux homme qui peut rien faire!"* Talleyrand is an old man who is not able to do anything! Napoleon was said to have answered, "I have some affection for him because he has been with me since the days of Brumaire."

"Your Excellency," Talleyrand was told that Fouche rejoined, "he still curries favors from those Royalists who are loyal to him. I would be remiss not to advise you that he is capable of leading a *coup* against you."

"That's why I have you, Monsieur Fouche, as my minister of police!"

Had it not been for the extraordinary job Fouche and his men were doing, Napoleon would not have felt secure in Paris. It was well known that Fouche had secret agents in attendance at every major Paris salon, bribing valets, maids, servants, prostitutes, and others servicing the nobility. He had positioned agents in different divisions of the military and in countless police prefectures throughout the country. Fouche even had surrounded Talleyrand with spies who monitored his every activity. With all this security in place, Napoleon had good reason to feel comfortable.

The major issue that consumed Talleyrand during 1809 (and a goal upon which both my beloved and Fouche agreed) was Napoleon's impending divorce from Josephine. Both agreed that marriage into an established house of Europe, plus a male heir, was needed to guarantee the viability of France after Napoleon's death.

Three potential candidates were presented to the emperor: the sister of Czar Alexander, who had already been offered to him; a daughter of the King of Saxony; and, a daughter of the House of Hapsburg. After hearing from his ministers, Napoleon invited Talleyrand to his home at Rue de la Victoire to argue the respective merits of each woman and help him make his choice.

"Your Excellency," Talleyrand told the emperor while they stood together in the drawing room, "you must marry the Austrian. Albeit, she is not as attractive as the czar's sister, but you, better than anyone, understand the importance of a strong Austrian state for the political stability of Europe."

Despite what Talleyrand had led Czar Alexander to believe, marriage to the Austrian candidate would not only reconcile France with the powers of Europe, but it would also show that France was trying to expiate the crimes of the Revolution, especially the execution of Marie-Antoinette, who was an Austrian by birth.

"You have to admit," Napoleon retorted, "this Austrian cow cannot be compared to the fine porcelain features of the czar's sister."

"We have no differences in our appreciation of women's beauty," Talleyrand responded, "but you must bear in mind that France must have a male heir to succeed you, and Austrian women are known worldwide for their ease in bearing children."

"Damn you, Talleyrand," Napoleon exclaimed, unsure how many of his other ministers shared my beloved's opinion. "Isn't it enough that you have tried to determine my foreign policy? Now you want to determine the woman with whom I will share my bed?

"I am simply your humble servant." Talleyrand smiled his usual, unknowable smile and bowed his head. "All that concerns me, as you have known from the very first day of my service to you, has been the significance of France in European affairs."

It was another successful argument by Talleyrand. On November 30,1809, Napoleon Bonaparte divorced Josephine. Within the month, it was announced by the Senate. By January 1810, the church court of Paris annulled the marriage. In April 1810, the emperor married the Archduchess Marie-Louise of Austria in a religious ceremony at the Tuileries.

As a token of gratitude and appreciation, Talleyrand was invited to attend all balls and receptions at the behest of the emperor. Yet, my beloved's notes reveal he not only continued to disparage Napoleon to friends like Lafayette, with words like, *"Le petit Corsican est une maladie dans le center d'Europe."* The little Corsican is a sickness in the center of Europe, but he also continued his own duplicitous behavior. Metternich's dispatches from Paris to Vienna were filled with privileged information from an individual known as "X," his code name for Talleyrand, while the Russians received copious private notes from Talleyrand under the code name, "Henri."

"You must each be aware that you cannot trust Napoleon for one moment," Talleyrand wrote to both Metternich and Baron Nabakoff. "His sole intention is to go to war against your respective countries. My emperor is beyond mad. He is driven by an unexplained obsession for war. He needs to destabilize the world order so that he can reconstitute it in his own image."

While Talleyrand was well on his way toward convincing the world that Napoleon was power-hungry, I often wondered whether Talleyrand did not fit that description equally well. But once, when I dared infer it, it was met with a shouted denial, a personal tirade against me and days of silence between us. But Talleyrand would soon have another turn to exhibit his competence. The world was going to be remade according to my beloved's vision, and the Congress of Vienna would be his instrument.

CHAPTER 30

▼

In the summer of 1812, as I vacationed in the south of France with my sisters, my two children, and attending servants, Napoleon invaded Russia with 400,000 soldiers, high spirits, and great expectations. His soldiers' faith in their emperor was sacrosanct, as if he was the creator of a new religion in which the French Grand Army was its invincible and lethal instrument. Success was the keystone of their collective belief. Failure was a possibility that was never entertained. They believed the mere mention of the potential use of the army was sufficient to frighten an enemy from the battlefield. So it seemed that June when the emperor's Grand Army attacked Russia by invading Moscow.

Upon entering the city, Napoleon found no evidence of the Russian army. Moscow was empty and burning. There were no people, no food, and no military opposition. Napoleon immediately prepared his army for an ambush, but none came. His men thought it was an easy victory.

"Too easy," some said afterwards.

The brutal Russian winter, which Napoleon had underestimated, was just beginning. As the czar had anticipated, the gentle snow flurries of autumn accelerated into an avalanche of winter misery. Freezing temperatures took their toll on the Grand Army, as did frostbite, hunger, and unexpected attacks on retreating French soldiers by Cossacks on horseback, hidden in the dense woods surrounding Moscow. Of the 400,000 soldiers of the Grand Army who began the Russian campaign with Napoleon, only 30,000 returned to France alive.

For several months prior to the invasion, Napoleon had tried to negotiate a new peace treaty with the czar, but with no success. Once Napoleon entered an abandoned Moscow, it was obvious to Talleyrand, if not yet to Napoleon, that the czar had no need for negotiations. He was counting on the Russian winter to decimate Napoleon's forces.

Would I be a traitor to Talleyrand's place in history to divulge that the strategic mistake Napoleon made was one that Talleyrand had hoped for? I was appalled when Talleyrand related the facts of the army's difficulties with obvious good cheer. We sat on a bench in the garden behind Talleyrand's home while Edmond sipped sherry in the salon with his family. I physically recoiled when Talleyrand boasted he had encouraged Napoleon to undertake an expedition that would end in such tragedy. As callous as it may sound, my beloved had become convinced the only way to stop Napoleon was to guide him toward military defeat. To Talleyrand's amazement, the defeat was still not sufficient to stop Napoleon from attacking the Prussian King of Saxony. But here I race too quickly ahead of my story.

Despite history's claim that Napoleon was a great general, my beloved always insisted he was brutal toward his soldiers and callous about their well-being. During the last years of his life, between our morning coffee and our walks together in the gardens surrounding Valençay, Talleyrand obsessively studied the wars in which Napoleon had engaged.

"Over three million French dead," he would mutter repeatedly with a mixture of remorse and astonishment. *"C'est un merde que est un egoiste! Il s'en foux des autres, surtout ses soldat!"* This piece of shit is an egoist! He doesn't give a damn about anyone, especially his own soldiers!

Upon his return from Russia, Napoleon convened his ministers in a meeting room at the Tuileries palace and invited Talleyrand to attend. After an hour of bombast coming from the emperor and feeble excuses for answers being returned by his ministers, Napoleon focused his words on his former foreign minister.

"You must negotiate with the czar." Napoleon ordered Talleyrand. "Today you have something with which to bargain. Tomorrow you may have nothing."

"Will you then take my advice? Or am I simply being used as a fig leaf to cover other intentions?" Talleyrand retorted, eager to humiliate Napoleon in front of his ministers.

"For such insolence, I could have you executed!"

"That prerogative, Your Excellency, you have always possessed. My neck has become sufficiently supple. Your hangman will have no problem in executing me."

"Tu m'en bets?" You make me crazy! Napoleon screamed at him.

"I will assist you in the negotiations on the condition that you withdraw your troops to the boundaries I previously negotiated with the Austrians, Prussians, and British."

"How dare you give me preconditions!"

"If I don't prepare you now, then I have failed to begin to advise you properly."

Silence reigned until Napoleon dismissed his ministers, but he asked Talleyrand to reseat himself at the table, opposite him.

"You choose to humiliate me in front of my ministers so you can show them that Napoleon Bonaparte is no match for Maurice-Charles de Talleyrand-Perigord," Napoleon began, less harsh than Talleyrand expected.

"I apologize for my poor manners, my emperor, if that is how my advice appears to you!" Talleyrand realized the emperor was not dismissing his advice out of hand.

The minutes of silence that went by were deafening. Napoleon began to pace again. Talleyrand shined the gold knob of his cane with his handkerchief.

"I want you to return to the ministry of foreign affairs!"

"I cannot," Talleyrand replied brusquely. "I am no longer well-acquainted with the affairs of Your Majesty."

"You hypocrite," Napoleon hissed, "you know them well enough!" He stared into Talleyrand's eyes and saw nothing but scorn and calculation. "You are planning to betray me!"

"No, sire, I am not. But I also cannot assume the position of foreign minister," Talleyrand responded in his most compassionate, seductive voice, "because, in my humble opinion, your policies are contrary to my own conception of what is needed for the glory and happiness of our country."

"What if I order you, as your emperor?"

"Then it would neither satisfy me to do my best for you nor make you confident that your policies, which I have already told you I do not agree with, would be properly executed."

"Do you not understand that it is France that needs you now? Not only I?"

"Your Excellency, I fully comprehend the terrible situation you have placed France in at this very moment!"

"And you delight in that realization?"

"Not at all! But, as you have ridden the tide of French adulation, you must be willing to accept its condemnation. I think I speak for France when I state your unwillingness to make the country part of the group of nations that want to avert war."

"You have misread all, my arrogant man," Napoleon rifled through several papers on the table and handed Talleyrand a document. "I have received news that…"

"…Prussia signed an alliance with Russia and has declared war on France!" Talleyrand finished Napoleon's sentence.

"So, it is not only true that you are wrong in your assessment of the warlike desires of other countries, but you have spies all over my government!"

"The French government belongs neither to me nor you! It belongs to the French people."

"So, will you help me and your French people?"

"I am afraid it may be too late for my help." Talleyrand's voice was firm, as if he was lecturing a recalcitrant student. "The Confederation of the Rhine that you yourself helped to create among several states is in the process of dissolving. Saxony, one of those states and once a reliable ally, has withdrawn from its alliance with France."

He paused to assess Napoleon's response. Talleyrand calculated it was time that he not be spared the details of the consequences of his pyrrhic military victories.

"With all due respect, sire, your military adventures have facilitated an amalgam of countries that want to destroy, once and for all, the infamous General Napoleon Bonaparte. That means they are also intent on destroying France."

"I don't need to be lectured to by…"

"Your anger is directed toward the wrong target, Your Excellency! What I have told you was said not with malice, but with concern for your own personal future and, more importantly, the future of France."

Talleyrand's gestures, as well as his words, tried not to betray his feeling that Napoleon's love of self far outranked Napoleon's love for his adopted country. But, my beloved was convinced that maintaining the charade was to win the day.

"How are you so capable of making me so angry one minute and the next minute feeling as if I should fall on my knees and beg your forgiveness?"

"As you have pointed out many times, over our many years together, I am a defrocked priest, so I am not able to offer you absolution!"

"Your words are more lethal than any lancer's sword."

"The reality of the heinous situation you have created through your impetuous nature is far more lethal to our countrymen than any words I have uttered or deeds I have done."

Talleyrand refused to stop reprimanding Napoleon. It was my beloved's turn to appear victorious. "At this very moment, Austria is teetering between remaining neutral or joining the coalition against us. England is offering any country substantial subsidies to declare war on France."

At long last, Talleyrand stopped.

Napoleon began to pace the room again. When he showed no sign of continuing the conversation, my beloved rose to leave.

"I leave you to consider what I have said."

Talleyrand hobbled out of the room, forgetting his cane in the excitement of having spoken so boldly, unclear whether Napoleon's anger toward him would subside or whether his words about the need for reconciliation with the warring powers surrounding France would have been futile. Of one thing he was sure, war would beget more war, and France would be the ultimate loser. If Napoleon would not desist in his attacks on neighboring states, there was nothing that Talleyrand could do except help to overthrow him. My beloved recalled he spent the next three days and nights secluded in his home with headaches, awaiting word of Napoleon's decision.

True to his nature, and despite his appealing words about negotiation, I have already recorded that Napoleon had the Grand Army strike Saxony. He won a brilliant victory even though his troops were significantly outnumbered. Saxony was defeated and accepted an imposed alliance with France.

The victory, however, might now be seen as the beginning of the end for Napoleon. Although I gain on my story, by 1814, just as Talleyrand had predicted, without a treaty with its neighbors, France was irrevocably defeated. The armies of Prussia marched upon Paris. England's duke of Wellington advanced into France from the south. Napoleon was confronted with an ultimatum by the allies that he withdraw to France's original boundaries. By April, Napoleon had abdicated, and the map of France was smaller than at the beginning of Napoleon's fifteen years in power.

When Talleyrand left Napoleon pacing the room at the Tuileries and had not received any further messages from him, he concluded his emperor's days in power were limited and only the return of the Bourbon kings would fill the eventual political vacuum. It was a conclusion he came to with a heavy heart, as he wrote in his diary:

> France, in the midst of these invasions, cannot be respected. Only the return
> of the House of Bourbon can provide some legitimacy to the country. Europe,
> uneasy, wishes France to disarm and resume its former boundaries so that

peace would no longer need constantly to be guarded. The House of Bourbon alone can lift the bloody veil from the eyes of the French nation, so jealous of its military glory, to see the reverses that have befallen her flag. The House of Bourbon alone can cause the foreign armies that cover the soil of France to be withdrawn. The House of Bourbon alone can avert the vengeance that twenty years of violence has stored up against our country.

Consistent with both his beliefs and his statecraft, Talleyrand sent an envoy to the Bourbon king, offering him his personal allegiance if Napoleon was dethroned and his aid in promoting the king as head of France.

Weeks later, as Parisians began to flee the city in advance of foreign forces marching against it, Napoleon screamed at his most trusted aid, his brother Joseph, "If our forces have to evacuate Paris and Talleyrand attempts to persuade the empress to remain in the city, you will know he is plotting to overthrow the Bonaparte dynasty. Beware of that man. He is the greatest enemy of our house."

CHAPTER 31

▼

Dispensing with his habit of sleeping until eleven each morning, Talleyrand rose early in preparation for his fourth visit from Czar Alexander. He powdered his white wig, applied light rouge on both cheeks and added facial powder. Today, the czar was making his formal entrance into Paris as the leader of the military alliance that had defeated Napoleon, and he was soon to appear at Talleyrand's house on Rue St. Florentin.

At the age of twenty-eight, I was wise enough and interested enough to want to observe the czar's procession and can rely on my own recollection of how the day transpired. Edmond had brought me to the parade site near the point at which the dignitaries were expected to arrive. We had been married for seven years, and Edmond was still trying to impress me with his worldly knowledge, indulging in a long, dry speech about history being made this day. At this point in our married life, he had no knowledge of my periodic meetings with Talleyrand over the years or the extent to which my education in international matters had now superceded his own.

My husband was a curious sight to behold. He was not unattractive, but he was over-preened and extravagantly dressed in a ruffled shirt and *cravat*, which he insisted was the bellwether taste of a fashionable. Both overpowered his small frame. During his discourse, I did not know which was more inclined to wander, his undisciplined mind or his eye, which surveyed the fluttering skirts of the girls lining the nearby street.

A hush fell over the crowd at the expected moment. Only the clacking sound of horses' hooves could be heard as the czar rode on horseback through the Arc de Triomphe. He was elegantly dressed in an all-white uniform that (to his chagrin I am sure) was unable to disguise his considerable waist that was tightened by a girdle hidden by a vast, black belt. His narrow shoulders were expanded by his uniform and disguised by glistening epaulets of gold.

Given the hindsight with which I now write, I still find it difficult to believe that, after accepting Napoleon as the romantic savior of France, I was now as eager for Napoleon's demise (as was Talleyrand) and was mesmerized by Czar Alexander and his entourage. Surrounding the czar were Cossacks of the Imperial Guard with their sheepskins, lances, and thick, red beards. Bashkirs were armed with bows and arrows. Circassians were dressed in shining coats of steel mail and tall, pointed hats. Of course, it was Talleyrand who later identified which men (or should I say officers barely out of their childhood) belonged to which tribe. Then again, it was Talleyrand who completed my education in so many areas.

The czar's supporters were immediately followed by a scrawny-looking Frederik William, King of Prussia, also on horseback and with a retinue of guards, who went completely unnoticed by the onlookers. Prince Metternich of Austria, of whom Talleyrand had frequently spoken, was a lithe man of unobtrusive features who rode in a handsome, gilded carriage. Viscount Castleraegh, the British foreign minister, a portly, obdurate man with a colicky temperament, according to Talleyrand, peered through his carriage window and muttered profanities.

"Damn these temperamental whores they call the 'citizens of France.' They are nothing but lecherous, debauched, ignorant peasants, elevated in stature by a few intellectuals."

Behind Castleraegh's contingent followed ministers, generals, representatives of the allied powers, and a cluster of lesser noblemen.

All were there for the same reason—to create a permanent peace treaty that would establish the boundaries of the nation-states that had been obliterated by Napoleon's adventurism. Most of Europe now considered the French a warlike people, Talleyrand frequently reminded me, because of Napoleon's successes. Each head of state in Europe now distrusted the French and wanted to minimize France's role on the continent. The Congress of Vienna, to be planned over the next few weeks, was to return a balance of power to the continent. Had anyone told me that I would also appear in Vienna on my uncle's arm, I would have laughed and laughed at the suggestion…and then hoped it to be true.

At the moment of the czar's dramatic entrance on that sunny day in March, it seemed that he alone was to be the arbiter of both France and Europe's destiny. It was Russia, in large part, which had stopped the Corsican-turned-Frenchman who had created the greatest hegemony since Rome had ruled the world.

Many citizens of the city were sufficiently awed by the procession to doff their hats at the czar's approach. To these humble admirers, he responded with a bow and a wave of his plump, dimpled hand.

The Parisians whispered, "How handsome he is. How gracefully he bows."

Edmond merely thrust his chest forward, like some kind of rooster, proud to yield to the czar's imposing presence, but he was certainly too insignificant to be noticed by him.

As the allies made their victorious entry into Paris, Talleyrand was placing the finishing touches upon a proclamation to the people of the city that he thought Czar Alexander should soon deliver. As promised, after reviewing the troops in the Champs Elysees, the czar appeared at Rue St. Florentin. The two men conferred in Talleyrand's salon, a place where my beloved offered fine conversation and frequently made his greatest diplomatic (and sexual) conquests. On the highly polished, oak side table stood small dishes of pheasant, quail, *foie gras*, fruits from Valençay, and an assortment of pastries to sweeten their conversation.

"Count Talleyrand," the czar said, making his selection from the dishes, "you know France, its needs and its desires. You have my confidence and that of my allies. We will settle nothing until we have heard your views. Tell me what we should do, and your words will be heard by all."

Talleyrand had heard these words spoken by this man before. The czar was a master of rhetorical excess, as his career had proven. Yet, my beloved believed that beneath the czar's exaggerated *façade*, was someone who was sincere and well-intentioned. He was smart enough to understand that, as an outsider, he could not ascertain the wishes of the French people.

For historical purposes, I must note that there were many times in Talleyrand's life when he had doubts about the decisions he made and the strategies he pursued. Rest assured, this was not one of those times. This was the moment he had been waiting for, a moment he knew that would determine the course of history. Czar Alexander was the most powerful of all the allied sovereigns, and he was listening to my beloved about the direction France must take. He was acting just as Talleyrand had hoped, and, if I were presumptuous, I would have to say it was just as Talleyrand had planned.

"Your Bourbon king is old-fashioned, antiquated, bombastic, and, worst of all, incompetent." Czar Alexander repeated an opinion he had given at previous meetings with Talleyrand. "In the matter of royal succession, the allies are in full agreement. We must eliminate the Bourbon dynasty entirely from French politics."

Czar Alexander wondered whether Talleyrand realized he was expressing his personal feelings and not those of his allies.

"Then whom would you propose for the French line of succession, Your Excellency?" Talleyrand asked ingeniously, wondering how he could get the czar to alter his opinion.

"Let us substitute the young king of Rome to succeed as Napoleon II under the regency of Marie-Louise."

Talleyrand was stunned. They had had this very same conversation only days before. Didn't the czar yet realize the insanity of this idea?

"The French are used to the Bourbon dynasty, Your Excellency." Talleyrand persevered. "Stupidity and incompetence have never impeded the rule of any nation. While you know I concur with your assessment, bypassing the Bourbon dynasty would be a grave mistake."

"The French crown could be given to Bernadette, Crown Prince of Sweden," the czar offered, somewhat weakly.

"I'm sorry to say that Sweden would be too foreign, if not repugnant, to the French people."

"Eugene de Beauharnais?" Czar Alexander was obviously frustrated with Talleyrand's negation of his suggestions. "Perhaps the crown rightfully belongs to the duke of Orleans, head of the cadet branch of the Bourbons."

"Neither you, sire, nor I," Talleyrand responded quietly, "can or should impose a king upon France."

"With all due respect to your important personage, France is a conquered country."

"That is true, Your Excellency," Talleyrand responded defensively. "But, even though you are the conqueror of this country, I must inform you that you do not have the power to impose a line of succession *ad hominem*."

"Count Talleyrand." Czar Alexander's face was flushing again. "I am afraid you are treading on the very dangerous ground of insubordination."

"I am aware of that, sire," Talleyrand responded forcefully, "but I would be doing you and your allies a great disservice if we did not create a durable state of affairs, a state based upon principle."

He paused long enough to see the anger leave the czar's face and some intellectual interest return.

"With principle, we are strong. There will be no resistance. And there is only one principle by which to settle matters."

"And what may that be?"

"The principle of 'legitimacy' is the cornerstone of peace, and that requires the restoration of a French dynasty. Louis XVIII is the embodiment of that principle. He is the legitimate king of France."

"How are you so certain that France desires to recall the House of Bourbon?"

"It is the wish expressed by the only body that can speak in the name of the people." Talleyrand had anticipated the question. "I will take it upon myself to have a declaration made by the Senate. Your Majesty will see the effect immediately."

"You are certain?"

"I will guarantee it," Talleyrand proclaimed with the self-assurance that only a seasoned diplomat or successful liar could muster.

After Czar Alexander departed, apparently persuaded the restoration of the Bourbons was a necessary evil, Talleyrand could not contain his delight. As he had stood talking with the czar, the most powerful man in the world, he had thought of his own preceding forty years, punctuated by periods of activity and inaction, humiliation and success, danger and adventure, confusion and skillful planning, good luck and bad luck. All melded into this one moment of history in which he and the czar would determine the fate of not only France, but of the entire continent.

Talleyrand felt he was at the zenith of his career. He held a position more powerful and more responsible than he had ever held before. Destiny had passionately embraced him. There was only one man to whom the allies looked for guidance, and that was my beloved.

The result of this meeting was a manifest written April 1,1814, by Talleyrand and signed by Czar Alexander. In it, the allies agreed they would respect the integrity of the French territories as well as any legitimate king. They invited what remained of the French Senate to appoint a provisional government to draw up a new constitution the allies would review and, assumedly, accept.

Two days later, Talleyrand convened the Senate under his own sponsorship and persuaded his colleagues, those who had not fled to London for fear of execution, that they must release themselves from the pledge of allegiance to their emperor. He informed them that the allies had invited the Senate to draw up a new constitution. Using charm and shielded threats, my beloved persuaded them to appoint a provisional government with him as its president. The following day, the Senate formally offered the throne of France to the count of Provence, Louis XVIII.

Looking back on that period, as exciting a time as it was for my beloved, it was also a time that forever changed my life. No less deftly than he negotiated with

Czar Alexander, Talleyrand began a negotiation with me. One evening, at a festive gathering in his home, with a salon filled with admirers oohing and aahing over his collection of Egyptian artifacts, he called me aside. As we stood in the privacy of his cobblestone courtyard, he asked me a question that would forever change my world and his. Would I accompany him to Vienna for the Congress being planned? All the rulers of the world would be attending. Without giving me a moment to think, he continued quickly, as if his statements had been well-rehearsed. He said he needed a hostess. He said he needed someone to arrange the balls and someone to circulate gaily. He said he needed someone with eyes and ears open to all that was transpiring.

My immediate response was more naïve than I intended, but it was also sincere. "Why do you ask this of a woman married to your nephew? You have a wife."

"Because you are the most beautiful woman in Paris. And, over these past few years, I have learned to respect and trust you. We have discussed many things, and I find you well-educated in worldly matters. You have proved to be a good listener and an excellent interpreter of my ideas. I have also observed how well you put people at their ease," he responded.

"Is that all?" I asked, almost in a faint. Could it be true? Was this the person I had managed to become, despite the boring, wifely role I had played these many years?

"For now," he said without changing his expression.

The look in his eyes, the splendor of the occasion, and, I must admit, the chance to escape from Edmond and my marriage made going to Vienna at the request of the most respected man in France an intriguing opportunity. It was a dizzying time. I had to think, plan, and, ultimately, pack. I dreamed of Vienna every night.

CHAPTER 32

▼

On April 4,1814, the day government power was to be transferred, the Senate's representative, the count of Artois, visited Talleyrand at his home. Artois was elegantly dressed in a green satin jacket with a white crinoline shirt so stiff that he was always forced to keep his chin fixed in an uncomfortable position looking upwards at Talleyrand. He was embarrassed to find that, at mid-morning, Talleyrand was still in bed with his papers in hand, drawing up the details for the initiation ceremony of the new Bourbon regime.

Artois looked about the bedroom with its beveled mirrors in intricately carved gilt frames and its large paintings of naked women in provocative positions. He wondered, I am sure, whether one particular painting, characterized by lusty, frenetic exuberance, could be a Peter Paul Rubens. Or was he wondering how my beloved's bedroom, as I am wont to admit, came to look more like a bordello than the residence of a statesman? Talleyrand seemed to be in no rush to leave his bed and, according to my beloved, Artois was forced to speak to a prone man who lounged in his finest silk pajamas.

I found a very interesting passage in one of Count Artois' letters given to me after Talleyrand's death, in which he discussed that fateful visit. I quote the letter because it reveals so much about Talleyrand's style of work despite the nasty rumors being spread by others. Artois wrote:

> Even in this embarrassing situation, or perhaps because of it, I overcame my awe of this famous statesman for his reputation was far more imposing than his demeanor. He was easygoing, jovial even. Phantoms disappeared when close to him. It was in the simplest manner that Count de Talleyrand let fall the remarks to which he attached the greatest importance. He appeared to sow

these words carelessly, like the seed that nature scatters. But, unlike in nature, where most seeds perish without issue, each of his words had a purpose."

The reason for this meeting in my beloved's *boudoir* was of a very urgent nature. Artois was bringing news that, while Napoleon was under house arrest, he had called a meeting of several marshals of France, proposing that the 20,000 men under their command come together to drive the allies from Paris and reestablish his regime.

Artois reported the marshals "had sat like birds without tongues when Napoleon raved and proffered his plan. Still, these same birds, by their silence, conveyed more than adequately their opposition to any renewal of the campaign."

Napoleon, Artois continued, not blind to his marshals' opposition, offered a counter-proposal. He would abdicate in favor of his son, the King of Rome. As the emperor expected, once he no longer presented himself as holding the reigns of power, the marshals were no longer against him. In fact, Marshal Macdonald and Marshal Ney had already spoken with Czar Alexander, who was amenable to Napoleon's suggestion, his one-time friend and ally, of whom he still had fond memories.

Upon hearing this, my beloved rushed to the czar's temporary headquarters to dissuade him from believing the marshals, who were spouting nothing more than Napoleon's self-serving arguments. The czar, Talleyrand knew, tended to alter his opinion, depending upon who was last to whisper in his ear.

Czar Alexander met Talleyrand in the library. Though it was the middle of the day, the velvet curtains were drawn, and the sun, straining to get through its heavy creases, gave the room the shading of twilight.

"Your Excellency," Talleyrand began in an offensively firm tone, "I understand Napoleon is trying to create a regency for his son, the young king of Rome."

"You heard correctly," Czar Alexander responded. "Napoleon's marshals have assured me that a regency arrangement would end Napoleon's ability to make war. Yet, it would avoid the reintroduction of those Bourbon incompetents."

"Did these marshals also guarantee they can control Napoleon?"

"Did you, yourself, not negotiate and sign important treaties for him?"

"Yes, sire," Talleyrand responded, certain that what he and the czar had agreed to days earlier may already have been undone.

"Have you such little respect for the man who allowed you to redraw the boundaries of Europe?"

"I guarantee, sire, that, if power is given to his son, within one year, Napoleon himself will be in total control of both the civilian and military sector of the French government."

"How can you be so certain?"

"It is in his character. He can no more cease from amassing power than you or I can cease from seducing an attractive woman. Within a year, Napoleon will precipitate another war."

The czar said nothing, obviously confused.

"Sire, the only hope for the recovery of France and for the peace of Europe is to restore the Bourbon dynasty," Talleyrand continued. "I remind you this was your decision only days ago."

Czar Alexander took a few, long minutes to think and then responded as Talleyrand hoped he would. "Your arguments are compelling, as usual. I did conclude that Napoleon must abdicate, and I have heard nothing of such import to alter my judgment."

"That is a wise decision, Your Excellency." Talleyrand bowed his head in false humility. "But we must act quickly before Napoleon has a chance to act against us."

"Of course, of course. But, while we shall deprive him of his armies, we shall not deprive him of all hope of existence," Czar Alexander said, his compassion for his old friend obvious. "We shall give him a kingdom of his own."

"What sort of kingdom?" Talleyrand could barely suppress his anger. What more could he say to convince the czar that Napoleon was dangerous? Abdication was merely the first part of a process. Execution should be next, as it had been good enough for the king and Marie-Antoinette. While he sat wondering what it would take to steer the czar to a proper course of action, the czar answered his question.

"What do you think of exile to Corsica?"

'Too dangerous. He was born there. A new insurrection could well begin there with a returning prodigal son."

Talleyrand wondered how the czar could even have thought this an appropriate resolution. It was Napoleon's own birth isle.

"Sardinia?"

"Too close to France. Also, it is populated with Napoleon's sympathizers."

"Corfu? I don't know. Where do you think he should be sent?"

"I believe our prior conversation pinpointed the island of Elba!" Talleyrand answered, finally realizing the czar wanted Talleyrand to take responsibility for the location. "It is a large area, and there are inhabitants on the island with whom he could preoccupy himself."

Czar Alexander moved around the room as if heavy in thought. Nothing in the room moved. When a light breeze entered through the windows, even the dust on the thick curtains remained fixed. After five minutes of silence, my beloved took the initiative.

"Sire, should I assume Napoleon Bonaparte will be exiled to the island of Elba? It takes a week to reach the island by boat from France. Shall I start making preparations?"

Czar Alexander walked over to Talleyrand's chair and extended his long, thin hand, one finger bearing a golden ring with double eagles. "I often wonder what I would have done without your assistance throughout the Bonaparte madness that has destroyed nearly half of Europe."

"You are too gracious, Your Excellency," Talleyrand responded, kissing the ring to reinforce the symbolism of this contrived physical act of both contrition and gratitude. He felt an actor, performing on behalf of his countrymen. But, this seeming act of submission was endowing him with a legitimacy that, even if an illusion, had the aspect of reality. And, legitimacy, as my beloved knew, would be required for him to remain in the political arena.

Before Talleyrand's departure, Czar Alexander put into writing the declaration that would be passed to Napoleon, informing him he was being exiled to Elba.

When I reviewed my beloved's notes, I have to be honest and state that not everyone agreed Elba was the correct place of exile.

Over glasses of claret at Talleyrand's house one evening, Fouche said, "Napoleon should be sent to the land of the Franklins, the Washingtons, and the Jeffersons, an appropriate place for exile, considering he would have an association of revolutionaries with whom he has a lot in common."

Metternich, who had come to France prior to going to the Congress of Vienna, thought sending Napoleon to Elba was inviting a war within three years. Although Talleyrand had great respect for Metternich, he felt the sooner Napoleon was exiled from France, the less likely it would be that the czar would change his mind, and the safer it would be for the Bourbon king to return. And, if King Louis XVIII felt grateful and saw fit to make Talleyrand his primary international statesman, my beloved would not decline the honor.

It was at this time that Talleyrand manipulated Edmond in a way that bore the markings of his dealings with Napoleon. He led Edmond to his own disaster without my poor husband ever knowing what was happening. During an informal social gathering of the family at Talleyrand's home, he simply said to

Edmond, in a matter-of-fact way, "I am thinking of taking Dorothea with me to Vienna to act as my hostess. Care for some plums?"

Edmond, the fool, took the plums.

Normal social protocol would have required Talleyrand to choose his wife as his hostess. But, Talleyrand was as practical as he was opportunistic and understood all too well that Catherine would be a liability at a time when it was crucial to court success in every way he could. By 1814, Catherine had become an overweight, overdressed, gossipy woman who spent her days dreaming of her former beauty and her evenings boasting of it. The beauty that once obscured her absence of wit and intelligence had now disappeared. Attendees of the elite social parlors of Paris would relate to one another the absurdities they had heard from Catherine's lips. Noblemen and their mistresses placed bets on the number of *faux pas,* mistakes, she would make at a particular reception. Talleyrand, always the gentleman, ignored such talk with his usual imperturbable calm. But, if truth be known, he continually berated himself for having allowed Napoleon to persuade him to marry such an obviously inadequate woman.

When my beloved concluded Catherine was ill-suited to be his consort in Vienna, he scanned the social horizon for someone he felt he could trust to fulfill his social obligations there. If this Congress was to determine the destiny of France, Talleyrand was determined to offer it France's most beautiful face and clever head—or so he told me. Looking back to that time, I was dreadfully naïve. My beloved truly convinced me that no other person except I would suffice for that role.

Years later, when pressed for details, he added more sobering reasons for his decision. Although impressed by my youthful charm, he was also enamored by the social advantages I brought with me that could be of service to him. First, he knew the Prussian royal family was friends of my parents. Second, he knew the czar was an intimate of my mother's. Third, he saw roles for each of my three sisters, strategically placing them in Vienna to transmit information daily. Wilhelmina, duchess of Sagan, was to be a lover of Prince Metternich's and should aspire to the position of his exclusive mistress. Pauline, princess of Hohenzollern-Hechingen, already had a husband among the sovereign princes and a lover among the leading negotiators. Jeanne, duchess of Acerenza, was a designated candidate for the bed of Baron Friedrich von Gentz, secretary-general to the Congress and an unerring source of well-informed gossip.

I have no doubt that my beloved's detractors would decry his approach to selecting a hostess as one more example of his unabashed opportunism. Yet, perhaps the opportunism was as much mine as his. To me, it epitomized much that I grew to respect about how he made his decisions. Once he knew what he wanted, he used all of his skills and resources to acquire it. Of course, it is easier to say this now, twenty years later, when I no longer doubt the sincerity of his love.

CHAPTER 33

▼

All of Europe knew the Congress of Vienna would determine the fate of western Europe for decades to come, and Talleyrand was concerned that France would retain its rightful place. Representing a defeated country that had been the aggressor, he knew he possessed very little leverage. So, his days and nights were spent thinking about how to create a sense of legitimacy for France where only defeat and resentment existed among the allies.

On April 29,1814, King Louis XVIII arrived in France from England and went straight to a meeting at Compiegne that was being held to plan for the Congress. To Talleyrand, the king's presence on French soil was essential for anything Talleyrand negotiated with the allies to be viewed as legitimate.

Once Catherine heard of my invitation to accompany her husband to Vienna, she spent the next several weeks pouting and complaining to anyone who would listen that Talleyrand was a miserable husband and poor lover. Against this background of gossip, I made my formal acceptance.

Those were marvelous days. I was caught up in a swoon of daydreams in which I was finally a free woman. Free from the boring gossip of Parisian salons. Free from a boring husband. Excited to be close to those who were planning a new era for France. My decision to marry Edmond had not been based on love. While it is still difficult to admit it these many years later, our time together was sustained only by a lifestyle to which I was accustomed and needed. My children held some interest for me when newborn, but, by the time the youngest had reached two years of age, I had grown as tired of them, as I had of Edmond. There, I have said it. I was selfish for life. I loved my children, but I did not need them. I trusted they would be well cared for as they grew, for the house was filled with governesses and tutors. They would grow in many ways. If I remained at home, I would not. Yes, I lived with feelings of guilt throughout my life. But Talleyrand understood me and did not think any less of me for my decision. My children, if you ask them today, forgave me when they grew to maturity. At least my daughter did.

I had also tired of life in Paris. Although Talleyrand's invitation was to fulfill a needed role during the Congress, my decision to accept it signaled to the social world that the breakup of my union with Count Edmond of Perigord was inevitable. Talleyrand was already notorious as a libertine. I would be considered as opportunistic as he, and perhaps I was.

Although Edmond soon met with Talleyrand to ask him many questions about the nature of the services I was to perform, in the privacy of our own home, he asked me if I didn't agree his uncle was a turncoat who would betray anyone to safeguard his own interests. I am pleased to record for posterity that my response was swift and sure. I told Edmond I had no doubt Talleyrand's interests were the same as those of France. Yes, he had helped to depose of Napoleon, but he had also obtained from the allies the return of the Bourbons. Yes, he had become the head of the provisional government, but that only ensured that France would play a determining role in its own future.

I could not have made it more clear to Edmond that there was no one I so admired as his uncle. If he, Edmond, had any intelligence on matters of state, he would be pleased for Talleyrand's successes. Even I, still unschooled in governmental intrigues, had thought it an ill omen when Napoleon had taken up residence in the Tuileries and installed himself in the apartments of King Louis XVI. Did Edmond not care about the entire armies of men that were needlessly killed in so many military campaigns? As I spoke these words...no, almost yelled them...I realized I had already become someone Edmond no longer knew.

In order to minimize the vitriolic rumors being spread in the salons, Talleyrand and I made every effort to be discreet, meeting in a country house eight miles north of Paris to talk and plan. It is only now, as I look back on that frenetic period of my life, do I realize Catherine knew from the day her husband and I departed for Vienna that she would never see Talleyrand again. In time, she would be banished from his house, and I would be labeled an adulteress.

King Louis XVIII's arrival did not come without a modicum of suspense. The new monarch's visit was delayed by an extremely painful bout of gout. When my beloved finally met the king, however, Talleyrand was ecstatic for he was treated with kindness and, he imagined, deference.

Shortly after that meeting, he and the czar met mid-afternoon at Rue St. Florentin. Talleyrand was enthusiastic, relating his encounter to an attentive czar who had not yet met King Louis. There was a chill in the air, and the men sat close to the fireplace in the library, like two old friends. My beloved adopted an air of conviviality and intimacy, though he later told me his mind never relaxed that entire afternoon.

"So, you were content with your new king?" asked the czar.

"Content, Your Excellency, is not the proper word," Talleyrand responded. "Monsieur Duras escorted me to the king's study. Upon seeing me, the king held out his hand in the most cordial manner and spoke words that were so very kind to my ear. He said, 'I am exceedingly pleased to see you. Our houses date from the same epoch. It was simply fate that made my ancestors the cleverer of our two families. If yours had ascended more so than mine, it would be you who would be asking me to take a chair, draw near, and let us speak of our common affairs. But, today it is I who say it to you, let us sit down and talk.'"

Talleyrand paused, as happy with the memory of that meeting as he was amused by the king's words. "I then gave the king an account of the state in which he would find France. That first conversation was a very long one indeed."

"As beginnings go, it sounds as if it started well. I wonder whether your king understands how important you were in orchestrating his return," the czar asked.

"You are prescient, Your Excellency. The king thanked me for all past considerations and support and charged me with drawing up a proclamation on the subject of the constitutional charter to be promulgated before his entrance into Paris."

"Then I will pay a visit to your king, just to make certain he understands the importance of the terms of the agreement that you and your colleagues will put to paper."

After Czar Alexander left, Talleyrand was too excited to do his customary letters. Instead, he sat in his courtyard, surveying the hearty vines climbing its brick walls and sipping a glass of claret. Why shouldn't he have his own small celebration? He had accomplished what no other man in France could have done. With the art of statecraft—persuasion, flattery, intimidation, and innuendo—he had been able to rid France of Napoleon, select a new king, gain the loyalty of the army for this king, restore the right of law with a new constitutional charter, and have France included in the Congress of Vienna along with its conquerors. He took another sip and smiled. It was he, not Napoleon, who had survived the Napoleonic era. He wondered whether Napoleon thought exile would be worth the price of having had the obelisk brought to France from his Egyptian campaign, that monolithic stone monument of huge proportions residing very close to my beloved's residence at Place de la Concorde. Talleyrand took a last sip and went inside.

Talleyrand was predetermined to like Prince Metternich for all the kind words he had already uttered in his behalf. In person, he was a tall, lean, distinguished-looking man who exuded both the aristocratic refinement and *noblesse* with which my beloved felt comfortable. From what he had heard of the Austrian chancellor, he was *un homme distingue*, a distinguished man—judicious, shrewd, and of moderate temperament. To be honest, my beloved recognized within Metternich the traits he admired most about himself.

Once again, Talleyrand arranged a mid-afternoon meeting at Rue St. Florentin. The weather was surprisingly pleasant, so they walked through Talleyrand's well-tended gardens as they spoke. The Austrian chancellor, Talleyrand discovered, preferred the cool outdoor breezes, especially to logs they could not get to burn in the library.

"As you might imagine," Talleyrand began, "there will be major issues to discuss in Vienna concerning post-war France. I am told the Russians are insistent upon having the Bourbon dynasty and King Louis XVIII restored to the leadership of France."

"Both by nature and disposition," Metternich responded. "I am a man who deplores unnecessary battles. Whatever the czar might want, I will err on the side of complying with him. Otherwise, we will be wasting a lot of time."

Talleyrand smiled inwardly. Metternich's response gave no hint of suspicion that he knew my beloved had crafted the new Bourbon role, but Talleyrand had to make sure.

"Am I correct to assume you are in accord with the principle of the legitimacy of royalty as necessary for national stability?"

"Count Talleyrand," Metternich answered in French tinged with a guttural German accent, "I am not a man who believes in scholastic exercises. I am very practical. We won the war. France lost the war. Napoleon must leave. If France wants a king, it is of no concern to me—so long as he does not interfere with the internal affairs of Austria. That is the only principle I believe in. However..." Metternich took his time, as if he could not find the proper French words. "I have very little faith in the permanence of your king."

"Why?"

"Because he is known to be weak and lazy and was never present in France at crucial times," Metternich responded bluntly. "Napoleon was our enemy. But he at least was courageous, forceful, and understood how to lead his army."

"In principle then, you would prefer to have Napoleon Bonaparte rule France rather than King Louis?"

"In principle, yes. I believe that force is the most effective form of diplomacy. Maintaining the relative balance of power among the major countries to be represented in Vienna might dictate a role for Napoleon."

Talleyrand was now concerned. He was beginning to develop an understanding of Metternich that would be indispensable to the forthcoming negotiations, but he was not entirely sure that he liked what he saw. While pleased that Metternich preferred to withdraw from confrontation rather than engage, the prince respected force and did not want to give anyone the chance to use it over him. Metternich was neither an analytical thinker nor daring enough to be guided by principle, not even the principle of monarchy. As a result, he could become the unwitting victim of circumstance. My beloved was disappointed. Metternich's admiration of Napoleon might make it impossible for the Bourbon dynasty to be restored.

When they parted, after some desultory conversation that Talleyrand considered both unnecessary and unproductive, my beloved remained on the stone bench in his courtyard. This time a frown pinched his beautiful face.

When Talleyrand met with the British representative to the Congress, Viscount Castleraegh, the chairs before the fireplace in the library were once more the venue. Where embers flickered red under ash with the czar (and none could be lit for Metternich), for Castleraegh, the fire crackled and spread. Talleyrand took this to be a good omen. Fortunately, the viscount was a more simple man to understand than Metternich.

Castleraegh began with the pomposity of many of the British. He was a rotund man with a ruddy complexion, and he was responding to Talleyrand's general question about how he viewed Europe. "My dear count, the continent is defined by the parameters of force and legitimacy that Britain bestows upon each of the so-called European countries."

"Then Britain wants France to return to its antebellum status?"

"Precisely correct!"

"Are you aware of the forces of change that are sweeping through Europe?"

"The only forces Britain recognizes are those that try to confront her directly," Castleraegh laughed. "Those we will deal with, if we have to."

By the end of their conversation, Talleyrand had concluded Castleraegh was, quite simply, myopic in his foreign policy. He viewed Europe with blinders on. From the limited perspective of his island, he was unable to understand or appreciate the ideological transformation taking place all over the continent.

Within the grand drama being played out, Castleraegh saw only that Britain would thrive if France was forced to stay within her former borders. It was as simple as that.

"Let me summarize what I understand Britain's position *vis-à-vis* France to be," Talleyrand said as courteously as he could. "Britain would prefer the French Revolution never happened, Napoleon was an aberration of history, and France's proposed king is simply a continuation of a lineage that should have maintained its grip upon France had it not been for its own incompetence and the devastating effects of the French Revolution."

"Now I understand why you are considered a genius of statecraft. You have summarized precisely my position with the least amount of words. Quite impressive, I would say."

While my beloved's summary may have been impressive, Castleraegh's approach to international affairs was antiquated. His approach to his allies was mistrustful. Presented with a complicated situation, Castleraegh would retreat to an extremely narrow position.

The two men parted, however, on the same amiable tone that had run through their conversation. Talleyrand had tasks to look after; Castleraegh had social calls to make.

By early June, at our last meeting before going to Vienna, Talleyrand and I picnicked at the country house we used for our meetings. While I had supposed we would be talking about last-minute logistics, which were numerous, Talleyrand was infused with a passion I had never seen. He had taken stock of each of the men he would be dealing with in Vienna, and he was troubled.

"Viscount Castleraegh will be an insular empiricist. Czar Alexander will be brilliant, though mercurial. Prince Metternich will be indecisive. They are an uncontrollable lot."

"If anyone can manage them…" I started to say before I was interrupted, feeling that optimism was called for.

"You cannot imagine how my days and nights are filled," he continued, as if he had not even heard my voice. "I am spending most of my time constructing scenario after scenario, in which I take the part of each of these men and try to anticipate their reactions."

I decided to take another approach. "Do your adversaries agree with each other?"

Talleyrand looked at me as if he was seeing and hearing me for the first time that afternoon. "Brilliant, my beauty, brilliant," he remarked. He began to eat our *dejeuner* in earnest. Within the coming months, Talleyrand created a strategy of playing each ally against the others, which I like to think arose from my casual remark.

Unfortunately, we left Paris with an ill omen of what was to come in Vienna. The day after the czar had dinner with King Louis, he entered Talleyrand's house like a man possessed by a demon.

"By God, that Bourbon king of yours, for whom you have so laboriously worked, is nothing but a boor!" the czar shouted.

"What happened?"

"That man is even less pleasant than Napoleon Bonaparte," the czar responded, striding back and forth on the Persian rugs covering the floor.

"Please try to calm yourself, Your Excellency, so that I might understand what transpired."

Talleyrand, at this point, was only concerned that all the positioning of ideas and alliances he had created up to this moment would not unwind as rapidly as a cheap spool of thread.

"First of all, that..." the czar paused. He was trying to compose himself, but his face remained beet red. "First, I was shown into a tiny room in which to wait and rest. I must have remained there alone for a full ten minutes. Then I was shown into a small, poorly decorated drawing room, no better than a servant's room. With more effrontery, your king seated himself at the head of a long table in an upholstered armchair while I was given an ordinary wooden chair, without a pillow, at the other end. When I started to give my point of view on the constitutional charter we agreed to, your king proceeded to ramble on about some relatively minor social aspects of reestablishing the royal court. Before I took my leave, thoroughly frustrated at the insignificance of the meeting, the king handed me this note with reference to the constitutional charter."

Talleyrand picked up the note and read it aloud:

> After having carefully read the constitution proposed by the Senate in the Session of April 6, We are pleased to say that, although We value its fundamental principles, We are insulted by a great many of its articles, which bear signs of the haste with which they were drawn and which cannot, in their present form, become the law of the state. Being resolved to adopt a liberal constitution, but being unable to accept the one which was provided, We hereby convene for June 10 of this year the Senate and the Legislature, undertaking to place before these esteemed bodies the work We shall have accomplished with guarantees in the new constitution to be ensured by the Royal House of Bourbon.

Talleyrand looked up from the document and stared into the furious eyes of Czar Alexander. The king has decided to write his own constitution. My beloved uttered the most appropriate word he could think of, *"Merde!"*

CHAPTER 34

▼

Talleyrand frequently amused me with stories about fat, pompous, fifty-nine year-old King Louis XVIII that were whispered throughout the royal court, exemplifying attitudes that were ill-suited to the tenor of the times. Once, Talleyrand recounted, the king slipped to the floor in the midst of a large celebration at the palace and, because of his extreme obesity, was unable to raise himself. An officer of the guard rushed forward to help him, but the king was horrified and angered by this presumption.

"Non non, non, monsieur!" the king cried out, moaning on the floor, surrounded by nervous courtiers.

He stayed there for a full five minutes until the arrival of the captain of the guards, an officer whose rank was sufficient to permit him to help the king rise.

"Plus ça change, moins ça change." The more things change, the less they change. My beloved recited this many times during our years together.

Most meetings with the king took place in his lavish private quarters at Versailles, a palace Talleyrand felt was less a haven of domesticity than an ornate cage. Beyond the sweeping ambassadors' staircase and the planetary rooms, my beloved was frequently received in the *Salon de la Piax*, the Peace Room.

"My dear Count Talleyrand, it is so good to be home. It gives me such pleasure to greet you each day as your legitimate ruler. Clearly, the nobility and the people have banded together to beg me to return to France. The peace process I will oversee will have no rival among Europe's leaders."

"La droite de reigne!" Talleyrand thought in disgust.

It was the same argument he had successfully used with Czar Alexander. Only when he had used it for his own purposes, he had known it to be delusional. But self-delusion was obviously no stranger to the king. Talleyrand shuddered at his arrogance and concluded that, during their quarter century in exile, the Bourbons had learned very little. King Louis XVIII did not want to think he had returned to the throne because of my beloved's interventions, because he was the choice of the czar, or even because he was the choice of the citizens of France. He simply believed it was his due, the legitimate and indisputable successor to Louis XVII, entrusted by none other than God with the welfare of his people.

"This principle, which is the very essence of both of our heritages, will allow me to undertake the necessary changes that are required to return France to glory."

"And what would those be?"

"I would have the House of Bourbon adopt the tricolor of the Revolution."

"My admiration, Your Majesty, for a bold and important idea." Talleyrand was pleased for he had had that very same notion.

"As king, I would respect the prerogatives of the Senate." The king paused to observe Talleyrand's reaction. "I feel this would demonstrate that, as king, I accept and appreciate both the representatives of the Senate and their role in my government."

"I once again applaud you, Your Majesty." Talleyrand bowed low to demonstrate his respect, but he wondered how these ideas had come to such an incompetent.

It was only weeks later that my beloved found out that spies in the service of the king had entered his home and copied notes he had written on a piece of paper lying beneath his desktop. My beloved always suspected Fouche of organizing the episode, but no proof could be gathered.

As the weeks wore on, Talleyrand found everything the king had told him to be a lie and realized he...yes, my beloved...had underestimated his "legitimate" ruler. Here was a formidable adversary whose disguise as a lazy incompetent was deceptive. Beneath his *façade* lay a ruthless, cunning, wily aristocrat who had been spawned from the hypocrisy and entitlements of the *ancien régime*. The king was merely pretending to accept the will of the people until he figured out how to co-opt them and their representatives.

Another day at Versailles, after the difficult climb up the ambassadors' staircase, avoiding the plasterers and painters who were once again renovating Versailles, he stopped to marvel at the palace's magnificence. Its marbles, its painted ceilings recording France's triumphs, and its huge expanses of mirrors all conspired to produce awe in the emotions of the beholder. He stopped for a few moments to watch some workers on ladders remove the Napoleonic imperial eagles and bees from the ceiling and replace them with the *fleur-de-lis* of the Bourbon kings, claiming he felt no remorse for his role in the demise of the emperor. When he once again entered the *Salon de la Paix*, the king was relaxing on a satin-covered divan, looking too self-satisfied. As my beloved learned much later, the king had deliberately chosen to play a childish and frustrating game with him.

"Your Majesty," my beloved began in his most mellifluous tone, "I think you know why I am here."

"I would not deprive you the opportunity to inform me, Count Talleyrand."

The king's tone made it obvious to Talleyrand that the meeting was not going to be an easy one.

"I know you are wondering why you should make this degraded nobleman, this apostate, this married bishop, this former minister of the Directory, the Consulate, and the Empire, your minister of foreign affairs…" Talleyrand was hoping his display of both humility and experience would mollify what seemed to him an already recalcitrant attitude on the part of the king.

"Your reputation for self-honesty and your brutal assessment of reality is in no way exaggerated. But you must know that Count Artois has been loyal to me for several decades."

"That is true, Your Majesty. But, without detracting from the count's reputation, which is well-deserved, it is not Artois about whom we must talk."

"If not he, then you?" The king was unnecessarily sarcastic. "What would you add to the position of foreign minister that Artois cannot?"

"I will not compare myself to Artois for twenty years of loyalty to a king cannot be minimized in any way. And I am afraid that, if I were to compare myself to him, we would lose the focus of what you and what France requires."

"Am I to believe that only you know what I and France need?"

"Your Majesty misunderstands me…for you and France have once again become one."

"Thank you, my dear count," the king smiled, never immune to flattery. "Continue!"

"This, as you and I both realize, is no time for modesty or coyness. The case I must make to you has to be convincing." Talleyrand saw that King Louis delighted in watching him grovel. "More than anything else, France needs an individual with great influence with the allied sovereigns. As far as I know, I am the only man with my range of experience who has excellent relations with all of the allies, especially Russia."

"Your point is well taken!"

"And equally important," Talleyrand continued, "France must have an experienced negotiator who has shown his ability to resolve crises and settle them with treaties that remain binding and enforceable."

Despite what Talleyrand knew to be the king's innate ill will toward "that cripple," as he referred to Talleyrand in the company of his intimates, the king did realize that what my beloved said was correct. Artois had little experience with the allies.

On May 13, 1814, Talleyrand was, once again, appointed minister of foreign affairs. He set up his offices in the same public building in the Rue du Bac from which he had directed foreign affairs for the Republic and for the Empire. Immediately after his appointment, Talleyrand recorded the concerns that would shape his actions in Vienna:

> The king has appointed me minister of foreign affairs, and, in that capacity, I am supposed to occupy myself with treaties of peace. That is, to negotiate with the coalition made up of England, Austria, Prussia, Russia, Sweden, Portugal, and Spain...The representatives who I know are getting restless without someone at the rudder of France's external affairs...It will be a more difficult job than even I imagined. Napoleon has drained France of money, men, and resources. The country has been invaded on all frontiers by armies composed, not of mercenaries, but of ordinary citizens animated by the spirit of hate and revenge. Over a period of twenty years, these people have seen their own countries occupied and ravaged by the armies of France. They have been oppressed, insulted, and treated with profound contempt. There is no outrage that one can mention for which they could not seek revenge. And, if they are determined to take revenge, how could France oppose them? Surely not by the scattered remnants of its armies, dispersed as they are throughout the countryside and commanded by rivals who were not always obedient even under Napoleon's iron rule...It is under these terrible conditions that I must negotiate for a new France. The task, at this moment, seems overwhelming!

CHAPTER 35

▼

The constitutional charter my beloved prepared for the king, to which the czar had readily agreed, was based loosely on the new American Constitution, suffused with its democratic ideals. Legislative power in the French Constitution, however, would be divided between the king and two assemblies. Initiation of laws would be a function of the throne with the assemblies merely having the right to ask the king to initiate legislation. The document presented to the Senate by the king was so far in spirit from the earlier one that it not only resulted in Czar Alexander leaving Paris in a rage, but Prince Metternich and Viscount Castleraegh following suit soon after.

Talleyrand, always averse to confrontation, waited a few days before he sent an apologetic message to the czar:

> Sire, I regret most humbly that I did not see you before your departure, but I take the liberty of reproaching you for the hurried manner with which you left my country. With all the respect of my most affectionate attachment to Your Majesty and knowing how closely I have followed your Noble career, I ask you to reconsider the situation in France and my own position within it. Do not deprive me of my reward. I ask it from the hero of my daydreams and, dare I add, of my heart. You saved France. Your entry into Paris signaled the end of despotism. I only ask that your generous soul have a little patience! The situation will resolve itself appropriately, as we discussed weeks ago.

No return correspondence was received. The only information Talleyrand received was from his British agents. The czar and his sister, Catherine, who was also his mistress, had created a major scene in London with their boorish behavior. So, just as King Louis had managed to alienate the czar, the czar had now managed to alienate Castleraegh and the entire British public.

Any rift among the allies, however, could only benefit France at the Congress. Castleraegh was now united with Talleyrand, distrustful of Czar Alexander. Metternich had also allied himself with Talleyrand because he suspected the czar had secret designs on Polish territory that Austria coveted. In fact, Talleyrand's spies had reported to him that Metternich had done all that he could do in London to widen the existing breach between the British government and the Russian czar, ridiculing the czar when talking to Castleraegh and mocking Castleraegh when speaking to the czar.

At our last meeting before leaving for Vienna, at a café near the opera house, Talleyrand was ecstatic. "The bickering among the allies fits perfectly into my plans. I would have been helpless in Vienna if the sovereigns acted in unison."

"Now France can become the catalyst for a settlement, rather than its victim," I agreed. Our frequent discussions over the past months had not only educated me, but had convinced me Talleyrand was, in fact, essential to France remaining a major power on the continent.

"If I link the principle of legitimacy in succession to Louis, the countries currently annexed to France can return to their own legitimate sovereigns. Can you imagine what good relations and stability this will create for France?"

"If you are too good in Vienna," I interjected, "you may find a rival in your king."

Talleyrand looked up from his *brioche* and smiled. "Perhaps I have taught you too well."

I smiled back, realizing this was the highest compliment he could ever give me.

While my beloved's goals were nothing short of changing the face of Europe, I made my own list of items to be accomplished. Assemble toiletries. Buy a new fur hat for the cool weather. Decide on the proper wardrobe. Say good-bye to Edmond and the children. Edmond and I had agreed we would tell the children that the new king had requested their mother accompany their great uncle on a very important mission. And, when the mission was over, I would return. At that time, it was largely the truth.

When the day of my departure finally arrived, I was more than ready for the voyage to Vienna. Edmond had alternated the weeks prior to this day with heavy drinking followed by extravagant gifts of love, as if either could influence the quickly approaching change. Did I feel guilty? My days were taken with so many tasks, both large and small, that I answered the question by filling my lungs with the fresh air of escape. My husband had a private life to which I was not privy. My children would soon see far more of their governesses and tutors than they would of me. Did I feel guilty? It was a question I studiously avoided considering.

The voyage was not difficult, made simpler by the arrangements Talleyrand had made for us. We were to travel together in the utmost of comfort and luxury. Rather than chance an upset during the voyage in his elegant phaeton, he had hired a barouche with four wheels instead of the usual two. Wagons followed, well-stocked with provisions and attendants assigned to care for our every need. Arriving in Vienna in the early hours of the morning, it was hard not to be delirious with the promise of what lay ahead. With the sun coming up and the streets so comfortably quiet, I listened to bird songs on the wind and truly believed myself free.

There was much to do. Talleyrand was very clear about his expectations, but he laid them out in the gentlest manner. He would send me note upon note daily, describing whom I would be meeting, how they should be addressed, and the nature of conversation they would enjoy. I must have accumulated a hundred such notes that first week. Each began with *"ma cher,"* my dear, and ended with the simple *"Bises, T."* Kisses. A good hostess, according to one note, must be able to charm and disarm a diplomat with grace and wit. According to another, there would be balls and drawing room events that I would have to preside over. Still another informed me that as many major political decisions would be made in the drawing rooms and ballrooms as would be made at the conference tables. I often thought about those precious notes when my affair with Count Clam-Martinitz began. Looking back on those days, I am not proud to say that much of what I remember of Vienna has less to do with the proceedings that were to reshape the world as I knew it than with my own flirtations.

My beloved proved to be a formidable instructor, and I, so he told me, was a worthy student. But he did not anticipate quite all of the intrigues and plotting that would transpire, least of all those I am embarrassed to admit were crafted by me. What can I say? I was a girl with a fickle heart and warm blood racing through my veins. Talleyrand's days and nights were taken up by the serious affairs of the moment. I needed to find something or someone who would consume whatever free time I had. And not a woman alive in Vienna, including me, could have resisted the charms of young Count Clam-Martinitz.

CHAPTER 36

▼

"Le Congres ne marche pas. II danse." The Congress does not walk. It dances, thought Talleyrand, as he walked through the gardens of Schonbrunn Palace that October 1814. For my beloved, Vienna was more than a city. Like Paris, it was a state of mind where aesthetics, pleasure, sensuality, art, and architecture blended seamlessly into a fantasyland with the notion of work as a secondary consideration. It was a world in which Talleyrand felt perfectly at home.

The noblest men, the most beautiful women, the wealthiest merchants, and minor royalty had come together for the Congress, not to mention the entourage of military officers and elegantly bedecked servants. Their days were spent in meetings or parading the city, waiting for evenings devoted to an endless series of balls traditionally held during the *Fasching,* the winter carnival from New Year's Eve until the beginning of Lent.

The heart of the city, the *Innere Stadt,* was circled by a broad boulevard, the Ringstrasse, with imposing buildings, monuments, and parks, not unlike the baroque buildings scattered throughout Paris that were perforated by the broad Champs Elysees Boulevard. Along the Ringstrasse, Talleyrand walked daily past the imposing town hall, the Parliament, and the State Opera. But, unlike Paris, the Danube, the river that runs through Vienna, had murky waters that could not compare to the beautiful Seine.

Even as he passed Schonbrunn Palace, soon to be the site of great ceremonial balls and lavish banquets, the worries of the Congress tormented him. It was no small matter to place all the major dignitaries of the civilized world in one particular place at one given time. The host of the Congress, the emperor of Austria, was obliged to provide an opening ball that demanded both inexhaustible imagination and inexhaustible wealth—neither of which he possessed. The expenses of the Imperial table alone, at the start of the Congress, were 50,000 florins, the entire daily budget for the Austrian ministry of foreign affairs. To be fair to all, a committee was appointed to devise entertainments and amusements for the delegates, their wives, and their retinues—with each country paying its own expenses. Not a day went by without some new concert, banquet, masked ball, unmasked ball, hunting party, tournament, carousel, military review, or theatrical piece. The highlight of that time, for me, was the attendance of Ludwig von Beethoven at a ball Talleyrand held for Europe's nobility. This young man was already recognized as the greatest composer of the time, and it was amusing to see men and women, mostly women, of the highest station vie with one another to meet him.

Every evening, dignitaries gathered in the salons and ballrooms under the "jurisdictions" of Lady Castleraegh, the duchess of Sagan, Countess Zichy, Madame Fuchs, Princess Esterhazy, the amorous Princess Baration—and me. We all flirted, gossiped, ate, and danced. The ministers found time to talk, occasionally fight, reach agreements, and negotiate their differences. My beloved described it as a "human tapestry of activity, festivity, and diplomacy." But he was aware of only half of each day's activities. While he and the men were daily occupied with diplomacy, I and the other ladies were busy creating a kingdom of *l'amour,* where each day we set down the terms and times of our romantic encounters.

Talleyrand resorted to his *ancien régime* comportment. Each evening, he consumed the sparkling glitter of decorations and uniforms. He enthused over the imperial, royal highnesses and took note of the diligence with which the Viennese pursued their respective amusements. He suggested that he be addressed as Prince Talleyrand, having been named Prince of Benevento in one of Napoleon's ecstatic moods and wondered what his life would have been like if he had been born Viennese. Would he have been able to influence the course of history, as he was soon to do?

It was Talleyrand's moment to savor. He was the man considered by the Congress to be the foremost statesman of the time. The imperturbable calm he maintained, with his now slightly rotund face encircled by ringlets, gave him a certain cherubic quality. The persona he displayed was one of ease and manners, allowing him to mingle effortlessly amidst royalty. When he wanted to make a serious point, I noticed he accentuated his normally grave and deep voice. Occasionally, I would place my arm on his and whisper a word of caution so that he would not totally dominate the assembly before him by the charm of his person, the articulateness of his words, or the cogency of his arguments. Although I was often rebuked at the end of a *soirée* for my "sweet interruptions," as my beloved called them, it did not detract from the pride I felt at his side.

He was not in Vienna, however, to exhibit his charm or to be amused—although he did a good deal of both. The seriousness of the Congress came to the forefront upon our arrival in the form of an oral report by one of his spies, advising that the allies were planning to "put France in her place." The Congress was to be an elaborate charade, during which Talleyrand would be handed the demands of the conquering nations.

"So much for pre-Congress maneuverings," Talleyrand thought.

Forewarned does not necessarily mean forearmed. Talleyrand was quickly confronted with demands he sign two preliminary agreements acquiescing to conditions about which he had had no input. The first acknowledged that Great Britain, Austria, Prussia, and Russia reserved to themselves the final decisions on all territorial questions. The second acknowledged that France would not be consulted on any questions of territory until the four allies had reached "perfect agreement" regarding the disposition of the Duchy of Warsaw and the vacated territories of Germany and Italy.

Talleyrand understood all too well why the allies wanted him to sign these protocols before the Congress could proceed. It was nothing less than a strategy of *force majeure.* The four countries were hoping to turn away from the concept of a unified Europe and substitute that of an oligarchy with themselves as the rulers.

If France was to depart from the Congress with any power, my beloved knew the allies' demands had to be counteracted. He would have to force them to accept law and legitimate sovereignty as the basis from which to the settle all questions before them. Tactically, he would have to create breaches among the allies in order to succeed.

I smile when I write these words, for I still bask in the brilliance of his mind now, as I did during our time in Vienna. Perhaps it was during the Congress that my great respect and fascination turned into love. Perhaps years later, I do not know. Here was a man possessing a unique capacity to understand the mind and machinations of the world's statesmen, and he had chosen to spend his personal moments with me, to share his confidences with me, and to talk out his plans with me. I was definitely honored, even if love had not yet arrived. Years later, I wondered whether I loved this man because of how elevated he made me feel or because of his own attributes. I never dwelled upon the issue for we were both happy with the results, no matter the reasons.

My beloved first approached Czar Alexander in an attempt to create a rift between Russia and Austria over their competing interests in the Duchy of Warsaw and Saxony. If the czar and Metternich were adversaries, they would be less of a threat to France.

Throughout an incoherent, highly emotional diatribe by the czar sitting in his apartments at the Hotel Kaunitz, Talleyrand maintained a calm demeanor. He surveyed the lavishly decorated rococo room and wondered if the czar appreciated the curved lines of the furniture and its pieced shellwork. While Talleyrand tried to record the full range of subjects they addressed that day, there was also a repeated notation in the margins, *"Il m'en bete!"* He annoys me!

"You must understand, Prince Talleyrand, that, by nature, I am a rebel," the czar said matter-of-factly, flattering my beloved by using the new title Napoleon had bestowed upon him.

"Your Excellency," Talleyrand responded, "perhaps the idea that you might be a 'compulsive oppositionist' would be more appropriate."

"As usual," the czar responded, delighted, "you have an uncanny ability to capture the moment with just the right word."

"All one has to do is examine your pattern of behavior in order to predict what you will do next."

The czar focused his gaze on Talleyrand, awaiting the explanation of his words.

"After having been a liberal and a supporter of the Revolution and of Napoleon," Talleyrand continued, "you convert to legitimacy and conservatism."

Czar Alexander wagged his finger at Talleyrand. "Do such changes in my behavior lessen the intensity of feelings I might have had on a particular issue at a specific time and place?"

"Not at all," Talleyrand replied. "Your beliefs should be based on the principles you hold dear to yourself, whatever they might be."

"Are you trying to tell me consistency is the hallmark of small minds?"

"Quite the opposite. For example, you could choose to rule the Duchy of Warsaw, yet show your generosity to Saxony by allowing them a plebiscite to vote for their own ruler."

"I do have a moral duty to each of these countries. Is that not correct, Prince Talleyrand?"

"Yes, it is, Your Excellency."

"Then it behooves me on moral principles alone," the czar continued, "to do as you suggest."

"I certainly cannot fault you for your logic." Talleyrand responded. He was unclear what logic the czar was using, but he was pleased the direction of their discussion was as planned.

"Oh, you know how to flatter, dear prince. But, as you also know from our previous dealings with that dwarf Napoleon, that flattery will only allow you a certain amount of leeway with me."

"You mistake my words."

"Now, now," Czar Alexander interrupted him. "You are the master of words. Everyone at the French Court and at the Congress is well aware of your skills. But, flattery and principles are not enough to dissuade a czar or king from actions he might want to take on a moment's notice."

"I think I understand your meaning."

"Do you now?" the czar asked with a harsh tone of voice.

"I am simply a prince, and you are a czar," Talleyrand responded, swallowing his pride.

"You are also a clever man!"

By the way he said it, Talleyrand understood this to be the czar's concluding statement. He thanked the czar for the audience and left, pleased with himself for having created the beginnings of dissension among the allies. Given a plebiscite, the citizens of Saxony would certainly vote against King William of Austria. Animosity between the czar and Metternich was almost guaranteed. And none of the other allies would agree to Russia's rule over Warsaw.

Days later, the game of diplomacy continued. This time, it was in the gardens behind Schonbrunn Palace and between Talleyrand and Metternich.

"I have always admired your dexterity in the art of statecraft," Talleyrand began as he limped along a path in the baroque gardens.

"Your words are far more revealing than your sentiments," Metternich responded brusquely.

"Are you accusing me of prevaricating?"

"My dear prince," Metternich responded, "what is statecraft but an endless series of deceptions and duplicity."

"How cynical!"

"How disingenuous of you, Prince Talleyrand."

"Then let us play out our deceptions as if they were truths!"

"That certainly defies what you Frenchmen love to embrace, your Cartesian logic."

"With your permission, would it be fair to say that, over the past several weeks, you have made insinuations to all who would listen that, although you respect me personally, you do not want me to have a major voice in the meetings?"

"I have been approaching certain individuals with similar remarks on a confidential basis."

"Why are you trying to be so discreet when you know very well that the more one endows information with secrecy, the more quickly it spreads."

"Then I must admit to the use of a futile method," Metternich smiled, revealing a set of discolored teeth, "for certainly it did not achieve what was intended."

"Not at all." Talleyrand responded with a sardonic smile, "You are conspiring with the allies to keep me away from your meetings while you all formulate your plans for France. But are you certain the allies are not conspiring against you?"

"In a normal situation, I would consider what you just said to be offensive."

"No offense was intended!" Talleyrand lied. "I merely bring to your attention that your methods of manipulating and cajoling members of the Congress against France are being used, as we speak, by Russia and England against Austria."

Metternich took his time responding, obviously surprised by Talleyrand's words. "For a man known for his subtlety and charm, Prince Talleyrand, you seem to be trying to provoke me. And, if you know anything about me, you know I will not be provoked." Metternich rose abruptly and left, walking in the direction of the palace, leaving Talleyrand smiling.

Over the next few days, the czar boasted to a group of delegates to the Congress about his intentions for Warsaw and Saxony, while Metternich made it known to another group of delegates that neither was acceptable to King William. At their next meeting, the czar accused Metternich of being "boorish and indecent" in a voice that had a "tone of revolt," while Metternich stormed out of the meeting, swearing he would never speak with the czar again.

As for Castleraegh, Talleyrand made England so despised for not have taken a firm stand on any issue that the English were considered the "scourge" of the salons.

By December 1814, my beloved had accomplished what he had set out to do.

CHAPTER 37

▼

The frost of January 1815 reflected the nature of the relations among the allies as much as it did the weather in Vienna. As fear of a new war hung over the Congress, Talleyrand took advantage of the situation to present France as the champion of peace and justice. He argued vigorously against the allies' plans to destroy Saxony and Poland, using both his own voice and those who could be equally persuasive. He visited the ally leaders individually and in small groups. He spoke to larger groups of those participating in the Congress. So effective was his strategy that, by the end of the month, he had completely won over an ally more powerful than either Castelraegh or Metternich or Czar Alexander. He had won over international public opinion—the new arbiter of politics, morality, and taste—for both himself and for France.

Despite the constant strain of his work, each day as the sun set, Talleyrand and I would meet to share a glass of champagne in our apartments and confer about the day's events. Throughout our time in Vienna, he encouraged me to visit the literary salons while he worked so that my time and mind would be used wisely. He suggested I act in the plays I was organizing, despite my dread of performing, saying this would eliminate any shyness in front of strangers. He said he adored me for making a sixty-year-old man feel like a young man in his thirties. He told me my presence had rejuvenated his sense of what was possible for him at this stage in his life and my confidence empowered him, making him as productive as he had been earlier in his career. He told me, he told me, he told me...The fact I was married to his nephew began to fade from both our consciousness. At the end of our conversations, my beloved, who I beg you to remember was still "uncle" to me, visited the salons of Vienna for mostly political reasons, while I spent stolen hours enraptured by Count Clam-Martinitz.

I have to admit that I found it somewhat disturbing for Talleyrand to encourage my interest in the theatre, not knowing whether to take his suggestion as a compliment or an insult. I had always approached my own interest in the theater with a sense of forbidden sensuality. I cannot recollect my age when I first heard the name of the Marquise de Pompadour mentioned, although I know it was over tea during a conversation between my mother and some visitors. Although I was not privy to the entire conversation, it was clear to me that, while the ladies vilified her character, their regard for her accomplishments bordered on envy. Madame de Pompadour sang opera. Madame danced divinely. Madame was an accomplished horsewoman, an amusing storyteller, an engraver, and a woman with elegant taste in clothes. And I believe these accomplishments came years before she became the official mistress of King Louis XV. It is almost embarrassing to admit now that I also envied her. Less for her accomplishments than for the fact she seemed to be a woman unlike those around me. A woman who had created herself and was her own master. Was this an idealized view? No doubt. But a formative one for me.

As we sipped coffee one morning before Talleyrand left for his appointments, I felt the need to ascertain his view of my most irregular position as his live-in hostess for he was sure to have heard the gossip to which I was privy.

"I will also be out most of the day," was my response to his inquiry about my day's activities. "We are rehearsing for Thursday evening's performance."

"I know you will have great success…" he began, as I knew he would.

"I only hope our reception is as kind as that always given to those plays supervised and performed by Madame de Pompadour at the palace theater."

"Are you comparing yourself with that…that…" Talleyrand put down the documents he was reviewing and looked at me crossly.

"…that courtesan?" I finished his thought for him.

"She was a woman whose existence is no model for you." His tone was as indignant, as if I had just insulted generations of his noble family.

"I am not making any such a comparison, although she did separate from her husband and take up residence at court with the king. And she did have a particular interest in politics, as I now have. And…"

Talleyrand dropped his usual mask of indifference for one of incredulity. He was clearly uncomfortable with the conversation I had begun.

"Did she not protect and subsidize your own Voltaire and his comrades? According to Maman, she herself played an important role in bringing about the Revolution, through her relationships."

When I stopped speaking, the silence between us was almost audible. When Talleyrand responded, it was with a firmness of voice usually reserved for his adversaries.

"We both know there are gossips who, for reasons of politics or jealousy, will try to malign and condemn our relationship. But I submit to you that your allusion to that notorious woman is ill-advised. Yes, your knowledge of the world of politics and power is broad. As was hers. And yes, I look forward to hearing your opinions, as the king listened to hers. But we share these apartments as uncle and niece, and I will tolerate no aspersions on your character, even when entertained by you, because of this...circumstance." Talleyrand concluded his remarks by thumping his cane on the carpet as he rose to leave.

I sat back on the divan and smiled, pleased my words had elicited such a reaction.

I have to admit, looking backwards these twenty years, I was jealous of Talleyrand when we were in Vienna, even while I kept myself happily occupied. The intrigues, manipulations, and issues that he dealt with daily made the limits to my world all too clear. The conventional view was that a noble woman's duty lay in defending the honor and advancing the interests of her family. Her marriage was largely to create a suitable alliance, arrange for the suitable upbringing of her children, and use her social skills in support of a suitable husband. Yes, while social ambitions were certainly expected, political ambitions were barely acknowledged and would forever keep a woman like me from any importance in Talleyrand's world. Could I even dare to think I could affect the course of history? Catherine the Great of Russia was certainly a formidable woman with whom history had to contend. Married to a Russian imbecile when she was only a Prussian adolescent, she became the reigning power of a vast and foreign country despite formidable opposition. While Talleyrand was no ruler, I decided there must be ways for me to influence his decisions that, by proxy, would be influencing history. That thought brought me some peace of mind.

More and more, I began to turn my life over to my beloved, and he later admitted I became his best "student." Never appear to make great effort, he exclaimed, for one's work should appear effortless. Rise late in the morning after the proper sleep so that the business of the day is handled with equanimity. Conceal your efforts from the sight of others, lest they reveal the true intentions of what is undertaken. I listened and listened well. Perhaps I did become his best student. Certainly his longest one.

CHAPTER 38

▼

The Congress of Vienna was entering a chaotic state. Europe was clearly heading toward another war, and Talleyrand predicted an imminent crisis of grave proportions. Reassessing the players, he realized that he would have to be the one to act proactively. Castleraegh was poor at strategic planning. Czar Alexander was obstinate. Frederick William was weak. And it was Metternich's vacillations that had, in fact, created the "case of the most urgent necessity." Providence, however, would soon have its own surprise in store for everyone.

As I lounged on the divan in the drawing room, watching Talleyrand at his desk fully absorbed in writing the final agreements of the Congress, I knew I was beginning to feel something for him I never had felt for Edmond, and that was quite different from what I felt for Clam-Martinitz. With the distance of years, I now realize I was growing to love this uncle-by-marriage who, despite the urgencies of the Congress, had always remained gentle, considerate, and solicitous to me. The *nobless oblige* he manifested to all, excited me. His old world charm added a patina of royalty, as if he himself was to be the successor to the throne. Despite his foot deformity and what some might consider his "advanced" age of sixty, I found him extremely attractive. His intense brown eyes, set off by his now-light reddish eyebrows, gave him a seductiveness Edmond, in all his youth, never radiated. At the time, I still addressed him by the title of "uncle" for I was a married woman of thirty-one years, flirtatious with and enamored of many to whom I was introduced. If truth be known, the stolen kisses with the count had started merely as an innocent flirtation. I had not intended for it to escalate, nor could I have predicted the duel to which it would lead.

I must confess that those months with the count were wonderful. He was the offspring of an ancient dynasty, handsome, young, brilliant, and extremely amusing—everything a young woman could desire in a lover. By January 1815, Clam-Martinitz and I were an accepted couple in Viennese society. While Talleyrand seemed to be unconcerned by this occurrence, he later confided in me that it was only because he assumed that, once the Congress ended, the count would rejoin his military regiment and he and I would return to Paris together.

This February morning, my mind was on the rehearsal of a play I had organized for later in the day by a yet unknown playwright named Hercule Lemarches. A servant, bedecked in green livery, hurriedly entered our quarters and handed Talleyrand a correspondence. Talleyrand read it once and then again.

"Metternich is informing me that Napoleon has escaped from Elba!" were the ominous words that left my beloved's lips.

I look back on my reaction to his words, aghast at the selfishness that attended them. My first emotion was not for my country, but one of rage toward that rude Corsican who was inserting himself into our life once more. My first concern was for his interruption of my own plans.

"Oh uncle, my rehearsal!"

"Your rehearsal, my dear niece, will take place, notwithstanding this occurrence," Talleyrand replied, nonplussed.

"This horrible man will disrupt everything."

"Fear not, everything will remain as it is now." Talleyrand rose from his chair and proceeded to his *boudoir*.

The half-opened door allowed me to watch him apply a hint of rouge to his pale cheeks and lips, and some powder to his face and wig. I was vicariously enjoying the pleasure he himself took in applying his toiletry. He dabbed some cologne onto his cheeks, but only after he held open the bottle to his nose and deeply inhaled its scent.

"Remember, my darling niece," Talleyrand turned toward me, aware of my voyeurism, "let the fragrance be ever so subtle so that it is seductive rather than overpowering. Like everything else in life, there is a very fine line between dressing attractively and appearing overdressed."

As I watched my beloved take time with his appearance, I found myself becoming annoyed. Why was I serving this old man, who was trying so hard to give himself the color of youth and the comportment of a king? I wanted to live gaily and pursue my own life. Far away from home and family, I began to find my situation a burden. I did not hesitate to repeat my claim.

"Uncle, I must be able to attend my rehearsal."

"What's this?" asked my beloved. "My niece grows insistent with me? This is something new. Perhaps you forget that you and I are in Vienna for a reason, and that reason is more grave than organizing theatricals and balls."

"Is that so?" I asked, feeling the heat rise to my cheeks. "Perhaps there is more here in Vienna than you have decided to speak about."

"If you think that, my dear, then you must have the patience to wait and see if you are correct." Talleyrand spoke in the most tender of voices. "You will see, and you will not be disappointed."

Though I do not know why, his words and his manner calmed me. The moment of anger passed. I attended to my theatrical and Talleyrand to his toiletries.

When he finished, he set out for Metternich's home, an aristocratic palace referred to in Austria as an *Adelspalais.* The imposing outer shell of the building, however, was in stark contrast to the small, sparsely furnished drawing room with its startling red curtains. Talleyrand was not impressed.

"Here is the letter I received from the Austrian consul general at Genoa at six o'clock this morning," Metternich began, in an agitated state. "I will read you the highlights." He put on his spectacles and read aloud with the worst French accent my beloved said he had ever heard. "The English Commissioner Campbell's frigate entered the harbor and inquired whether anyone had seen Napoleon at Genoa in view of the fact he had disappeared from the ship. The answer, being in the negative, the English frigate immediately set sail again."

"Do you know where Napoleon was heading?" Talleyrand asked, purposely appearing calmer than the circumstances warranted.

"The report makes no mention of it."

"If I know him, he will ride straight for Paris in order to regain power!"

With the arrival of the rest of the allies, the message was read again by Metternich. Within minutes, the group's decision was unanimous. They were going to go to war against Napoleon. Talleyrand felt their resolve and knew it to be appropriate. But he sighed that history was repeating itself. Blood would flow again, as red as the unsightliness of the curtains guarding the room.

Talleyrand dispatched a letter to the king, in Paris, requesting he stay calm and assuring him the matter was being attended to by all the powers in Vienna. He, Talleyrand, would be leaving for Paris to consult with him within the day. Until, that is, my beloved was informed, *sotto voce,* by one of his servants that he was being summoned by the Countess Marie-Therese de Perigord.

It had been several decades since he had seen or heard from her. Or perhaps my presentation of his life has taken a path away from addressing his dalliances with women whom I believe he loved to the extent to which he was capable of loving. Whatever the true cause of this omission, I now feel obliged to write that my beloved felt he could not refuse her summons. He had never forgotten her original kindness, her generosity of spirit, and her courage to leave her husband so that she could be near him at the seminary.

The thirty-minute ride in his landau placed Talleyrand in front of a *château* whose grounds and buildings showed years of neglect, the remnants of a marriage settlement by a husband who had left Marie-Therese almost destitute. Talleyrand wondered why she had never contacted him for some assistance. For the first time in a very long while, he felt guilty for something to which he had indirectly been a party.

Accompanied by somber servants, he entered a bedroom whose centerpiece was at one time a resplendent giltwood canopy bed festooned with a floral fabric. Now, only faded silk clung to chipping wood. Tattered window curtains were tightly drawn. A priest stood at the bedside, administering the sacrament of last rites. The room reeked of carbolic acid mixed with the stench of excrement. The emaciated figure lying so still on the bed bore only a faint resemblance to the adventurous, amorous woman he had once loved. Talleyrand told me he stared at the hollow, jaundiced face, marred by its half-moon scar, and remembered his initial reaction to it as a boy fleeing his home in Perigord. Most of all, he recalled the wise words bestowed upon him by this woman, twelve years his senior, that had served him well throughout his life, exhorting him to ignore his own deformity.

As he stared at her ashen face, he tried to conjure up the intensity of her once-penetrating eyes and the sensuousness of her bosom, and remember the incredible excitement he had felt when Marie-Therese had raised her veil and placed a gentle kiss on his lips. For the first time in his life, he had felt like a man.

"Charles," Marie-Therese said, breaking Talleyrand's reverie, "it was good of you to come."

"I was only just told that…" he stopped in mid-sentence, not wanting to utter those terrible words that had been whispered to him.

"Yes, Charles, I am dying."

"I'm so sorry."

"For what?"

"For…"

"For the fact I am dying?" she interrupted him again. "That, unfortunately, is a reality the great statesman Charles-Maurice de Talleyrand-Perigord cannot change." When she paused to cough, my beloved said he could hear a "death rattle" that was louder than her words.

"I have been remiss…I should have…after all you had done for me."

"Perhaps I wasn't important enough."

"That's not true!"

"I'm only playing with you." Marie-Therese tried to smile, which only made her cough again. "Won't you let an old woman have her last laugh, even at the expense of the great Talleyrand? I promise not to make this last…tryst…too difficult. May I call it a 'tryst,' to recall old times?"

"Of course, my dear, you may call it whatever you like." He placed her fragile, alabaster left hand against his dry lips. Memories of reprimands by the priests at St. Sulpice flooded him, and his eyes welled up with tears.

"You have made me very happy by being here with me today."

"Please don't exert yourself. I will be next to you for as long as you need me."

"You were always such a good liar. But I never cared. I always knew I would see you again." She took another long pause to breathe deeply.

The priest stepped closer to Talleyrand, nodding his head as if to indicate they should end their conversation.

"Can you find it in your heart to forgive me for any injustices I have committed against you?" Talleyrand wiped his eyes with the back of his hand, perhaps for the first time in his life totally disregarding the etiquette of using his silk-laced monogrammed handkerchief.

"My dear Charles! Don't you yet understand I loved you without conditions?" She tried to raise her head and collapsed onto her pillow

"Shh…hh…hhh…Try to save your energy so that we can…"

"We can never make up for the time we have lost," she continued with increasingly greater effort. "Although I may have disapproved of many things you have done, I want you to know I have never, for a single moment, stopped loving you."

Talleyrand, whose impassivity was a legend in the courts of Europe, told me he was so overcome with emotion that he was unable to speak. He walked quietly out of the room and out of the house, choosing to sit down on a stone bench in Marie-Therese's overgrown garden. He bent his head into both his hands and sobbed. If there was ever a time when Talleyrand had questioned the choices he had made in his life or the ultimate importance of his life's maneuverings for fame and achievement, it was at this moment.

The next day, Marie-Therese died.

Talleyrand described this scene to me many times over the course of our years together. He always made it very clear that Marie-Therese was his first love and, in that way, would forever hold a special place in his heart, a place I could never occupy. At the time, his grief for her left me feeling alone and sad. It also had the effect of making me feel less conflicted about my flirtation with Clam-Martinitz, which could now be described as a *liaison dangereuse*.

CHAPTER 39

▼

With news of Napoleon's escape from Elba, the smell of war was like an electrical storm, dissipating the festivities that had dominated the Congress. Baggage, trunks, and valises were hurriedly packed. Coaches emblazoned with the heraldic arms of their owners rushed out of Vienna as if pursued by armies of uncivilized nations. The reason was none other than Napoleon Bonaparte, who had returned to France, disembarking on the southern coast at Cap d'Antibes and now gathering his troops. Talleyrand was appalled by the situation, but he grudgingly admired Napoleon's imagination and determination.

The newly formed Chamber of Deputies issued a declaration offering the king whatever assistance he needed to repulse Napoleon. When King Louis learned that Marshal Ney, whose troops had been given the responsibility of arresting Napoleon, had instead deserted and given his allegiance to his former commander-in-chief, the king raced out of the Tuileries palace and fled to the safety of Belgium to wait out Napoleon's capture.

England, Prussia, Austria, and Russia moved quickly to resolve their own differences and concluded an alliance subsequently signed by all major participants in the Congress of Vienna. My beloved was honored when they invited France to join with them and sign on behalf of France. A triumphant Talleyrand wrote to the king:

> The coalition that was initially formed against France has been completely destroyed. France is presently allied with Austria and England. More importantly, France is no longer isolated in Europe. It is now acting in concert with two of the greatest powers, three states of the second rank, and soon with all states that follow principles other than those of revolution. Moreover,

France will be the soul of this alliance, formed in defense of principles that it
has been the first to preach.

There is no doubt Talleyrand was pleased with what he had accomplished.
France was to come out of the Congress "whole," and the treaty gave the
continent a configuration of states my beloved thought should work well for years
to come. The concepts of legitimacy, civil society, and checks and balances were
essential elements in the treaty's wording, and political stability and enduring
peace seemed inevitable. With barely an *au revoir,* Talleyrand rushed to Belgium
to consult with the king.

When Napoleon's army invaded Bologna on a spring-like April morning in
1815, it promptly defeated the Austrian army. While an early victory, it was a
clarion call to the allies.

In the margins of his diary Talleyrand wrote, "Fear has now overtaken and
catalyzed those lethargic countries that had not been willing to participate in the
Congress, although I hope it is not too late."

On April 8, Napoleon's representative in Vienna had the audacity to present a
note to Metternich, complaining about the "unfriendly attitude" of the Austrian
Court and declaring he would soon be occupying the banks of the Po River.

"This will be Napoleon's downfall," Talleyrand recorded when he was made
aware of the message.

By June, the stage was set for a major confrontation. Napoleon's army of
300,000 was confronting 92,000 English, Dutch, and German units under
General Wellington's command headquartered near Brussels. An additional
120,000 Prussian soldiers led by General Blucher covered Wellington's left flank,
225,000 of General Schwarzenberg's Austrian troops moved westward toward
Alsace, and 168,000 Russian troops commanded by Czar Alexander himself
stood right behind Schwarzenberg's forces.

Although the newspaper *Le Moniteur,* in advance of the attack, published the
news that "Emperor Napoleon Bonaparte has just won a sweeping victory over
the English and Prussian armies," reality was quite different At dusk, while Paris
was celebrating the defeat of the alliance, Napoleon was first launching his attack.
Eight battalions of the Old Guard, protected by heavy artillery barrage, charged
lines of Wellington's professional soldiers, who stood firm and took heavy
casualties. They retaliated against Napoleon's troops with a devastating blow that
smashed through his lines. Having expended his last reserve of soldiers, Napoleon
had no choice except to retreat. When Wellington and Bucher pursued the
fleeing French soldiers, they turned the retreat at Waterloo into a massacre.

The day after the Battle of Waterloo, June 19, 1815, Talleyrand learned of Napoleon's defeat. My beloved was resting at Aachen, on the way to visit the king, when he received the news from an old rival, Prince Conde, as well as his congratulations on "impressive achievements in Vienna." My beloved was as gratified by Conde's courtesy call as by Napoleon's defeat because his friend was a Royalist who, like many of his class, had never ceased to mistrust him. That he would seek out Talleyrand, an ex-revolutionary and former Bonapartist, to congratulate him was a promising sign the winds of politics in France has shifted once more. By the end of their conversation, my beloved felt that could again become acceptable to the nobility, who would inevitably rule once the final details of Napoleon's defeat were settled.

Later in June, Napoleon abdicated for the second time and was exiled to the island of Saint Helena, where he died six years later. As far as I know, Talleyrand and Napoleon had no contact during those final years.

When the Congress of Vienna ended, my relationship with my beloved was still based upon familial ties and intellectual interests. We had shared some personal intimacy, but it was of the most innocent kind. Looking back on those days, I now believe my "friendship" with Clam-Martinitz allowed me to maintain my "distance" from Talleyrand and avoid confronting any unnatural feelings I might have felt at the time for my uncle. Even Edmond seemed unconcerned about my position of hostess in Talleyrand's apartments. Of course, Talleyrand, with his strong sense of himself, dismissed all rumors of my liaison with Clam-Martinitz as unlikely, unworthy, and unreliable.

I found I missed the heady atmosphere of Vienna—the balls, the dinners, and the possibility of extraordinary decisions being made. So, I decided to accept Talleyrand's invitation to accompany him to Valençay for a short while, happy to inform Edmond my hostessing services was still required by his uncle and pleased with an easy opportunity to relinquish my role as mistress of the count.

One morning, while we sat together in the sunny south drawing room at Valençay, a royal messenger informed my beloved his presence was requested by the king. I had been relaxing on the divan with a manuscript while Talleyrand had been overlooking papers spread out on one of his favorite pieces of furniture, an Empire console originally owned by Cardinal Fesch.

Talleyrand thought for a few seconds before politely dismissing the man with a yawn, saying, "There will be time enough tomorrow."

His bags had not yet been fully unpacked. The guests at Valençay were in need of attention. He wanted time to talk with me about all that had occurred in Vienna. He did not relish another trip so soon.

The king was so livid upon hearing of Talleyrand's response that Françoise René Chateaubriand, a close friend of King Louis, ordered the messenger to return to ask Talleyrand to reconsider.

"Please tell His Majesty that I express my sincerest regrets, but I am not able to attend to his request immediately. I am extremely fatigued. My accomplishments in Vienna, while extraordinary, were extremely burdensome."

The king's anger at Talleyrand's words, he later learned, was great. Readying to depart for Versailles, he left instructions that no one in the royal court was to receive Talleyrand that day, the next day, or any other day.

A close friend of Talleyrand's, alarmed by the king's words, rushed to Valençay to reprimand my beloved for his foolish behavior and warned him that, if he did not cure the situation, he would be *persona non grata* at court. This warning alarmed him sufficiently enough for him to arrange his *toilette* in haste and rush to Versailles without informing me of his journey.

Once in Versailles, he demanded a courtier stop the king's carriage because "Talleyrand is here to see him."

"Impossible!" the king replied to the breathless courtier. "You must be mistaken. Talleyrand is asleep at this very moment. I am certain of that because he himself informed me of his present state of somnolence.

"Your Majesty," Talleyrand interrupted, approaching the carriage as quickly as his limp would allow, "I think you misunderstood me or your messenger misinterpreted what I said."

"Is that so?"

"I apologize for my seeming insolence, but the relaxation I sought at Valençay was essential to allow me to calculate the proper strategy for Your Majesty to return to Paris as a conquering sovereign."

"Is that so? How interesting. Please elaborate then upon your well-rested thoughts. No one has ever accused you of not being inventive and clever with your tongue and your mind. Or is it the reverse? I'm never sure which part of your body controls your wit."

"After spending a most restless night," Talleyrand began, ignoring the king's sarcasm, "with my responsibilities as your foreign minister weighing heavily on my mind—not my tongue, sire—I decided I must advise you not to proceed to Paris until you can rule free of any threats from within France, from foreign saboteurs, or from foreign troops."

Before the king could use sarcasm again to belittle my beloved, Talleyrand handed him a long memorandum he had, in fact, been preparing for weeks.

The king's response was not what my beloved had hoped it would be. He took the document, but he did not attempt to look at its contents. Instead, he spoke in a scornful tone to both Talleyrand and the courtiers who had gathered within earshot of the carriage.

"Prince Talleyrand, you and I are from very old and highly respected families. In that sense, you must consider me not to be just your king, but also a distant cousin who is extremely concerned about your state of health. You yourself have informed me you are fatigued by the events of recent months. I would like to thank you for your service on behalf of the long line of Bourbon kings to whom you and your family have been most loyal."

Talleyrand bowed his head in acceptance of the king's favor, yet uncomfortable with his tone of voice.

"I have been informed you are about to leave us," King Louis continued in a voice that no longer tried to disguise his contempt. "I appreciate your need for rest and contemplation. We will miss you. You will write to us frequently with news of yourself."

With an imperial nod, Talleyrand was summarily dismissed from his audience with the king—and so it seemed—from the court. For the first time in his life, my beloved was speechless.

C H A P T E R 40

▼

When Talleyrand returned to Valençay, he entered a state of isolation. He took his meals and spent most of his waking hours alone, in the library. Reflecting upon the embarrassing episode with King Louis, he feared he would no longer be able to participate in his life's overriding love, international diplomacy. Yet he was certain the king could not survive without his skills.

On those evenings, he dined alone and then chose to join me in the salon afterwards. I knew he was in need of an understanding and accepting ear. He would talk—usually about how right he had always been in understanding France's needs and how little he had been appreciated by those he served—and I would listen. I rarely had to ask more than three questions or raise my eyebrows at a provocative statement for him to continue until his disappointment and frustration dissipated. He would return to his study calm.

When he went into the garden after dinner, I knew he wanted to be alone with his thoughts. I would watch him choose a path through the window and then walk it twenty times over, nodding and shaking his head, gesturing with his arms, as if in deep debate with a nearby companion.

After Napoleon's defeat and exile, it was not a foregone conclusion that King Louis would be restored to the throne of his ancestors. Among the allies and within France itself, there were many who favored a Republic. Others believed a permanent peace could be obtained only if Napoleon's son, the King of Rome, was allowed to mount the throne under the aegis of a responsible regency. Still another group, led by the Russians, felt only the House of Orleans, in the specific person of the duke of Orleans, could maintain a permanent peace in Europe.

Talleyrand remained convinced that France could find peace and freedom only under a constitutional monarchy. The key to that peace lay in Paris, and the man who controlled Paris at that time was none other than Joseph Fouche, Napoleon's minister of police. But Napoleon was now deposed, and it was likely Fouche would be next.

Regicide, my beloved always said, ranks in history as one of the most unforgivable sins one could commit against the state. Despite Fouche's new ducal title, the nobility considered him a murderer. None in the entourage of the Bourbon kings had forgotten that, as a member of the Assembly in 1793, Fouche had voted for the death of King Louis XVI. Yet, if my beloved held any hope of regaining power under King Louis, he needed to make an ally of Fouche once again and help him gain the confidence of the king.

Through charm and persuasion, Talleyrand was able to obtain an audience for himself and Fouche with King Louis XVIII, albeit an informal one. I think back fondly to the evening at Valençay when Talleyrand and I orchestrated an intimate dinner to convince the king and his advisors that keeping Fouche as the king's minister of police was as essential to a him as it had been to Napoleon.

We had planned the dinner together, as co-conspirators. We discussed every detail that was important—from the placement of individuals around the table to the best way to respond to embarrassing questions. While the dinner party was to unite the guests in their regard for Fouche, the time and effort Talleyrand and I shared planning the party served to deepen our loyalties to each other.

The dining room, well-suited for small receptions, was already animated by walls covered with pastel-hued Flemish tapestries and a floor covered by a Persian rug from the Ferejhan district, its medallion and stylized flowers alight with color. I had ordered the best flowers from de Marche, new table dressings from Madame Ledroit, and figs from St. Luc. The table, which accommodated three dozen guests that evening, was set with my beloved's most ostentatious crested china dinner service and Jacobite goblets, the latter having been purchased precisely because they commemorated the English Jacobite rebellions. Talleyrand frequently laughed at the irony of the toasts to the king's health that were proffered throughout the evening with goblets that honored rebellion.

That night, all we touched was of silver, not only the spoons and forks, but vases, gravy boats, salt shakers, tureens, and serving platters. At least a dozen silver candelabras graced the table, although they paled when compared with the Greco-Egyptian silver centerpiece, a gift from Napoleon, with its sphinx supporting a base from which six branches held candles.

I have taken the liberty to describe in detail the luxury of the appointments for two reasons. The first is that I am very proud to have been "schooled" so well by Talleyrand while we were in Vienna and wish to show off my own accomplishments. Second, my beloved's cherished possessions created an atmosphere we both concluded was necessary to manage the situation.

We sat as thirty-six around the table and burned a huge number of candles that night. I have to admit, without any humility, that everything turned out to perfection. His eyes smiling, my beloved nodded in my direction more than once during the evening. Some time after the last course was served and before the piano recital by a yet-unknown Polish pianist, Talleyrand nodded to me that the time was right and took control of the conversation.

"Tell us, Fouche," he began, gently tapping his spoon on a crystal goblet, to gain everyone's attention, "what is the state of security for our new king?"

All at the table stopped their gossiping and strained to hear the response. The king appeared the least interested.

Fouche surveyed the elegantly arranged table and the noble personages seated around it, flattered he had been invited to sit among them.

"As usual, there are many disturbing elements surrounding the current situation. I fear the citizens of Paris are preparing an uprising against Your Majesty in this time of transition."

"You see, my friends," Talleyrand interrupted, "like all trusted professionals, my dear friend and colleague is ahead of the times." Talleyrand started to applaud, encouraging his guests to follow suit.

"One would imagine our good citizens would be grateful for having our king return. Unfortunately, that is not the case."

"You must elaborate on what you mean." Talleyrand waved his hand toward Fouche, hoping the hours of preparation before the dinner had convinced him this was his chance to separate his loyalties from Napoleon's regime.

"There is an intricate maze of political intrigues that my men are watching that are taking place around the city," Fouche continued, trying hard to impress. "Armed conflicts among Republicans, Orleanists, and Royalists break out daily at the slightest provocation. My men are being trained to handle these matters with discretion, when appropriate, but with harshness when that is the only reasonable approach."

"Shocking!" Talleyrand responded ingenuously. "Clearly, if we are to remain a viable country, what the king needs is a strong chief of security, someone like you, who is well acquainted with the current betrayals and deceits ongoing. Such a man would be appreciated by all true Frenchmen."

"With all due modesty, Your Majesty," Fouche turned toward the impassive face of King Louis, unable to resist Talleyrand's lead, "I offer you my humble services to protect you and the royal family and to maintain the sanctity of our beloved France. My allegiance is with you and the France you will create."

Talleyrand stood up and started to applaud once more. He and I could not help but notice the effect of Fouche's flattery upon the king.

"France could never reward you sufficiently for the sacrifices you have already made for her and those you will make in the future."

When I rose, goblet in hand, the other guests stood and applauded, as if on cue. King Louis did nothing and said nothing, although I distinctly remember seeing him take a long look at Fouche.

Within the week, the king appointed Fouche his minister of police. Within two weeks, and despite continuing reservations on his part, he re-appointed Talleyrand his minister of foreign affairs.

True to his nature, upon receiving his appointment, my beloved proceeded to help King Louis create a well-balanced group of advisors and ministers, but it was men he could control. He set up a board of peerage that assigned royal titles to those who had been loyal to the House of Bourbon, making certain those who were knighted knew they owed their allegiance to him. He dissolved the assembly of deputies and the Electoral College so that the king would have no political resistance.

When my hostess duties were completed to both Talleyrand's and my own satisfaction, I made a decision that was almost as difficult as the one that allowed me to leave my family for Vienna. I recall that Talleyrand and I were walking after dinner in the lush gardens behind the *château* when I told him I would soon be leaving for Paris, but for a fashionable house of my own. He appeared shocked, as if someone had informed him Napoleon had once again escaped his island of exile.

"Have I not made you happy in Vienna and here in Valençay?" Talleyrand began. "Could you have accomplished more, learned more, been more useful to any other man in any other place?"

I knew better than to attempt an answer. The questions were rhetorical, and Talleyrand believed the answers to be self-evident. As the good listener I had become, I knew it best to allow him to finish.

"You are a unique young woman, my beauty. You came to me with a curious mind and have allowed me to fill it with people of the world and ideas you had never considered. Unless you say differently, I believe we have lived well together. You have had your friends and independence. I have accomplished what was needed for France." He hesitated before adding, "And you have been most helpful in my accomplishments."

At the time, I wondered whether he flattered me so, knowing it would bind me to him or whether he truly meant what he said. But, the intent was not as important as the result. My cheeks reddened. Heat came into my chest. My heart beat loudly. When he came closer and took my hand, it was nearly too much emotion to bear. Did I desire him in the same way I desired the count? Not at all. But I felt his power, and it excited me.

It took all of my emotional strength to take my hand from his. I told him all he had said was correct. But I needed some distance from him, as well as from the count, if I were to know where, or with whom, I belonged. I must have been convincing because he did not reach out for my hand again and we ended the walk in silence. Any thoughts I may have entertained about being swept up in the arms of this most celebrated man and how I would feel were not realized.

Within the week, I left Valençay, alone, for Paris.

CHAPTER 41

▼

When Talleyrand returned to Paris, he was confronted with a problem that shook the foundations of the new government and his own position in it. If for no other reason than his demanding and tiring work schedule, our paths did not cross for months.

Talleyrand wanted to fill the new Lower Chamber of Deputies, as he had filled the Upper Chamber, with a fair representation of Constitutional Monarchists (the majority), laced with a representation of Bonapartists, Republicans, and Jacobins. The results of the August 1815 elections, however, were extremely disturbing. All of these groups lost seats. In their place were elected Royalists of the most extreme and reactionary type, who regarded the established government with great suspicion. All equally mistrusted Talleyrand, whom they viewed as a traitor to their aristocratic class. So, my beloved found himself caught between an unsympathetic monarch and a hostile Lower Chamber.

Confronted with a crisis, my beloved usually thrived. It was his genius to always know how to handle it. If the constitutional monarchy was to survive, he knew he would have to take a drastic measure. With some misgivings, he decided to make a sacrificial offering to the Royalists. And, of all people, it was to be Fouche, the man Talleyrand had just placed in power.

Not wishing to spend an inappropriate number of pages on Fouche, please take my word that, within the month, the new minister of police was dismissed. A mistake here, an innuendo there, a well-placed rumor at the right salon…and King Louis and his advisors were suddenly questioning their decision to depend on an appointee of Napoleon for their security.

Once Fouche was dismissed, Talleyrand knew his own neck, literally, was at risk. From the viewpoint of the Royalists, Fouche and Talleyrand had been collaborators. They had both been leaders of the revolution and ministers under the Directory and the Empire. Napoleon had regarded both of them highly and then had been betrayed by each.

Many of my beloved's colleagues were already whispering to each other that Talleyrand always appeared tired and was beginning to feel the approach of old age. They gossiped that even the best attention to one's *toilette* could not disguise a decrease in energy.

Talleyrand, on the other hand, decided that his *ennui,* listlessness, was due to an affair of the heart and not of advancing age. Years later, we were able to look back at our time together in Vienna and laugh at how blind we had been to the nature of our growing feelings for each other. Talleyrand, as busy as he had been with his own intrigues at the Congress, had been suppressing a great deal of anger at the discovery that I had found time to "entertain" Count Clam-Martinitz. Although I maintain there is no truth in it, Talleyrand is convinced I used Clam-Martinitz to make him jealous.

At our first meeting in Paris, at a reception given by Madame Stendhal, Talleyrand spoke of a future with me. I tried to explain to him I was still confused, but I was content with my new independent state. I had obligations to my own children, but I was now very certain I wanted a life for myself. I was legally bound to a husband, but I had always known he was a man who cared less for me than for his reputation. I still had ties to the count, but I claimed my own freedom for now and perhaps for the future.

Talleyrand could barely hide his anger when he said, "In a city where gossip provides the underpinnings of society, your situation has become, even by French standards, an outrage."

Upon hearing this, I did something I would never think to have done while living with Talleyrand. I rose from my seat, told him what a pleasure it was to have seen him again, and walked over to join a group of acquaintances. Knowing Talleyrand as I did, I had made him both angry and frustrated. And it pleased me.

I had no acceptable excuses to give Edmond, however, for why I was not returning home. I had been informed by friends that my children were thriving, so Edmond could not use their well-being as leverage over me. Not really knowing what to do to maintain his family's honor, Edmond challenged Count Clam-Martinitz to a duel, the duel with which I began this document. I now believe it was Talleyrand's growing love for me, more than his sense of duty as an elder relative, that prompted him to oversee the duel. When my husband lost, our relationship officially ended. And, with a tarnished and unclear future in Paris, I left with the count and returned to Vienna.

When I left Paris, so my beloved later told me, he was in complete anguish. This was the upset his colleagues blamed on age and energy. In fact, my beloved was so hurt by my "desertion" that he acted in a most unusual way. Instead of maintaining his famous impassivity, he wrote me directly, imploring my return for the "good of my noble reputation." He knew, of course, his excuse was as transparent, as were the emotions he was trying to hide.

When I refused to return to Paris, Talleyrand paid an agent to find me and persuade me to return. When his agent's entreaties failed, my beloved, in a plaintive tone, requested I grant him a meeting with the count so that they could "negotiate a settlement in which all parties might be accommodated." I believe those were his words. As far as I knew, he was the only "party" who was not happy with the current situation. I did not grant Talleyrand's request.

It was I alone who met Talleyrand in a park in Vienna, not far from the Hotel Kaunitz where we had stayed during our happier days at the Congress. It was a gray, cold day, and we each sat stiffly on a bench, as if we were the heads of two enemy countries trying to find common ground. It was Talleyrand, as I should have guessed it would be, who quickly came to the "heart" of the issue.

"Dorothea, my dear," Talleyrand implored, "you were born to govern some very powerful man. You and I both know that neither my nephew nor your count have the ambition nor the means to be great."

"Although your statement may be true, I fear your notion of "govern" is really a prelude to submission. What I wish to forget about my life as a daughter, mother, and wife was my capacity for submission," I retorted.

"Be frank with me, as you have always been in the past." Talleyrand responded, somewhat fearful of the answer he would receive, "Would you ever consent to live with an old man, such as myself, again? You and I both know Count Clam-Martinitz is merely a passing pleasure. At some point, you will be alone."

"When we lived together in Vienna, having so many functions to perform as the companion to "an old man," as you say, I realized I had my own desires, my own need for independence, that my words be taken seriously, that..."

"Then my response to you is this," Talleyrand said, now knowing exactly what would deliver me to him wholeheartedly, "you must develop those features within yourself that will allow you to become whatever you must. And I will help you."

Talleyrand took my hand in his and held it fast. To my own surprise, I did not withdraw it. His eyes scoured my face. He pulled me close to him, and his warm lips brushing against my cheek caused the hairs on my neck to straighten. When he circled my waist with his arms and forced our lips together, I realized he wanted me with him at any price. He whispered in my ear he would make whatever concessions necessary if I would leave the count and return to Paris with him.

My beloved was a formidable negotiator that day, relentless in his pursuit of his goal. It was my obligation to the *ancien régime,* he pointed out. He would never be able to effectively accomplish his international tasks without my presence at his side, he stated. I enjoyed being at the center of power, he observed. We loved each other, in our own way, he concluded. Weren't these enough reasons, he asked, to leave Clam-Martinitz?

After several more afternoons of what we later called his "love diplomacy," Talleyrand succeeded in garnering my consent to return to Paris and live with him at Rue St. Florentin.

One week later, as I bid a fond farewell to the count, in the same gardens in which Talleyrand had won both my heart and my mind, I could barely contain the anticipation of my new life. Using my formidable acting skills, I explained to the count that my duties to both Talleyrand and France transcended our indulgences we always knew would one day end.

"Ainsi soit-il!" So be it! Talleyrand muttered under his breath, as I entered the carriage that would take us to Paris.

CHAPTER 42

▼

The thought of returning to Paris as the companion of the most interesting and powerful man I had ever known was intoxicating. I saw images of rooms to redecorate in my favorite colors, new linens to be purchased, furnishings to be ordered, and, once finished, enchanting evenings at Rue St. Florentin filled with the most stylish and knowledgeable people in Paris.

The most difficult part of my decision to live with Talleyrand as something more than his hostess, was informing my family…no, Talleyrand's and my family…I would not be returning to my wifely and motherly duties. Over the years of separation, short notes and timely gifts had been exchanged with promises of return when my services were no longer required. Since the duel, Edmond had resigned himself to our permanent estrangement. My children, I was informed by friends, had stopped inquiring about their mother. Talleyrand, as he was prone to do, dismissed the need for any apology or excuse.

It was with a guilty heart that I chose to make my final explanations by letter: one to Edmond and one to the children. While I admit the act was cowardly, I feared any exposure to the family would lessen my determination to start a new life.

Of course, our physical relationship changed once I moved into Talleyrand's home. But I have made the decision that recounting our personal pleasures and disappointments would serve no historical purpose. Let me just state that, while Talleyrand's age had stolen much of his passion, his years of experience more than made up for that loss. He was a patient teacher, but he was open to new explorations. He was assured, but he allowed me to test my own limits. Ultimately, he was more tender and accommodating in his lovemaking than I would have imagined this commanding, opinionated, manipulative man to be. In some ways, I may have been the most fortunate of his lovers because he knew he was going to need me for the rest of his life. And, as he taught me in the area of diplomacy, need is a strong motivator.

To quote my beloved, "History has no mercy for those who fall from power."

Once again, he proved correct. Before we were able to unpack my trunks and settle into our new life in Talleyrand's home, he found himself no longer part of the royal court and no longer minister of foreign affairs. To me, this meant fewer invitations to important balls, fewer evenings at the opera, fewer callers to our home bringing gifts, fewer dinner parties to hostess for royalty, and fewer possibilities to participate in discussions of important issues. To Talleyrand, this meant a loss of power and influence, a blow to his self-esteem and usefulness to the state from which I am sorry to say he never recovered. Even today, I am unsure whether my beloved resigned his position based on principle, as he claimed, or was dismissed by King Louis XVIII for a lack of confidence.

This is my understanding of the events that transpired. Prior to our return to Paris, my beloved had been at the center of renewed negotiations with the allies over what he considered particularly harsh terms of surrender in the First Peace of Paris. The armies of Russia, England, Prussia, and Austria still occupied France, and my beloved gladly took on the mantle of negotiating a more honorable peace. The clever strategy he devised for this second round of talks was to insist the war the allies had waged against France had really been waged against an individual—Napoleon—and not against a nation. It followed from his reasoning then that, because Napoleon no longer ruled, France should be free of the terms of the first peace treaty.

"France is willing to cede any territory," Talleyrand wrote on behalf of the king, "which does not form part of ancient France, plus pay an indemnity, and accept a provisional occupation by a certain number of troops for a limited period of time." When the allies counter-proposed a devastating set of terms, decrying Talleyrand's "principle of inviolability of the territory of France," Talleyrand found his position to be without the support of his king.

On September 24, 1815, Talleyrand, in his position as president of one of the king's councils, told King Louis that if he was unable to support the position of the existing government of France, then he and his ministers would have no other choice but to resign. According to Talleyrand's notes from that day, the king looked to the ceiling with an air of complete indifference, as if accessing a greater power, and replied, "Well then, I suppose I shall have to find new ministers."

There are those who claimed this dismissal, or "maneuvered resignation," to be kinder and crafted by the king to appease the mercurial czar, who was still furious with Talleyrand after uncovering a secret treaty my beloved had signed in Vienna. Others decided that "elements" in the now-dismissed deputies of the Assembly considered Talleyrand's past behavior so reprehensible that they had placed pressure on the king for his dismissal. Still others suggested the king had never felt comfortable with his choice of Talleyrand as foreign minister and had been unduly influenced in his appointment by fine wine and Fouche, both of which wore off quickly.

No one knew better than Talleyrand, however, why he was no longer part of the government. According to my beloved, the dismissal revolved around one factor alone—King Louis's personal fears for his own future. The king was aging with difficulty, weeks upon weeks spent ill and immobilized with gout. Many of my beloved's meetings with him had taken place in the anteroom to his bedchamber in the presence of his physician. Both age and infirmity had led the king to fear another exile. He wanted nothing more than to be left to rule in peace and allowed to die in the royal palace. With Talleyrand as his foreign minister, neither would be likely to occur. The possibility of an internal conspiracy against the crown would always remain high, as would the likelihood of another confrontation with the allies.

"What King Louis needs is Talleyrand's policies without Talleyrand," my beloved said of his own political demise. I must admit he was probably correct. But Talleyrand could not have done anything differently once a principle was at stake.

Not wanting to handicap his successor's future negotiations, Talleyrand insisted on all public occasions that he had resigned for personal reasons, allowing the gossips of the salons to lasciviously infer it was to allow "an aging man more time to school his young niece in the art of life in Paris."

Talleyrand was dismayed, however, upon receiving the news the duke of Richelieu had been appointed his successor. Only three months earlier, the duke had refused a post in Talleyrand's government on the grounds that, "I have been absent from France for twenty-two years, and I am a stranger there, both to men and institutions."

"What a perfect choice! He knows Russia better than France," Talleyrand wrote in his diary with more than a touch of sarcasm. This was the very same duke who had held a commission as lieutenant general in the Russian Army and a position as the czar's governor of the province of Crimea.

However strange this appointment may have seemed to the general populace, Richelieu was in possession of something Talleyrand knew he did not have, the confidence of the king. And I would add, even if Talleyrand would not, my beloved did not have the support of the czar.

As Talleyrand predicted, Richelieu was forced to retreat from the firm line my beloved had drawn for the allies. The resulting Second Peace of Paris gave both Switzerland and the Netherlands a small strip of France's frontier and, to Prussia, the Saar. Piedmont received part of Savoy. An indemnity of 700 million francs was imposed, in addition to one billion francs necessary to settle the claims of private citizens for losses sustained during various Napoleonic invasions. That sum was truly outrageous, and, after torturous negotiations with the king, the allies settled for a fraction of that amount. An army of 150,000 allied soldiers was to occupy the northern regions of France for five years, and the expense for this occupying army was to be borne by France.

Perhaps the crowning indignity for Talleyrand, who had always appreciated fine possessions, was the low value Richelieu had placed on objects owned by the state. While he maintained he had no choice in the matter, the allies repossessed almost all the works of art the Napoleonic wars had brought to France. Even the Vatican, through a papal emissary who Talleyrand dubbed the "Holy Father's shipping clerk," took back the lavish presents it had bestowed upon France and its kings over the decades.

To relieve the air of despair I found settling on our home in Paris, I suggested we take up residence at Valençay for a while, a place that always seemed to bring peace to my beloved. With a half-hearted "yes" from Talleyrand, I organized the journey. We were gone within the week—before my beloved had a change of either heart or mind.

I am pleased to be able to write the change of location was exactly the remedy needed. The season was winter of 1816, and we were alone together for the first time in our lives. Instead of the daily messengers and the never-ending meetings, we spent time watching the local artisans repair our carriages and the stable boys condition the horses. The tailor could take his ease with his measurements and stitches. The wigmaker, while shocked by the styles of Paris I described to him, delighted us with tales of life in the area.

What I remember most fondly from that time, however, were the walks Talleyrand and I took together over the property. Talleyrand, having shed his gold-knobbed cane for one carved for him out of a fallen branch we chanced upon one day, seemed to stand taller and walk more briskly, as if the world's problems were slowly being shed from his shoulders. As this happened, the words that tumbled out of his mouth were a joy to hear. He talked of history, philosophy, art, his mistresses, his successes, and his failures. He talked and talked and talked.

I listened a great deal over those months, and I could not have been happier to do so. Of course, I offered opinions, counterarguments, questions, and conclusions. But largely, I listened and learned. It is not surprising that what I have incorporated into this manuscript had their seeds planted during that glorious time at Valençay. Any questions I might have asked myself after his "dismissal" about the wisdom of my decision to stay with him had vanished, never to return. The irony of the love he gained from me, as his political power diminished, was not lost on either of us.

King Louis, sensitive to the proprietary manners of the *ancien régime,* informed Talleyrand one day he was naming him his grand chamberlain. The position was not more than a sinecure, but it was a dignified one that allowed both of us access to the royal apartments and a place of honor at state functions. Talleyrand was also to receive 100,000 francs per year, for the remainder of his life. *Quel honour!*

It was with a heavy heart that I agreed to return to Paris.

CHAPTER 43

▼

Talleyrand's loss of power soon became only a gnawing memory. To my great happiness, he sought solace, if not refuge, in my company. In addition to being his lover, I happily played the role of companion for a man who was now well into his sixties. If I had ever entertained thoughts of unbridled independence—taking on more lovers, acting in theatricals, traveling alone to exotic countries—I gladly surrendered them to being an important part of the world of this most complex and intriguing man.

In comparison to Talleyrand, most men bored me, Edmond especially so. Young, dashing bachelors like Count Clam-Martinitz, with whom I continued to flirt at balls, were little more than handsome faces whose conversations focused on either the glories of battle or the delights of fashion and gaming. A surprising number were either frivolous, self-absorbed, or both. While I cannot say I never again questioned the strength of my desire to remain with an aging lover, the answer always remained the same: I loved him as he was!

His fame was fleeting. His age was advancing. There was little chance of his return to power so long as King Louis remained on the throne. But, none of that mattered. While the initial attraction to my uncle-by-marriage may have been to gather glory to myself by remaining beside a famous and powerful man, as I grew older and wiser, the reasons for staying with him became more pure as they became more complex. If Talleyrand was alive as I write these words and would choose to share his feelings, he would also tell you, what might have started for him as a need for freshness and youth in his life, grew into admiration and love. We had, for the last two decades of his life, a unique partnership.

Always sensitive to the importance of appearances, however, especially in Restoration France, Talleyrand was disturbed by the gossip that was our constant companion. The entire court knew the countess of Perigord was not living under the roof of her husband, but residing in the home of his uncle. They were also aware neither Edmond nor I had attempted to obtain an official divorce from the state or an annulment from the Pope. Although I had begun to receive regular reports from relatives about the disposition of my children, the comments made about their abandonment hurt me the most and are too difficult to record.

To minimize public scandal, Talleyrand created an elaborate ruse that, in fact, fooled no one, but it gave my beloved some peace of mind. He renovated his already expansive home on Rue St. Florentin to create the appearance of propriety. His bedchamber was placed on the mezzanine, opening onto the Rue de Rivoli, while my suite of rooms was placed on the second floor, facing the Tuileries. He surrounded us with friends and family to the extent that, at one time, we had living with us his cousin, his cousin's secretary and manservant, a musician, several children of friends from Valençay, and an assortment of other guests who were unknown to me. When this elaborate stage set was complete, Talleyrand was pleased. I must admit that much of the gossip appeared to subside. The king's generous stipend, and the extensive financial resources Talleyrand had amassed over the years allowed us to easily maintain the lifestyle my beloved had coveted since childhood.

I have no doubt that, as I come toward the end of this manuscript, you are wondering what had become of Talleyrand's wife, Catherine. So, you shall wonder no more. Catherine, on her own volition, had fled to England, intending to return to France only after Napoleon was defeated. I must admit her absence allowed us to live contentedly with each other for many years.

Friends in London reported to Talleyrand from time to time, and that is how we learned the years had not been kind to her. She had grown into a corpulent, red-faced, colicky individual who had not retained any of her original beauty.

My beloved, fearful to have his wife complicate our relationship, tried everything he could to keep Catherine in London once he received news of her impending departure for Paris. He implored one of his appointees, the marquis of Osmond, the French ambassador to London, to make Catherine "understand the dilemma she presents if she returns to France." Catherine, to her credit, was as clever in devising reasons to leave London as Talleyrand was in finding them to keep her there. For a period of time, messengers sent by Catherine arrived at Rue St. Florentin at all hours of the day and night. Some said she could no longer afford to live in London. Others mentioned her unhappiness at not fulfilling the duties of the wife of a prominent statesman. Still others blamed the weather and how the cold and wet of London did not suit her disposition.

One evening, returning from a performance of a symphony at the royal palace by that ruffian, Ludvig von Beethoven, my beloved's manservant greeted him with yet another message. This one informed him Catherine was now residing in Pont-de-Sains, in the home on the outskirts of Paris that Talleyrand had given her at the time of their marriage. The note upset my beloved enough for me to suggest we retire to the library for a glass of claret and discuss the situation. I remember, even today, how we sat facing each other, near the fireplace, and how my thoughts could not help but wander to those ecstatic days and the conversations Talleyrand had had in this room, in these same chairs, with Czar Alexander.

"Catherine writes it is her intention to remain in Paris," Talleyrand offered, folding the letter and placing it in his waistcoat pocket. He thought for a moment and then said what was on both our minds. "I wonder if there is anything I can do to dissuade her from living so near to us. Our paths are bound to cross."

"Since money is a primary reason that Madame Talleyrand does anything," I responded with more anger than I intended, "perhaps we should deal with her from that vantage point."

"You are absolutely correct, my dear." Talleyrand said, pretending he had not already had the identical thought.

We ended the evening by agreeing on an offer of an annual stipend and a new home in a warmer climate, only to regret the generosity we had shown. Catherine took the money, but she remained in Paris and continued to bemoan her fate to all who would listen, making my beloved somewhat of a laughing stock in the city. Even King Louis could not resist teasing Talleyrand one day at court.

"Is it true, Prince Talleyrand, that Madame has returned? If so, I assume it is a situation to which you can hardly pretend your usual indifference."

The king sat in his red velvet seat, beneath the overhanging banner of the Bourbon dynasty. The occasion was the signing of a minor treaty that needed my beloved's signature, although he had had no responsibility for its making. The ministers observing the king began to snicker.

"Sire," Talleyrand responded, trying to appear unperturbed, "it is indeed true my wife is back in Paris. I, too, have my March 20."

The king blanched, according to Talleyrand's description of the incident, and then turned red with anger. He had no suitable reply to Talleyrand's reference to the date of Napoleon's triumphant reoccupation of the Tuileries and his own embarrassing flight to Ghent. From that day forward, no one at court, including the king, ever mentioned Catherine's name in the presence of Talleyrand.

Catherine had the good sense not to exacerbate a delicate situation by appearing at our door or at any gathering to which we were invited. Within the year, she sold her house at Pont-de-Sains to Talleyrand in order to fatten her purse and moved to the town of Auteuil, where I understand she lived well for the eighteen years that were left to her. Talleyrand, as far as I knew, never saw her again.

CHAPTER 44

▼

Our life together between 1815 and 1830 was filled with travel between Talleyrand's homes in Paris and Valençay, state functions, dinners, recitals, the opera, and the theater. I even took my beloved's advice and appeared in several theatricals. But, despite his attempt to enjoy the life of a retired diplomat and his assurances to me he no longer desired to return to "an ineffectual government," all of Paris knew the new grand chamberlain to be restless and angry. His political carping became increasingly intolerable to both friends and colleagues.

During a state function one evening in November 1816, for example, Talleyrand ignored my meaningful stare as he began to inveigh against the government. He started with the minister of police…

"Descazes is nothing more than a *masquereau*, pimp, with whom the Chamber of Deputies cannot have any dealings without degrading itself."

…and ended with the Minister of Foreign Affairs:

"The Richelieu ministry is everywhere despised. Nothing it does escapes public contempt. And Monsieur de Richelieu himself is the most despised of all."

King Louis, understanding all too well the restlessness and anger of impotency, explained to his courtiers, "It is the wounded vanity and disappointed ambition of a talented man who is beset with his own mortality."

The years 1817 to 1821 witnessed the death of a number of Talleyrand's friends and associates, and my beloved was "left with the burden of listening to or writing eulogies for others, yet feeling the death I was acknowledging was my own." Especially troubling was the passing of Madame de Stael, for Talleyrand now felt guilty about causing unnecessary years of estrangement from a woman who had shown herself to be a true friend in many ways.

After so many years of being educated on worldly issues by my beloved, I found it satisfying to be able to help him at this very emotional time. One morning, as he sat in the library reading, I took two small volumes from a high bookshelf, both written by Madame de Stael. While they brought tears to his eyes, an occurrence I chose not to notice, he soon collected himself and began to discuss the most important part of their relationship, the intellectual bond they shared. Ideas on revolution. Ideas on religion. Ideas on the Enlightenment. While they did not always agree, Talleyrand had found her thinking analytical and her thoughts stimulating. By the time his monologue on her virtues ended, his sadness had turned into nostalgia.

Then he paid me the highest compliment he could have, saying my interests had broadened so immeasurably over the years and our discussions had taken on the same character as those he always looked forward to with de Stael. While not obvious to him, I nearly wept as he spoke his words. De Stael would no longer be my competitor, in death as in life, but a colleague.

The notice of Napoleon's death, all alone on the isolated island of Saint Helena, finally softened my beloved's disappointment with the general who he had hoped would use his sword to create democracy for France. In his diary, he wrote:

> That Napoleon was a genius is undeniable. He had no equal in energy, in imagination, in intellect, in his capacity for work, in his extraordinary productivity, in his ability to lead men. He was not equally gifted in judgment, but, even here, when he was willing to pause long enough to listen, he knew how to make use of the good ideas of others. His career was one of the most astonishing in a thousand years of history.

As I read this entry several years after it was written, I imagined my beloved to be speaking about himself, as he would have wanted others to remember him.

In 1830, life's fortunes reversed themselves once more. At the age of seventy-six, Talleyrand was again thrust into the forefront of public affairs. Applying the same methods he had used against Louis XV and Napoleon—secret coalitions among politicians, security officials, and military officers—he helped to overthrow King Louis XVIII and install one of his old friends, the duke of Orleans, as the new king. For Talleyrand's help in acquiring the throne, King Louis-Philippe appointed him ambassador to the court of St. James.

My beloved was overjoyed once he resolved his initial concern that his advanced age would limit his ability to carry out his duties in London. I believe my own prodding resulted in his accepting the post, and I have no doubt that additional years of life were presented to him along with the appointment. In his memoirs, Talleyrand wrote the appointment would allow him "to implement my long-held theory that France's strength lay in a close association with Britain. I preached this principle to Mirabeau, I urged it on Napoleon, and now I will impress it on Louis-Philippe."

As expected, Talleyrand's appointment created great controversy throughout the diplomatic ranks. Reaction in France was more negative than my beloved had expected. His association with the new French government was viewed by some as still another example of his diplomatic manipulations. Russia was opposed to the nomination on the basis that Talleyrand had played a role in the unsuccessful assassination of a previous czar. Metternich, still in power, was indifferent, viewing Talleyrand as a potentially moderating force for Europe. The British, to our joy, were quite pleased to be receiving Europe's senior statesman, believing my beloved could foster the stability Europe needed after all the turbulence caused by France over the preceding fifty years.

To his chagrin, Talleyrand was unprepared for the political scene he encountered once we landed in England. King George IV, England's popular ruler, was soon replaced by his brother William IV, a simple-minded man who had no particular ideology except to acquiesce to the relentless bombardment of the liberals who advised him. A revolution of the upper classes was in the making by members of an aristocracy that was reputed to be the most rigid and exclusive in the world. King William was so taken by their revised notion of "legitimacy" that he began to consider France's new King Louis-Philippe a "scoundrel" because of the conditions under which he was crowned.

Talleyrand took note of the change and, as was his genius, transformed himself to fit into the new British society. He followed the dictum that years before had helped him win the position of delegate from Autun: be all things to all men. Addressing the British crowds, he was a French revolutionary whom they cheered and revered. Within the houses of the nobles, he acted the senior diplomat of a conservative Europe. He even took to wearing a caped traveling coat that was newly waterproofed by a man called Macintosh, a very popular style in England.

For the next few years, Talleyrand and I made significant inroads into a stultified British society. The invitations became more frequent and the occasions more opulent. My beloved took up cigar smoking, much to my distress, merely because of its novelty. The English had recently invented wooden matches, and the last hour of every ball found all male attendees filling the rooms with a putrid smell. We ignored the ill manners of some, like Prince Leviers, the representative of Czar Nicholas, who continually gossiped that our illicit relationship had "incestuous" qualities.

When I look back at our four years in London, I am convinced my beloved's diplomatic successes outweigh the one failure he decried for the rest of his life. One of his most difficult and successful negotiations concluded in the Conference of London in November 1830, when he convinced Britain, Prussia, Russia, Austria, and the Netherlands that Belgium should remain independent, rather than be unified with the Netherlands. In an almost impossible feat, he managed to allay the fears of each country that France would not take advantage of the existing movement in Belgium to reunify with France, having been annexed to it in 1794.

Once the Belgium crisis was resolved, he successfully negotiated an alliance in which France became a full partner with Britain, Spain, and Portugal in defending the continued rule of Spain's queen.

My beloved's spirits took a tragic downturn, however, when he could not transform France's current, informal *entente* relationship with England into a formal defensive alliance, what had been his personal goal for decades. Try as he did, such an alliance alluded him. When we left London in August 1834, his relationship with Prime Minister Palmerston, who had replaced Wellington in that position, was severely strained. In November of that year, at eighty years of age, Talleyrand officially resigned his position, using ill health as his excuse.

After Talleyrand and I returned to France, we spent most of our time at Valençay, the home to which he was most attached. Talleyrand rose fairly late each morning, continuing his lifelong habit. Increasing problems with his deformed leg now prevented our customary walk together in the gardens after breakfast. Instead, he used the time to read the classics, history, and the funeral orations of Bousset. Often, he would retire to his study to write. He sat for hours each day, recording his thoughts and impressions at his new mahogany writing desk, which I believe he bought largely because its cleverness intrigued him. It served as a dressing table as well as a desk for the long top drawer opened to reveal a mirror, glass bottles, lidded boxes, compartments, and secret drawers. Several times a week he received friends, admirers, and enemies alike, all welcomed irrespective of accidents of birth, wealth, or rank.

When there were no guests, we filled our time with discussions of books that each of us was reading. When there were guests, he would greet them in the library, seated in a large upholstered, open armchair we had brought back with us from England. His hair was powdered in the old style. His cane lay across his legs with his bad leg, which he now called his "horse's hoof," propped up on an ottoman. His eyes sparkled as ever, while the rest of his face remained frozen in a mask of indifference. He was no more or less than a prince, always courtly and gracious.

Occasionally, he would ride through the property in his open carriage with a visitor and point with his cane to the deer that had presented themselves for their amusement. In the evening, a harpsichordist would play for us, whether or not there were guests. All who visited felt honored and listened to my beloved in fascination. His tongue was as sharp in old age as it had been decades earlier, and he still dominated every conversation.

He received honors, such as his admittance into the Académie Française, which recognized him as a man who embodied the achievements of France over the past half-century. At a reception in his honor, a gathering of France's most eminent thinkers, writers, and leaders all rose to their feet to applaud his entrance. My beloved was overwhelmed.

It was a sad day, and there were a great many of them when my beloved dwelled on the fact the future was no longer his. The entire household would be draped in a curtain of gloom. Mistakes of the past would be replayed endlessly in his mind. Some days, he would be in anguish that, as a senior statesman in his eighties, he had been asked to resign a ridiculous post at the British Embassy. Then, an all too frequent cycle of emotions would begin with anger, followed by resentment, finally followed by bouts of depression. How he would be remembered in history became his final obsession.

Sitting in the morning room, as we were wont to do early each day, Talleyrand would read aloud the dispatches that had arrived the prior day and ask for my opinion. This particular day, I believe the subject we were discussing was Prince Metternich's difficulties with the Hungarians, over whom the Hapsburgs ruled. As he spoke, Talleyrand's eyes began to water, and he put the remaining documents on his lap.

"Dorothea, eighty-three years have passed!" he said, as if it was crossing his mind for the first time.

"You are fortunate you are in good health and have been able to obtain such a noble age."

"Don't patronize me!" he retorted in mock anger.

"Self-pity does not become you, dear."

"Hold your tongue for a moment and indulge me." Talleyrand limped, without benefit of his cane, to the divan upon which I lay and seated himself at my side. "I no longer feel strong enough to bear the devils that lurk inside. As I look back on my life, I wonder how many useless intrigues there have been." He took my hand to his lips, as if needing a coverlet for his words.

"Those were as much a part of your life as were your manipulations of people and events," I countered, always the optimist.

"Think of all the failures."

"And what about the successes?"

"At what price were those successes achieved? How many have I betrayed? Who have I deceived? When have I not lied to achieve my purpose?"

"It was always for a greater good, for something more important than yourself. For France." I pressed my hands to his face and brought it to my breast. I knew he needed reassurance. We lay together on the divan in silence. My sadness that he would die from the demons that were stirring was almost too much to bear.

"How many complications did I have to create or untangle when simplicity might have been the best alternative?" my beloved continued, unable to excise his tormenters.

"That, my dear, is nothing but distorted hindsight."

"You are trying to console me, and, as always, I appreciate it. But I keep asking myself how much emotion and energy has been wasted on enemies that were not necessarily there. Or on self-aggrandizing illusions that were maintained that could never be achieved. All so that I could continue feeding my sense of self-importance."

"Soon, you will complain about having met and lived with me!" I responded, my words desperate to alter the subject and his mood.

But, there was no answer to his cry. We both knew it. I watched the pulse in his neck beat at a very fast rate and was concerned for him. I needed him to stay with me forever. Didn't he know that?

"Dorothea, it is time for me to reveal a secret to you that I have kept my entire life."

I smiled, doubting any secret was still being kept from me.

"I have always had the gift of understanding those around me. I think I used it as effectively as I could in the service of my country. But, I have also always known more than I needed to know. And, more often than not, I could do very little with that knowledge. *Quel dommage.* What a pity."

I was feeling such sadness at that moment that I wanted to run to my favorite outcropping on the estate and weep there in solitude. My beloved was doubting the verdict of history, what people would think of him, what people would remember of his deeds. And we both cried.

CHAPTER 45

▼

Talleyrand died quietly in his bed at Valençay, with few by his side, in May 1838 at the age of eighty-four. His death was the saddest event of my life for I had lost the man I had grown to love, without reservation, in my own maturity.

It was almost too disheartening for me to bear the manner in which the world responded to his passing. His death went largely unnoticed by the courts of Europe and by the vast majority of the French. King Louis-Philippe was proper in his sentiments and gifts, but nothing more than proper. I am ashamed to record what the satirical revue *Le Charivari,* read by all Parisian society, published following his death:

> M. de Talleyrand was at death's door this morning, and everybody was wondering whether the sly devil was playing some sort of practical joke. We know he never acts without a purpose, but no one could figure out what advantages there were in suffering the pangs of death.

I was both insulted and shocked by those words, probably more so than Talleyrand might have been. He would have admired the writer's perceptiveness because, only several days before his death, Talleyrand had met with Father Dupanloup, who represented the Pope, in what might be termed my beloved's "final negotiations." It was the Pope's desire that Talleyrand renounce his many sins before he could be interred in consecrated ground, sins such as living with me in an unmarried state, "stealing" church property on behalf of the revolutionary government, and performing the ordination ceremony for constitutional bishops. The writer of the satiric piece would have guessed correctly that, wanting to gain all the advantage he could in heaven, Talleyrand struck his final deal. Yet I have always felt Talleyrand saw his position no different than that of his idol, Voltaire, whose deathbed conversion was also claimed.

Behind the critical review lay the sad fact the youth of France had come to scorn the values for which my beloved stood. They saw his life as embodying little more than corruption, secret deals, and undeserved privilege. Yes, Talleyrand swore allegiance at least fourteen times in his life, created intrigues to help one government overthrow another, and was responsible for the dismissal of friends and enemies alike from public office. But, his actions were always in behalf of a stable France. Such an ungrateful attitude on the part of France's youth represented to me a serious lack of knowledge of the time and events of their own country, and it was certainly no appreciation of what Talleyrand did to enable them to be born into a free, stable society.

Should my beloved be blamed because none of the governments he helped put into place lived up to his expectations for them? Not the post-Revolutionary Directory, not the Napoleonic Empire, not the Constitutional Monarchy of King Louis XVIII or its continuation by King Louis-Philippe. The promises that had come with the fall of the Bastille in 1789 remained largely unfulfilled at the time of my beloved's death.

Perhaps Talleyrand would not have cared what the youth of France believed to be true about his role in shaping their country over a period of forty-five years. But he certainly did care how history judged him because history was what Talleyrand had always hoped to shape, if not control. With history as his measuring rod, I think he would have been disappointed. As I write this last chapter to my manuscript, thirty-eight years after the Congress of Vienna and ten years after my beloved's death, I think it is accurate to state that many of his colleagues believe, as I do, the civilized world is now governed by rulers who have created little more than police states for their countrymen. This was not my beloved's hope for either France or the continent.

What are now called the March Days have passed over the land like a tornado. Perhaps I should not have been so surprised that month when a messenger from the court arrived, in an anguished state, to inform me King Louis-Philippe had abdicated following rioting in the streets of Paris. Two weeks later, another messenger arrived, informing me Prince Metternich had fled to England. Talleyrand had been right again. Revolutions do begin in spring. This year, March, a month when the weather typically brings new beginnings, brought riots to Berlin, a declaration of autonomy from Hungary and Bohemia, wars throughout Italy, and I do not even know what else! I was just about to flee Paris for Valençay to quiet my nerves when those hideous March Days were over almost as quickly as they had begun.

As I sit here in my beloved's favorite armchair in his favorite room, the library of Rue St. Florentin, this June 1848, I am sixty-four years of age, and the revolutionary month of March is already a fleeting memory. If Talleyrand were here next to me, polishing the gold knob on his favorite cane, a simple act that allowed him to clear his mind of the day's serious matters, I suspect he would tell me the power of a revolution is only as strong as its control over the military. And, once again, he would have been right. All of the outbreaks in March that strove for independence and justice have now been crushed. This new movement toward what people are calling "nationalism," which seems to be sweeping over Europe, has been crushed as well.

I am glad Talleyrand is not here to see how little of what he felt he accomplished at the Congress of Vienna remains. Perhaps history has its own rules and designs and merely creates the illusion in a man like Talleyrand that he is able to shape events. Perhaps not. Time will be the judge, and I do not know whether I shall live to know its verdict.

As I come to the end of my manuscript, unsure of what will occupy my time tomorrow or the days and years that will follow, I realize that, as a young woman without any discernable skills of negotiation, I had struck an enviable deal. I had the good fortune to live with an extraordinary man with a rapacious appetite for life. I took from Talleyrand what I needed in my youth, support for my independence, excitement, influence, and knowledge. And Talleyrand took from me what he needed in his old age, youth, passion, loyalty, and love.

What an adventure my life has been. As I put down my pen for the last time, I hear the arrival of my coach on the cobblestones of the driveway. It is time for my drive through the Tuileries. Next to my writing time, it is the most enjoyable hour of each day. My daughter, with whom I have finally reached a reconciliation, frequently accompanies me. My beloved Talleyrand always does.

—Paris, June 1848

Selected References

Atterbury, Paul and Lars Tharp, eds. *The Bullfinch Illustrated Encyclopedia of Antiques,* New York: Little Brown and Company, 1994.

Bergeron, Louis. *France Under Napoleon.* Princeton, NJ: Princeton University Press, 1981.

Bernard, Jack F. *Talleyrand.* New York: Putnam, 1973.

Carter, Michael, ed. *Encyclopedia of Popular Antiques.* London: Octopus Books Limited, 1980.

Castelot, Andre. *The Turbulent City-Paris, 1783–1871.* New York: Harper and Row, 1962.

Cooper, Duff. *Talleyrand.* London: Phoenix Press, 2001.

Davenport, Millia. *The Book of Costume.* New York: Crown Publishers, 1948.

Dwyer, Philip G. *Talleyrand.* London: Pearson Education Limited, 2002.

Garrioch, David. *The Making of Revolutionary Paris.* Los Angeles: University of California Press, 2002.

Holtman, Robert B. *The Napoleonic Revolution.* New York: J. B. Lippincott Company, 1967.

Kemske, Floyd. *The Third Lion.* New Haven, CT: Catbird Press, 1997.

Kostof, Spiro. *A History of Architecture.* London: Oxford University Press, 1985.

Lefebvre, Georges. *The Coming French Revolution*. Princeton, NJ: Princeton University Press, 1989.

Lever, Evelyne. *Marie Antoinette*. New York: Farrar, Straus and Giroux, LLC, 2000.

Perrot, Philippe. *Fashioning the Bourgeoisie*. Princeton, NJ: Princeton University Press, 1994.

Raeburn, Michael. *Architecture of the Western World*. New York: Rizzoli, 1980.

Rense, Paige, ed. *Châteaux and Villas*. Los Angeles: The Knapp Press, 1982.

Tung, Anthony M. *Preserving the World's Great Cities*. New York: Three Rivers Press, 2001.

About the Authors

Steve Pieczenik is a critically acclaimed author of psycho-political thrillers and the co-creator of the best-selling *Tom Clancy's Op-Center* and *Tom Clancy's Net Force* book series. He is also one of the world's most experienced international crisis managers and hostage negotiators. His novels are based on over thirty years experience in resolving international crises for four U.S. administrations.

Dr. Pieczenik trained in Psychiatry at Harvard and has both an M.D. from Cornell University Medical College and a PhD. in International Relations from M.I.T. He served as a Deputy Assistant Secretary of State and/or senior policy planner under Secretaries Henry Kissinger, Cyrus Vance, George Schultz and James Baker.

During his career at the State Department, Dr. Pieczenik utilized his unique abilities and expertise to develop strategies and tactics that were instrumental in resolving major conflicts in Asia, the Middle East and Latin America, Europe and the United States. He developed conflict resolution techniques that were instrumental in saving hundreds of hostages in different terrorist episodes, including the Hanafi Moslem seizure in Washington, D.C., the TWA Croatian hijacking, the Aldo Moro kidnapping, the JRA hijacking, the PLO hijacking, and many other incidents involving terrorists such as Idi Amin, Quaddafi, Carlos, FARC, Abu Nidal and Saddam Hussein.

In addition, Dr. Pieczenik helped develop negotiation strategies for major U.S.—Soviet arms control summit meetings under the Reagan administration. He was also involved in advising senior officials on psycho-political dynamics and conflict mediation strategies for President Carter's Camp David peace conference. In 1991, Dr. Pieczenik was a chief architect of the International Paris Peace Conference which prevented Pol Pot and the Khmer Rouge from creating another "killing field."

Dr. Pieczenik has started companies in industries as varied as investment banking, publishing and television, and was Executive Producer of two four-hour television mini-series.

For Further Information about Steve Pieczenik
Website: www.stevepieczenik.com
Email: SRLiterary@aol.com

Roberta Rovner-Pieczenik received her BS from CCNY, her MS from Cornell University, and her PhD. in Sociology from New York University. She is the author of books and monographs in the fields of criminology and evaluation research. She also edits the novels of Steve Pieczenik and Alexander Court.

978-0-595-34208-2
0-595-34208-6

Printed in the United States
48017LVS00004B/109-177

9 780595 342082